ALSO BY MATTHEW BAKER

Hybrid Creatures: Stories

If You Find This

Why Visit America

Why Visit America

Stories

Matthew Baker

HENRY HOLT AND COMPANY
NEW YORK

Henry Holt and Company
Publishers since 1866
120 Broadway
New York, New York 10271
www.henryholt.com

Henry Holt ® and ® are registered trademarks of Macmillan Publishing Group, LLC.

"Fighting Words" originally appeared in *Missouri Review* under the title "A Cruel Gap-Toothed Boy" in 2012; "Rites" originally appeared in *One Story* in 2015; "The Transition" originally appeared in *Conjunctions* in 2016; "Life Sentence" originally appeared in *Lightspeed* in 2019; "A Bad Day In Utopia" originally appeared in *Lightspeed* in 2019; "The Sponsor" originally appeared in *Salt Hill* in 2018; "Appearance" originally appeared in *Michigan Quarterly Review* in 2013; "Lost Souls" originally appeared in *Conjunctions* in 2020; "Why Visit America" originally appeared in *The Paris Review* in 2019; "To Be Read Backward" originally appeared in *American Short Fiction* under the title "The Wrong Chemicals" in 2011.

Library of Congress Cataloging-in-Publication Data

Names: Baker, Matthew, 1985– author.
Title: Why visit America : stories / Matthew Baker.
Description: First edition. | New York : Henry Holt and Company, 2020.
Identifiers: LCCN 2019031315 (print) | LCCN 2019031316 (ebook) |
    ISBN 9781250237200 (hardcover) | ISBN 9781250237194 (ebook)
Subjects: LCSH: United States—Civilization—Fiction.
Classification: LCC PS3602.A58664 A6 2020 (print) | LCC PS3602.
    A58664 (ebook) | DDC 813/.6—dc23
LC record available at https://lccn.loc.gov/2019031315
LC ebook record available at https://lccn.loc.gov/2019031316

Our books may be purchased in bulk for promotional, educational, or business use. Please contact your local bookseller or the Macmillan Corporate and Premium Sales Department at (800) 221-7945, extension 5442, or by e-mail at MacmillanSpecialMarkets@macmillan.com.

First Edition 2020

Designed by Meryl Sussman Levavi

Printed in the United States of America

10 9 8 7 6 5 4 3 2 1

for my country

Contents

Why Visit America

Fighting Words

A sudden reversal. In seventh grade this "Nate Vanderveen" chose to lavish our niece with flowering weeds, with vending-machine jewelry, with convenience-store chocolates, with love notes written on the back of homework he hadn't done, but now in ninth grade this "Nate" chooses to lavish her with curses ("Go fuck a dog you freak"), ridicule ("My tits are bigger than that bitch's"), and slander ("Emma sucked me off once too"). He is what in the eighteenth century would have been called a lout, a brute, a ruffian, what in the twenty-first century is now called a thug. Stewart thinks the boy is antisocial, meaning psychopathic, once saw the boy perched on the roof of his family's cottage, preparing to hurl a stray cat onto his driveway two stories below. We live in a village on the shore of the Great Lakes. I am a lexicographer; my brother is a professor of dead languages. His expertise is the words from these languages for which English has no equivalent. Stewart uses these words when he can, although it is rare that he finds the occasion. This "Nate" is such an occasion. Stewart refers to the boy as *kimlee*, which best translated means "foe-who-has-chosen-you"; this makes Stewart the boy's *kimloo*, or "foe-you-have-chosen." We live in a state once enriched by its industries of handcrafted furniture and gasoline automobiles, a state now impoverished as plastic and polyester replace wood and leather, as the pumpjacks of other states drain what's left of the dwindling petroleum in our nation's reservoirs. It is a state in which it is rare for a forty-something man to refer to a fourteen-year-old boy as his foe, regardless of the language used to do so. In the eighteenth century we might have challenged the boy to a duel by pistols, but it is the twenty-first century, and in Michigan, as in most states in our nation, dueling is illegal—dueling and all other "consensual altercations."

But the boy spits in Emma's face in the cafeteria, bullies her friends into deserting her, scribbles elaborate drawings of an elderly and childless Emma living alone ("like your gay uncles used to") with labels attached to the symbols of loneliness he's chosen to include there ("cats" "hate mail from your neighbors" "cat food that you have to eat too cause you're so poor" "more cats" "dildo you hump thinking about wrinkly grandfather dicks" "more cats") and slips these drawings through the slot in the door of her locker and then walks away whistling as if he were a kindly old mail carrier instead of a cruel gap-toothed boy who reeks of mildew and reeks of sweat and has just found another way to traumatize the same girl he's left sobbing in various classrooms and hallways several times this week alone.

The school principal is of no use, cannot do or refuses to do anything other than occasionally suspend this "Nate" from a handful of school days, which for a boy of that sort is more holiday than exile, giving him schoolless days on which he must do nothing aside from wander the beach throwing rocks at boats he doesn't own and plotting how he might next make Emma hate herself a little bit more. The boy has powers of transformation: in a matter of weeks he has transformed her, from a girl who loved reading books with dragons on the covers, a girl unashamed of her braces, a girl unashamed of her brother, into a girl who refuses to enter the public library, a girl who will not sit next to her brother on the bus, a girl who will not smile out of fear of showing her teeth. Stewart and I, too, are transformed. We were timid men, not prone to brooding, not prone to fantasies of batting at a fourteen-year-old's knees with a shovel, of snapping teeth from a fourteen-year-old's gums with pliers. We were men who drank twig tea, who planted petunias in our windows, who grew rhubarb in our gardens, who left apple cores on our porch railings for the squirrels to eat if they pleased. We were men who, when our sister fled to the capital of our nation to be with her new lover and asked if we would move into her cottage to care for her children, each said simply yes, despite that we knew she would not be returning soon, despite that we knew she might not be returning ever. We did not say yes because we meant yes; we said yes because we were too timid to say the no we meant. But now this boy has transformed us into something other than timid. We have decided we will hurt him. We will hurt the boy in a way that he will feel and keep feeling and never stop feeling, mutilate his psyche in a way that will make him fear us and what we are capable of even after we are dead. We want to hurt him in this way because we are afraid that this is the way in which he has already hurt Emma—he has transformed her, and we are unsure how to restore her, unsure if we are even capable of changing her back.

★ ★ ★

I have worked for over two decades as a lexicographer. Unlike most lexicographers, my task is not to write definitions for existent words, nor to revise definitions that have already been written by others. Instead, my task is to write what are known in my industry as "mirage words."

Publishers of dictionaries are fearful of plagiarism; it is undesirable for somebody to copy the definitions from our dictionaries and then to begin printing dictionaries of their own. But with dictionaries theft is difficult to monitor. When lexicographers write a definition for an existent word, we are not creating—we are articulating some abstract idea that already exists in the collective consciousness of English speakers. When lexicographers write a definition for *unwanted*, we are all defining the same *unwanted*—similar to a crowd of artists painting portraits of the same face, artists who are paid to re-create that face as realistically as possible. Overlap is inevitable, theft difficult to prove.

Thus it is my task is to write mirage words: fictional words with fictional definitions. *Othery* is a word I recently wrote, a noun I defined as "suffering experienced through empathy for another's suffering, more painful than that original suffering." Including mirage words such as *othery* in our dictionaries does not undermine their credibility. Dictionaries are not read; dictionaries are used only to look up certain words, for meaning or spelling. Dictionary users will not look up *othery*, because *othery* does not exist. But if *othery* appears in another dictionary, then we will know that the publishers of that dictionary have stolen from our work—*othery* could have only come from our dictionary.

It was only after moving in with Emma and Christopher that I was able to write *othery*. Never before had I experienced that suffering. Back when I lived alone, I did not experience this pain. I suspect that even when our sister did live here she did not feel *othery* for the children—otherwise I doubt she ever could have left.

My understanding of the world is shaped by these words I have written. If not for *othery*, I never would have agreed to Stewart's plan to hurt the boy. It is not Emma's pain I am trying to end so much as my own. Like Stewart, I carry a private language, words that in our village I alone am capable of speaking or thinking. But while he carries words written by the dead, mine are words of my own making.

★ ★ ★

We begin by tailing this "Nate" after school, during the hours when Emma is rehearsing for the fall play over in the high school auditorium and Christopher is practicing for marching band in the field behind the high school. Marching band is for high schoolers only, but Christopher displays such a rare talent with the clarinet that the director of the marching band has promoted him to "honorary high schooler." For us this is ideal—if Christopher were not in marching band, we would be stuck at home after school, supervising Christopher like responsible *tians*, unable to study the movements of this "Nate Vanderveen."

Tians is a word that, if my work were read, would be useful to many in our village—*tians* is the plural form of *tian*, a noun I wrote for our student dictionary that I defined as "a relative responsible for a child's upbringing." Many children in our village are raised not by mothers or fathers but by aunts, cousins, nanas, stepbrothers. Words such as these are offensive in that what the words truly mean—*aunt, cousin, nana, stepbrother*—is "not-mother," "not-father," and therefore "not-parent." For one parenting a child, this implied "not-parent" can be hurtful.

Stewart parks the pickup at the high school alongside the station wagons and minivans and sedans of other *tians*. Many of these station wagons and minivans and sedans were built by our *tian*, the grandfather who raised us, who retired from the automobile factories to the lake only months before the bankruptcies came, before the factories were shuttered and abandoned, before the factories were overrun with squatters, before the factories were converted into laboratories for manufacturing the psychoactive chemicals that in our nation are illegal to make or sell and doubtless are now our state's primary source of income. Our *tian* fed us, bought us books when he sometimes didn't even have the money for his own cigarettes, but otherwise ignored us; he had discovered that we were boys who had no aptitude for working with oil sockets, spanner wrenches, alignment pins, boys who loved words instead. It was only once our sister was older that he discovered a child who loved tools.

"Books aren't going to feed you," our *tian* would say, wielding some drill or torch, shouldering through the door to work on his motorcycle in the driveway with our sister. "Come on out. You boys might as well learn now." But we would stay on the floor, where we lay among our piles of books, not daring to look up from the words on the pages until the spring on the screen door had snapped the screen door shut and we were sure our *tian* was gone and could not force us to come out into the sun to run him tools back and forth from his toolbox.

But now the boys who'd had an aptitude for working with automobiles are working in apple orchards, liquor stores, grocery stores, gas stations pumping what's left of our nation's petroleum into the automobiles their fathers built—men skilled in an extinct trade. Still, it is this useless aptitude that separates them from us: they are masculine in a way we have never been. This is what scares us about our desire to hurt this "Nate Vanderveen," to knock his head against brick walls, to press his face into smoldering embers, to fling him from the tip of the pier and let him drown among the rocks. It is a masculine desire; we are unaccustomed to such masculinity. We distrust it, decide to study it before acting. We will follow "Nate" and make note of his patterns, so that when we are ready to ambush and attack him we will know where and when he will be alone. Whatever we do, we do not want to be caught.

The boy comes slouching out of the high school, wearing no backpack, carrying no homework, having likely left it behind in his locker, indifferent to completing it. He makes a vile gesture at somebody in the window of a bus, hops onto the stone fence that separates the school from the road, and then walks along the fence, as if walking across a tightrope, toward downtown. I make note on a pad of paper: "Friday September 26 departs school at 2:37 p.m. walks into town via fence." I mark an x on our map of the village and record the day and the time the boy was sighted at that location. The buses caravan out of the parking lot, and the boy pauses on the fence to extend that same vile gesture at each of the buses, then moves along again once the buses have passed.

"The *kimlee* prowls," Stewart says, twisting the key in the ignition, "unaware his *kimloo* prowls the same streets." He shifts into drive. The pickup sputters away from the curb. We ride.

★ ★ ★

The bulk of the words I write—*nostalgian, unvoy, gensong, hoggle*—are works of fancy, unrelated to my experiences. As other lexicographers at my publisher sometimes ask to read my work, I generally avoid writing words that are personal. The most notable exception to this was *impsexual*, which I wrote only after many years of trying to define my own sexuality. None of the existent words for orientation represented my own: in high school, I felt no heterosexual lust for the breasts and hips of the girls, felt no homosexual lust for the arms and butts of the boys, felt therefore no bisexual or pansexual or poly. Asexual was perhaps nearest to what I was, but still imprecise, for although I felt no lust for girls or boys or any gender at all, I did feel lust. The lust that I felt, however, and that I feel, was for some nameless, indescribable thing, something that I have never seen and that I am now convinced may not exist. It was not zoophilia—I felt no lust for dogs, sheep, grazing horses—nor was it paraphilia—I felt no lust for teddy bears, shoes, trees. My lust was for something human—some sort of human that perhaps had once existed, or might one day evolve, but in the twenty-first century was a nonentity.

I did not notice that anything was amiss until Stewart, four years my younger, began to develop crushes on different classmates at school, keeping record of these crushes in an old yearbook. I discovered the yearbook one night while he was taking a bath. Staring at the cartoony hearts and exclamation points that he had drawn around different faces, I realized that whatever feelings he was having were feelings that should have come to me years ago, if the feelings were ever going to come. The yearbook had been hidden with a stash of lingerie catalogs, which somehow was even more unsettling, discovering that like me, he must have masturbated sometimes, but that unlike me, when he did he could actually picture what he wanted. I had never before felt so intensely ashamed. Hearing the water draining from the tub, I quick hid the yearbook and the catalogs back under the bunk bed we shared, and then sat alone in the moonlight on the carpet in silence and despair.

I published *impsexual* in our medical dictionary, a noun I defined as "one who sexually desires a nonentity (or nonentities)." I meant *imp-* to suggest *impossible*, to connote an unworkable desire. Only after publishing the word did I realize that *imp-* more likely suggested *imp*, and therefore connoted a desire for fictional creatures.

When Stewart was in high school he was outspoken about the

disgust he felt toward our principal, who was rumored to be asexual. So I did not tell him about my own orientation, for fear my orientation would evoke even more disgust than that. When I did tell him—only after we had both moved away from our village and back again, only after Stewart had been married and divorced twice, only after I had published and been paid for *impsexual*—Stewart told me that a dead language he had once studied, a language that had evolved and died in a peninsular nation on the other side of the planet, had possessed such a word.

"*Kawa-mashka*. It meant sexual desire for something that doesn't exist. See, you aren't that original," Stewart said.

It was then that I realized that although I lived alone and had always lived alone and had never loved another human, I had never been alone entirely. Others had felt this lust that I felt, this unworkable desire, and had lived and died with it centuries ago, or had not yet been born.

★ ★ ★

Except for afternoons when Stewart has faculty meetings, we trail the boy every weekday until 6:17 p.m., when we drive back to the cottage to await the arrival of the extracurricular bus bringing home Emma from rehearsal and Christopher from practice. Our method is one of patience. Stewart parks the pickup near wherever "Nate" chooses to prowl; I take notes on the various activities that "Nate" undertakes. As a rule we do not leave the pickup. When the boy disappears into a store or the arcade, we do not follow. In the pickup we are simply two brothers in an automobile—we are doing nothing wrong. Stewart grades papers with a fountain pen. I revise definitions for an upcoming deadline. We stay in the pickup and we wait. The boy knows our faces, knows whose *tians* we are. We do not want to alert him to our plot.

The exception to this comes several weeks after our study of "Nate Vanderveen" has begun. The pickup is parked downtown, a single street lined by quaint shops with shiplap siding. "Nate" is rooting through a trash bin behind the bookstore, a new but not entirely unexpected behavior. Stewart wears khakis with suspenders over a rumpled dress shirt from teaching; he naps slumped back with his hands resting on his stomach. I wear a vest from the office; I've just noted "Monday October 13 roots through bookstore trash bin 4:27 p.m." on the pad of paper, consulting my pocket watch before logging the official time.

When I see what's happening I try to wake Stewart because I don't know what to do.

"Stewart," I whisper. "Stewart, Stewart, Stewart." Stewart blinks awake, scratches his stubble, falls asleep again. I elbow him. "Stewart, one of us needs to get out of the truck."

Stewart blinks awake again, says, "We aren't—" but then looks through the windshield and sees it too: our nephew tiptoeing along the bookstore toward the trash bin beyond, muttering something to himself, wielding his fully assembled clarinet like a sword. "Nate" is still headfirst in the trash bin, his legs wiggling as if he's falling and looking for somewhere to land. Stewart says, "Is that?" I say "It is," and then he tumbles out of the pickup and runs after our nephew, hissing, "Christopher! Dammit, Christopher!" Christopher is crouched at the gutter at the rear of the bookstore, peeking at "Nate" in the trash bin, but when he hears his name he turns, his eyes growing wide, then growing even wider, looking as if he's either about to cry or take a swing at Stewart with the clarinet.

Stewart gestures for him to come to the pickup. Christopher glances at me in the pickup, then at "Nate" in the trash bin. Christopher shakes his head. He's not going to come. Stewart creeps slightly closer. Christopher hesitates. Stewart creeps closer yet, then snatches the clarinet, throws him over a shoulder, and comes lurching back to the pickup.

Stewart shoves him between us in the cab, shuts the door, hits the lock.

"Aren't you supposed to be at band?" Stewart says.

Christopher scowls at the dashboard. "Nate Vanderveen spit on Emma again today at lunch," Christopher says. "So I took the day off from band to fight him."

We stare at our nephew like he's a word with a new definition. This is a boy who likes to play with the dolls his sister keeps boxed in the basement, a boy we once found sitting on a stump in the woods singing a song he had written about "handsome elves" and the "sparkly fairy potions they keep on their shelves." He is even skinnier than we were at his age, and on his nose has three freckles, which, as far as we can tell, outnumber his friends.

"With a clarinet?" I say.

"He's two years older than you, you idiot," Stewart says. "He's the sort of kid who plays with knives, not his sister's ballet slippers."

"Stewart," I say, feeling *othery* for Christopher. Stewart is in the habit of saying things he regrets, which is why he also is in the habit of getting divorced.

Stewart says, "He would've sent you to the hospital. What did you think you were doing, trying to jump a goon like that?"

In the eighteenth century a child of Christopher's meager size likely would have already succumbed to some minor illness—measles, whooping cough, influenza—but it is the twenty-first century and we have paid for the necessary vaccines to protect Christopher's delicate body. In the eighteenth century Christopher also would have been blind, and thus even if he had survived his various illnesses probably would have had his fingers or his arm wrenched off by the gears of some machine in whatever factory he was working, and afterward would have lived as a beggar before starving in the snow and the filth of some gutter, but it is the twenty-first century and we have bought him eyeglasses so he can see. If Stewart is angry with him it's because we've just caught him out seeking an untimely death when we've been working so diligently to prevent one.

"I don't care what he would have done. He gave Emma the nickname 'Smelly' and now nobody will talk to her or sit by her or call her her real name," Christopher says.

Stewart starts the pickup just as "Nate" squirms backward from the trash bin, holding a mouse by the tail. The boy lifts the mouse, squinting as the rodent sways back and forth, paws scrabbling at the air. We pull away from the curb, sputtering toward the lake. The trees in our state have already gone from green to gold and then gold to red, the leaves starving, growing season over. Wind blows through the branches, knocking leaves adrift.

"And what do you mean, aren't I supposed to be at band?" Christopher says. "What were you two doing there? Aren't you supposed to be working?"

"It doesn't matter why we were there," Stewart says.

Christopher scowls at the dashboard. I stare at the paint-chipped cottages along the shore. The weathered docks. The bobbing sailboats. The beachgrass swaying in the dunes. Christopher mutters, "And I don't play with her ballet slippers," even though he knows that we know that he does.

★ ★ ★

One of Stewart's dead languages has a series of words for human demeanor. The word that Stewart says describes my own personal mien is *weyrey*. Best translated *weyrey* means "demeanor-of-invisibility"; Stewart says the reason I was ignored instead of bullied when we were younger is that I have an aura of insignificance. I often think of us as a "we," but Stewart prefers to focus on the ways in which we are a "you and me."

"You're the opposite of the person who, when he walks into a room, everybody drops whatever they're doing just to watch him, wishing that they could know him," Stewart said. "When you walk into a room, even people who aren't doing anything don't bother to watch you. They're more interested in doing nothing."

This is one of the things he has regretted saying. He later told me he did, although he still thought *weyrey* was my mien.

"It's not because you're quiet. Talkative people can be *weyrey* too. People who think they're social," Stewart said.

Stewart says his own mien is *nipfay*, which best translated means "irritant-demeanor." When we were younger he was as quiet as me, wore the same secondhand sweaters and castoff jeans, but while I was ignored, he was bullied by everybody in our village with a fondness for bullying, and even by some without.

"You walk into a room and nobody notices you," Stewart said. "I walk into a room, and even if I don't say a word, or even look at anyone, everyone gets this feeling that they'd hate me if they knew me. They're irritated by my very existence."

As his older brother, I should have been the one to defend him from the boys who emptied his backpack out the windows of our bus—his sci-fi novels bouncing off the railing on the bridge and tumbling into the creek—the boys who broke into his locker and peed into his gym shoes, the boys who bloodied his nose with fists. I was even more afraid than he was, though. When boys would shove him at the bus stop, I would pretend not to notice, standing with a book near enough to my face to smell the pages. So instead he went to our *tian*, begging him for help.

"So hit them back," our *tian* said, biting a steel nail between his teeth as he spoke, pressing a measuring tape against the windowsill with his thumbs. Our sister stood nearby holding a hammer. "I'm not going to fight your fights."

The next week a boy Stewart's age was throwing pinecones at Stewart when our sister, two years his younger and six years mine, tripped the boy and kneed the boy in the mouth. The boy rode to school with a cut tongue and a mouthful of blood and didn't speak a word to Stewart for months. Stewart likewise went months without speaking to our sister, furious that she had fought a boy he had been too afraid to. In the state in which we live, a boy can grow into a man only if he is unafraid to hurt another boy with his hands. A boy who is afraid to hurt other boys cannot grow into a man; he becomes something else, something neither boy nor man, something we have no word for.

That is why Stewart feels so guilty about what this "Nate" has done to Emma; Stewart believes that if our sister were here, she never would have allowed this to happen.

In the same way that a trauma can leave somebody with a physical impairment—a limp, a sightless eye, a stump arm—a trauma can also leave somebody with an emotional impairment. I believe that Stewart has several. One of my first publications was *hurden*, a noun I defined as "a permanent emotional impairment." When our *tian* was forty-something, an engine tipped off a conveyor belt and fractured the bones in his foot; even after our *tian* retired, his gait was still marked by a limp. Stewart's limp is not a physical one—not a limp of the feet—but still he is marked by it. Before, he'd had one wife or another to fight for him as our sister had—to menace the plumbers and mechanics and supermarket cashiers who attempted to cheat him, to browbeat the colleagues who snubbed or belittled him. But now Stewart is Stewart alone. He wants to believe he is capable of defending Emma in a way he has never been capable of defending himself. But a *hurden* cannot be undone—by definition, a *hurden* is a thing of permanence.

I was uneasy publishing a word based on Stewart's suffering. But it is vital my words seem authentic. Plagiarists will skip a word that is an obvious fiction. My words must seem to serve some purpose in the English language that no other word is capable of serving. Those are the words plagiarists will copy. When the mirage seems solid.

★ ★ ★

The boy has no patterns whatsoever, lives by a policy of whim. Stewart scissors apart my notes and rearranges the entries, first by day of week, then by time of day. Regardless of how the notes are arranged, the boy's doings appear utterly arbitrary.

By day of week:

"Thursday October 16 eats butterscotch candy at 4:37 p.m. on bench outside of gas station."

"Thursday October 23 takes magazine from neighbor's mailbox at 5:02 p.m., tears single page from magazine, deposits torn page in mailbox, departs with magazine."

"Thursday October 30 steals onto sailboat at 2:53 p.m. at wharf, beckons for friend (same as previous week, boy from arcade) to join him upon boat, friend refuses (seems afraid), boy climbs out of boat and shoves friend off of dock, friend flounders, swims toward shallows, boy helps friend from water, depart together into town."

"Thursday November 6 at 6:08 p.m. sets street on fire with aid of gasoline."

By time of day:

"Tuesday October 21 attempts to take bicycle parked outside of bookstore at 5:51 p.m., caught by other high schoolers (older), flees into alley with bloody lip."

"Friday October 24 behind high school at 5:50 p.m. hits small dog with stick."

"Wednesday October 29 at 5:53 p.m. assists *tian* with automobile repairs in driveway, yelled at by *tian* for kicking tires of automobile."

"Friday November 7 5:51 p.m. instructs friend (same as last week, boy from wharf) to stand outside antique shop with back to windows, boy disappears into alley toward rear of antique shop, reappears on roof of antique shop (friend unaware, still facing street) and pees onto friend from roof; friend curses boy, ducks into doorway of antique shop to avoid spray, boy laughs, zips pants, disappears from roof, reappears in alley; friend is accosted by owner of antique shop for standing in doorway; boy and friend curse the owner, spit on windows of antique shop, depart together toward arcade."

The retired have already abandoned their cottages for the season, driven from freshwater peninsula to saltwater peninsula, to the southernmost state on the continent, if they have the money to afford a condo for the winter. The retired too poor to migrate have holed up in their cottages with firewood and space heaters and electric blankets, waiting for the snowdrifts to settle in, the dark months of rime and ice. Our map becomes overrun with x's, marking where and when the boy has been, which by now is almost everywhere. Christopher skips marching band again, following us while we follow "Nate." The pickup is parked at the general store, where "Nate" is inside either shopping or shoplifting, when Christopher appears at my window, bundled up in a coat and mittens and one of his sister's pink scarves. Christopher knocks on the glass. Stewart blinks awake, mumbles, "Huh?" I lean on the crank until the window snaps through the frost and then roll the window down.

"Why aren't you at band?" Stewart says.

"Because I'm following you," Christopher says. "Are you following Nate Vanderveen?"

"No," Stewart says.

"Are you going to beat him up or something?" Christopher says. "You know you can't beat up a kid."

"He's not a kid," Stewart says. "He's fourteen and clinically psychopathic."

"Fourteen is a kid," Christopher says.

"We're not going to hurt him," I say. "Just scare him."

"You better not tell Emma," Christopher says. "Maybe you think that by beating him up you'll be telling her you love her, but she's not going to get that."

"We caught you trying to do the same thing, you idiot," Stewart says.

"All I'm saying is, if you do it, don't tell her, because she's going to hate you for it," Christopher says. "Mom knew how to tell her she loved her, which is just to say it. Also, if you're going to beat him up, I want to help."

Stewart looks at me and then says, "*Vivixixi*," a word from one of his dead languages that best translated means "ill-advised plot."

"I know you're saying in your freak language that you don't want me to come, but too bad," Christopher says. He climbs into the pickup, scrambling over me to sit between us. "Today he took Emma's necklace with Mom's ring on it and flushed it down the toilet. Just tell me when you're actually going to get out of the truck, because I'm going to come and I'm going to kill him." He buckles his seatbelt. "But I've been hiding behind that streetlight watching you for probably an hour, and my face is numb and my hands are numb and my feet are numb and I don't want to walk all the way home on frozen feet, so for now can you just drive me home?"

"No," Stewart says. "We're waiting for the *kimlee* to come out of the store."

"You two are the worst parents," Christopher mutters. He yanks his sister's scarf over his mouth and nose and then huddles into himself, wrapping his arms around his chest, tucking his mittens under his arms.

★ ★ ★

Christopher skips marching band daily, comes with us while we follow "Nate," drinks from a mug of steaming cocoa while we drink from mugs of steaming tea. Before, our afternoons had been soundless, the noise outside the pickup—the howling of the wind, the honking of the geese, the creaking of worn brakes on buses, the clanging of chimes on porch awnings, the katzenjammer of "Nate" tossing his *tian*'s tools from the roof of his family's cottage onto the driveway below—muffled from inside the cab. Now our afternoons are full of endless chattering, this from a nephew who formerly behaved toward us as if we had abducted him from his mother rather than adopted him in her absence, a nephew who had not deemed us worthy of even the most mundane updates about his life. For once he talks to us like *tians* instead of "not-parents"; he references what our sister would have done less every day, seeks our opinions instead.

We sit across from this "Nate's" cottage, slumped low in the cab so the pickup will appear empty if the boy happens to glance in this direction. The boy has crawled under his *tian*'s automobile, doing something to the underbody with a pair of pruning shears. Stewart and I like when the boy vandalizes his *tian*'s belongings—it is thrilling to anticipate the moment his *tian* will see what the boy has been doing, exciting to discover how his *tian* will react. Sometimes his *tian* finds the tricks funny. Other times not.

"When can we actually fight him?" Christopher says.

"When we're sure he's alone and nobody will see us," Stewart says.

"He's alone right now," Christopher says.

"His *tian*'s home. That's his automobile the boy is under," I say.

"Are you afraid of his dad?" Christopher says.

"No," Stewart says.

"His dad is enormous," Christopher says. "If we beat up Nate, won't his dad come after us?"

"We've already seen him come after this 'Nate' with a belt, a wheel wrench, a wooden paddle, and what looked like the leg of a chair," I say. "It's not like we want to do anything to the boy that his *tian* hasn't done already."

"Just because he does it to Nate doesn't mean he'll like us doing it," Christopher says.

Later this "Nate" bicycles to the wharf wearing a wool beanie. He rides down the pier, making a vile gesture at each of the yellow signs that prohibit bicycling on the pier, and disappears behind the lighthouse. Stewart and I hope his friend will come—sometimes the boy and his friend meet at the lighthouse. We like when the boy and his friend are together—it is intriguing to see what new cruelties he will perform upon his friend, moving to see him and his friend reunited again after the cruelties have ended. We park between trucks with rusted motorboats on hitched trailers.

"Would you rather stab him in the stomach, or stomp on his throat so hard that it literally crushes his windpipe?" Christopher says.

"I am not answering that," I say. "Stewart, do not answer that."

"I can't decide which is better," Christopher says. "Why can't we fight him? He's alone now."

Stewart gestures at the yachts and the speedboats moored along the docks.

"We can't jump him here. Somebody might see us," Stewart says.

"Fine," Christopher says. "Would you rather punch him in the face until his eyes are swollen shut, or drag him across some broken glass?"

The boy rides back down the pier, pumping along the boardwalk back toward downtown. Stewart waits until the boy has disappeared before starting the pickup. We find the bicycle dumped on the pavement outside the gas station, "Nate" prowling the aisles inside. Stewart and I hope the boy is getting candy—it is confusing to feel as we do, as if we would like to give him both candy and bruises. But we have never seen anybody as happy as this boy when he is chewing a candy.

Instead he emerges empty-handed, gathers a handful of rocks from the alley behind the arcade, flattens against the wall. He peeks, flings a rock at a passing automobile, and then ducks back into the alley. A rock pings off the bumper of the next automobile as the brake lights flash red. The elderly driver throws his elbow over his seat, twisting around, frowning, looking for the source of the noise. The boy peeks, flings another rock. The rock cracks against the rear window. The driver curses, yanks the gearshift, and speeds away. The boy peeks again, huffing into his cupped hands, warming his fingers with his breath.

"I can't understand why anybody would want to hurt people like the *kimlee* does," Stewart says.

"You want to hurt him," Christopher says.

"I mean hurt somebody like Emma, who hasn't done anything to him," Stewart says.

"You hurt Emma," Christopher says.

"He does not," I say, feeling *othery* for Stewart, knowing he, like me, hates nothing more than seeing Emma unhappy.

"He does too. So do you. How about when you said that our mom must have loved her boyfriend more than us if she left?" Christopher says.

"I never said that," I say.

"We heard you," Christopher says.

I have no memory of having said it, which makes this an instance of *diffiction*, a noun I defined as "a memory inconsistent with the shared reality of others' memories; something nonfictional to an individual but fictional to the individual's society." *Diffiction* is my most successful work, in that since its publication it has appeared in new dictionaries by three separate publishers, each appearance prompting a lawsuit, the lawsuits far beyond profitable.

"If he said it, it was only because he believed it," Stewart says.

"That doesn't mean she didn't cry about it later," Christopher says.

"Okay, so one time he said something that hurt her feelings," Stewart says.

"You also told her not to get her hair cut any shorter than last time because if it was any shorter she'd look like a boy," Christopher says to me, then says to Stewart, "and you ate the chocolate she bought with her own money, and also you told her that if she was an animal she'd be a mole."

"She laughed when I said that," Stewart says.

"She wasn't laughing about it later in her room," Christopher says.

★ ★ ★

Our weakness is the same it has always been—the books we read as children, the books we read still. We study "Nate" too long: see him following his *tian* around the yard, imitating his *tian*'s lumbering stride; see him ducking the balled-up homework flung at him from buses; see him mocking a younger boy holding a grown-up's hand downtown; see him shoved against his garage by his *tian* after having punched his friend in the face, struggling as his *tian* growls at his friend to hit the boy back, shouting as his *tian* gestures at his friend that the boy will not be released until his friend has struck him in the face in retribution; see him peeing against the trash bin behind the bookstore after the owners of the bookstore and the antique shop and the gas station and the arcade have all refused to let him use the bathrooms inside; see him sitting alone on the rocks along the pier on days his friend doesn't come, hood up, shoulders hunched, feeding the gulls from his hand. Stewart and I suffer *othery* for this "Nate," still hate him, and try not to love him, but love him anyway, unable to kill our aptitude for *othery*, the skill we learned as children—a skill our *tian* never learned, nor our sister, nor even this "Nate" himself.

Stewart pretends nothing is wrong, insisting that when the opportunity arises he will fight him, with or without me. I say we should forget the boy, should devote our afternoons to other pursuits, but Stewart says our afternoons are for Emma, shaming me into coming.

Stewart pretends nothing is wrong, I pretend nothing is wrong, and Christopher is utterly unaware that we have been changed—unaware until the afternoon that "Nate" bothers to look at the pickup and wonder who's inside.

★ ★ ★

The pickup is parked across from the boy's cottage, windows tinted with frost. Stewart is napping under a blanket; I'm sipping tea from a mug; Christopher sits between us, rubbing his mittens together to warm his hands, talking about what he plans on doing to this "Nate" once we finally have him cornered.

I feel the bed of the pickup bob.

Christopher spins, I spin, and together we peer through the cracks in the frost and see the boy creeping along the bed toward the rear window of the cab, breathing mouthfuls of fog.

"Stewart," I whisper, nudging him, "start the truck!"

"Let's get him, let's get him!" Christopher says, diving for the handle of the door.

I hit the lock and shove him back. "Sit still," I hiss at Christopher, then shake Stewart, whispering, "Stewart!"

The boy squats at the rear window, wiping at the frost with his hands until his palms have melted patches back to glass. Stewart blinks awake just as the boy peeks into the cab.

"*You* faggots?" the boy shouts, squinting at us.

Christopher scrambles for the other door, shouting, "Let me out!" I snatch him by the ankles and yank him back again as "Nate" climbs onto the cab—we hear him fumbling around above us—and then leaps back down onto the bed, slamming down hard with his boots, making the pickup shudder. The boy hops around, shouting something too muffled for us to make out.

"How'd he find us?" Stewart shouts.

"What do you mean, how'd he find us?" Christopher shouts, kicking at me, lunging for the door again. "We're parked outside of his house! Let me out of here already!"

Stewart glances at Christopher, then looks at me, and can't pretend anymore. He grabs Christopher by the collar, so roughly that it chokes him, and shoves him back between us. Christopher hunches in the seat, holding his throat, coughing, as Stewart fumbles in his pockets for his keys.

The boy appears at the window next to me wielding a branch the size of a bat. He cocks back and takes a swing at the door, and the branch hits the door with a jarring thud. "Fuck all of you!" the boy shouts, spittle flecking his parka. "You dogfucking faggots! Fuck you and fucking Emma and everyone in your fucking family! I'll kill all of you fuckers!" The branch splinters against the door and the boy stoops at the fender, digging around in the snow for another. Stewart starts the pickup.

"Run him over!" Christopher shouts.

But "Nate" is back, swinging at the window. "Get the fuck away from my house!" he shouts as the branch cracks against the glass. "Gutterfucks! Pixielovers! Buttsnobs!"

The door to his cottage slams open and his *tian* stomps out into the snow in gym shorts and shoeless just as Stewart shifts the pickup and floors the gas. The tires spin in the snow, the window shatters, the pickup lurches into the road. Christopher and I turn, watching through the rear window as the boy's *tian* jerks the branch away from him, the boy shouting words at us we're too far away to hear, words we wouldn't understand even if we weren't. The boy has a private language of his own; he has the words he needs to hate us. His *tian* quiets him with the branch, and then the pickup dips with the road into a thicket of trees and Christopher and I can't see anything anymore and turn back around.

"Take me back," Christopher says. Stewart says we won't. Christopher calls us cowards. He doesn't speak another word to us until we're home.

A fox with snowy fur scampers away from the garage as we pull into the driveway. Stewart tosses his jacket onto the stool by the door, I hang my jacket from the knobs on the wall, but Christopher keeps his coat zipped, with clumps of snow melting on his shoulders.

"Even if you were afraid to get out of the car, you could have at least let me out," Christopher says, crying now, voice cracking. "I quit band for the chance to get back at him. I quit band, I lie to Emma about why I'm not on the bus anymore, we sit in your stupid truck every stupid day waiting for the perfect stupid opportunity, and then when it finally comes you let him say whatever he wants and then just drive away after he's finished."

"Shouldn't you be happy, you idiot?" Stewart says. "We didn't fight him, we aren't going to fight him, and now she won't have to hate us like you said she would."

"Just because she wouldn't have understood what it meant doesn't mean it wouldn't have meant it," Christopher says.

Christopher slips out the door, shuffling off into the snow. We watch him hike into the woods. It is irrelevant what this "Nate" has done, irrelevant what more this "Nate" might do. We cannot think of him as a foe, a *kimlee*, anymore, can think of him only as somebody with his own *hurdens*. Not merely a "Nate," but an actual boy who would actually feel whatever we did to him. We are men who in the eighteenth century would have been called incapable, pitiful, spineless, men who in the twenty-first century are called those things still. We could not defend our niece from the evils of the world. We could not defend even those evils from other evils.

Stewart won't talk to me, instead carries a flattened box from the garage to the driveway, tapes the cardboard over the broken window, then brushes the snow from the cab. I stand at the kitchen window, waiting for the extracurricular bus to bring Emma home from the latest performance of her play. While I wait, I take an empty vase from the cabinet and pour in some water. Every night somebody has been going to watch her; every night some boy has been bringing her flowers.

Rites

Months before the rites, they began arguing about who would bring great-uncle, cousin-in-law, brother Orson.

They argued on the blanketed bleachers of football stadiums, on sunbleached driftwood along the lakeshore, over rusted grills of smoking meat. While they argued, they fiddled with nearby objects. Shifting umbrellas, swiping at handfuls of sand, nudging the lids of ketchup bottles. Moving things from here to there. The impulse of the animate to manipulate the inanimate. To reposition, to rearrange.

They were a big family.

Among them there were those who affected the rigid silence of their Polish ancestors, those who affected the wine-drunk gestures of their Sicilian ancestors, those who affected the dour sneer of their French ancestors, those who affected the wind-beaten posture of their Manx. They bore Belgian lips under Irish noses, beneath Scandinavian foreheads. They wrinkled like Luxembourgers. They wrinkled like Turks. They were the product of thirteen generations of immigrants intermarrying. They were everything, which felt very much like being nothing.

They lived in Minnesota.

Some dwelled in gated manors, on leafy estates. Some dwelled in cluttered bungalows, among suburban sidewalks. Some dwelled in apartments above restaurants in the city. Pearl lived in a farmhouse, on untilled farmland, in the countryside, which was where the rites were to be held.

The argument was resolved in the back of a taxi, where Pearl's sons were crammed, wiping rainwater from their eyes. Everybody except Zack agreed it should be Zack.

"He won't come," Zack argued.

"You'll have to make him," said bearded Morgan.

"Tell him lies, if that's what it takes," said bearded Lauren.

"Remember, he took you fishing once when we were younger," said mustached Alexander. "He never took any of us fishing."

Everybody agreed it should be Zack, because once Orson had taken Zack fishing.

Next they argued about who would pay for the gasoline.

★ ★ ★

The internet said the weather would be foggy on the morning of the rites.

On the morning of the rites the weather was foggy.

Zack drove to Uncle Orson's apartment. Zack's wife was layering a mask of cosmetics over her face. Zack's daughters were bobbing their heads and singing along with an advertisement.

Zack parked the car at the curb.

Zack's wife uncapped some lipstick, said, "Hurry."

Zack's daughters sang, "Drinking—it's—my—life!"

Zack buzzed Uncle Orson's apartment.

★ ★ ★

Uncle Orson was wearing a pale violet bathrobe and a discolored pair of boxers. His fingers were wrapped with a bandage. His nostrils and ears and nipples were sprouting whitish hair.

"I don't like rites," Uncle Orson said.

"It's going to be more than pills and champagne," Zack said.

"I don't care what it's going to be," Uncle Orson said.

Uncle Orson's apartment reeked of leeks and cabbage. Piles of unwashed dishes stood tilting against piles of faded magazines. An envelope with a gold seal and stamped postage (the invitation to the rites, signed by Zack's mother, Orson's sister, Pearl) lay crumpled on the sofa, stained with a smear of snot or mustard.

"It's an honor for the family," Zack said.

"It'd be better if I didn't come," Uncle Orson said.

"She's only sixty-seven," Zack said.

"The age is irrelevant," Uncle Orson said.

"Don't you love her?" Zack said.

"That's what I'm saying," Uncle Orson said.

★ ★ ★

Orson sat between Zack's daughters.

Zack's daughters weren't singing anymore.

It wasn't Orson's apartment that reeked of leeks and cabbage.

It was Orson.

★ ★ ★

They drove through the city. They drove through buildings tattooed with graffiti and through buildings capped with billboards and past plastic bags hurrying together onto a bridge. They drove under stoplights lurching in the wind and past flags with gold stars hanging jerking from balconies. They drove past blinking signage. They drove past gutters weeping steam. They drove from the city into the woody countryside roads, drove through the fog to the barren unplowed fields where Pearl lived in the farmhouse with its painted shutters. And the other cars were there already, and Zack's daughters ran into the house and through the unlit rooms of empty cupboards and boxed belongings and latched windows and shrouded mirrors and out of the house again, the screen door slamming shut as Zack's daughters galloped from the deck into the trees, stumbling panting to a stop along the shore of the marsh, where everybody was standing with the dew blackening their shoes. And mustached Alexander was lugging a can of gasoline onto the dock. And bearded Lauren and bearded Morgan were talking to their mother's roommates from university, the roommates who hadn't had their own rites yet, a pair of women with gray bouffants and suits wrinkled from the train, and Lauren and Morgan were nodding and smiling. And their mother in her blue dress and gold pearls was laughing with the children—the neighbors' children, and Lauren's children, and Morgan's children, and the daughters of a man with a port-wine birthmark who had worked with their mother at the theater, and some cousins' children, and now Zack's daughters—and a few of the children were weeping, but Zack's daughters scolded them. And Alexander's husband was doing a dance for the cousins. And Zack was pouring himself, and then their mother's wrinkled childhood sweetheart, a glass of champagne at the rickety tables propped along the birch trees. And the tablecloths fluttered with the wind. And golden balloons bobbed on strings. And loafers squelched through mud. And the rowboat creaked in the marsh. And the fog drifted through reeds. And Orson stood against the rough bark of a maple tree, and the tree had a scar in its limb from the clothesline it had worn there for years and years and years, but now the clothesline had been unknotted, and wound, and boxed. And now everybody had a glass of champagne except for Orson.

Zack made a speech about their mother's moods.

Alexander made a speech about their mother's quirks: about what Pearl had liked watching (horror films, usually bloody, often with zombies, which had given Alexander nightmares), about how Pearl had dressed the brothers (matching shirts, as children, always), about where Pearl had kept spare sheets (inexplicably, Zack's closet).

Lauren and Morgan made a speech about different memories: a memory of her taking them to a parade; a memory of her taking them to a waterfall; a memory of her giving a speech at her own mother's rites; a memory of her chasing Alexander through the house with a ladle after Alexander had sworn at her; a memory of her nursing Zack during a fever and Zack's hallucinations during that fever and the braces on Zack's teeth in those days; memories of things she had worn that were now unfashionable.

And again their mother was laughing.

And others made speeches. And when their mother saw Orson, she clapped her hands together, and said his name, and hugged him. And wrinkles made maps in the skin of her face. And she thanked him for coming. And he whispered something to her. And Zack's daughters were teaching the other children the words to an advertisement. And the children were singing advertisements. And their mother offered a toast, and the champagne glasses clinked, tipped, emptied. And when their mother was ready, bearded Lauren and bearded Morgan shook gasoline into the rowboat, and shook gasoline onto their mother, and their mother stepped dripping from the dock into the boat. And the boat pitched from side to side. And their mother's bouffant had wilted from the gasoline. And their mother's dress had been blackened by gasoline. And Zack untied the boat, and their mother clutched the oars, and their mother rowed into the marsh. And the boat slid through the reeds into darker waters. And their mother stood, then, in a swaying rowboat, in a foggy marsh, facing the family. And lit the match. And dropped it. And the rowboat became a fire the shape of a rowboat. And their mother became a fire the shape of a mother.

The fire was waving.

Everybody clapped.

Alexander cheered.

The wives of Lauren and Morgan shouted their goodbyes.

But Orson wept, as if Orson were one of the children.

★ ★ ★

The paperwork was submitted. Pearl's belongings were variously inherited, or donated, or sent to the landfill. The farm, its vast acreage, had been sold months before.

Afterward they gossiped, the family, about how Orson had cried.

"A disgrace."

"Almost ruined the celebration."

"I said from the start, he's unsociable, he's antisocial, just don't invite him."

"Why was he crying? Does he think her life was a failure, unfulfilled, unhappy somehow? Doesn't he understand that she was quite successful, actually?"

"She certainly chose painful rites."

"No worse than a twelve-hour wedding day in heels."

"And she looked so lovely."

"You don't think she saw him, do you? From the boat? Her triumphant moment, spoiled by her own sibling?"

Even with Orson's tears, everybody agreed that Pearl's rites had outdone any rites to date—even the rites of William, Orson and Pearl's grandfather, who had imported a crate of fungus from Japan, bright scarlet toadstools the shapes of coral, and at dawn had eaten the toadstools, seated atop a throne of piled rocks, and then throughout the day had chatted with the family, until by dusk the toxins had killed him.

William's had been clever, but something about Pearl's—about seeing grandmother, great-aunt, cousin Pearl transform into a creature of fire, in the same rowboat in which her dead husband once had proposed their marriage, above the marsh at which she had stared so many mornings over mugs of tea—had captivated the family. To the last, they preferred sentiment to cleverness.

Orson had cried then too—when chinstrapped William had collapsed, in agony, from the rocks into the grass—but Orson had been a child then, and the family hadn't worried.

Now, however, the incident at the marsh had incited a growing animosity toward Orson, and therefore a growing interest. After years of being avoided, or ignored, or honestly forgotten altogether, Orson's standing had shifted from embarrassment to curiosity. At the rare event at which he would grace the family with his presence—a Memorial Day cookout, a Thanksgiving Day banquet, a Labor Day potluck—a gang of children would creep after him, peering at him from behind furnishings or shrubberies, studying his every tic. Gabe, a towheaded toothy boy who excelled at firing fireworks, insisted that Great-Uncle Orson could speak to animals. "He talked to the squirrel, and the squirrel *nodded*." Abby, a chubby pigtailed girl with an allergy to peanuts, claimed that Great-Uncle Orson had broken a plate. "But it was *broken*," Abby whined, although the remains of a plate were never found, and nobody, other than Abby, had heard the plate hit the floor.

Boxes were hauled from attics, photographs dusted with shirt-sleeves. "That's him as a kid?" asked Dylan, who was pathologically suspicious and often would force adults to repeat things, as if checking for inconsistencies. "That's him," said mustached Alexander. Dylan and his brothers squatted over the photographs to rummage through. Orson and Pearl standing sweaty, grinning, behind a lemonade stand. Orson and his parents at a horseshoe pit, pointing, exclaiming. Chin-strapped William helping Orson roast a frankfurter over a bonfire. "He looks so *average*," said Dylan's youngest brother, chewing a candy skull. Dylan frowned. Dylan squinted at the photographs. "That's him?" Dylan asked, again. Alexander confirmed, again, that the child was Great-Uncle Orson, and then Zack's daughters appeared in the doorway in baggy superhero capes and said that anybody who wanted to trick-or-treat had about one second before they got left behind.

There were those in the family who claimed they would be boy-cotting Orson's rites—bearded Lauren and bearded Morgan among them—as punishment for the disrespect that Orson had shown to Pearl. But the truth was that there also was a certain amount of anticipation now for Orson's rites, this secret feeling that something about Orson's rites might be exceptional, or memorable, or unusual somehow. When they were together, none of them spoke of it. Only when they were apart—in line at the supermarket with a certain sister, playing cribbage in the lamplit kitchen of a certain aunt—would they speak of it, confidant to confidant. As the secret spread, however, the truth became clear. They all had the same feeling. They couldn't wait.

Other rites were held, those years, the last of Orson's generation's.

Special permits were required if the departing had chosen a method other than pills, but the departing rarely chose other methods. Orson's cousin Jennifer chose pills, her fireplace, a frosty midwinter evening; Orson's cousin Benjamin chose pills, a rainstorm, his old deer blind; Heath, Orson's cousin-in-law, chose pills; and like that, Orson's generation vanished, leaving only Orson.

The family waited for the invitation to Orson's rites, but the invitation never came.

The traditional age for rites was seventy.

Orson, now, was seventy-three.

Their feeling shifted from anticipation to concern. Orson, they realized, was stalling.

★ ★ ★

They argued along the banks of a frozen pond, scarved with scarves, gloved with gloves, watching their children skate in loops across the starry ice. Stalling wasn't uncommon—hadn't great-grandmother, grandmother-in-law, great-aunt Winnie delayed her rites for over a year, canceling them, rescheduling them, canceling them, until she had found, finally, the courage?—but stalling was nevertheless uncomfortable for all involved. And, pointed out bearded Morgan, set a bad example for the children. And, pointed out bearded Lauren, was tremendously unpatriotic. And, pointed out bearded Morgan, was socially, and environmentally, and fiscally irresponsible, and arguably borderline criminal.

The family decided to send somebody to address the situation. Everybody except Zack agreed it should be Zack.

"Remember, he listened to you about Mom's rites," said mustached Alexander.

Alexander's husband offered to come and help, but Zack grunted, waved the offer away, and then lurched onto the ice with a goalie mask and hockey puck to the jeers of the children.

The next day, after work, Zack drove to Uncle Orson's apartment.

At the door, Uncle Orson's face was streaked with stripes, the aftermath of a nap on corduroy pillows. His cheeks had hollowed, as if he wasn't eating properly, and his hair was plastered to his brow. He was wearing his bathrobe over a pair of sweatpants and a ragged sweater.

Uncle Orson gathered magazines from a battered steamer trunk—limping with every other step—dumped the magazines on the kitchen counter, and set out a plate on the trunk, of crackers, which were stale, and which Zack ate out of politeness nonetheless. Chewing a cracker, surveying the apartment, Zack tucked his hands into the pockets of his suit coat and felt some unknown object there. Peeking into the pocket, Zack spotted a bottle of glittery nail polish. His daughters sometimes hid objects in his suits that they knew would embarrass him if discovered at work. His revenge was hiding baby photos of them in their textbooks to spill out onto their desks at school.

Uncle Orson seemed glad to have a visitor, but also had nothing to say. Uncle Orson just sat there, staring at the balcony, beaming, as if enjoying how the view was altered when shared with Zack. From the sofa, Zack could see into the darkened bathroom. The gleam of tiles. A glint of mirror. Boxed eye drops, grimy bottles of antacid tablets, gnarled tubes of hemorrhoid ointments. An unwashed cup brimming with multicolor painkillers. These were good signs. Stallers often became eager to quit stalling as their health worsened, as rites became less of a menace and more of a relief. From a purely selfish position, that was what rites offered: escaping the intensifying pain of living within a deteriorating body.

The internet had said today the wind would blow toward the lake.

The wind was blowing toward the lake.

Water dripped, dripped again, into the sink.

Zack explained that the family was wondering about Orson's rites.

Uncle Orson's face collapsed, like the flimsy frontage of a run-down building.

"Wouldn't you say it's time?" Zack said.

Fingers trembling, expression flickering between a scowl and a wince, Uncle Orson reached for a cracker.

"If you're afraid nobody will come, we'll make sure everybody comes," Zack said.

"I'm not going to do the rites," Uncle Orson said.

"If you need money, we'll help you pay for the ceremony," Zack said.

"I'm not going to do the rites," Uncle Orson said.

Zack started to speak again, then actually heard what Uncle Orson was saying.

Zack frowned, confused. "You're what now?"

"I'm not going to do the rites," Uncle Orson muttered, as if ashamed, and then slipped the cracker between his lips.

"You can't not," Zack said.

"There isn't any law," Uncle Orson said through a mouthful of cracker.

Zack unbuttoned his suit coat, leaning forward, elbows to knees. "How many years has it been since you taught? Nine? Ten?" Zack said. Uncle Orson gulped the cracker down. Zack hunched even closer yet, trying not to become upset, gesturing vaguely. "You can't keep on, just, consuming resources, creating waste, without contributing anything to society. There are eleven billion of us on this planet. A family planning policy helps prevent drought, prevent famines, wars over energy. By stalling, you're hurting everybody, you're hurting my generation, you're hurting the kids' generation, you're hurting their kids' generation, you're living like a primitive."

Now that Uncle Orson's secret was out, Uncle Orson seemed to relish saying it.

"I'm not going to do the rites," Uncle Orson said.

"Doing rites is a privilege we haven't always had," Zack said.

"I don't care what it is," Uncle Orson said.

"Our ancestors, your ancestors, fought for these rights," Zack said, angry now.

Uncle Orson gathered the plate.

"I don't want them," Uncle Orson said, and limped to the kitchen for another box of crackers.

★ ★ ★

When Zack reported that Orson wasn't stalling but in fact refused altogether, the family exploded, as across the stands rival fans erupted, with cap-waving applause, at a home run.

"Troglodyte!" shouted Morgan.

"Oh, what, he's going to cling to every last scrap of a second? Rot away, wither up, until he's incontinent, blind, demented? How much is he really going to enjoy those last few years, that he won't even hear, or taste, or remember?" shouted Lauren.

The rivals sat down again, some still applauding. Zack's daughters, one over at shortstop, one in the outfield, were mouthing words at each other, gossiping between plays.

"But he must understand the alternative!" said Morgan's wife.

"Forget his duty to society. How about his duty to himself? Because the outcome, if he refuses rites, is going to be inhumane. Hasn't he seen pictures of how—how *wasted*, how *ruined*—people became in those *barbaric* homes?" said Lauren's wife.

Mustached Alexander, standing, was booing the unpaid umpire.

"He was a history teacher," Zack said, yanking Alexander down. "He's seen the pictures."

By sundown, everybody knew. The family—several cousins especially, with municipal political positions, wary of any potential scandal—insisted Zack talk sense into Orson, through whatever means necessary, before Orson became conspicuously overage. Zack didn't know how. "Just go back," smiled Zack's wife, popping a pan of popcorn in the kitchen, slapping Zack's butt, "and make him understand."

So Zack did. He went back—several times—and every time found himself unable to talk to Uncle Orson about the rites. Instead, Zack sat on a wobbly foldout chair on the balcony and watched Uncle Orson feed seeds to birds. A wren with speckled plumage would alight on the chipped railing. Uncle Orson would offer a handful of seeds, nibble a seed as an example, try to encourage the bird to eat. Beyond the railing, sunlight gleamed on the windows of the relish factory. Clouds made shapes. Sitting there next to Uncle Orson, Zack felt very much like a child. Like a bulky, lumbering, hairy orphan, wearing a work suit like a costume. Zack didn't often have time to think, to sit and think and reflect, which was perhaps why he was so often so happy. He rather fiercely wanted to live a moral, responsible, good life. But those evenings on the balcony, as he tried to find the words to reason with Uncle Orson, he began to admit that he didn't understand, exactly, why everybody did things how everybody did. It made him feel very lost. As if he weren't a member of any family, but was ultimately just himself, bewildered, alone.

Afterward, Zack would drive home and pretend to have made some progress.

And in the brownstone apartments across from Zack's office, a hunched balding woman hung herself with an extension cord while Zack tried to balance an account. And as Zack jogged through the misted streets of the city, sweating through sweatbands, breathing steam, the kin of a gaunt bespectacled woman huddled beneath umbrellas to watch as the woman leapt from a bridge and then tumbled, coattails flapping, toward the water below. And Zack's barber celebrated a birthday—a seventy-first—by carving his arms with a razor and bleeding himself dry, and after that Zack's hair was cut by a younger barber with tattooed arms who told no jokes. A stranger buttoned and fastened and zipped himself into soaking clothes, and then sat on the pier, alone, until the clothes froze and he froze. A muttonchopped retiree leapt from the roof of a hotel, landed on an empty taxi, broke his spine, his pelvis, multiple ribs, and both heels, and failed to die, until his rites were completed by a doctor with a syringe. Elsewhere in Minnesota, among the thousands who died in those years of alcohol poisoning, several were seventy-year-olds who had chosen whiskey or brandy for their rites. Another poisoned herself with caffeine, another poisoned himself with cocaine, another with insulin. Another with oxygen. Another with water. Another ate a colorful blend of monkshood seeds, nightshade root, and yew berries, with a demitasse of foxglove tea. In Idaho, a lifelong conservationist opted to be eaten by wolves. In Pennsylvania, a former flyweight boxing champion elected to die of heatstroke in a sauna. In Arkansas, a renowned painter painted herself, her skin, sole to brow, with silver paint, and thereby suffocated. In Florida, a court-martialed general disemboweled himself with a dagger. While in Minnesota, across the street from Zack's home, a retired librarian was starving, ate nothing, as her friends came and went, saying hello, checking how she was, with rites that lasted almost a month. And as Zack and his daughters loaded sacks of sausage and eggplant and detergent into their trunk, the sound of a pistol firing echoed across the parking lot of the supermarket, the sound of rites completed, followed by a family applauding, from a fenced yard nearby. And as Zack and a coworker bought espressos from the stand in the park, a faint tart smell of smoke lingered above them, the odor of a house fire, accidental, caused during the rites of an electrician who had chosen electrocution. And as Zack jogged through the dripping streets of the city, splashing through puddles, panting, a withered stubbled man pinned with a brittle corsage lowered himself gingerly onto train tracks below, while the conductor of the oncoming train sounded the whistle, and sounded the whistle, cheering him on.

People became bodies. The animate the inanimate. Zack jogged home and began setting the table for supper as his daughters, clutching worksheets, begged for help with math.

★ ★ ★

They ate gelato sometimes, the family. Raspberry, hazelnut, pistachio, lemon. Kaleidoscopic plastic tubs, strewn across the heavy oak table, with wine from their cellarage. As their spoons flashed, they obsessed over Orson, like a child unable to leave alone a loose tooth. What did Orson live for? What was it that had given him this mania for life? A lover, a drug, a hobby? A goateed cousin who rented a studio in

Orson's neighborhood reported that Orson was often sighted walking along the relish factory, gathering speckled pebbles. Could somebody please explain that? Another cousin reported once spotting Orson sitting on a bench in the park, appearing to be taking extreme pleasure in the temperature of the paper cup of coffee clutched between his bare hands. The cousin hadn't said hello. A pimpled nephew, who had an internship that summer at the offices of Orson's physician, and who normally had only the utmost respect for the confidentiality of patients' records, had peeked at Orson's, and reported now that Orson suffered from a recurring affliction that was downright nauseating. Zack mentioned the hemorrhoid ointments, but the pimpled nephew laughed these off, as if, compared to this, hemorrhoids were nothing. The pimpled nephew bounced his eyebrows. Did they want the details? Did they? Huh? Nobody did. Bearded Lauren, waving a wallet, claimed to be willing to wager anything, any amount whatsoever, that Orson had a total of zero friends, companions, and acquaintances. Bearded Morgan dared somebody to make a wager. The goateed cousin was slapping Zack on the back, pointing at their spoons, comparing flavors. What was it? What was it that had given him this mania for life? What did Orson live for? Zack's daughters were obliterating the other children at table tennis in the garage, using spin moves Zack had taught them that they claimed to have invented.

At work, Zack often would stare in a daze across the street at the arched window where the woman had hung herself with only cats for an audience. After the rooms were emptied, the apartment was rented by a curly-haired woman with curly-haired children, who moved taped boxes into each room, and untaped the boxes, and unpacked the objects stowed there, carefully choosing a place for each object to rest—a china cabinet just shy of a radiator, a record player on the windowsill—this *here*, this *here*. Zack worried not only that he had failed to persuade Uncle Orson, but that Uncle Orson had managed to persuade him. Zack worried constantly. Raking leaves, dusting windows, forking frosting from birthday cake. Zack wasn't sure anymore whether he could go through with the rites when his own time arrived.

But, then again, Zack never had to.

The week after his fiftieth birthday, while jogging at dusk across a bridge, Zack became nauseated, Zack's vision blurred wildly, and Zack collapsed, dead, of an aneurysm, on the concrete. Sneakers still knotted. Sweatbands still damp.

The moment before the blackout, as Zack began to stumble— Zack's thinking was getting muddled, Zack's vision was going foggy— Zack clung to a memory from years before, of the cloudy morning that Uncle Orson had taken Zack fishing.

As Zack's younger brothers had slept, Zack's mother, bleary-eyed, in a nightgown, had toasted Zack a slice of bread. Then Zack— holding the toast in his teeth—tied his boots, zipped his jacket, and ran from the farmhouse across frosted leaves to Uncle Orson's sputtering car. And they drove together under the stars to the lake, where they sat with fishing poles in a metal rowboat and waited for something to bite. Zack ate the toast, Uncle Orson gave some pointers, and then they cast the poles, again and again, into the pale fog. And dawn broke. And the sunrise cracked. And clouds settled across the sky. And the fog scattered. And they still hadn't caught anything. And, that whole time, the exact same gull had been circling overhead.

"Nothing's happening," Zack complained.

But Uncle Orson smiled at the clouds, and smiled at the rowboat, and smiled at the gull, and smiled at the poles.

"Nothing has to happen," Uncle Orson had said.

Then Zack hit the concrete and Zack was gone.

Darkness had fallen by the time the medics carted off the body.

Zack's wife wasn't home yet.

Zack's daughters took the call, moments after hiding a plastic unicorn in a suit coat upstairs.

That was the night that they learned, Zack's daughters, that there was a difference, a noticeable difference, between rites and other death.

Because, with rites, you could brace yourself. Because, with rites, you knew the person was ready. Because, with rites, you could say goodbye.

The internet said stars would fall from the sky.

Stars fell.

★ ★ ★

Zack's wasn't the only unscheduled death of that generation. A cousin, Dylan's mother, died of kidney cancer a few years later, and mustached Alexander of a fall from a ladder a few years before his rites were due. Burials, compared to rites, were quiet, gloomy, lonely things. Nobody liked them.

The rest of that generation, however, did live to do their rites. Zack's wife chose pills; bearded Lauren, bearded Morgan, chose pills; they all chose pills, the cousinage, because pills were painless, and dependable, and clean. And like that, Zack's generation vanished, leaving their children to run the family.

Some inherited money.

Some inherited debts.

They all inherited Orson.

Orson aged—septuagenarian, octogenarian, nonagenarian—and Orson's body broke down. His skin thinned; his glasses thickened; his jaw hung open constantly, shutting only when chewing; he shrank from bony to spindly to skeletal, a sweater hanging on him like a sheet on a broom; he moved about with the reckless stooped hobble of somebody barely capable of withstanding everyday forces like gravity, somebody for whom a level floor was a trampoline springing. The warpage of his spine, the wastage of his jowls, were staggering. He was conspicuous, had blatantly surpassed the traditional age, was obviously flaunting the rites, and in the city was persecuted accordingly.

The local grocer refused to sell him food. The cashiers at the supermarket didn't outright refuse, but instead bullied him into taking his patronage elsewhere, mainly by overcharging him for everything in his cart, ringing up, for example, a can of peas as a snowblower, and ignoring his protests. As for the local convenience store, that was staffed by surly lipringed teens who offered to hold his rites then and there. The museum banned him. The cinema barred him. The library, less rigorous, had him use the back door. Even at places where the family worked, Orson was unwelcome. Zack's daughters, who taught together at the same school in neighboring classrooms, had witnessed other teachers on the playground urging the children to look away or shut their eyes as he passed by on the sidewalk. Gabe, still towheaded, still toothy, but whose prowess with fireworks had peaked at age eleven, now owned a storage company, and sometimes overheard employees heckling him through the chain-link fence, and never intervened. Abby, whose allergy to peanuts persisted even into her middle age, now worked reviewing mortgages at a local bank, where every week from her cubicle she would spot him entering the lobby to withdraw money from a machine. Using the machines gave him some difficulty, but the tellers had stopped serving him years ago. Sweating, murmuring, trembling, he would struggle through the prompts and options. Managing to complete the withdrawal could take him as long as an hour. After prying the cash from the machine, Orson finally would count through each of the bills to verify the total before hobbling out again. Orson's salary had always been modest. How long he had been saving, and planning, for his act of rebellion, his life after retirement, they didn't know.

They sat through power outages, around the flickering stumps of scattered candles, under heaps of blankets, watching blizzards bury porches.

Other families—led by the grandchildren of immigrants, by the children of immigrants, by immigrants themselves—celebrated Pakistani holidays, told Guatemalan myths, wore Nigerian jewelry.

They were a family who entire generations before had abandoned any pretense of participating in the cultures of their ancestors' homelands. They had only the culture of their homeland. Which felt very much like a nonculture. Like no culture at all.

Which perhaps helps explain why they took such an interest in other cultures. They often traded facts, the family, that they had heard about other countries. Articles, legends, rumors. Unusual reports. Their favorites including a certain story about China.

In China, in graveyards, meals were often left on the graves as offerings to ancestors. But, they had heard, these meals often disappeared. Not eaten by ghosts. Eaten by the homeless. The homeless there survived by sneaking into graveyards and eating the offerings. Chestnuts, dumplings, pickles, noodles. Meals meant for the dead.

Orson seemed like that to them.

But the opposite.

Like a ghost, stealing from the plates of the living.

They delivered packages, and managed portfolios, and designed bridges, and waited for Orson to die. But he didn't. He ate crackers. He drank coffee. He looked at rocks; he looked at birds; he sat on benches. Sometimes, on rare autumn mornings, on rare spring evenings, he might even call them, asking somebody for a ride to someplace, a family gathering, a birthday party. And somebody would—somebody always, always would—would drive across town, and help him into the sedan, and drive back across town, and help him out of the sedan, and lead him along the stone pathway and up the brick steps and through the doorway and the hanging streamers and the bobbing balloons and the wrapped presents buried beneath wrapped presents, into those warm rooms of chatting people. There he would be, drifting through clusters of men in bow ties smiling hello and men in buttoned vests chopping apples and men in colorful sweaters feeding infants from plastic bottles and women in shimmering blouses waving hello and aproned women ladling cider and monocled women reading aloud from illustrated fables and teenagers in sweatshirts playing the piano and cowlicked boys sneaking cake and ballcapped children spilling marbles and girls in dresses chasing after balloons—there he would be, for the whole party, not speaking to anybody. He was the unhappiest person they had ever met. And he was theirs, somehow. He belonged to them. Their undying mystery, and their great shame.

The Transition

Of course, his family had heard of the operation, knew not only that such a thing was possible but that there were actually people doing it, and although his family was conservative, his family wasn't radical by any means, in fact his family was really quite moderate, so much so that during elections in which the conservative candidate seemed especially intolerant or corrupt or feebleminded his family was occasionally even known to vote for the liberal alternative, and although his family was religious, his family certainly wasn't the type to speak of issues in terms of good and evil, and for instance had no qualms about nudity in the media, and sometimes drank to excess, and wasn't opposed to gambling, and believed in evolution, and although his family was poor, not destitute exactly, but decidedly working class, and held no college degrees, his family possessed no prejudice against people who elected to have vanity surgeries like liposuction and rhinoplasty, and were always heartened to meet people benefiting from bionic modifications such as pacemakers and prostheses, and enjoyed watching programs of an educational nature, and took naturally to new technologies—and yet there was something that set the operation apart from other issues, something that repulsed his family almost instinctually, something that filled his family with contempt, a fact his family had made no effort to hide, like back when the news had been flooded with stories about a famous architect who had transitioned and his family had spent an evening sitting around out on the stoop ridiculing the architect, or back when the news had been flooded with stories about a former model who had transitioned and his family had spent an evening sitting around out on the stoop bashing the model, and so the fact that his family found the concept utterly loathsome certainly would have been clear to Mason.

Then there was also his personality. He was profoundly reserved. He rarely smiled. He seldom laughed. He spoke clearly, without any animation. Although he often complained, he never became angry. He never seemed gloomy. He never appeared excited. He must have cried occasionally as a child, but no incidents came to mind specifically, and regardless he certainly hadn't cried in the presence of his family since. He never showed signs of feeling powerful emotions.

So, considering that he was showing signs as he sat there at the table, that his hands were trembling, that his voice was shaking, that he was so nervous that the feeling was actually affecting him physically, and that he really wasn't in the habit of joking about this type of thing—or, quite honestly, joking about anything—there seemed to be no doubt that he was serious when he interrupted a moment of silence to announce, or rather confess, that he was planning to have his mind converted to digital data and transferred from his body to a computer server.

Mason's father, who was wearing his favorite apron, with the cartoon pelican across the chest and the maroon stain just beneath the pockets, gaped at him from the counter in the kitchen, frozen there in the midst of dipping a silicone spatula into a container of the latest batch of his secret sauce. Mason's brothers, who planned to drive the motorboat down to parkland at dusk to go shrimping on the bayou, were reclined around the table in athletic jerseys and camouflage cutoffs, squinting at him with expressions of confusion. Mason's mother had come in from the backyard when she had heard him arrive, wearing the straw hat and baggy caftan that she'd been sunning in, and she felt such a jolt of panic when he said what he said that she had to set her iced tea down onto the nearest surface, the stove, or else she surely would have dropped the bottle onto the floor.

Mason stared at the table, and then, as if suddenly daring to hope that the idea might be met with no resistance, looked up and blurted, "We'll still be able to talk or whatever."

His mother crossed the kitchen toward the table, feeling past the counter with her hands, her eyes never leaving him. He must have been coming from a shift at the supermarket. His uniform was rumpled. His nametag was askew. He'd always been scrawny, but recently he seemed especially frail. His eyebrows were so light in color that he didn't seem to have eyebrows at all, which had caused him untold trouble on the playground as a child. He had watery eyes, a delicate nose, thin lips, and a weak chin. He looked like the type of person who'd probably have a milk allergy. She couldn't explain what that was supposed to mean exactly. A neighbor had said it about him once though, and as soon as she'd heard it, she'd known it was true. She loved his face. As she slid into a chair at the table, she had to resist an urge to reach over and cup his jaw in her palms. The thought of losing him was terrifying.

"I mean, I'll be able to chat whenever you want, I'll be online literally all of the time," Mason said, gaze falling back to the table.

His mother turned toward the counter, searching for some indication of how his father was reacting to the announcement. The heat from the sun was already leaving her skin, and the sensation seemed almost like a manifestation of her fear, as if the emotion were sapping the warmth from her skin as the feeling spread. She had been relaxing in a canvas lawn chair all morning, sipping from that bottle of iced tea, watching with amusement as sparrows hopped along the branches of the tree, basking in the occasional gust of wind that rushed across the backyard, letting loose tremendous yawns, stretching her limbs out, rubbing her eyes with the heels of her hands, scratching her belly periodically when the urge struck, savoring the tart aroma of the charcoal burning in the grill, enjoyably conscious of being dressed in a bright caftan and floppy hat. Coming in from that realm of bodily pleasure to be confronted with somebody who wanted to leave all of that behind was intensely jarring. She didn't understand what he could be thinking.

Over by the counter his father set down the spatula.

"You do realize that not having a body would mean not having a body?" his father said.

"Yes."

"As in never again?" his father said.

"Yes."

"What the hell is wrong with your head?" his father said.

His father swore only when he was deeply afraid, which told his mother that she wasn't the only one taking the announcement seriously. Despite how grave the situation was, however, his father apparently really did need to check on the grill before the ribs burned. Scowling, with the hem of his apron flapping at his shins with every step, his father marched out the door into the backyard.

Mason, who had been staring intently at his knuckles during that brief exchange with his father, glanced back up again. His cheeks were flushed; sweat pitted his shirt. His mother suddenly felt sure that this discussion, albeit awkward, would be easily resolved. Years from now, his family was going to look back on this moment and laugh about his mistake, like how the family still joked about the time that one of his brothers had considered quitting his job in order to sell dietary supplements for a company from door to door until the family had explained to him that the operation was obviously a scam, or how the family still joked about the time that one of his brothers had considered starting a jazz group until the family had explained to him that yes he might love the drums but honestly he had no rhythm and he didn't belong anywhere near a stage. Certainty spread through her, and a bit of pride that she had been the one to realize that this was all a misunderstanding. She felt so relieved that she had to suppress a grin.

"You're just not thinking," she announced.

"About what," Mason said.

"I don't know what put the idea in your head, but you're not like those other people doing it, there's too much you'd miss about having a body," she said.

She could tell from his stare that she hadn't yet convinced him, and she folded her hands together, searching for an example.

"Like dancing," she exclaimed.

"I hate dancing," Mason said.

"Oh you do not," she said, and then she fell silent, because she knew of course that he did.

Until now his brothers had been sitting back observing the scene, picking their teeth, biting their nails, but his brothers finally exploded.

"What the heck bro?"

"Where did this even come from?"

"How could you actually want something that messed up done?"

"Our own flesh and blood?"

His oldest brother leaned in.

"You'd even give up sex?" his oldest brother said.

Mason didn't reply, just gazed at the centerpiece, a vase of wildflowers.

"What about sex?" his oldest brother demanded.

Mason gave a faint shrug.

"More trouble than it's worth," Mason said.

She had never seen his brothers look so offended.

His oldest brother sat back, knitting his fingers behind his head with his elbows thrown wide in a posture of dismissal, and sneered, "Well, who cares if you want it done, you'll never have enough money to pay for it."

"I already do," Mason said.

Mason apparently had been setting aside a substantial portion of each paycheck for years now. His mother fiddled with the bangles around her wrists in distress. Back when his family had sat around mocking the celebrity chef who'd transitioned, back when his family had sat around trashing the piano prodigy who'd transitioned, he must have been saving up money for the operation even then. He had sat there and had listened to his family call people like that monsters and had secretly believed that he was a person like that all along. The thought stunned her.

Mason stared at the table, then glanced back up with a desperate look, exclaiming, "I hate having to deal with clothing. I hate having to go shopping and trying to find things that fit and having to put together an outfit every single day and worrying about what matches and having to drag everything down to the coin wash. I hate getting sick. I hate getting headaches and getting backaches and getting earaches and getting toothaches and puking especially. I hate having to get checkups at the doctor and the dentist and the optometrist every single year. I hate always having to make meals and eat the food and wash dishes afterward. I hate having to shower. I hate having to sleep. I'm tired of wasting so much of my life on taking care of a body. I just want to be able to read stuff and talk to people all of the time."

"Sweetie," his mother said. She leaned across the table, her heart beating frantically, and laid her hands over his hands. "I know you might feel like that right now, but if you'd just stop and think about it for a couple days, you're going to change your mind."

"I've been thinking about it for over twenty years," Mason said.

He eased his hands out from under her hands, pulling away, as if ashamed.

"I don't belong in a body," Mason said.

He lowered his head.

"I've always known," Mason said.

He left before the meal was served, slipping out the door with his shoulders slumped, then sputtering off down the road in his rusty hatchback. While his brothers sat around the table bitterly rehashing that comment about sex, his mother drifted in a daze out into the backyard, where his father was squatting over the grill. Looking up from the ribs with an expression of fury, his father confessed that he had come out to the backyard not so much out of concern for the ribs as out of fear that he had been about to cry, which he had never done in the presence of the children before and didn't want to.

Mason had scheduled the operation for later that February, just a month away, taking the earliest available appointment the local clinic could offer. As his mother brushed her teeth that night, an activity in which she usually found much enjoyment—the tingle of foam on her tongue, the prick of bristles against her gums—she couldn't focus on the experience at all, but instead was gripped by a feeling of dread. She had driven past the local clinic before, a nondescript facility with screened windows and tinted doors, and the place always seemed to have a sinister aura. Although he had asked his family to be there for the operation, there was no way that she could go. She found the concept disturbing enough when the procedure was done to a stranger, let alone her youngest son. What frightened her most was imagining the actual transition. The exact moment when his body would be empty. The exact moment when his mind would be gone.

She had never suspected he might want something like that, but now that she knew he did, she couldn't help feeling like she should have suspected all along. He had always been different than his brothers. He had been a puny, feeble, pallid child. Even back then he had whined about everything. He hadn't liked doing puzzles. He hadn't liked making crafts. As an eater he had been picky, declining to eat fruits, refusing to eat vegetables, not even liking candy, subsisting mainly on cereal and macaroni. He'd sipped reluctantly at colas. He'd grudgingly nibbled at cookies. His brothers in contrast had eaten with gusto, devouring multiple helpings apiece of whatever she'd cooked, praising the flavors in exultation, licking salt from lips and grease from fingers. His brothers had been playful too, wrestling each other and racing each other and spinning each other dizzy and taking great joy in both resisting and surrendering to gravity, climbing trees and leaping from roofs and soaring and plunging back and forth on swings, but he'd had an aversion to physical activity. He hadn't even liked walking. He'd had a listless gait, walking about with his arms limp and his feet dragging, as if having to walk was an arduous task, simply onerous. Getting him to make the walk from the front door of the house to the bus stop at the corner on weekday mornings had been nothing short of a miracle. He hadn't liked going outdoors at all. If she had tried to take him bicycling, he would crank at the pedals a few times, then grumble, gradually coast to a stop, slide off of the seat, let the bicycle fall onto the pavement, and flop down on the curb, refusing to go any farther, complaining that pedaling made his legs hurt. If she had tried to take him canoeing, he would heave on the paddle a few times, then mutter, slump over on the seat, and stare at the bottom of the canoe, complaining that paddling made his arms hurt. If she had tried to take him swimming at the ocean, the water had always been too hot or too cold or too salty or too wet. While his family had tossed a foam ball around in the shallows, he had sat on the beach with his arms wrapped around his shins and his chin propped on his knees, either in the sun, complaining that the light was too bright, or under the umbrella, complaining that the shade was too dark. Sitting on the sand had made his butt hurt.

He was remarkably annoying. Yet despite how finicky he was—or maybe even because—he had always been her favorite. She adored him. The only time he had ever seemed content as a child was when he had been left to his own devices. He had preferred to stay indoors, hunched over a screen on his beanbag in his bedroom, poring through online encyclopedias. Compared to how reserved he had been in person, he had seemed to come alive when exchanging messages with people over the internet. Occasionally she had even heard him chuckle or snicker in there at something he had read. She had taken pains to keep him from being disturbed.

Now she couldn't help blaming herself for what was happening. She had only wanted him to be happy, but in the process she had ruined him. She should have forced him to play with other children. She should have forced him to eat whatever she had cooked instead of letting him prepare meals of bland grains. She should have forced him to bike and she should have forced him to canoe and she should have forced him to swim until he had learned how to love the world. It was her fault that he had ended up like this. She had failed him as a mother.

She spit toothpaste into the sink, rinsed the toothbrush under the faucet, shut off the lamp in the kitchen, set an alarm for work the next day, and then climbed into bed. His father was lying there on his back with the blanket thrown off. Moonlight coming through the window illuminated the strip of gut exposed between the band of his briefs and the hem of his tee. She stared at the silhouette of the fan on the ceiling for a while.

"I reject the notion that somebody can be born that way," his father grumbled.

She felt the mattress dip as he shifted to look at her.

"If you're born in a body, then you belong in a body, and that's that," his father said.

When she didn't respond he swiveled back toward the ceiling.

"He's just lazy. Doesn't want to work anymore. Just wants to live for free. God knows we've got enough of those types in this country. Well, okay, he's paying for it himself. So maybe he'll be more like somebody who's retired than like some freeloader on welfare. Fine. But you can't turn somebody into data. They can turn his memories to data, they can turn his beliefs to data, they can turn his knowledge to data, and his particular mannerisms, and his thought patterns, and his exact vocabulary, but even if they put all of that stuff into the computer, there's still going to be something missing. I'll tell you this much, those things in the computers don't have souls. Because you can't turn that to numbers. You just can't. And for the record, he could have at least stayed for supper," his father exclaimed.

And she knew he needed to rant, so she let him rant. And later, she stuck her face into her pillow and wept so violently that the bed shook, and he knew she needed to weep, so he let her weep. And then for the rest of the night she alternated between fidgeting and lying as still as possible, too upset to sleep.

From then on that became her norm, both at night and during the day, just constant worrying. Even when she wasn't thinking about it she was thinking about it. No matter where she was at, no matter what she was doing, whether she was searching through the envelope of coupons in her purse to pay for tampons at the pharmacy or she was concentrating on the descriptions of the various deductions that her accountant recommended making before filing taxes, an awareness of the situation was always there in the background of her other thoughts, interrupting. I am losing my son. I am losing my son. I am losing my son.

Since graduating, Mason had been renting a house with some roommates, who no doubt would claim his belongings after the operation. But there wouldn't be much to claim. His furnishings were spare, just a bed with a sheet, stacked crates with folded clothes, a battered plastic hamper, dirty bowls on the windowsill containing flecks of dried milk and crusted cheese, a framed photo of his family on the wall, the tangled cords of his chargers on the floor, and his beanbag. She had been over there a number of times, once to bring him chicken broth when he had the flu, once to bring him emergency funds after he had been mugged. The roommates that he'd found were strange—women with glazed looks who played video games excessively, shifty men who were always busy mailing and receiving mysterious packages and constantly reeked of curry and patchouli, aggressively chatty people who believed that the moon landings had been a total hoax and that astrological systems were indisputably factual—and she had worried about him living there. That his roommates might pressure him into doing something risky, like heroin, or orgies. Activities so pleasurable that the activities were addicting. And there had in fact appeared to be cause for concern. He had seemed unwell in recent years. Not just because of how frail he had become, but the bags that had formed in the skin beneath his eyes, and the furrow that had formed in the skin between his eyebrows. She had wondered if he was depressed.

After confessing his plan to his family, however, Mason immediately seemed to improve. In the coming weeks he occasionally drove over in the evening to hang out on the stoop with his family, sitting there in his regular chair with his usual slouch as if everything were normal. Sipping from a bottle of iced tea, his mother would study the changes in his appearance from across the stoop. The bags beneath his eyes had faded. The furrow between his eyebrows had disappeared.

Some of the color had actually returned to his skin. In fact, the nearer the day of the operation came, the healthier he seemed, and that alarmed her more than the symptoms of depression ever had, because his growing excitement seemed like proof that he genuinely believed he needed the operation.

She set her bottle of iced tea down onto the stoop, then shifted in her chair to turn toward the street, returning a wave to a neighbor in a passing car. She had always assumed that once hormones hit he would finally become interested in the lively social network at school, but even as a teenager he had preferred digital interactions to relationships in person. His brothers had been daredevils in those years, exploring abandoned factories with friends, egging the vehicles of enemies, roaming around heckling tourists for fun, constantly coming and going from the house with every departure and arrival announced by the thwack of the screen door and stomps on the front steps, but he had been as much of a homebody as ever. He had dated a few people—the longest had been a timid mathlete with a strand of hair dyed aquamarine—and the romances had at the very least been earnest sexually. Sorting through his dirty laundry, his mother had occasionally discovered a sock stiff with dried semen; dumping the contents of his trash can into the garbage container in the garage, his mother had sometimes spotted a condom wrapper in with the mix. Yet he had never seemed truly enamored with anybody, speaking of the people he dated with the same reluctant preference he showed for cereal and macaroni, as if sex were merely another appetite to be sated. And otherwise he hadn't shown much interest in his schoolmates at all. For the sake of convention she had wished that he would join some extracurriculars, maybe try out for a musical or run for student council, but for selfish reasons she also had been glad that he had spent most weekends hunched over a screen in his bedroom. She had loved having him nearby, just getting to glance at him as she walked past the room to fetch a sponge from the kitchen, or getting to dust the mirror in the bathroom knowing that he occupied a room just down the hall. Stopping to visit him between chores, she would see apps flashing across his screen at an almost blurry rate as he switched between chats and forums and the comments beneath articles. She had marveled at how many conversations he could engage in simultaneously.

"What are you talking about on there?" she had asked him once, standing over his beanbag with a vacuum cradled in her arms.

"Everything," Mason had said, drawing out the syllables of the word for emphasis.

And he had in fact seemed to be interested in everything, occasionally sharing at supper what he had learned throughout the day, the topics ranging from subjects like oceanography and astrophysics to bits of gossip about mods and other friends from online. Puberty had added a lump to his throat that dipped when he spoke. His scalp had shed dandruff that his mother was forever having to brush from the back of his shirt, and though she had insisted that he and his brothers be asleep by midnight during the school week, on the occasions when she had risen in the wee hours to use the bathroom and while padding down the hall had spotted the faint glow of a screen shining through the crack below his door, she had never asked him to go to bed. She had taken any chance to accommodate him, even when that had required breaking her own rules.

Thinking of that, she actually could remember a time he had cried. When he was a teenager a particularly catastrophic hurricane had blown through, and though the house had been spared any significant damage, the power had been out for weeks afterward, with no way to get online. His brothers had always thrived during outages, enjoying the novelty of eating canned goods by the light of a gas lantern and flushing the toilet with water stored in plastic milk cartons, and had treated those weeks like an extended camping trip, lounging around the living room spooking each other with urban legends and playing board games that hadn't been pulled from the closet in years. Mason, however, had struggled. The longest the power had ever been out before was a few days at a time, and he must have assumed that would be the case again, because he had spent the first few days after the storm sitting on the windowsill in the living room with his arms folded across his chest, watching the street with an intent expression, as if utility trucks from the electric company were due to arrive at any moment. As the outage had dragged on, his bearing had gone from impatient to agitated, with a set clench to his jaw and his lips pursed tight, and he had become increasingly anxious, replying to questions with distracted grunts, ignoring requests to join activities, just pacing around the window in the living room kicking at the carpet, or for hours sometimes simply slumping across his beanbag with a blank screen clutched in his hands, until finally one morning after waking up to discover that the power still hadn't been restored, he had broken down weeping at breakfast, burying his face in his arms, with the descending knobs of his spine protruding through the stretched fabric of his shirt as he sobbed. His brothers had stared at him with mild shock.

"The power has to come back on eventually," his mother had said, trying to reason with him from across the table.

But he had been inconsolable, his body trembling in frustration.

"This is the worst thing that's ever happened to me," Mason had cried.

At the time, she had dismissed the statement as a bout of melodrama, just another complaint from a child prone to complaining, but now she realized that he might have meant what he had said: that the worst he had ever felt was being cut off that long from the internet.

Her name was Hailey, but she was a mother—even before giving birth to the boys, she had always felt that was what she was meant to do, her identity—and his mother especially. She loved his father, she loved his brothers, yet the family hadn't felt complete to her until he had come along. When she had first held him, a bleary newborn with a wisp of pale hair, she had been struck by that exact thought. This is everybody. And she still felt that way, sitting around on the stoop, like the family wasn't complete without him. He balanced out everybody else, that gawky figure over by the railing. She loved how he would set his ballcap in his lap to fuss with the snaps on the plastic adjuster for a while absentmindedly. She loved how he would tuck his hands into the webbed cupholders attached to his chair as if the holes had been included for that exact purpose. She loved how when she accidentally bumped the bottle of iced tea by her feet while laughing at his brothers, he lunged to catch the wobbling bottle before the iced tea could spill. When she slipped indoors to blow her nose, the gentle lilt of his voice drifting in through the screen door gave her a sense of well-being. When she returned outdoors with a file for her nails, the sharp odor of the sneakers he had kicked off by the front steps made her swell with contentment. He had a presence she could feel even when she wasn't looking. And now all of that was tinged with dread. She knew what the stoop was like when he wasn't there, from days he was at work, or days he was home sick. On those days there was an empty space. An absence over by the railing that she was constantly aware of, no matter how hard she tried to be happy with what she had. And after the operation, that empty space would be there forever, the rest of her life.

His family avoided talking about the operation around him without exception. His father, who had never understood him but had always made an effort to understand him anyway, had given up, maintaining a polite yet firm silence on the matter, as if acknowledging the choice might count as consent. His brothers, who had defended him from any accusations of weirdness when he was younger with a ferocity that had sent critics running, now just sat back looking embarrassed if the issue was mentioned, as if too humiliated to speak. His mother, who in truth usually couldn't resist a topic that promised a bit of drama, was struck dumb with fear when given the opportunity to join a discussion about the decision. Even Mason himself avoided the subject. Although he might have been relieved to have confessed his plan, he was obviously still ashamed of his plan too. Whenever anybody brought up the operation, his hands would tremble and his voice would shake, the same as when he had made the initial announcement. And the operation came up often when he was on the stoop. By now word of his plan had spread through the neighborhood. He was a spectacle, like somebody out on bail for a crime that would mean life in prison, a local landmark about to vanish from the neighborhood forever in a sensational fashion. Neighbors would wander over to the stoop under the pretense of talking with his family, chatting about basketball or landscaping or potholes or the weather until enough time had passed to be able to turn to him casually to ask about the operation, as if the subject had only just then come to mind.

In general the neighbors seemed less interested in hearing his perspective than in reporting what they personally felt was so worthwhile about having a body and then explaining that he actually liked having a body just as much as they did. He would tug uncomfortably at the collar of his tee while a neighbor expounded on the wonders of bubble baths; he would fidget uneasily with the rips in his jeans while a neighbor testified to the greatness of scented lotion. And his mother thought that he did seem to give serious consideration to what the neighbors said. Yet whatever the neighbors insisted would be worth keeping a body for, he always responded that he would still prefer to live as data. He wouldn't miss driving with the windows down. He wouldn't miss wearing slippers, dressing up for weddings, or changing out of wet clothing into dry pajamas. He wouldn't miss jambalaya, peanut butter, mustard on pretzels, burritos bursting with cheese and beans and salsa bundled up in wrappers, pepperoni pizza with the crust flavored subtly like cardboard from the box, lobster so tender that the meat flaked apart, the maraschino cherry off the crown of a banana split, the extra portion of milkshake in the steel cup that always felt like a surprise bonus after you had finished the serving in the glass, pancakes drenched in maple syrup and waffles dolloped with whipped cream, bacon dripping with so much grease that the oil had soaked the paper towel underneath, popcorn coated with so much salt that a layer of crystal had formed at the bottom of the bucket, chili dogs heaped with onions and seasoned with the smell of cut grass at a ballpark, buffalo wings slathered with cayenne and seasoned with the smell of lit candles at a pub, toasted marshmallows oozing out from between slabs of chocolate and graham cracker with the scent of campfire on your fingers, toffee so buttery you had to wipe your lips afterward, fudge so rich you would feel your toes curl involuntarily, the tang of a bite of pickle with the peppery aftertaste of a pastrami sandwich still fresh on your tongue, hot fries with cold ketchup, chocolate chip cookie dough, fried green tomatoes, pecan pie, grits, or beignets. He wouldn't miss getting buzzed on coffee, wine, or cigarettes. He wouldn't miss the shiver of ecstasy after scratching a mosquito bite. He wouldn't miss roller coasters. He wouldn't miss wave pools. He wouldn't miss turnstile gates. He wouldn't miss funnel cakes. He wouldn't miss souvenir hats. He wouldn't miss anything about amusement parks whatsoever. He wouldn't miss the rush of adrenaline after running a stoplight, the almost giddy relief following a bout of hiccups, sucking drinks through straws, having caricatures drawn, feeling drowsy, collapsing into a mound of blankets and pillows, naps so intense you woke up drooling, the sound of rain, the smell of rain, or wind chimes.

"It's unnatural," a neighbor grimaced, speaking of the operation, which was the closest that any of the neighbors ever came to condemning him in person. When he wasn't around, his mother knew, the neighbors gossiped about him constantly. When he was around, the children on the street weren't allowed on the property, as if the neighbors were afraid his thinking might be infectious.

"The internet is a beautiful place," Mason murmured.

He had never left New Orleans. He had lived in the same neighborhood in the same district in the same city his entire life. He had always had his family nearby to protect him. The internet wasn't a beautiful place. The internet was a dangerous place. His mother stayed up late into the night, sitting alone in the kitchen with the lamp lit, searching the news for stories about postcorporeals. Earlier that month a postcorporeal from Indianapolis had been infected with a virus that had damaged her programming so severely that she had crashed and hadn't been able to be revived, effectively killing her. And only the week prior a postcorporeal from Baltimore had been attacked by hackers, had her memory looted for credit card information and social security numbers, had random sections of her data vandalized apparently just out of spite, and been left in the digital equivalent of a coma. While the year before in a highly publicized case a company in Salt Lake

City that hosted postcorporeals from across the country had failed to maintain its facilities properly, not out of negligence but rather in a deliberate attempt to increase profits, regularly skipping the safety inspections standard to the industry, which had come to the attention of the public only after the servers at the data center had been fried by a power surge from a lightning strike, resulting in hundreds of postcorporeals vanishing from the world in a flash, in a disaster the magnitude of a collapsing hotel or a crashing plane, an event that never would have happened had the place been up to code.

She wouldn't have any way to watch over him anymore.

How long would he survive out there?

For Mardi Gras his family had a tradition of spending the day together, which was an important event every year but this year had taken on particular significance, because the operation was scheduled to take place the following morning. It was going to be her last chance to be with him. She tried to suppress her sense of grief to focus on making the day as perfect as possible. That was all she wanted, a perfect day, so that after losing him she could at least always remember that her last day with him had been special. She shook her head at his father and sent him back into the bedroom to change out of the tank top and cargo shorts he had picked out into something nicer. She made his brothers promise not to pick any fights with tourists. She loaded her purse with spray-on sunscreen and bottled waters.

And the day was perfect. His family looked beautiful, proud parents and polite children dressed in fine clothing made by respected brands, and in the morning his family snagged prime spots for viewing the parades and saw floats so spectacular as to be truly among the best in living memory, and in the afternoon his family got ice cream cones piled high with generous scoops of butter pecan and rocky road and vanilla bean and blue moon and then strolled along the riverfront cracking jokes, and in the evening his family stumbled onto a live performance put on in a park by an unassuming band and heard a funk concert that wowed the crowd to such an extent that afterward members of the audience formed a line to shake hands with the musicians. And then after dusk his family set up on the patio of a cafe, splitting a platter of nachos and sipping from pints of ale, people-watching over the fence, and that was perfect too. The temperature was mild, the breeze was pleasant, and dazzling stars filled the sky above the street. The road was strewn with colorful debris. Metallic noisemakers, cracked to-go cups, a trampled bouquet, tangled strings of beads, fluorescent dildos, an acrylic bong. Revelers streamed past the patio, people grinning behind feathered masks and people primping rainbow wigs and people whose skin was painted with mesmerizing swirls and people in sequined outfits twirling jeweled canes that glittered under the streetlights and people breathing fire to the cheers of people riding by on unicycles and people embracing strangers and people chanting nonsense with friends and people in billowing capes skipping with each other down the street, and even in the midst of all of that pleasure and joy and happiness, Mason still seemed faintly bored. Eventually he took his phone out of his jacket, hunching over the screen, responding to messages, sending new messages, ignoring the carnival completely. He had only nibbled at the nachos. He had merely nipped at the ale. And at the concert he hadn't clapped between songs and instead of watching the performance had just fiddled with his phone, and along the riverfront he hadn't even wanted an ice cream cone and instead of watching the steamboats had just fiddled with his phone, and during the parades he hadn't bothered to catch any of the throws and instead of watching the floats had just fiddled with his phone. The day had been perfect, and the day had been ruined anyway, because he had been too distracted to experience any of it. His mother leaned back in her chair with a frown. She had worried that she might get so sad tonight that she would cry, but all that worrying had been for nothing, because she wasn't sad. She was furious. He might as well have already been gone. He couldn't look away from that fucking screen.

She stood from the table so suddenly that her chair toppled over backward with a smack.

"You disgust me," she spat.

Mason glanced up with a startled look.

"I want no part of whatever type of life you plan to have after tomorrow," she said, walked out of the cafe, and drove home alone.

Back at the house she changed into baggy sweatpants and a shirt that had been washed and dried so many times that the fabric was soft and wispy, an outfit which generally gave her great pleasure to wear, but which of course now she was too angry to enjoy. She had meant what she had said. She hadn't planned to say it, but she didn't regret saying it, either. She was done with him. She was livid. She grabbed a bag of caramels, popped the cap from a stout, and sat down at the table in the kitchen with the lamp on to eat and drink and enjoy it, not just out of spite for him, but out of spite for all postcorporeality. She was still sitting there when headlights swung into the driveway and a key rattled in the door and in walked his father, who could see that she was in no mood to talk, so kissed her head, patted her shoulders, and then went into the bathroom to get ready for bed. Snoring soon filled the house, but she was too restless to lie down, too wired on beer and sugar, so she cleaned instead. She scrubbed the toilet, she scrubbed the tub, and she scrubbed the grime that had formed around the faucet of the sink, trying to avoid thinking about him, which she couldn't, so eventually she gave up. She thought about him. She wandered the house in the glow of the streetlights coming through the windows, inspecting the contents of cabinet drawers and closet shelves, examining different mementos from his life. Here were the stuffed animals that he had tolerated sleeping with. Here were the action figures that he had endured playing with. Here were the hand casts that he had complained about posing for even after having finished posing. And, oh, here, this was the container full of messages he had written to her at school during lunch. She peeled the lid from the container with a sense of awe. When packing lunches, she had always slipped a note into each lunchbox. And at a certain age he had begun writing her back, shutting a reply into his lunchbox for her to find when she later opened it to empty out the used baggies. His messages had been written on scraps torn from the corners of notebook paper, using whatever type of utensil he had favored at the time. Crayons, then colored pencils, eventually markers, and gel pens as a teenager. The messages had never said anything memorable, just remarks about his classes, or comments about his schoolmates, but she had loved those notes. None of his brothers had ever written her back.

She remembered now, that was the last thing he had said to her at the cafe before becoming engrossed in his screen. He had been explaining the logistics of the operation. He had smiled, "I'll message you after it's finished."

She dozed off on the couch at some point during the night and ended up with an arm and a leg dangling over the side and her face pressed into the crack between a pair of cushions. His father woke her just before leaving for work. Rain was drizzling. She brushed her teeth, tied her hair back, threw on some eyeliner, put on some lipstick, and got dressed in her uniform for the motel. By then the rain was a downpour. The wipers on her car needed to be replaced, and her breath was fogging the windows, so she could hardly see as she drove. She felt terrible. Mason would be at the clinic by now. Nobody had gone with him. She should have kept her mouth shut the night before. She had just been so angry, but even if his choice was abominable, he was still her son. The guilt was awful. The wipers thocked back and forth. She swiped at the fog with the cuff of a sleeve. Her pulse sped up as she made the decision. She had to go. She was terrified by the thought of being there for the transition, the moment when his body would be suddenly empty, the moment when his mind would be suddenly gone, but she needed to hold him one last time before she lost him. She drove past the motel and merged onto the highway.

The clinic was locked. After buzzing her in, the receptionist asked for her identification and checked a list for her name and then led her down an empty hall into the operating room, where he had already been sedated. Tears welled in her eyes. The procedure was underway. She wouldn't have a chance to say goodbye. A machine enclosed his head completely, with the rest of his body extending out of the machine onto a gurney. His palms were crossed over his chest. A neon pink plastic wristband identified him for the operators. Aside from a pair of plain white boxers, he was naked. Seeing him in there like that was so upsetting that she almost turned to leave, but instead she wiped the tears from her eyes and forced herself to take a seat on the stool next to the gurney. She leaned her umbrella against the wall, she set her purse on the floor, and then she held his hands in her hands. The operators nodded at her, and then went back to work, adjusting dials and skimming scans. There was nothing to do but wait, and the wait was terrible. The constant feeling of dread that she had been living with since his announcement was so much worse than ever before. Rain pelted the roof. Indicator lights blinked. The operators murmured to each other. She kept wondering whether the moment had passed, waiting for some sign that the transition had occurred, but there was no way of telling. Her muscles were tensed. Her teeth were clenched. And her dread just kept building.

She was bracing for the moment of the transition, squeezing his hands with a tight grip, breathing so fast that she was slightly dizzy, staring at his body, when she became aware of a faint beeping coming from a monitor on the machine. The sound made her think of her phone, tucked into the breast pocket of her uniform with the volume on high. She actually would know when the transition had occurred, she realized. When he messaged her, her phone would chime. She glanced down at her uniform, looking at the bulge her phone made in the pocket, and when she did, the strangest thing happened. She felt a burst of joy. Excitement so intense that a shiver passed through her. This sense that she wasn't about to lose him forever, but instead was finally about to meet him, truly meet him, for the first time. The feeling confused her, but the longer that she stared at the pocket expecting her phone to chime at any moment, the stronger that the feeling grew, until she was nearly overcome with anticipation. His hands were still warm, but whether the life had left his body yet didn't matter. She felt certain of that suddenly. It wasn't him. It never had been.

Life Sentence

Home.

He recognizes the name of the street. But he doesn't remember the landscape. He recognizes the address on the mailbox. But he doesn't remember the house.

His family is waiting for him on the porch.

Everybody looks just as nervous as he is.

He gets out.

The police cruiser takes back off down the gravel drive, leaving him standing in a cloud of dust holding a baggie of possessions.

He has a wife. He has a son. He has a daughter.

A dog peers out a window.

His family takes him in.

Wash is still groggy from the procedure. He's got a plastic taste on his tongue. He's got a throbbing sensation in his skull. He's starving.

Supper is homemade potpies. His wife says the meal is his favorite. He doesn't remember that.

The others are digging in already. Steam rises from his pie as he pierces the crust with his fork. He salivates. The smell of the pie hitting him makes him grunt with desire. Bending toward the fork, he parts his lips to take a bite, but then he stops and glances up.

Something is nagging at him worse than the hunger.

"What did I do?" he says with a sense of bewilderment.

His wife holds up a hand.

"Baby, please, let's not talk about that," his wife says.

Wash looks around. A laminate counter. A maroon toaster. Flowers growing from pots on the sill. Magnets shaped like stars on the fridge.

This is his home.

He doesn't remember anything.

He's not supposed to.

★ ★ ★

His reintroduction supervisor comes to see him in the morning.

"How do you feel, Washington?"

"Everybody keeps calling me Wash?"

"I can call you that if you'd like."

"I guess I'm not really sure what I like."

Lindsay, the reintroduction supervisor, wears a scarlet tie with a navy suit. She's got a bubbly disposition and a dainty build. Everything that she says, she says as if revealing a wonderful secret that she just can't wait to share.

"We've found a job for you at a restaurant."

"Doing what?"

"Working in the kitchen."

"That's the best you could get me?"

"At your level of education, and considering your status as a felon, yes, it really is."

"Where did I work before?"

Lindsay smiles.

"An important part of making a successful transition back to your life is learning to let go of any worries that you might have about your past so that you can focus on enjoying your future."

Wash frowns.

"Why do I know so much about mortgages? Did I used to work at a bank?"

"To my knowledge you have never worked at a bank."

"But how can I remember that stuff if I can't remember other stuff?"

"Your semantic memories are still intact. Only your episodic memories were wiped."

"My what?"

"You know what a restaurant is."

"Yeah."

"But you can't remember ever having eaten in a restaurant before."

"No."

"Or celebrating a birthday at a restaurant. Or using a restroom at a restaurant. Or seeing a friend at a restaurant. You've eaten in restaurants before. But you have no memories of that at all. None whatsoever." Lindsay taps her temples. "Episodic memories are personal experiences. That's what's gone. Semantic memories are general knowledge. Information. Names, dates, addresses. You still have all of that. You're a functional member of society. Your diploma is just as valid as before. And your procedural memories are fine. You still know how to ride a bike, or play the guitar, or operate a vacuum. Assuming you ever learned," Lindsay laughs.

"Did you do anything else to me?"

"Well, of course, your gun license was also revoked."

Wash thinks.

"Did I shoot somebody?"

"All felons are prohibited from owning firearms, regardless of the nature of the crime."

Wash turns away, folding his arms over his chest, pouting at the carpet.

"Washington, how do you feel?"

"Upset."

"That's perfectly normal. I'm so glad that you're comfortable talking with me about your feelings. That's so important."

Lindsay nods with a solemn expression, as if waiting for him to continue sharing, and then leans in.

"But honestly though, you should feel grateful you weren't born somewhere that still has prisons." Lindsay reaches for her purse. "Do you know what would have happened to you a century ago for doing what you did? The judge would have locked you up and thrown away the key!" Lindsay says brightly, and then stands to leave.

★ ★ ★

Wash gets woken that night by a craving.

An urgent need.

Was he an addict?

What is he craving?

He follows some instinct into the basement. Stands there in boxers under the light of a bare bulb. Glances around the basement, stares at the workbench, and then obeys an urge to reach up onto the shelf above. Pats around and discovers an aluminum tin.

Something shifts inside as he takes the tin down from the shelf.

He pops the lid.

In the tin: a stash of king-size candy bars.

As he chews a bite of candy bar, a tingle of satisfaction rushes through him, followed by a sense of relief.

Chocolate.

Back up the stairs, padding down the hallway, he pit-stops in the bathroom for a drink of water. Bends to sip from the faucet. Wipes his chin. Stands. A full-length mirror hangs from the back of the door. He's lit by the glow of a night-light the shape of a rainbow that's plugged into the outlet above the toilet.

Wash examines his appearance in the mirror. Wrinkles around his eyes. Creases along his mouth. A thick neck. Broad shoulders, wide hips, hefty limbs, and a round gut. Fingers nicked with scars. Soles hardened with calluses. The body of an aging athlete, or a laborer accustomed to heavy lifting who's recently gone soft from lack of work.

He can't remember being a toddler. He can't remember being a child. He can't remember being a teenager. He can't remember being an adult.

He stares at himself.

Who is he other than this person standing here in the present moment?

Is he anybody other than this person standing here in the present moment?

His wife stirs as he slips back into bed. She reaches over and startles him with a kiss. He kisses back, but then she climbs on top of him, and he pulls away.

"Too soon?" she whispers.

Mia, that's her name, he remembers. She has a flat face, skinny arms, thick legs, and frizzy hair cut off at her jawline, which he can just make out in the dark. Her nails are painted bright red. She sleeps in a plaid nightgown.

"I barely know you," he says.

Mia snorts. "Didn't stop you the first time." She shuffles backward on her knees, tugging his boxers down his legs as she goes, and then chuckles. "I mean our other first time."

★ ★ ★

The restaurant is a diner down by the highway, a chrome trailer with checkered linoleum and pleather booths and ceiling fans that spin out of sync, featuring a glass case of pastries next to the register and a jukebox with fluorescent tubing over by the restrooms. The diner serves breakfast and lunch only. Wash arrives each morning around dawn. The kitchen has swinging doors. He does the dishes, sweeps the floors, mops the floors, and hauls the trash out when the bags get full. Mainly he does the dishes. Dumps soda from cups. Pours coffee from mugs. Scrapes onion rings and pineapple rinds and soggy napkins and buttered slices of toast and empty jam containers and crumpled straw wrappers into the garbage. Sprays ketchup from plates. Rinses broth from bowls. Racks the tableware and sends the racks through the dishwasher. Stacks spotless dishes back onto the shelves alongside the stove. Scours at crusted yolk and dried syrup with the bristly side of sponges. Scrubs skillets with stainless steel pads for so long and with such force that the pads fall apart and still there's a scorched residue stuck to the pans. Burns his hands with scalding water. Splashes stinging suds into his eyes. His shoes are always damp as he drives home in the afternoon. He shaves, he showers, and he feeds the dog, a moody mutt whose name is Biscuit. Then he sits on the porch step waiting for the rest of his family to get home. His house is modest, with small rooms and a low ceiling, and has no garage. The gutters sag. Shingles have been blown clear off the roof. The sun has bleached the blue of the siding almost to gray. Across the road stands a field of corn. Beyond that there's woods. The corn stalks sway in the breeze. The dog waits with him, curled up on the grass around his shoes, panting whenever a car drives past. He lives in Kansas.

Sophie, his daughter, a ninth-grader, is the next to arrive home, shuffling off of the bus while jabbing at the buttons of a game. Jaden, his son, a third-grader, arrives home on the later bus, shouting taunts back at friends hanging out the windows. His wife works at a hospital, the same hours that he does, but she gets home last since the hospital is all the way over in Independence.

Wash tries to cook once, tries to make meatloaf. He knows what a meatloaf is. He understands how an oven functions. He gets the mechanics of a whisk. He can read the recipe no problem. But still the attempt is a disaster. He pulls the pan out when the timer goes off, and the bottom of the meatloaf is already charred, and the top of the meatloaf is still raw. He hadn't been able to find bread crumbs, so he had torn up a slice of bread instead, which doesn't seem to have worked. He samples a bite from the center of the meatloaf, that in-between part neither charred nor raw, and finds some slivers of onion skin in among what he's chewing. When his wife arrives home, she surveys the mess with a look of amusement and then assures him that this isn't a skill he's forgotten. She does the cooking. At home, the same as at the diner, he does the dishes.

Other items that his wife assures him were not accidentally erased during his procedure: the date of her birthday (all he knows is the month, August); the date of their anniversary (all he knows is the month, May).

"Here's a clue. My birthday was exactly a week before you came home. Borrow a calculator from one of your delightful children if you need help with the math," Mia says, dumping a box of spaghetti into a pot of roiling water while simultaneously stirring a can of mushrooms into a pan of bubbling marinara. "If you'd like to know how long you've been married, your marriage license is in the filing cabinet in the basement. In fact, if you're really feeling ambitious, your children have some birth certificates in there too. Heck, check your immunization record while you're down there, you're probably due for a tetanus shot."

There are moments so intimate that he can almost forget he's living with strangers. His daughter falls asleep on him one night while watching a show about zombies on the couch, her head lolling against his shoulder. His son leans into him one night waiting for the microwave to heat a mug of cider, his arm wrapping around his waist. Late one night after the kids are asleep, his wife hands him a rubber syringe and a plastic bowl and asks him to flush a buildup of wax from her ears, an act that to him seems far more intimate than intercourse.

But then there are the moments that remind him how much he must have lost. One night, during a supper of baked potatoes loaded with chives and bacon and sour cream, his family suddenly cracks up over an in-joke, a shared memory that's somehow related to mini-golf and bikinis. His wife is laughing so hard that she's crying, but sobers up when she realizes how confused he looks.

"Sorry, it's impossible to explain if you weren't there," Mia says, thumbing away tears.

"But he was there, he was the one who noticed," Jaden protests.

"He can't remember anymore, you ninny," Sophie scowls.

And then the subject gets changed.

Wash does know certain information about himself.

He knows his ancestry is part Potawatomi. He knows his parents were named Lawrence and Beverly. He knows his birthplace is near Wichita.

But taking inventory of what he knows isn't as simple as thinking, "What do you know, Wash?"

He has to ask a specific question.

He must know other facts about himself.

He just hasn't asked the right questions yet.

"Wash, were you ever in a fight before?"

"Wash, did you like your parents?"

"Wash, have you seen a tornado?"

He doesn't remember.

He tries asking Sophie about his past one afternoon. Wash is driving her to practice. Sophie runs cross.

"What was my life like before the wipe?" Wash says.

Sophie is a plump kid with crooked teeth, a pet lover, and has a grave demeanor, as if constantly haunted by the fact that not all kittens have homes. She's doing history homework, flipping back and forth between a textbook and a worksheet, scribbling in information. She's got her sneakers propped on the dashboard with her ankles crossed.

"Huh?" Sophie says.

"What do you know about my life?"

"Um."

"Like tell me something I told you about myself before I got taken away."

She sneers at the textbook. Bends over the worksheet, forcefully erases something, and blows off the peels of rubber left behind. Then turns to look at him.

"You never really talked about yourself," Sophie says.

He tries asking Jaden about his past one afternoon. Wash is driving him to practice. Jaden plays soccer.

"What was I like before I went away?" Wash says.

Jaden is a stringy kid with a nose that dominates his other features, a soda junkie, and constantly hyper, regardless of caffeine intake. He's sitting in an upside-down position with his legs pointed at the roof, his back on the seat, and his head lolled over the edge, with his hands thrown across the floor of the truck. He's spent most of the ride listing off the powers of supervillains.

"I dunno," Jaden says.

"You must remember something about me."

"I guess."

"So what type of person was I?"

Jaden plucks at the seatbelt. Frowns in thought. Then turns to look at him.

"A grown-up?" Jaden says.

Wash tries asking his wife, but her taste in conversation is strictly practical, and she doesn't seem interested in reminiscing about his life before the wipe at all. No photos are framed on the counter. No snapshots are pinned to the fridge. If pictures of his family ever hung on the walls, the pictures have long since disappeared.

But other artifacts of his past are scattered throughout the house. In his closet hang flannel button-ups, worn tees, plain sweatshirts, a zip-up fishing vest with mesh pouches, a hooded hunting jacket with a camouflage pattern, a fleece, a parka, faded jeans on wire hangers, and a suit in a plastic garment bag. Who was that person who chose these clothes? In his dresser mingle polished turquoise, pennies smashed smooth by trains, a hotel matchbook lined with the stumps of torn-out matches, an assortment of acorns, ticket stubs from raffles, wooden nickels, a pocket knife whose blades are rusted shut, and the marbled feather of a bald eagle. Who was that person who kept these trinkets? There's a safe in the basement where his guns were stored before being sold. He knows a combination, spins the numbers in, and the handle gives. But aside from a bungee, the safe is empty. No rifles, no shotguns, no pistols. Even the ammunition was sold.

Who owned those guns?

And then there are the artifacts of his past that he sees in his family. Sometimes in the driveway he'll glance up from the car he's washing or the mower he's fueling and see his daughter watching him from the door with an expression of spite. Was he ever cruel to Sophie? Sometimes as he drops his boots in the entryway with a thud or tosses his wallet onto the counter with a snap he'll see his son flinch over on the couch. Was he ever rough with Jaden? When he sets his cup down empty, his wife leaps up to fetch the jug of milk from the fridge, as if there might be some repercussion for failing to pour him another glass.

He has a beat-up flip phone with nobody saved in the contacts except for his wife and his kids. Were there other contacts in there that were deleted after he got arrested?

At cross meets and soccer matches, the other parents never talk to him. Was that always the case, or only now that he's a felon?

How does he know that trains have cupolas? Where did he learn that comets aren't asteroids? Who taught him that vinegar kills lice?

Wash is at the homecoming football game, coming back from the concession stand with striped boxes of popcorn for his family, when he stops at the fence to watch a field goal attempt. A referee jogs by with a whistle bouncing on a lanyard. Cheerleaders in gloves and ear-muffs rush past with pompoms and megaphones. Jayhawkers chant in the bleachers. Wash glazes over, he's not sure for how long, but he's still standing at the fence when his trance is interrupted by a stranger standing next to him.

"You did time, didn't you, friend?"

The stranger wears a pullover with the logo of the rival team. His hair is gelled. He's got pleated chinos and shiny loafers.

"Do I know you?" Wash says.

"Ha. No. You just had that look. We all get the look. Searching for something that isn't there," the stranger says.

Wash cracks a smile.

The stranger grumbles, "I don't know why people even say that anymore. Doing time. That's not what happens at all. Losing time. That's what happens. Poof. Gone." The stranger glances down and gives the ice in his cup a shake. "I lost a year. Let's just say, hadn't been totally candid on my tax forms. Couldn't have been worse timing though. I'd gotten married that year. No joke, I can't even remember my own honeymoon. Spent a fortune on that trip too. Fucking blows." The stranger turns away to watch a punt return, sucks a gurgle of soda through his straw, and then turns back. "How long did you do?"

"Life."

The stranger whistles.

"No kidding? You lost everything? From start to finish? How old were you when you got wiped?"

"Forty-one."

"What'd you do to get life? Kill a cop? Rob a bank? Run a scam or something?"

"I don't know," Wash admits.

The stranger squints.

"You aren't curious?"

"Nobody will tell me."

The stranger laughs.

"To get a sentence like that, whatever you did, it must have made the news."

Wash stares at the stranger in shock. He could know who he was after all. All he'd have to do is get online.

"We don't have a computer though," Wash frowns.

The stranger passes behind him, giving him a pat on the shoulder, and then calls back before drifting off into the crowd.

"Going to let you in on a secret, friend. At the library, you can use a computer for free."

★ ★ ★

Lindsay, his reintroduction supervisor, is waiting for him at the house when he gets off work the next afternoon. She's wearing the same outfit as before, a scarlet tie, a navy suit. She's sitting on the hood of her car next to a box of donuts.

"Time to check in," Lindsay says through a bite of fritter.

Biscuit stands on the couch, paws propped against the window, peering out of the house.

"Have a seat," Lindsay says brightly.

Wash takes an eclair.

"How are you getting along with your family, Washington?"

Wash thinks.

"Fine," Wash says.

Lindsay leans in with a conspiratorial look. "Oh, come on, give me the gossip."

Wash chews, swallows, and frowns.

"Why'd you have to give me life? You couldn't just give me twenty years or something? Why'd you have to take everything?" Wash says.

"The length of your sentence was determined by the judge."

"Just doesn't seem fair."

Lindsay nods, smiling sympathetically, and then abruptly stops.

"Well, what you did was pretty bad, Washington."

"But my whole life?"

"Do you know anything about the history of prisons in this country?" Lindsay reaches for a napkin, licks some glaze from her fingers, and wipes her hands. "Prisons here were originally intended to be a house of corrections. The theory was that when put into isolation criminals might be taught how to be functional citizens. In practice, however, the system proved to be ineffective at reforming offenders. The rate of recidivism was staggering. Honestly, upon release, most felons were arrested on new charges within the year. And over time the conditions in the prisons became awful. I mean, imagine what your situation would have been, being sentenced to life. You would have spent the next half a century locked in a cage like an animal, sleeping on an uncomfortable cot, wearing an ill-fitting jumpsuit, making license plates all day for far less than minimum wage, cleaning yourself with commercial soaps whose lists of ingredients included a variety of carcinogens, eating mashed potatoes made from a powder and meatloaf barely fit for human consumption, getting raped occasionally by other prisoners. Instead, you get to be here, with your family. Pretty cool, right? Like, super cool? You have to admit. And the wipe isn't simply a punishment. Yes, the possibility of getting wiped is meant to deter people from committing crimes. Totally. But wipes are also highly effective at preventing criminals from becoming repeat offenders. Although there is some biological basis for things like rage and greed and so forth, those types of issues tend to be the psychological byproducts of memories. And a life sentence is especially effective. Given a clean slate, felons often are much calmer, are much happier than before, are burdened with no misconceptions that crimes like embezzlement or poaching might be somehow justified, and of course possess no grudges against institutions like the government or law enforcement or former employers." Lindsay glances over, then turns back toward the road. "For example."

"So I'm supposed to feel grateful?"

Wash didn't mean to speak with that much force.

"Do you even know how much a wipe like yours costs?" Lindsay says, her eyes growing wide. "A fortune. Honestly, most people in your zip code would need a payment plan for a simple vanity wipe. You know, you do something embarrassing at a party, you overhear somebody saying something mean about you that rings a bit too true, so you just have the memory erased. And then there are survivors of truly traumatic incidents, who often have to save up for years after the incident if insurance won't cover the cost of having the incident wiped. And alcoholics and crackheads and the like have no choice but to shell out, as a selective memory wipe is the only possible cure for addiction. Veterans with post-traumatic stress disorder are generally treated with wipes as well, although those wipes, as was the case with yours, are covered by taxpayers." Lindsay leans back on the hood of the car, propped up on her elbows, and squints into the sun. "It's a better deal for taxpayers anyway. Wiping your memory may have been costly, but was still nowhere near as expensive as paying to feed and shelter you for half a century would have been. That's the problem with prisons. They're overpriced, they underperform."

Wash scowls at the driveway.

"How are you feeling, Washington?"

"Frustrated."

"Tell me more."

"I don't even know what I did to get wiped."

Lindsay smiles. "The less you know about who you were before, the greater your chances of making a successful transition to your new life." Beneath her cheery tone there's a hint of uncertainty. "I would particularly recommend in your case that you avoid asking people about the details of your arrest."

★ ★ ★

Wash has to drive by the local library, a squat brick building with a flag hanging from a pole, whenever he drops off the kids at practice, and he tries to avoid wondering whether whatever he did to get arrested made the news. He notices that other parents stick around during practice, so occasionally he stays, watching Sophie stretching out at the track between intervals, knee braces on, or Jaden dribbling balls through a course of cones, shin guards crooked. Wash likes his kids. He doesn't mind being their parent, but he wants to be their friend, too. To be trusted. To be liked. The desire is so powerful that sometimes the thick fingers of his hands curl tight around the links of the fence out of a sense of longing as he watches the kids practice. Becoming friends with the dog was simple. Biscuit sniffed him and licked him and that was that. He's the same person he's always been as far as the dog is concerned. The kids are distant though. He doesn't know how to jump-start the relationships.

On other days he drives home during practice. The wallpaper in the kitchen is dingy, there are gouges in the walls of the hallway, the ceiling fan in the living room is broken, there are cracks in the light fixture in the laundry room, but not until the constant drip from the sink in the bathroom has turned to a steady leak does he actually stop, think, and realize that the house must be in such shabby condition because of how long he was gone, in detention during the trial, when his wife would have been living on a single income. That faucet is leaking because of him.

He knows how to fix a leak. Leaving the light in the bathroom on, he fetches the toolbox from the basement. He's emptying the cupboard under the sink, stacking toiletries on the linoleum, preparing to shut off the water, when his wife passes the doorway.

"What exactly are you doing?" Mia says.

"I'm gonna fix some stuff," Wash says.

She stares at him.

"Oh," she says finally, and then carries on down the hallway, followed by the dog.

By the time the corn in the field across the road has been harvested and the trees in the woods beyond the field are nearly bare, he's got the gutters hanging straight and the shingles patched up again. He takes a day off from the diner to tear out the stained carpeting in the hallway, wearing a dust mask over his face with the cuffs of his flannel rolled. Afterward he's rummaging around the shelf under the workbench in the basement, looking for a pry bar to rip up the staples in the floor, when he notices a quiver of arrows.

Wash tugs the mask down to his neck and touches the arrows. Carbon shafts. Turkey fletching. He glances over at the safe.

Did he have a bow once?

Was the bow sold with the guns?

Turning back to the shelf under the workbench he sees that there's an unmarked case clasped shut next to the quiver.

Wash pops the lid.

Though he doesn't recognize the bow itself, he recognizes that it's a bow, even in pieces. A takedown. A recurve. And before he even has a chance to wonder whether he knows how to assemble a bow, he's got the case up on the workbench and he's putting the bow together, moving on impulse. Bolts the limbs to the riser, strings the bow, and then heads up the stairs with the quiver. Drags a roll of carpet out the back door and props the carpet against a fence post to use as a target. Backs up toward the house. Tosses the quiver into the grass. Nocks an arrow. Raises the bow. Draws the string back toward the center of his chin until the string is pressing into the tip of his nose. Holds. Breathes.

Leaves are falling.

He lets go.

The arrow hits the carpet with a thump.

The sense of release that washes over him is incredible.

Wash is already exhausted from tearing the carpet out of the hallway, but he stands out in the backyard firing arrow after arrow until the muscles in his arms are burning and his flannel is damp with sweat, and arrow after arrow buries deep into the carpet. Fixing leaks, hanging gutters, patching shingles, he can do stuff like that, but the work is a struggle, a long and frustrating series of bent nails and fumbled wrenches. But this is different. Something he's good at. He can't remember ever feeling like this before. The pride, the satisfaction, of having and using a talent. Biscuit watches from the door, panting happily, tail wagging, as if sensing his euphoria.

Wash is scrubbing dishes after supper that night while Mia clips coupons from a brochure at the table.

"I want to go hunting," Wash announces.

"With the bow?" Mia says.

Wash thinks.

"Do you hunt?" Wash says.

"No," Mia snorts.

She sets down the scissors, folds her arms on the table, and furrows her eyebrows together, looking up at him with an inscrutable expression.

"Why don't you ask your children?" Mia says.

Jaden and Sophie are in the living room.

Jaden responds to the invitation by jumping on the ottoman, pretending to fire arrows at the lamp.

Even Sophie, busy working on a poster for a fundraiser to save stray cats from getting euthanized, wants to come along.

"You're okay with killing animals?"

"I only care about cute animals."

"Deer aren't cute?"

"Deer are snobs."

Last weekend of bow season. Hiking off-trail on public land. The dawn is cloudy. Frost crusts the mud. Wash leads the way through a stretch of cedars, touching the rubs in the bark of the trunks, explaining to the kids about glands without knowing where he learned that's why deer make the rubs. Finds a clearing. Sets up behind a fallen log at the edge of the trees, Jaden to this side with a thermos of cocoa, Sophie to that side with a thermos of chai, whispering insults back and forth to each other. Waits. Snow begins falling. The breeze dies. The kids go quiet as a deer slips into the clearing. A buck with a crown of antlers. A fourteen-pointer. The trophy of a lifetime. The arrow hits the buck so hard that the buck gets knocked to the ground, but just as fast it staggers back up, and then it bounds off into the woods, vanishing. With Jaden and Sophie close behind, he hurries over to where the deer fell. Blood on the snow. Tracks in the mud. Wash and the kids follow the trail through the pines, past a ditch full of brambles, down a slope thick with birches, until the trail disappears just shy of a creek. By then the sun has broken through the clouds. And no matter where he searches from there, the buck can't be found.

He's just about given up looking when he notices some trampled underbrush.

Beyond, on a bed of ferns, the buck lies dead.

Jaden and Sophie dance around the kill, doing fist-pumps and cheering, and that feeling before, shooting arrows into the carpet in the backyard, is nothing compared to the feeling now.

★ ★ ★

Driveway.

Weekend.

Icicles hanging from the flag on the mailbox.

Jaden, in pajamas, boots, and a parka, is sucking on a lozenge, occasionally pushing the lozenge out with his tongue, just far enough for the lozenge to peek through his lips, then slurping the lozenge back into his mouth, while helping him shovel snow.

Wash chips at some ice.

Jaden starts to wheeze.

Wash glances over.

"What's wrong?" Wash says.

Jaden shakes his head, reaches for his throat, and falls to his knees.

Both shovels hit the ground. Wash grabs him by the shoulders and thumps his back. Jaden still can't breathe. Wash spins him and forces his mouth open in a panic. Sticks a finger in. Feels teeth, a tongue, saliva, an uvula. Finds the lozenge. Claws the lozenge. Scoops the lozenge out with a flick.

The lozenge lands in the snow.

Jaden coughs, sways, blinks some, then looks at the lozenge.

"That was awesome," Jaden grins.

★ ★ ★

Backyard.

Weekend.

Buds sprouting on the stems of the tree beyond the fence, where a crow is perched on a branch, not cawing, not preening, silent and still.

Sophie, in leggings, slippers, and a hoodie, is helping him to clean rugs.

Wash holds a rug up over the grass.

Sophie beats the rug with a broom.

Dust flies into the air. Coils of hair. Clumps of soil. Eventually nothing. Sophie drapes the rug over the fence, being careful to make sure that the tassels aren't touching the ground, as he reaches for the next rug. Just then the crow falls out of the tree.

The crow hits the ground with a thud.

Wash looks at the crow in shock.

The crow lies there. Doesn't move. Twitches. Struggles up again. Hops around. Then flaps back into the tree.

"Was it asleep?" Wash squints.

Sophie stares at the crow, and then bursts out laughing.

"Nobody's gonna believe us," Sophie says.

★ ★ ★

Ballpark.

Minor league.

Chaperones on a field trip for the school.

His wife comes back from a vendor with some concessions.

She hands him a hot dog.

Wash inspects the toppings with suspicion. Rancid sauerkraut. Gummy mustard. What might be cheese.

The meat looks greasy.

"You used to love those," Mia frowns.

She trades him a pretzel.

"Guess that was the nostalgia you were tasting," Mia says.

★ ★ ★

Basement.

Jaden is hunched in the safe.

Sophie is crouched under the workbench.

Biscuit is leashed to a pipe on the boiler.

Tornado sirens howl in the distance.

"This is taking forever," Sophie says.

"I want to play a game," Jaden whines.

"We should have brought down some cards," Sophie says.

"There's nothing worse than just sitting," Jaden grumbles.

Wash presses his hands into the floor to stand.

"Don't you dare," Mia says.

Wash freezes.

"I'll be fast," Wash says.

And then, after glancing back at his wife at the foot of the stairs, goes up.

Noon, but with the lights off the house is dim, like today dusk came early. Wash hurries down the hallway toward the living room. There's a pressure in the air. In the living room he pinches his jeans to tug the legs up, then crouches over the basket of games, digging for a deck of cards.

Rising back up, tucking the cards into the pocket of his flannel, he glances over toward the doorway.

He can see the door lying in the yard next to a can of paint, where he had been painting the door when the sirens had begun to wail. The windows in the door reflect the clouds above. Through the glass is flattened grass.

The screen door, still attached to the doorframe, is rattling.
Wash crosses the living room.

He stands at the door.

He touches the screen.

Sky a mix of gold and green.

Leaves tearing across the yard in a rush of wind.

He can feel his heart beat.

The screen door opens with a creak.

Wash steps out onto the porch. His jeans snap against his legs.
His flannel whips against his chest. Beyond the corn across the road,
past the woods beyond the field, a tornado twists in the sky.

★ ★ ★

The anniversary will be their twentieth, but their first he can remember. Having to plan some type of date makes him nervous. He would
just take his wife out to eat somewhere fancy, which he knows is the
standard move, but aside from the diner the other restaurants in town
are all chains: a burger joint, a taco joint, a pizza place that doesn't even
have tables or chairs. Besides, he feels like this anniversary should be
special, something memorable, above and beyond a candlelight dinner. Wash agonizes for weeks, at a loss what to do, worrying that he
won't think of anything in time, and then while leaving work after an
especially brutal shift the week before the anniversary, he notices a
brochure tacked to the corkboard by the door. Wash reaches up, fingers pruny from washing dishes, and plucks the brochure down from
the corkboard. The brochure advertises cabin rentals in the state park
at El Dorado Reservoir.

His wife looks shocked when he tells her what the plan is, but
moments later she's jotting down a list of supplies to buy and gear to
pack, which seems like a form of approval.

Sophie gets left in charge of watching Jaden, with cash for emergencies and a fridge full of food, and he and his wife clear out of
town. Mia paints her nails teal over the course of the drive, her frizzy
hair trembling in the breeze through the windows. Wash stresses,

convinced that the cabin won't be as nice as the pictures in the brochure, afraid that his wife might secretly consider the plan too outdoorsy, but the cabin turns out to be just as perfect as promised, and his wife is beaming before the duffels have even hit the floor. He's never seen her like this. At home, she never drinks alcohol, she never plays music, she's stern and practical and tireless, emptying hampers and folding laundry and cleaning the fridge and washing the dog and checking the kids did their homework and helping the kids with their homework and scheduling appointments and reading mail and paying bills and organizing the junk drawer and lugging bags of garbage out to the bin without ever stopping to rest, as if the home, not just the house but the family and the lives contained within, would completely fall apart if she allowed herself to relax for even a moment. But at the cabin she's different, already loosening up, sipping from a can of beer, cranking up the bluegrass on the radio, dancing in place at the stove as she cooks up a feast of steak and mushrooms and roasted potatoes crusted with rosemary, giving him a glimpse of who she might have been when he met her twenty years ago, a twenty-year-old girl with a sense of humor and a lopsided smile and few if any responsibilities. He's liked his wife for as long as he can remember, but watching her dance around at the stove makes him feel something new, something powerful, tender, warm. He can tell that the feeling is strong, but even though he knows how strong the feeling is, and though he can't imagine how a feeling could possibly be any stronger, he's not sure whether or not there's still another feeling that's even stronger out there. He can't remember being in love. Has no spectrum to place the feeling on. Doesn't know what the limit for emotions is. Does he like her, or really like her, or really really like her, or really really really like her?

After the meal he leans back with his bare feet flat on the floor and his hands folded together on his gut, stuffed with starch and butter and meat and grease, buzzed from the beer. His wife usually doesn't involve him in parenting decisions, just signs the consent forms and checks the movie ratings herself. But for once she's actually consulting him about the kids, leaning across the table with her chin on the placemat, toying absentmindedly with the tab on a can.

"There are these acne pills Sophie keeps asking to try."

"She gets like a single pimple at a time."

"Should we let her or not?"

"For one zit?"

"So no."

Then:

"Do you think Jaden is getting picked on?"

"What makes you say that?"

"He keeps coming home with ripped clothes."

"He's just wild."

"You're sure?"

Wash feels a flush of pride. He likes when his wife asks his opinion. Maybe it's only because of the anniversary weekend, but he hopes it signals a permanent change.

"I got us something," Mia says suddenly, pushing up off of the table to stand, looking almost giddy. She goes out to the car, pops the trunk, digs under a tarp, and comes back lugging an unmarked cardboard box topped with a silver bow. The present is nearly as long as the table.

Wash takes ahold of the flap and rips through the tape.

Lifts the lid.

A rifle.

"Whoa," Wash says.

The gun lies on a pad of foam. Carbon barrel. Walnut stock. A repeater. A bolt-action. He reaches into the box, but then hesitates, looking to her for permission.

"Take it out," Mia laughs.

The moment he picks up the rifle a sense of relief washes over him. Like having a severed limb suddenly reattached. A natural extension of his body. Automatically he pulls the bolt back to check whether the chamber is empty, then shuts the breech and raises the gun, butt to his shoulder, stock on his cheek, his eye at the scope, testing the sights. The smell of the oil. The feel of the trigger. He can already tell that he's skilled with this thing.

"Are we allowed to have this?" Wash says.

"You're not, but technically I'm the owner, I did all the research, and as long as you don't have access, we're in the clear, so we'll just keep the gun in the safe and if anybody ever asks then we'll say that you don't know the combo. And honestly, on my honor, I did want to have a gun in the house again just in case of intruders. A pistol or a shotgun probably would have been better for that though. I went with this because of you. You can use it for target shooting out back, even use it for deer hunting if you want. I thought it all through. We'll just be careful. Nobody's going to know."

His chair creaks as she settles onto his lap.

He's overwhelmed.

"I love you," Wash says, without meaning to, the words just coming out.

He sets the rifle onto the table to kiss her, but an expression of alarm flashes across her face, and before he can lean closer she drops her head, with her chin to her sternum. Confused, he waits for her to look back up. Her hands rest on his shoulders. Her ass weighs on his thighs. She's trembling suddenly. No, he realizes, she's crying.

He can't remember ever seeing her cry before.

The sight scares him.

"What's wrong?" Wash frowns.

When she finally responds she speaks in a murmur.

"You're hardly you at all anymore."

"What does that mean?"

"You're just so different."

"Different how?"

Mia goes silent for a moment.

"You never did dishes before."

"Well, it wasn't my job back then, right?" Wash says.

"I mean at home," Mia explodes, shoving him in frustration, startling him.

"But after the meatloaf, you told me that's how things worked, was you doing the cooking and me doing the dishes," Wash says.

"I was kidding, I didn't think you'd actually do them, but then you got up from the table after we finished eating and you just started washing dishes, you'd never washed a dish in that house before in your life, you never used to play games with the kids, you never used to bring the kids along hunting, I always had to nag you to fix things around the house and even after you were done fixing things then you'd get on me for nagging you, I could barely get you to give the kids a ride somewhere without you throwing a fit, all you wanted to do was work and hunt and be alone in the woods, or rant at me about political stuff that there was nothing I could do anything about, we don't even fight anymore, I tried to pretend that you're the same but you're not, you're the same body, you move the same, you smell the same, you talk the same, you taste the same, but the rest of you is gone, you don't remember the tomato juice when I was pregnant with Jaden, you don't remember the fire alarm after I gave birth to Sophie, everything that used to have a secret meaning between us now is just a thing, to you a hay bale is just a hay bale, a batting helmet is just a batting helmet, a mosquito bite is just a mosquito bite, and that's not what they are to me," Mia cries, hitting his chest with her fists, "we lost our past, we lost our history," hitting his chest with her fists, "and you deserved it," a fist, "I didn't," a fist, "not me."

Wash sits there in terror, letting her beat on him, until finally she clutches his tee in her hands and sinks her head into his chest in exhaustion. His skin tingles with pain where the blows landed. His heart pounds from the shock of being struck. Wash glances at the blotchy sunspots on his hands, the faint scars on his fingers, the bone spurs on his heels, the brittle calluses on his soles, relics of years he can't remember living. He's never felt so much like a stranger in this body.

He's almost too shaken to speak.

"Which one do you want?" Wash says.

"Which what?"

"Which me?"

Mia heaves a sigh, then lifts her head, turns her face away, and rises off of him. She shuffles toward the bathroom. "I never would've gotten a gun again if you were the way you used to be."

Midnight. He lies next to his wife in the dark. The sheets are thinner than at home. The pillows are harder than at home. He can't remember ever having spent a night away from home before. He's gotten so used to falling asleep with her nuzzled against him that trying to fall asleep with her facing away from him is intensely lonely. His feet are cold. An owl hoots down by the reservoir.

Does he love his wife?

Did he ever love his wife before?

★ ★ ★

Lindsay is sitting on the chair in the living room. She's wearing the same outfit as every month. She tucks her hair behind her ears, then bends to grab a toy from the floor, a plastic bone that squeaks when squeezed.

"This is the last time we'll have to meet," Lindsay says.

"We're done?"

Lindsay looks up with a smile.

"Next month will mark a full year since your wipe. By the standards of our justice department, you've been officially reintroduced to your life. Congratulations."

Lindsay tosses the toy down the hallway.

Biscuit takes off running.

Wash thinks.

"There's something I don't understand."

"What's that?"

"What happens if you commit another crime after you've had a wipe like mine? What else could they even do to me if they've already taken everything?"

"They took the memories you had back then. You have new memories they could take."

Wash frowns.

"If you're being sentenced to a partial wipe, a shorter sentence is better than a longer sentence, of course. But for a life sentence, the numbers are meaningless. Is it worse when a sixty-year-old dies than when a six-year-old dies? Of course not. The length of a life has nothing to do with the weight of the loss."

Wash settles back into the couch, folding his arms across his chest, tucking his hands into his pits.

"That's important for you to understand," Lindsay says.

Wash glances over.

"You have another life you could lose now," Lindsay says.

Biscuit drops the bone back onto the floor.

Lindsay reaches down.

"How do you feel, Washington?"

"I feel really good," Wash says.

★ ★ ★

Mia calls him into the bathroom. She's sitting on the lid of the toilet in drawstring sweatpants and a baggy undershirt. The pregnancy test is lying on the side of the tub.

"We're both going to remember this one," Mia says, smiling up at him.

His kids barge into the bathroom a moment later, already fighting about what to name the baby.

Wash goes shopping for a crib with his family, pushing a cart down the bright aisles of a department store as swing music plays over the speakers. Wash reclines on a checkered blanket at the park as fireworks burst in the sky above his family, shimmering and fading. Wash hunches over the wastebasket in the bedroom, clipping the nails on his fingers as his wife pops the battery from a watch on the dresser. Wash leans over the sink in the bathroom, tweezing a hair from his nose as his wife gathers dirty towels from the hook on the door. Wash shoots holes into a target shaped like the silhouette of a person as his kids watch from the stump of an oak tree, sipping cans of soda. And wherever he's at, and whatever he's doing, there's something that's stuck in his mind like a jingle, nagging him.

He sits on the porch with the dog. Rain drips from the awning. Silks are showing on the husks of corn across the road. Summer is already almost gone. Behind him, through the screens in the windows, sounds of his family talking drift out of the house.

Sometimes he does want to be alone. Sometimes he feels so lazy that he wants to refuse to help with chores. Sometimes he gets so tense that he has an urge to punch a wall.

But maybe all of that is trivial compared to how he used to be.

Is he a different person now?

Has he been becoming somebody new?

Or does he have some soul, an inborn nature, a congenital personality, that's bound to express itself eventually?

The academic year hasn't started yet, but the athletic seasons have begun. He's on the way to pick up the kids from practice when he passes the library. His eyes flick from the road to the rearview, watching the library fade into the distance as the truck rushes on toward the school.

Knowing who he was might not even be an option. What he did might never even have made the news. And he's already running late anyway. But still his hands clench tight around the wheel.

Swearing, he hangs a u-ey, swinging the truck back around.

He parks at the library.

"I need to use a computer," Wash says.

The librarian asks him for identification, registers him for an account, and then brings him over to a computer. All that time he's thinking, what are you doing, what are you doing, what are you doing, imagining his kids waiting for him by the fence at the school. The librarian heads back to the reference desk.

His hands are trembling as he reaches for the keyboard.

He logs onto the computer, pulls up a browser, and searches his name.

The screen blinks as the results appear.

Nothing. A pop star with his name. A goalie. A beach resort with his name. A monument. He's not there.

He skims through again to be sure, and then laughs out loud in relief.

The temptation was a mirage all along.

Wash swivels on the chair to stand, then thinks of something, and hesitates.

He turns back around.

Puts his fingers on the keyboard.

Tries his name plus his town.

The screen blinks as the results change.

His heart leaps.

He's there.

The list of articles seems to scroll on forever.

The headlines alone are enough to send a beat of rage pulsing through him.

Wash runs his hands over his mouth, glancing at the daylight streaming into the library through the door beyond the computer, trying to decide whether to leave now or to keep reading, flashing through all of the memories he has from the past year that he could lose. Jaden grinning in amazement after choking on the lozenge in the driveway. Sophie cracking up laughing after the crow fell out of the tree. Mia treading water at the reservoir in a white one-piece, glancing at him with a casual expression before suddenly lunging over to dunk him. Jaden lying on the linoleum in the kitchen in cutoff shorts, gripping him by the ankle, begging to be taken to the go-kart track. Jaden whirling around the yard with a lit sparkler. Mia swinging by the diner on a day off from the hospital, hair piled into a bun, trench coat damp with rain, splitting a slice of cherry pie with him while he's on break. Sophie standing under the light in the kitchen in pajamas, holding him by the arm, upset by a dream about a ghost. Sophie singing into a lit sparkler like a microphone. Mia arranging gourds on the porch. Mia brushing icicles from the awning. Mia sweating into a damp washcloth, deliriously rambling about how much she loves him, as he crouches by the bed with the wastebasket, waiting there in case she pukes again. The dog watching a butterfly flutter down the hallway, then turning to look at him, as if waiting for an explanation. His kids dancing around the dead buck, boots tromping through snowy ferns, gloved hands raised in celebration, lit by the dazzling sunbeams spiking through the branches of the trees, and afterward driving back to the house with the deer in the bed of the truck, the mighty antlers rising into the air out the window behind the cab, the kids chattering to each other on the seat next to him, hats both off, hair all disheveled, and later eating bowls of cornflakes in the kitchen in thermal underwear together as the kids recount the story of the hunt with wild gestures, while his wife sits across the table in a plaid nightgown, smiling over a mug of black tea. The secret experiences that nobody else shared. The joy of discovering the chocolate stash hidden in the aluminum tin in the basement. The habit he's made of visiting the glittering display of chandeliers and pendants and lamps and sconces whenever he goes to the hardware store, marveling at the rich glow of the mingled lights, filtered through the tinted glass and the colored shades. The sense of destiny when a bottle of cola suddenly plunked into the dispenser of a vending machine at the shopping mall as he was walking out of the bathroom. The fear and the awe and the wonder of seeing a monstrous tornado churn in the sky above the town, the funnel spiraling down from the clouds, the tip just about to touch the ground.

Wash sits back in the chair, looking from the door to the computer, biting his lip as he wavers, torn between the possibility of having a future and the possibility of having a past. But only for a moment. Because when he thinks about it, he knows who he is. He already knows what he'll do.

A Bad Day In Utopia

She'd had a hard day. Earlier that morning she'd discovered that the game her company was developing, which was already months behind schedule for release, had a glitch somewhere in the code that caused the game to crash if the player character was equipped with diamond armor on the level with the meteors, and nobody could figure out why. It didn't make any sense. It was a total nightmare. Anna, her boss, was mad at her for leaving dirty dishes in the kitchen again. Lucy, her supervisor, kept ignoring her emails about the status of the new health plan. Indira, the latest intern, had spilled coffee all over the table in the conference room, and the coffee had gotten onto her blouse and her skirt, and though the coffee had been iced and hadn't burned her, her blouse was white and her skirt was peach, and she hadn't been able to get the stains to wash out completely, leaving faint blotches on the fabric, and her clothes were still damp from trying. Her landlord, Kayla, had sent her a message that she wouldn't replace her garbage disposal, despite that her disposal was indisputably broken. Her therapist, Sofia, had sent her a message that she was raising her hourly fee, even though her fee was already outrageous. Danielle, her neighbor, still wasn't talking to her after last weekend. And all of the women at the company were running around the office, desperately trying to pinpoint the exact cause of the glitch, which made her so anxious that she could physically feel the stress tingling through her body as she typed code, and her breast had a lump that she was trying not to think about until the results came back, and her wrist was still tender from the spill that she had taken on the track at the gym, and she had a pimple on her shoulder that was sore and swollen and seemingly resistant to every known variety of acne cream, and that morning the governor had announced a plan to substantially raise the income tax in California, which meant that she'd have less money to put toward savings every paycheck, and that she wouldn't be able to afford a baby for another year. Fuck, she thought. Fuck, fuck, fuck. By the end of the day she was just sitting at her computer in a daze. She was supposed to meet some of her friends for dinner. She wasn't hungry. She felt depressed. She didn't want to go. She messaged her friends that she had to cancel.

Mackenzie called her.

"Why aren't you coming?" Mackenzie said.

"I had a shitty day," she said.

"Maybe going out would help?" Mackenzie said.

"I'm just going to go home," she said.

Mackenzie made a sympathetic noise.

"You sound miserable. I'm going to have a care package delivered to your apartment. Expect wine and cupcakes. I love you, I miss you, get some sleep. I'll see you this weekend," Mackenzie said.

After hanging up she tried calling her mother.

"I had a terrible day," she said.

"I'm sorry, baby, I'm just walking into a surgery," her mother said.

"Oh," she said.

"I'm sorry, really, I'll call you back when we're done," her mother said.

"I'll just be at home," she said.

She hung up. She felt awful. She left. In the elevator she realized she had forgotten to shut off her computer. She was too exhausted to go back. She walked through the revolving door in the lobby out onto the street. The sun was out, but rain was falling, a light scatter of drops pattering down from a blue sky. Fluffy clouds were floating above the city. She paused at the curb, full of despair. The street was full of people. A mail carrier at a drop box, a woman in tortoiseshell glasses, sorting through envelopes. An electrician on a hydraulic lift, a woman with tattooed hands, repairing a utility pole. A pair of cops, a couple of women with blond ponytails, ticketing a parked convertible. Women striding down the sidewalk with briefcases and clutches and backpacks and satchels and colorful wheeled suitcases. Women gliding through the intersection in buses and taxis and pickups and sedans and gleaming delivery trucks. Students on a field trip from out of town, a line of girls in matching shirts, following a pregnant chaperone across a crosswalk. Teenagers in dresses and denim jackets doing kickflips and nosegrinds on battered skateboards. Women holding hands at marble tables on the patio of the cafe across the street, sipping at foamy cappuccinos, flirting with each other. Seeing the women holding hands made her think about sex. And suddenly all that she could think about was sex. She wanted to be touched.

She wasn't lucky enough to be attracted to women. She had tried a couple times, in school, in college, and had been forced to admit that women just didn't interest her sexually. She had only ever fantasized about men. Men from classic movies. Men from vintage comics. Men from paintings and statues at the museum. She had other straight friends, Mackenzie especially, who liked to go to android clubs, having sex with robots designed to look like men, with cocks and balls and hairy chests, skin as soft and warm as the flesh of a human. The robots could talk and laugh and flirt, but the technology was still relatively unrefined, and tended to induce that uncanny effect, seeming vaguely creepy to her. She preferred to get off with simpler machines, generally. Vibrators. Dildos. Showerheads. She could satisfy herself like that for weeks at a time.

But sometimes there were days when machines weren't enough, days when she felt like cuddling, days when she felt like kissing, days when she felt like being caressed and squeezed and held by another person.

And so when she got into her car that day, instead of going home she drove to the local menagerie.

San Francisco's menagerie was a glass dome on the shore of a sandy cove along the ocean, out past the redwood forest in the hills. She drove with the windows down so that her hair danced around her head as her car flew over the bridge. Electronica was playing over her stereo. Rain was still falling in a scatter. The sky was turning orange and yellow. Fluffy clouds were floating above the hills. She felt a tingle of excitement, of anticipation, as she arrived at the menagerie. Sunlight reflected off of the dome in iridescent shimmers of color. The only other car in the lot was an antique roadster. The primary purpose of the facility obviously was to serve as a safeguard, to prevent the extinction of the human race in the event that civilization collapsed, if artificial fertilization was suddenly rendered impossible by an asteroid impact or a geomagnetic storm. The men created for the menagerie were living sperm banks. Redundant machines that would only be useful in an emergency. Like an oil lantern that nobody would ever need unless the power went out and the batteries went dead in the flashlights. She rarely ever thought about that, though, as the possibility was so unlikely. For her the primary purpose of the facility was to provide women the opportunity to have sex with men. Her straight friends preferred to have sex with robots because having sex with men was so much more expensive, but she didn't mind paying extra. Technically the money was a donation. All of the proceeds went toward buying the men special treats, like sorbet and pastries. She liked feeling generous. The doors to the lobby slid apart automatically. She paid the receptionist, accepted a glass of chilled cucumber water, selected a couch in the waiting area, and sat sipping the cucumber water in the waiting area as the receptionist paged a guard. Even for a weeknight, the menagerie was strangely quiet. Aside from the receptionist, the lobby was completely empty. Recently a man had attempted to escape from the menagerie in Detroit, had become violent when the guards had tranqed him, and had attempted suicide with a belt upon awaking in his cell. Another man had recently attacked a visitor at the menagerie in Atlanta, had been beaten by the guards in retribution, and never would be allowed to have a visitor in his cell again. She had read about it in the news. Incidents like that didn't scare her, though, being so rare. The global population of men was strictly regulated, just over a hundred thousand in the world, and all of the men had been raised in captivity from birth, were familiar with the bite and the sting of batons and stunners. In her experience the men at the menagerie knew better than to cause trouble. And in a way, she liked the thrill. Entering the lair of the most violent, ruthless, destructive creature that had ever walked the face of the planet.

San Francisco's menagerie was an average size, from what she'd heard, although she had never been to any other. Boys at the menagerie lived in cells on the upper floor. All of the men lived in cells on the ground floor. The hallway had a white floor and white walls with a white ceiling. A guard with a radio and a gun and a black uniform led her down the hallway, passing the glass doors looking into the cells where the men lived. Duke, a man with a button nose and dimples, who was cute. Earl, a man with freckles and a cleft chin, who was gorgeous. Marquis, a man with a buzz cut and an enchanting singing voice. Prince, a slender man with a tongue piercing and prominent cheekbones, who was gay and rarely interested in sleeping with visitors. Malik, a chubby man with a sexy laugh. Amir, a shy man with a fine ass. Baron, a charming older man who was bald and bearded and spoke with a stammer. The doors were staggered so that none of the men could see each other through the glass, only the passing guards. Tonight the men were all occupied playing video games, doing crosswords, stringing guitars, folding origami, sniffing socks, watching the news, making pour-over coffee. The one she liked best was kept in the cell at the end of the hallway.

"I'm so glad that you're here," Rex said with a surprised smile, looking up from a sketchpad full of designs for flying machines.

The guard strolled back down the hallway as the door slid shut, leaving her alone with him. Rex strode over to the door barefoot, wearing a brown linen tunic over tight beige pants. He was younger than she was, probably early twenties, a tall, broad, muscular man whose face was angular and handsome, with dark wavy hair and a pair of bright hazel eyes that shone with intelligence and curiosity. His voice was deep. His stubble was hot. His tracking bracelet was an attractive silver band, the same as the rest of the men's. Like the other cells at the facility, the suite where he lived was pleasant and spacious and elegantly decorated, with a king-size bed, a desk for writing, a chair for reading, and a dresser for clothes. A bookcase full of novels and atlases and encyclopedias and tattered volumes of poetry. A bathroom. A kitchenette. A yoga mat, a weight bench, and a stationary bicycle for exercise. A grand piano, which he had been learning to play since early childhood. A canvas on an easel, since lately he had been interested in art. All of the furniture in the suite was minimalist and modern. A couple pairs of boxers were strewn across the floor around the laundry hamper, and an apricot pit sat on a plate by the sink, but overall the appearance of the suite was clean and tidy. The wall across from the door was made of glass, overlooking the beach and the tide pools and the glittering green and indigo water of the ocean stretching off to the horizon. Rex kissed her. His lips were very soft. His mouth tasted like sugar. He'd been eating caramels.

"You got a new haircut," she said.

"Do you like it?" Rex said.

"Did you pick it out?" she said.

"I saw it on a man in a book," Rex said.

She set down her purse by the door. Usually she wore lingerie when she visited the menagerie, but she hadn't been planning on coming, so that day she had on a discolored bra and a pair of cotton panties with a couple of ratty holes along the waistband. Rex didn't seem to notice any difference, stripping off her blouse and her skirt and her bra and her panties with a passionate urgency, kissing her skin everywhere. She was small enough that he could carry her over to the bed. She had sex with him. Afterward she cuddled with him. A light rain was still falling beyond the windows. The sky had turned pink. Fluffy clouds were floating above the ocean. Her cheeks felt flushed.

Her heart was pounding. She was naked now except for her watch, an heirloom from her grandmother, a simple timepiece with gold hands on a gold face and a gold band. Rex stroked her head, gently caressing her hair, massaging her scalp with his thick fingertips, which she had told him before that she liked. His skin was slightly lighter than her skin, and she liked the visual contrast. When he'd taken off the condom, tossing the condom into the wastebasket, some of his semen had spilled out onto the sheets. She liked the smell of his semen in the air. She liked the smell of his deodorant. She liked the smell of his sweat. She felt fantastic. She liked talking to him.

"I've been learning about the history of architecture," Rex said.

Watching the bulge in his throat bounce when he spoke exhilarated her.

"Tell me something you learned," she said.

Rex hesitated. "Is it true that most of the buildings in the world were built by men?"

"I don't think very many women got to be architects under the patriarchy," she said.

Rex frowned at the ceiling.

"That makes me angry," Rex said.

"Me too," she said.

"It's just so unfair," Rex said.

"I guess everything was like that," she said.

"I bet the world would be so much more beautiful if all of the cities had been built by women," Rex said.

She thought about that for a while.

"Well, every building put up in the past fifty years was built by a woman, and a man will never build a building again," she finally said.

Rex seemed satisfied with that. She ran her hands over his skin absentmindedly, feeling his tiny nipples, the firm muscle in his pecs, the rigid grooves between his abs, spreading her fingers through the scratchy bristles of his pubes. His buttocks were round and smooth and nice to touch.

"Will you tell me what it's like outside?" Rex said.

Rex always asked her that when she visited him. He had never felt sunshine. He had never felt rain. He had never felt wind. He had never felt grass or dirt or sand. He was obsessed with the outdoors. Mountains. Icebergs. Flowers. Weather.

"It's warm today," she said.

Rex was captivated.

"And it's raining. But a light rain. A very light rain, so light that you barely feel it. And the wind is light too. The perfect breeze. And the city smells like rain and steam from all of the humidity and the water. And the rain brings out the smells of the grass and the dirt and the flowers. And all the birds are flying north for the summer, so that when you walk down the street you hear birds chirping everywhere, all around you. And the rain is so light that when a drop falls on you it feels almost special, and you have to reach up to wipe it off of your cheek," she said.

Rex turned toward the windows with a look of longing.

"I wish we could feel it together," Rex whispered.

She ate a fig from the platter of fruit on the nightstand next to the bed.

"Will you go down on me again?" she said.

Rex said he would, eager to please her. She spread her knees, taking hold of his head, enjoying the feel of his hair between her fingers, the feel of his tongue pulsing against her clit, the feel of his hands wrapped around her thighs, gripping her tight. Tasting her must have aroused him, because when he finally rose back off of the bed, his cock was hard again, standing stiff in the air. She had sex with him again. He came with a moan, digging his fingertips into the skin on her back, gently calling out her name.

Afterward she cuddled with him again. Twilight was falling across the ocean beyond the windows. The clouds had vanished. Stars were appearing in the sky. She felt comfortable. She felt happy. She had a sudden craving for nachos. She glanced at her watch. She wanted to watch a couple episodes of a new show before she went to sleep.

"I'd better go," she said.

She got dressed. Rex looked distraught. He quick fumbled to put on his pants and his tunic. As she pulled the strap of her purse over her shoulder, he reached for her.

"Take me with you," Rex whispered, glancing at the door with a wild look.

She was startled. He was serious. She stepped back.

"No, honey," she said.

"I want to run away with you. We'll live together. Somewhere out in the wilderness, where nobody will find us. We'll build a home. We'll have a family," Rex said.

"No," she said.

"I love you," Rex said.

"You barely know me," she said, stunned.

"You're beautiful. You're smart. You're kind. You are, I know you are. That week after the earthquake, when you found that lost dog on the side of the road, you carried him to your car to bring him to a shelter, even though he was all muddy and got your clothes and your seats dirty. When you told me about that, I fell in love with you. That was the moment. That dog could have had fleas, or worms, or rabies, but you saw he was alone, that he needed help, and you helped him. Because that's the type of person you are. I love how you look when you laugh, when you really laugh, so hard that you can't breathe. I love how happy you get when you eat something sweet, the way that your eyes get small and crinkle with happiness while you chew. I want to make you happy. I want to live with you. I think about it all the time. I want to be with you forever," Rex said.

"Rex, no," she said.

"Please," Rex said, becoming teary.

The sight of the tears made her hesitate, and suddenly he looked desperate, as if he could sense her wavering. The tears shimmered in his eyes as he stepped closer.

"Please, don't leave me here. I can't take it anymore. Just take me with you. I won't be violent. I'll respect you. I'll be kind. I'll be peaceful. I'm not like the other men," Rex said, begging now.

She had fantasized before about sharing a life with him. Standing there at the door, she imagined helping him sneak out of the menagerie, past all of the guards. Cutting off the tracking bracelet with the pliers from the emergency toolbox in her trunk, and then driving away in her car, to someplace far away. Moving into an abandoned farmhouse in the country. Growing vegetables. Raising chickens. Keeping bees. Waking in the same bed every day. Being outside together. How he would smile, how he would weep, when he knelt down to touch the soil for the first time. How he would laugh in wonder. She thought about how much she loved for him to touch her. How much she loved to talk to him. How much she loved to be with him. She thought about her friends. She thought about her mother. Like all of her friends, every member of her generation, she was a stem-cell baby, fertilized in vitro with artificial sperm, her gender preselected, and then transferred from the petri dish into her mother. She had been born long after the purges. Long after men had become obsolete. She had never lived in a world where men roamed free. A world where assault and murder and war were all an everyday occurrence. Her mother had been too young to remember. But before her grandmother had died, her grandmother had told her stories, sitting around the firepit behind the trailer, roasting marshmallows over the embers. The worst day she had ever had under the matriarchy, her grandmother had said, was still better than the best day she had ever lived under the patriarchy. A former soldier and retired housekeeper, her grandmother had fought off an attempted rape by a friend of her father at the age of thirteen and had been called a liar when she had finally dared to confess to her father what had happened, had once been bending for a suitcase at a luggage carousel when a man had pinched her ass with his fingers, had once been holding the pole on a bus when a man had pressed hard into her hand with his groin, had once been taken to a med center by a friend after an unidentified predator had slipped a date-rape drug into her beer at a concert, had had her body remarked upon by men on a daily basis, as a teenager had been rejected from the high school wrestling team solely on the basis of being a girl, as a soldier had regularly been passed over for promotion in favor of male candidates who were considerably less qualified, as a housekeeper had never been paid a comparable wage to male housekeepers at the hotel, had been sent countless pictures of erect dicks from friends, coworkers, acquaintances, neighbors, and total strangers, completely unsolicited, had dated a man who had enjoyed mocking her whenever she made any type of mistake and had left her feeling pathetic and stupid, had dated a man who had tried to control what she ate and had called her disgusting and ugly whenever her weight had fluctuated, had dated a man who had habitually provoked arguments with random men at bars, getting into vicious fistfights, hurling stools, shattering bottles, throwing punches, shouting with hormonal rage, scaring the hell out of her every time, and had eventually married a polite, helpful, affectionate, sensitive man, who like all husbands had taken a vow to be faithful, and who had cheated on her on over a dozen occasions. Her grandmother's aunt, a chemistry professor who had never been paid a comparable wage to male colleagues at the university, had had an abusive husband who had spread rumors that she was an alcoholic after she had finally divorced him. Her grandmother's sister, a nurse anesthetist who had never been paid a comparable wage to male colleagues at the hospital, had been harassed by a stalker who for years had periodically sent her videos of him masturbating to her headshot. Her great-grandmother, who in her youth had seen a boy with a rifle go on a shooting spree at a shopping mall that had claimed the lives of dozens, had routinely been beaten by her father. All of her friends had stories like these. Mackenzie's great-grandmother, who had gone on to become a famous pilot, in her youth had been assaulted by a college quarterback at a frat party, and despite that her testimony had been corroborated by multiple eyewitnesses, her rapist had never been convicted, had just gone free. Anna's grandmother had been molested by her band instructor. Lucy's grandmother had been fondled by her loan officer. Indira's grandmother had been pressured to send nude photos to her boyfriend, had been called a slut when he had posted the photos online in revenge for dumping him, and years later had been pressured to give her manager a blowjob, and then had had her hours cut back after she had refused. Danielle's grandmother had once been raped by her own husband. And that was only a random sampling of women from a single generation, in a single community. Humans had been living in organized societies for over ten thousand years. Ten thousand years of tribes and kingdoms and nations. Ten thousand years that men had ruled the world. Ten thousand years that women had suffered without change. Had been treated as inferiors, and simpletons, and burdens, and temptations. As mere property, like a cow or a donkey. As mindless objects. She thought about that. She thought about all of those women, not as a group, but the individual people, each of whom had been unique and complicated and remarkable, each of whom had had hopes and dreams and feelings, a single precious life, and had been oppressed from her first breath to her deathbed. The billions upon billions upon billions of women. She thought about the genital mutilations, and the forced pregnancies, and the forced abortions, and the bride burnings, and the boy clubs. All of the abuse. All of the bullying. All of the shaming. All of the belittling. All of the gaslighting. All of the catcalling. All of the stalking. All of the groping. All of the rapes.

"No meant no," she said, and walked out the door.

Testimony Of Your Majesty

I remember leaving a shopping mall once as a child, strolling across the sunny parking lot with my family, my father carrying shopping bags full of ties and corduroys and aftershave, my mother carrying shopping bags full of shawls and clogs and potpourri, my sister, hardly older than a toddler, lugging a shopping bag crammed with boxes of headbands. I had a shopping bag too, and as we drove back down the highway with the shopping bags heaped cozily around us, I gradually became aware of the people in passing cars. A couple in a minivan. A teenager in a pickup. A family in a sedan. Staring at us.

"Are we different from other people?" I asked.

★ ★ ★

I am a parent now too, and live a very different life. My children run through the aisles of the public library, cheering with excitement at book displays, getting gently hushed by smiling employees. My youngest daughter is the last to decide on a book for the week, coming to the counter with a graphic novel about a beautiful werewolf. The cover is tattered from all of the people who read the book before her. Pages are bent in makeshift bookmarks. Colorful notes are written in margins. She's frowning thoughtfully as she places the book in my hands.

"Is healthy the same as happy?" she asks.

★ ★ ★

Who would ever guess, looking at me now. I wouldn't know how to explain to my children. How to explain the shame. How to explain the urges. I never even speak of it to my husband. And yet, some days, I'll be washing the dishes or sweeping the porch when the memories will suddenly overwhelm me. The breathtaking ecstasy of consumption.

"She's grotesque," another teenager once whispered, watching me walk past.

I was a very pale child, strangely gangly, whose face often had a faraway expression, as if in the midst of communicating telepathically with invisible creatures. I loved to wear dresses. I liked to wear flats. I had a habit of walking around with my hands balled into fists, like somebody expecting an ambush at any moment. Although this probably radiated a sense of anxiety, the causes were physiological rather than psychological. My circulation was poor, especially in my fingers, and keeping my hands in fists was warmer.

I did also have a lot of anxiety.

My family lived in the suburbs of Nashville, in a house that can only be described as gigantic, just gargantuan. Slate shingles, dark brickwork, flanked by a pair of turrets. Three stories, plus an attic and a basement. A proper mansion. My bedroom was circular, overlooking the driveway from the top of the east turret. In the west turret, my sister overlooked the net hammock hanging between the magnolias. When the blossoms got blown down from the trees, the grass around the hammock turned pink with petals.

If the exterior seemed excessive, the interior was even worse.

A popular measure of spiritual health in those days, perhaps you'll recall, was that known as "the ratio." We were taught the ratio in school. Belongings per person, of course. At the time, 100:1 was considered the healthiest. A ratio of 1000:1 was considered inexcusably high. A ratio of 10:1 was considered irrationally low. 100:1 was about the ideal proportion.

Well, our ratio was staggering. Including clothing, shoes, jewelry, tableware, furnishings, appliances, decorations, knickknacks, toys, and etcetera, our ratio was approximately 9000:1. A grossly unhealthy figure.

For anybody, doing anything, having a ratio of that size would have meant suffering a certain amount of prejudice. For a thirteen-year-old girl attending a private school in Tennessee, having a ratio of that size meant being an absolute pariah. Schoolwide my nickname was "Her Highness." Kids sometimes taped dollar bills to my locker to mock me. I kept every last one, I am ashamed to say, which only made the bullying worse.

The common belief was that families like ours were afflicted by an appetite of the eyes—that we simply stuffed our spaces with things to look at. My family, however, if not a contradiction to the rule, at the very least contained an exception: my mother was blind. (My father often joked that she never would have agreed to marry him if she could have seen him, although she of course had touched his face and said she found his features quite appealing: slick graying hair brittle with mousse; a wide forehead lined with creases; a broad angular nose with a lump at the bridge, a healed fracture, from a college wrestling tournament; rather plump lips; a boxy jaw with a cleft chin. A landscape pleasant not only to touch, but also to look at. My mother in contrast was plain: straight black hair, an unremarkable nose, and thin lips.) My mother could read Braille, and had an unusual hobby. My father owned, had inherited, a department store, and at that time every register in the department store contained a roll of paper that the register would punch for each transaction. The holes punched into the paper weren't Braille, of course, but rather a code that could be fed to computers, which were then used to compile purchases and calculate profits. ("$176.86," "$97.45," "$231.07," etcetera—that's what the dots meant.) But when my mother could get him to remember, my father would bring home spools of that punched tape for her, and as she swung with us in the hammock or lay with us by the fireplace, she liked to run her fingertips over the holes, reading—not what the computers read, but instead searching the spools for patterns she recognized, like some type of game, shouting with pleasure whenever she did find letters or words or phrases, such as "love," in the endless strings of empty holes. The exercise perhaps was similar to a girl fluent in Morse, standing at the checkout in the department store and searching for meaning in the dings and trills of the registers, finding words such as "love" in the sounds, when what the registers were truly saying was simply "cancel sale" or "transaction completed." (Or is what the registers were truly saying "love"? What dictates meaning: intent or interpretation?)

Regardless, my mother, though blind, was just as bad as the rest of us. Just as we felt intense longing at the sight of new bicycles on display, she too was overcome by sensations: the noise of a new electric fan; the scent of new teak bowls; the flavor of a new latex balloon; the texture of rippled bottles of perfume. Our appetite was visual, aural, olfactory, gustatory, tactile, and indiscriminate especially. Weekends, driving home from brunch, I would feel the tension mounting in the sedan, our unspoken struggle to suppress a swelling craving to shop, an almost bursting desire. There was never any question of whether we would break. We always broke. Passing the shopping mall, we would beg my father to stop, lost whole days there, basking in the dusty warmth of the skylights, trembling with the faint quiver of the escalators, buying mounds of blazers and polos and blouses and skirts, fragrant candles, spongy luffas, opal sunglasses, crystal armlets, a brass spyglass, a framed chalkboard, an iron luggage rack, a hardwood table with fluted legs. At the supermarket, we would toss spare placemats, novelty mugs, fuzzy slippers, board games that we would never play, into the cart with the groceries. At gas stations, we would follow my father inside, impulsively shoving packs of baseball cards onto the counter, random magazines, used videos, gaudy mood rings. My father, who never smoked, always bought a plastic lighter. We spent as much on merchandise as gasoline.

We weren't without conscience. And we weren't unconscious of the economics. Bringing home shopping bags, dumping piles of superfluous belongings onto my bedspread, I would feel nauseous with shame. Truly, hideous, just utterly gross. All of us did. We understood that in a society where many still lacked everyday essentials, to live as we lived was simply abhorrent. Barbaric, even. But our yearning to consume—to possess new objects, something, anything—was insatiable. We couldn't help ourselves.

I have a memory of lying sprawled across the carpet in the master bedroom, watching my parents in their bathroom, my mother flossing, my father shaving—carefully maneuvering the razor over the cleft in his chin, then flicking cream and flecks of stubble from his razor into the sink—as he talked to us, trying to comfort us. In the mirror, my sister was jumping on the canopy bed behind me, making the sheets flail with every bounce.

"Just look at history," my father argued, rinsing his razor. "Having lots of stuff used to be considered a mark of prestige. Noble. Desirable. Sexy. The ultimate ambition."

He told us to ignore the bullies at school, saying that feeling guilty about buying extra things was "silly," merely "cultural." But his voice had a tremor, and his cheeks had suddenly flushed—regardless of what he said, he was embarrassed of our lifestyle, the same as the rest of us.

But honestly, there was also an intense feeling of pleasure, of fullness, that came from our lifestyle. Inanimate things, just like animate beings, have a presence, a powerful presence. In my bedroom in the turret there was an elevated window seat. And sitting there—looking, not outward, but inward, facing the bedroom—I was often given the distinct feeling of being embraced. By all my belongings. Felt held by everything. The sparkling waterfall chandelier suspended by a chain from the center of the ceiling, the painted armoire standing cheerfully against the wall, the wire mannequin heaped with hats and caps, the bookshelves crammed with novels with gleaming jackets, a quartz geode, an empty birdcage, a golden clock shaped like an hourglass, coats and dresses and jeans and sweatshirts stuffed into the closet on wooden hangers, dirty laundry overflowing from a wicker basket, colorful beanbags, a tufted chaise, the cashmere throws my mother insisted on buying for me, which were always folded in a neat arrangement on the lid of the cedar chest, a rainstick, a bike helmet, a bocce set, jump ropes, golf clubs, a lacrosse stick bought on a whim, a sturdy walnut chair, a matching rolltop desk, a cushioned stool, a mirrored vanity, bubbling lava lamps in a range of colors and sizes, elastic hair ties, scattered bobby pins, glass fairies, rhinestone tiaras, various pairs of swimming goggles, the gigantic fake butterflies my father had strung above the bed for me, which sometimes quivered in the breeze from the vent in the ceiling, a nightstand cluttered with bejeweled rings and diamond chokers, a pogo stick lying on the rug, towers of unread magazines, piles of unwatched videos, decks of playing cards, packs of sidewalk chalk, yo-yos with tangled strings, twisted belts, glittering wands, jars crammed with crusted paintbrushes, a hairdryer, another hairdryer, a purse, a purse, a purse, a purse. A world of things, and every day the world was changing, the character of the bedroom constantly shifting, old objects disappearing into drawers or boxes as new objects appeared. I was protected there, kept safe from any feelings of boredom or emptiness. I felt very near to content.

I could have been happy hiding away in that turret forever, pretending nobody existed except for my family.

Weekday mornings, the thump of the school doors behind me felt like the thud of an executioner's blade.

I did have one friend at school, Madison Gates, a toothy redhead with a latex allergy. The school nurse had once touched her throat while wearing latex gloves, and her entire face had broken out into a rash. Madison had thought the rash was hilarious, if somewhat painful, but that incident—that and her hair—was the origin of her personal nickname: "The Red Queen."

Madison's family lived a block away from mine, in a gated mansion with an antebellum design. Marble driveway, sculpted hedges, a pillared awning over the porch. Four stories, plus an attic and a basement. Their ratio was simply beyond estimation. Madison was an only child.

Madison's windows overlooked the swimming pool and the wading pool and the pool house in the backyard. Her bedroom was twice the size of mine, and equally crammed. (Her belongings aren't necessary to list in entirety. Just picture mine, but with a touch of adventurer. Bottled ships, model carriages, a longbow with a quiver of feathered arrows. Etcetera.) Madison was the one who forced me to learn Morse. She had learned the code from an old military manual that she had inherited from her grandparents, and during sleepovers, in the moonlight, lying with me on her waterbed, she would drill me on the alphabet by tapping my forehead with the code. I can distinctly remember lying there: happy, tired, smelling of chlorine, blinking drowsily at her face as her fingertip softly tapped the alphabet into my skull. Madison would refuse to let me sleep until we had gotten through each letter. She would always fall asleep facing away from me, but when morning came, I often awoke to find her clinging to me, like a drowning girl to some passing wreckage, with sweaty hair matted to her face. I really loved that.

Madison had a reason for drilling me—at school there were times when we needed to talk confidentially, without any fear of being overheard. This was generally whenever she caught sight of Cody Walden. During our lunch hour, for instance, Cody had shop class, and he somehow always managed to sneak out—would come roaming into the cafeteria, grinning impishly, wearing plastic safety glasses flecked with sawdust, to the cheers of his friends. Cody was a squat stocky boy with wide shoulders and a thick torso and a mess of hair so fair that the color seemed almost white. He had developed a reputation for being intensely emotional: a fierce temper, a moody humor, passionate loyalty to his friends. He loved to discuss obviously implausible hypotheticals. He delighted in stunts. He rejoiced in pranks. He earned grades that were utterly abysmal. There was nobody as popular. As he roamed past where we sat, Madison would clutch a fork or spoon, frantically tapping a coded message into the laminate surface of the table: "love of my life."

Her fear of being overheard wasn't paranoid. Cody's ratio was perfect. A girl like her daring to aspire to a boy like him was a joke—one that other kids would have found hysterical—in moments her social status at the school would have sunk from outcast to laughingstock. Our ratios were by far the largest in the school. Even the other rich kids shunned and mocked us. Madison didn't stand a chance.

Even my parents felt some embarrassment about how we lived. Madison, however, felt no shame. She truly believed there was nothing wrong with her lifestyle, and shopped without qualms. Together we were monsters. Our sprees were legendary. We ravaged outlets; we plundered boutiques. Lugging shopping bags through the parking lot toward where my parents were parked, we would be taunted by strangers, kids in basketball jerseys leering from pickups, spitting, "Y'all are gross." Madison would snap, "Go fuck yourselves." (She never would have been so brave at school—kids we had never seen before were nowhere near as frightening as kids we had to see daily.)

Madison's parents were bankers—a mother with rusty hair who habitually wrung her hands, a father with a faint voice and a receding hairline, rather timid people—themselves the children of bankers. Giving money away, modest living, was not in their blood. Her parents must have suffered some ostracism too: when speaking of other adults, her parents referenced only coworkers, neighbors, hairstylists, physicians; like my parents, her parents didn't seem to have any friends.

Nevertheless, her parents did have certain aspirations for their daughter, socially. (Also for me perhaps: her parents treated me like an adoptee, and seemed genuinely concerned for my welfare.) I don't think her parents ever had any ambitions of their daughter becoming "popular." Her parents simply wanted her to fit in, belong. To be accepted by her community, rather than abhorred.

Thus, at the conclusion of the school year, these rather timid people concocted a bold plan. That summer, without her consent, her parents announced that she would be having "a pool party."

Nine girls from our grade were invited—girls who held student council offices, who starred in theater productions, who excelled at debating competitions, who took camping trips together, who had actual love lives—the same girls who curtsied to us in the hallway and the cafeteria and the gymnasium, crooning "Her Highness" and "The Red Queen." I would have been mortified, absolutely humiliated, if my parents had mailed those girls invitations to "a pool party." I felt just nauseous, imagining the confused murmurs, then shrieks of laughter, as the girls slit the envelopes and read the invitations. Madison, however, didn't really care. "They won't come, and that's all that matters. They won't even reply, and the party will never happen," Madison said.

Yet the girls did reply, and unanimously accepted.

I still cringe at the memory of that fateful day.

Madison made me swear to come, which she was wise to do—that morning of the pool party, only my loyalty to her could have gotten me into a bikini and over to her house. I was terrified. Madison looked miserable, flopped across a wicker couch in her solarium, holding a pillow to her face as if attempting to smother herself, while her parents bustled about excitedly, dusting mirrors, sweeping bathrooms, squeezing lemons for homemade lemonade. Their cheery mood suggested they expected this gathering to be the beginning of a new era. Madison was wearing a glittery silver bikini that sparkled in the sunlight, complementing the dark speckle of freckles on her arms; her knees were streaked with sunscreen; I realized suddenly that her feet were tapping a message into the wicker couch, over and over, a single word: "doomed."

I was worried the girls were planning some type of prank, or had decided that the party would be an amusing diversion, like tourists agreeing to visit a zoo of especially grotesque creatures. But when the girls arrived—and they arrived together, leaping from the bed of a truck—the looks on their faces made the truth quite plain. They had come because they had been guilted, or forced, into coming, by their parents. They were not tourists. They were knights, ordered out onto a battlefield; they stayed huddled close together, because they were not ready to die.

Madison's parents had resisted the urge to buy balloons, streamers, paper lanterns, silk leis, any frills whatsoever. But the house itself was frills. The girls—Scarlett, Leah, Adriana, Brianna, Reagan, Emmylou, Jasmine, Chloe, and the puny waif, Dolly—advanced cautiously through the great room, avoiding touching any of the furniture. In the kitchen, the girls accepted lemonades but refused straws—nonessential, wasteful—and greeted us politely but warily, then ventured out into the backyard. Even wearing only swimwear, the difference between us was stark. Our swimsuits were brand-new, never worn. As for them, some wore faded bikinis, bleached nearly colorless by years of sunlight and chlorine, while most simply bathed in bras and cutoff shorts. Likely none of them had ever swum in a private pool before. The girls stood uneasily in the shallow end, clutching the lemonades, whispering.

Standing on the tip of the diving board, Madison made an attempt at a peace offering.

"There are towels in the pool house," she called.

The girls huddled together to discuss the offer, and then nudged their tiny spokesperson to speak.

"We dry off with the sun," Dolly beamed.

Madison rolled her eyes, bounced once on the diving board, and did a cannonball.

Ultimately the party was uneventful, and a disaster. I spent the afternoon floating around nervously on an inflatable swan, trying to turn invisible, wishing the other girls weren't there so that we could actually enjoy ourselves. Madison alternated between performing hostile maneuvers on the diving board and flinging her vast arsenal of pool toys into the water—beach balls, dive rings, foam noodles, plastic donuts—as if attempting to overwhelm her enemies with belongings. By then the girls seemed to have forgotten about us altogether, gossiping and snickering by the ladder, occasionally batting away approaching pool toys. Madison's parents watched the scene from the windows in the parlor. Whatever her parents had hoped to witness—cultural differences overcome by the power of youth, social prejudice vanquished by the fabled magic of teenage spirit—remained a fantasy. The girls did not want our friendship, and were experienced at avoiding unwanted possessions.

When their ride honked in the driveway, the girls quick gathered their crumpled shirts, then withdrew en masse, leaving a smattering of damp footprints that shrank and disappeared in the sun.

"That was awful," I murmured, draped limply over the neck of the inflatable swan.

"Who'd want to be friends with those snobs anyway?" Madison laughed.

She was trying to seem upbeat. I could tell she was rattled. I left shortly after, slipping on my sandals to walk home. Madison was firing her longbow at a target behind the pool house, refusing to speak to her parents, scowling as arrows skewered the bullseye. Her parents were collecting empty lemonade glasses from the poolside, having a hushed discussion. "Goodbye, dear," her mother said to me, smiling tightly.

In the end what made the pool party fateful was its failure. Her parents had truly believed the pool party would improve her standing. Its failure didn't discourage them, however; instead, its failure only emboldened them. They had learned that ordinary gestures were inadequate—that what they wanted would require drastic measures.

The week after the pool party, over a dinner of spinach and seared tuna, her parents announced that their family would be changing their "consumption habits."

Madison nearly choked on what she was chewing. She was outraged, and that was when she thought "changing" meant they would be buying fewer things; when she was told that "changing" also meant they would be giving things away, she was dumbstruck.

Her parents aimed to scale down to a ratio of 100:1.

Over the next few days, as her parents began boxing their belongings, Madison fluctuated between different tactics: vowing, at any
cost, to resist the new policy; desperately begging her parents to spare
her room; questioning their fairness; questioning their resolve; questioning their sanity; tirelessly reminiscing about the origins of prized
spatulas and beloved socks; pleading for some deferral, postponement,
anything; boycotting family activities; denouncing humanity; threatening to run away; barricading her door; ranting; babbling; weeping;
and periodically disowning her parents. I was her only ally. She made
me come over to her house every day, "just to be here," like a witness
she might someday need to testify in court.

This must have been difficult for her parents, of course. They
had to give up heirloom china, handcrafted globes, antique mirrors,
astonishingly expensive colognes. But for her prosperity, her parents
seemed willing to sacrifice anything. Even her love. Thus, they drifted
grimly through the great room, tagging furniture with stickers, bright
colorful dots meaning "this one goes," as beyond the windows their
daughter pretended to be floating dead in the swimming pool.

Inadvertently, I was the one who brought about her surrender.

One twilight, lighting handfuls of sparklers with her on the roof
of the pool house, I mused, "Maybe Cody will fall for you, now that
you'll have less stuff."

Madison never reacted, just stared as her sparklers burned down
toward her fist.

But that next day found her wielding sheets of those stickers,
wildly tagging objects in her bedroom. That adventurer spirit—bottled
ships, model carriages—had finally been roused. She may have been
afraid to let go, but seemed simultaneously elated, thrilled at the pros-
pect of overcoming some unbearable task to win her one true love.
"What?" Madison said, shrugging at me. Then tagged my forehead
with a sticker, grinning.

I will never forget, the morning the movers were coming to haul
everything away, she kicked over a stickered jewelry box. Laughed,
triumphantly. Said, "Look at all of this junk!"

She offered me a silk ribbon with a gold locket shaped like an egg. I took it, and she frowned, as if disappointed. I took nothing else.

We sat on the porch together, sharing a can of ginger ale, watching movers in tan uniforms load stickered furniture into a semi. The pinball machine left the movers panting; the billiard table left the movers cursing; the jukebox the movers nearly dropped. And then there were boxes, seemingly endless boxes, brimming with pillows, her father's vintage rangefinder cameras, her mother's gleaming track trophies, her own unused bowling shoes and unworn pumps. There were a dozen boxes of towels alone.

After the movers had driven off, Madison galloped through the rooms with her longbow strapped to her back and an arrow clutched in each hand, whooping with pleasure at the freedom, the absence of obstacles, while in the parlor her father plunked chords on the grand piano, playing a ragtime song, and her mother watered a potted sunflower in the solarium, smiling with a look of satisfaction. I stood backed into a corner of the great room like a lamp the movers had forgotten to take away. I hadn't realized until that moment, but that house had come to feel as much mine as theirs. My home away from home. I felt shaken by the loss of so very many things. Still, I could see that there was something chillingly beautiful about the house now. An elegant starkness. A breathtaking austerity. In the context of so much empty space, the remaining belongings were striking, each item seeming somehow remarkable. The mantel of the fireplace had been swept bare except for a single object, a nondescript photograph of their family in a silver frame. I recall staring. I had never noticed that photograph before.

Their ratio wasn't as low as 100:1. By their estimate, they had only managed to come down to 391:1. But that was healthy, indisputably healthy. The excessive size of their house wasn't, but that only emphasized their new proportions, like visible ribs under shrunken flesh.

I had imagined the summer before high school going very differently. We spent the rest of that summer trying to establish new patterns. What had once been our favorite pastime, shopping, was now awkward for both of us. With the ruthless finality of bankers long accustomed to following through—foreclosing buildings, repossessing vehicles—her parents had scissored her credit cards to slivers of plastic. Madison did sometimes tag along with me to the shopping mall, but she could merely spectate, now. I would offer to buy things for her, but she would only shrug. "I'd have to give up something else to keep it, and there's really nothing left that isn't essential," Madison would say. We had bonded together over the fanatical pleasure we took in shopping; now, shopping bored her. At her house, too, our traditional entertainments had vanished. Her television was gone. Her karaoke machine was gone. Her disco ball was gone. The swimming pool remained, but the pool toys: gone. Without inflatables, I had nothing to float around the pool on. I was too feeble for sustained swimming—lacked the muscles for paddling and kicking, the lung capacity for deep exhales, deep inhales, held breaths—now could only sit slouched on the diving board, watching as she swam about underwater, trailed by a stream of bubbles. We didn't know what to do with each other. At my house, she looked uneasy, like a rehabilitated alcoholic visiting a home with a wine cellar, a pantry stocked with gins and rums.

"So you've cut back," my father boomed, standing among the fireflies in our driveway one night toward the end of summer that her parents had driven over to fetch her. Her parents looked embarrassed—that their family had cut back so effortlessly, that their family had cut back so drastically, that their family had cut back at all. Humble as always. "A healthy choice," my father nodded, his face plastered with a rigid fake smile that was probably as painful for him to wear as for me to see. Madison glanced at him from the backseat with a hopeful look. "Are y'all going to cut back too?" Madison asked. My father hesitated. "Us, well, we'll probably always be big spenders," my father admitted, then patted the roof of their car, and bellowed goodnight.

By the time that high school began that autumn, all of the other kids had heard about her new ratio. Madison wore the same pair of jeans every day that first week. She volunteered to hang posters for the clothing swap happening that month. Once she had scoffed at spiritual education activities like prayer and meditation, but now she tackled the exercises in class with a genuine vigor. To the other students she suddenly seemed attractive. I saw her talking with other girls waiting in line for chicken nuggets in the cafeteria, smiling nervously, and when she turned to wave at me, the other girls all nodded at me too. I dared to hope that this would be the beginning of a new life for us. That high school would be different. That her new cachet would finally win us the acceptance of the rest of the grade. Our community. I truly believed that. I was that naive.

One brisk autumn morning, I slipped out of geometry to fetch some homework. Rounding the corner, I discovered a gang of girls gathered in the hallway. Whispering conspiratorially, taping dollar bills to the door of my locker. Scarlett, Reagan, Emmylou, Jasmine. That puny waif, Dolly. Madison was standing there too, but instead of the burst of warmth the sight of her face usually gave me, I felt a sinking horror. As she pressed a thumb to a strip of tape, smoothing the edges, she glanced over toward me, then saw me, and she froze. For a moment we both were motionless. Then the other girls burst into laughter. I fled to a bathroom, locked myself in a stall, and cried.

Earlier, I withheld certain details about my nickname, "Her Highness." I will just tell you. The nickname did have a diminutive form, which was used rather frequently, and in especially disparaging tones of voice: "Her Heinie."

Well, after that Her Heinie was alone.

★ ★ ★

I became quite familiar with that bathroom stall over the course of that autumn. I was too insecure, too ashamed of having no friends, to eat alone in the cafeteria. Each table was big enough to fit a dozen students—which drastically emphasized your lack of company when eating alone—and worse, was circular, forcing you to face every single space that could have been a friend, should have, and wasn't. Without

Madison, I didn't dare. Instead, I ate in the bathroom across from the gymnasium, sitting on a toilet in a locked stall. I always hid in the stall furthest from the door to the hallway. Graffiti had been scrawled across the walls of the stall in vivid streaks of nail polish. Cryptic messages. Arcane drawings. Chewing the carrots my mother had packed, the rye sandwich, the oatmeal cookie, I would contemplate the bizarre graffiti, along with my own hideous nature. I fantasized about somehow getting sent into the past, into those eras that my father had spoken of, when somebody like me would have been considered desirable. I longed so desperately to live in a society like that, my fantasies often left me blinking back tears. Simply put: I had reached a previously unimaginable low. However pitiful that my social status had been before, I had always had Madison. Anything I had suffered, she had suffered; anything she had suffered, I had suffered; we had suffered together. I wasn't mad at her—I couldn't blame her for wanting to be accepted—I missed her though, and also was terrified that all of my secrets were now circulating the school. Hiding there in the stall, I sometimes heard a shuffle of boat shoes and penny loafers as girls entered the bathroom. I would sit very stilly to avoid detection, afraid even to chew or swallow, as the girls jabbered together at the sinks, agonizing over their ratios. "I should scale back somehow." "*You* should? Please, I just had a birthday! I made my parents *swear* not to get me anything, and what do they do? Get me a bunch of stuff anyway!" "How could they do that?" "It's like they don't even care!" Hand dryers would whoosh, and then those girls would shuffle out of the bathroom, only to be replaced moments later by another pair, these girls with husky whispers: "You're getting a *hot tub*?" "But look, you don't think people are going to think that we're rich now, do you?" "Of course that's what people will think." "I swear, it's not a splurge, it's essential, my doctor is practically forcing my parents to get it for me for my fibromyalgia. Plus it's not even that big. It's barely bigger than a bathtub." "That doesn't matter. That doesn't matter. Seriously, do you know *anybody* who cracks as many rich-girl jokes as Nick? Unless for some reason you *want* to break up, you'd better donate some shit, like, *tonight*." "I know, I know, you're totally right." In retrospect, overhearing those conversations must have had an effect on me. Because, along with eavesdropping, that was the other thing I spent that autumn doing: purging.

The purging always felt strangely exhilarating. Instinctively, I did not want my family to know about the habit, and there was what can only be described as a pleasurable terror, being engaged in a secret undertaking that felt simultaneously both so very right and so very wrong. Once a week my parents would go out on a date together, to the symphony usually, my father dressed in a seersucker suit, my mother wearing a gown and pearls. Ostensibly, I was expected to babysit my sister, but by then my sister was nearly a teenager herself and required no supervision. Typically she spent date nights watching movies about star-crossed vampires. I spent date nights purging. After verifying that my sister was occupied, I would sneak a garbage bag from the kitchen to my bedroom, frantically hurl belongings into the garbage bag—crystal balls, chintzy necklaces, fanny packs, snow globes, feathery boas, costume wigs—then creep back down the spiral staircase, through the kitchen, into the garage, and lift the lid of the waste receptacle, standing on tiptoes, dangling in headfirst, cramming the garbage bag beneath the other garbage bags already there, where nobody would notice. Some evenings, I would dare to repeat the whole procedure, throwing out belongings multiple times a single night. Afterward, I always felt lighter, becoming dizzy, almost giddy, at the thought of what had been accomplished. I bought absolutely nothing during these purging phases, determined to keep shedding belongings until my ratio was healthy. Afternoons that my family stopped at the shopping mall, I wouldn't even touch the merchandise. If my parents became insistent, urging me to try on new cardigans, new windpants, new crewnecks, new scarves, I would feign a stomachache, heartburn, anything to excuse myself from having to participate. I could go on like this for weeks.

Yet inevitably my resolve would falter; I could suppress my appetite for objects only so long. Eventually my cravings would overwhelm me; every purge ultimately led to a binge that resulted in me owning even more than before. Frenzied, ravenous, I begged my parents for things at random, wildly filling shopping carts, desperate to fill the empty spaces left by the latest purge. I bought a dreamcatcher, a kaleidoscope, an aquarium, a kazoo, a kitten calendar, a mermaid calendar, a gnome calendar, an astronaut pen, a set of poker chips, junk that there was never any chance of me actually using. After having denied my cravings for so long, these binges would leave me feeling intense relief. An amplified ecstasy. I bought clutches. I bought satchels. I bought capris, pinafores, leotards, turtlenecks, miniskirts, bomber jackets, crop tops, leather pants. Back home, I would stagger into my bedroom lugging heaps of shopping bags. Afterward, surveying the shredded packages and ripped wrappers and snipped price tags scattered across my bedspread, I would feel sick. I was hopeless. I was disgusting.

Psychologically, swinging back and forth between periods of strict denial and rampant excess was just hell. I couldn't stand to look at myself. During purges, I hated myself for the binges. During binges, I hated myself for the purges. Being rich seemed like a curse. I fantasized about being born poor, jealous of the kids at school who had low ratios simply by virtue of not having enough money to buy surplus belongings, rather than any form of goodwill. Being born rich required actual self-control. I had the resources to buy nearly any object that caught my attention. I didn't have enough self-restraint to resist the constant temptation, and even if it might have helped me at school, it would have alienated me at home. My family wasn't close, but my parents and my sister were the only people in the world who cared about me, and shopping was our family pastime. Nothing made my father so excited. Nothing made my mother as euphoric. Buying junk with my sister was how we bonded, the only mutual interest that we had, the only time that we genuinely connected. It was at the heart of every relationship in our family. I drifted through the mansion with an afflicted expression, a mess of conflicting urges: intense cravings to shop, a desire to be healthy, a longing to be seen as beautiful instead of revolting, a desperate yearning to be accepted at school, still wanting to fit in at home. I honestly think my family never knew about the purging and the binging. My parents rarely visited my bedroom in the turret, my sister even less, and even then would only peek through the door, asking some question. The wild fluctuations in my ratio wouldn't have been obvious anyway, with that many belongings in my bedroom to keep track of. My parents never showed any signs of concern, probably assuming that my tormented demeanor was just typical teenage behavior. I had always been moodier than my sister. I was probably just hormonal. My father tried to cheer me up, relieving tension with jokes and chatter. My mother expressed affection with hugs and caresses, drawing me in to cuddle. My sister cheered ecstatically at reality shows on the television and told me to smile more, saying nobody liked a sourpuss. Nobody in my family ever actually talked about emotions, or admitted having problems, or revealed any vulnerability. (Even watching television together was an exercise in denial. My parents never changed the channel when something uncomfortable came on—that would have acknowledged that there was something making us uncomfortable. Instead we always suffered through the moment in silence. A music video for a popular hip-hop song that was notorious for a line that dissed a rival rapper as rich. A sitcom about a rich doctor whose ludicrous excesses were a recurring gag on every episode. A cartoon about a group of kids who were constantly lampooning the rich industrialist in town. A commercial for a glossy lifestyle magazine with beaming celebrities on the covers, surrounded by colorful captions promising tips on how to cut back, scale down. My entire body would go stiff until the moment had passed.)

I still remember, after a particularly brutal cycle of purging and binging that winter, spending an evening with my mother on the love seat in the great room. My father had taken my sister to a concert, some teenybop band, leaving my mother and me home alone. We were sprawled across both cushions of the love seat, snuggled together to fit. I had spent the afternoon locked in my bedroom, secretly weeping into a pillow, and now took a profound comfort in being held. My mother had a spool of that punched tape from the department store, running her fingers over the holes. Gazing out between her arms, I stared through the spotty panes of a window, looking at what she couldn't. The twilight was a pale violet color; in that light the blades of grass, already coated with frost, were shades of blue. "Were you rich when you were a kid too?" I asked suddenly.

The wording was insensitive: "affluent" would have been less offensive, or maybe "wealthy." The question had spilled out of me without any warning though, "rich" and all. I expected my mother to correct me; instead she only smiled. The slight furrow to her eyebrows, the faint pucker to her lips, suggested sympathy, even regret. "Yes," my mother murmured, still running her fingers over the spool. "But in those days rich wasn't as rich as rich is now."

Just then she gasped, having found a message in the spool. She guided my fingers over the holes, helping me to feel the letters she had discovered: "beware," the spool read. "How creepy," my mother cooed, pleased. She later gave me the spool to keep.

★ ★ ★

Winter went, spring came, and flurries of pollen covered the fire hydrants and the parked cars with a fluorescent grit. Every April the high school hosted a donation competition on the football field; tradition dictated that a boy and a girl would be chosen to give a speech during the festivities. A speech about charity and goodwill and spiritual health. The boy and the girl were always chosen from the freshman class. This wasn't something that our school had invented— the tradition was observed by every school in Nashville, and seems to have been widespread throughout the South. (Its range may have extended even further, but it was probably a regional phenomenon; I have never seen the tradition referenced in books or movies, and online references are scarce.) The boy and the girl were chosen on the basis of votes. All students voted. The positions were coveted; popularity determined who won. Cody Walden of course would win for the boys. For the girls, despite everything that had happened between us, I found myself secretly rooting for Madison. Winning might have led to a breakthrough for her with Cody. The boy and the girl wrote and delivered the speech together, met outside of school to prepare—if she won, she finally would have been given a chance to be alone with him. Even with her new ratio, however, there were still far more popular girls in the freshman class; realistically, she had little chance of winning, short of somebody rigging the election.

As it happened, though, somebody did rig the election.

To this day, I can scarcely imagine the pleasure my classmates must have taken in organizing the scheme. The announcement interrupted a lecture in econ. As the winning students were announced, I was rooting so intently for the name Madison Gates—silently mouthing the syllables to myself, for luck—I was initially bewildered when my classmates swiveled in unison to look at me. Some looked confused; most were smirking, or stifling laughter. I realized, then, that my name had been announced over the intercom. I had won. I had won. I had been elected to give the speech.

"Well. My. What an honor!" the econ teacher offered, looking somewhat confused himself.

In a panic, I grabbed my textbooks, snatched my backpack, walked out of econ without even asking for permission to leave, and moments later was seated on a chair in the office of the principal, begging to resign.

"Resigning isn't an option," the principal said. The principal was a graying sinewy woman who spiked her bun with pencils and favored pinstripe dresses. She had a pensive, solemn demeanor, denounced all irritants as fascists—for example, muttering "fascist!" at a pen in retaliation for the pen running out of ink—and was unwed, a fact that students often attributed to her ratio, which was notoriously unhealthy.

"But they only voted for me as a joke," I said, clutching my textbooks to my sweater.

"Yes, that's really the only explanation," the principal agreed, perhaps more bluntly than necessary, folding her hands under her chin. "And that's why you'll have to go through with the ceremony. They wanted to humiliate you. If you resign then they've won. You're going to have to do the brave thing here."

"I'm not that sort of person," I said, slumping backward, feeling ready to burst into tears.

"Well, darling, now might be the time to change that," the principal said.

I stared past my brogues at the speckled motif scattered across the floor.

"We'll need to look over a copy of the speech beforehand," the principal said, standing, and then shooed me out the door.

I shuffled down the hallway, feeling miserable, getting stares and snickers from every classroom.

Cody found me at my locker after school.

"You're the one who won?" Cody said with a confused squint.

I was too intimidated to do anything but nod.

"Huh," Cody said.

We walked to his house to write the speech. He had offered to come to my house instead. I had rejected that idea, for obvious reasons. Leaving school, I trailed him down the hallway with my head bowed toward the floor. Cody chatted briefly with passing friends. His speech was interspersed with slang acquired in spiritual education: he concurred with amens; he dissented with mus; he greeted and parted with salaams and namastes. He cursed with pleasure, relishing fuck especially. Occasionally he paused at the lockers of certain intimates, discussing, in undertones, the particulars of stunts and pranks: a ruse that would require gaining access to the janitor's closet; mischief planned for the principal's convertible. I mostly stared at the linoleum. Despite having no feelings for him, I still felt a degree of terror, standing in the presence of somebody whom so many people desired—the desire was so thick in the air that the accompanying emotions could be experienced secondhand. As we passed through the swinging doors into the breezy spring weather, kids congratulated him from the windows of buses while hailing me sarcastically.

"Your Highness, we salute you, we sing your praises!"

"Hey Heinie, you gonna buy a new dress for the speech?"

"New earrings, new heels, why stop there?"

"For an occasion like this, you've gotta treat yourself!"

After we had left the school grounds our walk was silent.

Cody lived only a couple blocks from school, in a modest bungalow with white columns and faded siding, shaded by gigantic chestnut trees. Hummingbirds were flitting around the yard. Walking up the driveway, I thought the house looked like a fairy-tale cottage, the type that would belong to a reclusive magician, maybe kind, maybe wicked. The inside of the bungalow was just as enchanting. Madison had once dragged me to the public library to examine a copy of his family's latest tax filing—his parents were bigwigs in the country music industry, with a combined income nearly identical to that of my parents. In contrast to my parents, however, his parents elected to donate the vast majority, primarily to infrastructure initiatives and healthcare programs. Their ratio was rumored to be exactly 100:1. The bungalow was furnished in the wabi-sabi style that most families back then idealized: simplicity, roughness, weathering, tarnish. The wooden seats were rubbed pale and glossy from years of use; the leather cushions on the couches were darkened and cracking; the teal paint on the cabinets was chipped and peeling. The floors and the surfaces looked swept and dusted; the feel of the house was bright and cozy. In the kitchen, the scent of baking lasagna wafted from the oven beneath a rack of gleaming copper pots. Passing through the dining room, I noticed that each member of the family had a designated set of tableware: a plate, a bowl, a cup, a mug, a fork, a spoon, a butter knife, a steak knife, and a cloth napkin apiece, stored on individual shelves above the ancient credenza. The dishes were porcelain, decorated with bucolic scenes; the cutlery was silver. When guests came, presumably additional tableware was rented—or the children ate after the adults had eaten—as there appeared to be no extra.

His bedroom was tucked between the bathroom and the laundry. Cody dumped his backpack on the floor and then sat down in his chair, automatically assuming a padmasana pose. I stood back in the doorway, gazing at his bedroom in wonder. Madison would have swooned. Eleven articles of clothing hung in his closet—nine shirts, a random assortment of sweatshirts and tees, all faded shades of indigo and green, plus a spare pair of jeans and a scarlet windbreaker with a drawstring hood—from eleven hangers. Scattered across the carpet lay rumpled socks and upended boots. For furnishings he had a full-size bed draped with a richly colored quilt, the chair, a desk, and a rustic dresser. Like his clothing, his furnishings were all of exceptional quality, and fantastically worn. His desk was bare except for a loaner cassette tape scrawled with the underlined surname of a friend, a gunslinger movie in a plastic rental case, and samurai manga labeled with library call numbers—not, technically, his belongings. His only visible belonging that wasn't categorically practical was a skateboard, propped against his dresser, that was bedecked with an image of a roaring dragon either attacking or defending a castle tower.

"I guess we should get to work," Cody said.

I didn't know where to sit, which caused me to begin to sweat. I didn't dare sit on his bed; he would have been so revolted he probably would have had to wash his bedding afterward, quilt and all, if somebody like me had sat there. I considered just standing, maybe leaning against the wall, but that seemed too awkward. Ultimately, I decided to sit on the carpet, which proved to be fairly awkward too.

Cody stared at me a moment, frowned, and then stood back up again.

"I can't think all cooped up in here," Cody said, grabbing his skateboard.

Across the road from his house lay a wooded park with a deserted playground. While we brainstormed, I sat on the edge of the merry-go-round, slouched over my knees and gripping my ankles; Cody skated around the playground, leaping overturned garbage cans, skirting picnic tables, dodging barbecue grills, making the skateboard buck and flip beneath his sneakers. With a figure as burly as his, he didn't appear to be built for something like skateboarding, but he was agile, and he was limber, and he possessed miraculous balance. I couldn't have articulated this back then, but the difference between him on a skateboard and other kids on skateboards was the difference between art and sport. For him skating didn't seem to be about competition. I was given the sense that he was expressing himself through every grind and twirl, using that skateboard the way a dancer would use a stage.

Madison would have been spellbound, getting to watch him move that way. I felt only self-pity. Kids with low ratios always seemed to be like he was: breathtakingly talented at some art. After examining his bedroom, I finally understood why. He had been forced to choose. That was his only toy, a skateboard, and so that was what he did: skateboard, skateboard, skateboard. As for me, I had no talents, no skills, no abilities at all. I owned a skateboard too—and ballet shoes, and tap shoes, and roller skates, and ice skates, and soccer cleats, and softball cleats, and a bicycle, and a scooter, and a flute, and a harp, and a fiddle, a magic kit, a sewing kit, a chess set, a calligraphy set, and acrylic paintbrushes, and watercolor paintbrushes, and instant cameras, and pottery wheels, and gardening tools, and finger puppets, and a marionette. I had sampled every one of them, and thereby had mastered none of them. I had tried riding my skateboard exactly once. I had become frustrated, and had had the option of giving up.

Watching him give such elegant whirling forms to whatever emotions had accumulated during his day, I longed for the ability to do the same. I briefly imagined kissing him, which was idiotic. I didn't even like him, and he definitely didn't like me.

"I really don't even know what to say," I shouted.

"If you want, I can get copies of speeches kids have given before, and we can just throw together a speech from that. If you haven't noticed, the speech is pretty much exactly the same every year: 'Charity is an essential part of spiritual health, by working together we'll end poverty and homelessness. Yadda yadda yadda, blah blah blah,'" Cody called, swooping past me crouched low on the skateboard.

"You say it like you don't mean it," I shouted.

"It's not that it isn't true. It's just so obvious that giving a speech about it seems kind of pointless," Cody called.

He hit a twig, swore, wobbled, and crashed, tumbling across the sidewalk as the skateboard clattered across the pavement.

"Are you okay?" I said.

Grinning, he rose gingerly off the pavement, bleeding from scrapes on his chin and his elbows. He brushed pebbles from his shirt, looking embarrassed, somewhat proud. Then his smile fell.

"You know you only got elected as a joke, right?" Cody said.

"I'm not an idiot," I said.

"You're going to go through with the speech anyway?" Cody said, frowning.

I pressed my face into my legs, peering through at the chipped paint on the merry-go-round.

"Resigning isn't an option," I said.

★ ★ ★

The next day those scabs on his chin and his elbows got him a lot of attention at school. Passing through the cafeteria, I overheard him narrating his fall to a table of laughing girls. When he glanced in my direction, I hurried on to the bathroom, clutching my bagged lunch, and ate in my usual stall.

As if having the speech to look forward to somehow wasn't enough to satisfy the masses, the bullying at school only got worse in the weeks leading up to the donation ceremony. Kids stapled advertisements to my backpack. Kids threw crumpled receipts at my head. Returning to my locker to fetch my jacket at the end of each day, I'd find my locker plastered with dollar bills, some crusted with dried flecks of snot, some wet with phlegmy globs of spit. In the bathroom, kids chiseled cakes and guillotines onto the walls of my usual stall. I tried just to ignore it. I was cracking under the strain. Back at home, I binged, I purged, I binged, I purged, I binged, I purged, and otherwise wandered through the house in a constant state of depression, picking fights with my parents over insignificant incidents, snapping viciously at my sister over trivial comments. My family tried to be patient with my explosions. My relationship with my family continued to deteriorate anyway. As usual, nobody talked about the issue. My parents understood that having to give the speech was meant to embarrass me, and pretended not to understand, acting as if the donation competition was any other school event, awkwardly changing the subject whenever the topic happened to be raised. My family wouldn't be at the ceremony. My family never went to the ceremony. I had never been either. I lay awake at night, gripped with dread and fear, imagining the scene at the football field. The stage and the crowd. The humiliation of having to stand there as a rich kid and make a speech about charity and goodwill.

Cody cobbled a speech together as promised, scribbling out the text on ruled paper. The principal had some trouble deciphering his messy scrawl—denounced her reading glasses as fascist—but ultimately approved the speech, essentially the same speech she had approved every year before.

As we were supposed to deliver the speech together—periodically alternating paragraphs, even occasionally finishing a sentence that the other had begun, for dramatic emphasis—we met again the day before the ceremony to practice. Meeting at his house that night wasn't an option, he said; his parents were entertaining potential clients, some folk musicians from Charleston.

I tried protesting that meeting at my house wasn't an option either. "Why not?" Cody said.

"It's just not like yours," I said, lamely. He knew exactly how we lived. Our assets were a matter of public record the same as anybody's. He had probably even seen the photocopy of our tax filing that kids sometimes passed around for entertainment.

A friend delivered him by bicycle that afternoon. I was perched on the window seat in my turret and watched as he arrived, hopping off the handlebars and waving goodbye to the friend with a laugh. Sunlight, both reflected and refracted by my belongings—perfume bottles, earrings, crystal balls, pendants, snow globes, wristwatches, hand mirrors, gemstones, the waterfall chandelier—projected glimmers of light across my bedroom, flickering. I remember picking nervously at a hangnail. Cody climbed the stairs to the turret with a glass of soda, still fizzing, that one of my parents must have poured for him. He whistled as he stepped through the door.

"You really do have a lot of shit," Cody murmured.

Gently, he flicked a pinwheel, sending the rainbow vanes spinning. When the pinwheel stopped, he turned, looking around the bedroom.

"Do you actually use all of this junk?" Cody said.

"No," I said.

"Doesn't having all this stuff ever feel like a burden?" Cody said.

"I don't know," I said.

"Huh," Cody said, nodding and squinting, as if trying to imagine having to live among so many belongings.

I couldn't tell if he was mocking me, but while we rehearsed, he wore my pinwheel, tucking the rod into the pocket on his shirt like a boutonniere.

★ ★ ★

A dusting of snow is falling across the city tonight. Blues is playing over the radio on the kitchen counter. I'm chopping celery. I'm making gumbo. I didn't mean to think about him again. I barely even knew him. I never loved him, didn't even like him, not romantically. And yet there was something about him. Something spellbinding about being around him. Because of what he did, I'm linked to him forever. I twist the knob for the burner. Flames erupt beneath the pot on the stove. I stare at the flames for a moment before reducing the heat. He got into trouble after graduating, eventually moved out of the country. I never had the chance to ask him about that day. About his motives.

I remember being gripped by a feeling of desperation, walking down to the football field on the afternoon of the donation competition. I wore the humblest outfit possible, no jewelry, just a plain sack dress—with deep hip pockets, notably—my hair in a simple updo, and my oldest pair of flats. The sun was shining, but rain had fallen earlier that morning, making the air feel wet and humid and the grass all damp and muddy. Rented trucks were parked on the track, staggered like runners waiting for the crack of a pistol, with the rear doors raised and the loading ramps extended. Rented tables were arranged in rows on the football field, parallel to the yard lines, gradually getting buried beneath donations. Wearing latex gloves, teachers sorted through the piles, organizing the donations into boxes. Madison somehow must have come into contact with the latex gloves. Concerned friends had gathered around her in the end zone to examine an outbreak of rashes on her arms. Dolly was rushing back from the concession stand with a waffle cone of frozen custard to comfort her. I felt a glimmer of loneliness, seeing her surrounded by all of her friends. By then most kids had been there for hours, and parents were already trickling into the stadium, claiming seats over in the stands. Behind the podium on the stage, the principal was tinkering with the microphone. The scoreboard was dark. The competition was a competition in name only. There was no home team; there was no away team; the donations were not points, were never tallied.

I can't explain what happened with the unicorn. I obviously should have known better. I should have shown more restraint. I was wandering the field with my hands stuffed into the pockets on my dress, trying to avoid thinking about the speech, trying to avoid glancing toward the stage, and failing, and the size of the growing crowd in the stands terrified me, was even bigger than imagined, was even louder than imagined, and noticing the sun was sinking toward the scoreboard, I realized that the ceremony would be starting soon, any time. Even after all of those years of bullying, I'd never had a feeling like that before. A sense of being truly in danger. I wasn't even on the stage yet and was already trembling, experiencing simultaneous bursts of anxiety and dread and fear so intense that my legs felt weak and my stomach felt queasy—and in a state of panic, on instinct, without thinking, I calmed myself the only way that never failed me.

Shuffling through an aisle of tables, past heaped mounds of donations, I noticed a sparkle—light twinkling on the glittery horn of a plastic unicorn.

I paused and gazed at the figurine. There was nothing special about the unicorn in particular. I had similar figurines back at home.

Nevertheless, in the grip of that silent hysteria, I suddenly found myself slipping the unicorn into a pocket.

The panic subsided immediately. I felt a sense of relief. I was in possession of a new belonging. I was not alone. I was not alone.

That brief solace was interrupted by the cry of a girl with a pixie cut holding a box of hats.

"Her Highness just took a donation!"

I backed away from the table with my heart pounding as her cry was joined by a chorus of others.

"Even Heinie wouldn't dare!"

"I swear, she did, right off of that table!"

"Hear ye, hear ye, you won't believe this fucking shit!"

"The majesty has imposed a tax!"

"The majesty is stealing from the needy!"

A mob of kids swarmed me, led by the girl with the pixie cut. Already irritable from having to lug around heavy boxes, the kids looked furious. The girl with the pixie cut set down the box of hats and then stepped forward, rifling through the pockets on my dress. Triumphantly, she pulled out the unicorn.

"Thought you were entitled to this, eh?" she sneered, brandishing the unicorn.

The others looked scandalized. Mortified, I spun around to flee and bumped straight into Cody. He was wearing his scarlet windbreaker, his usual jeans, his usual sneakers, and an expression of contempt. He had witnessed everything. At that moment—seeing his look of disgust—I discovered a hope, some pitifully desperate hope, had been nesting inside of me: that maybe he was beginning to think of me as a friend. I became aware of the feeling at the exact instant the hope died.

The speakers above the stands suddenly screeched with feedback as the principal called us onto the stage.

"Can't wait to hear what you have to say," the girl with the pixie cut smirked, tossing the unicorn back onto the table.

Minutes later the principal was leading us up the steps onto the stage. The stage was vast and intimidating and utterly empty except for the podium. The walk to the podium was terrifying. I glanced sideways at the crowd and immediately regretted looking, because now that the stands were full, the crowd was immense and frightening, a mass of shirts and blouses and jackets and ballcaps and snapping cameras, hands shading eyes from sunlight, hands fanning cheeks with programs, seemingly endless rows of familiar faces. Cody strolled ahead of me in his scarlet windbreaker with his notecards clutched in a fist. I trailed behind him with my head bowed low and my notecards tucked in a pocket. I had practiced so many times for that speech. I had never practiced that hard for anything. I had the speech memorized by heart, my lines and his lines, and was glad to have the speech on notecards anyway, just in case my mind blanked from the terror. My heart was racing. As we reached the podium, turning to face the crowd, I remembered to smile. My smile must have looked fake and petrified. The orchestra standing on the track between the stage and the stands finished playing a processional march, capping off the song with a dramatic burst of trumpets, and then even the orchestra turned to stare at us.

I remember thinking that if we could just get through the speech, everything would be over, everything would be fine.

After some brief remarks about the wonderful turnout and the favorable turn the weather had taken, the principal introduced us to a round of halfhearted applause, then strolled back down the steps, leaving us alone on the stage.

Taking out my notecards, my hands were quivering. I had seen most of the people in the audience before somewhere, but never all at once. Being stared at by so many silent expressionless people was like a scene out of a nightmare.

Cody was supposed to speak the first line. Standing next to me at the podium, he leaned toward the microphone, then opened his mouth, then shut his mouth, gave the audience a strange smile, and looked down at his notecards, cocking his head as if reconsidering something. He stared at the notecards. He frowned at the notecards. Glancing from him to the crowd, nervously waiting for him to speak, I was struck by a sense of foreboding.

Somebody in the audience coughed.

Cody glanced up at the crowd.

"We wrote a speech, but, uh, honestly it's pretty boring," Cody said.

Somebody laughed at the back of the stands and then fell quiet.

"It's probably better just to speak from the heart anyway," Cody said.

The audience stared at us.

"I like rich people," Cody said.

I glanced sideways at him without swiveling my head or moving my body in the slightest, desperately trying to keep smiling, and then glanced back at the audience, which was utterly silent.

"I think there's something beautiful about owning lots of junk," Cody said.

Somebody laughed again at the back of the stands, a hearty chuckle, while the rest of the audience held blank expressions.

"I think it's awesome," Cody said.

At the back of the stands, somebody laughed and then whooped enthusiastically, while faint grins began to appear in the crowd.

"I don't think there's anything wrong with having extra stuff," Cody said.

I stood frozen on the stage with my ears ringing and my skin crawling and the notecards shaking in my hands. Across the stands, kids were now grinning with delight. Always so trusting, always so naive, I suddenly realized something that had never occurred to me before. I had originally assumed that the election had been rigged by the usual bullies—maybe Dolly, even Madison. But none of those kids had experience organizing a scheme on that scale.

There was somebody, though, who did: Cody.

"I mean, there's nothing inherently unethical about owning multiple homes," Cody said, to scattered laughter.

I'll probably never know what he intended. Only years later did the possibility occur to me that he genuinely might have been trying to defend me by what he said that day on the stage. In retrospect, he did seem like the type of person who might have empathized with an outcast, who wasn't afraid of breaking rules or rebelling against social norms. I like to imagine that after spending time with me, he might have come to pity me, might have come to care about me, and that witnessing the incident with the unicorn had somehow upset him, provoking him to try to protect me. That he was only trying to help me by what he said. At the time, though, standing there on that stage, I assumed that he had been the one to rig the election, and that he had never planned on giving the speech on the notecards in the first place. That he had planned to use the ceremony as an opportunity to attack me all along. I was trapped on that stage, and now he could mock me with an audience of hundreds of people. All for the sake of getting some attention. The sake of pulling off a legendary stunt. He seemed like that type of person too.

Regardless, whether he intended what he was saying to be sincere, whether he intended what he was saying to be sarcastic, the audience clearly interpreted what he was saying as a joke. As yet another prank by a notorious prankster. Out of politeness, some of the parents in the audience were trying not to smile, even looked disapproving, but as he continued to speak, insisting he thought greed was attractive, scattered laughter passed through the stands, then ripples of laughter, then waves of laughter, until finally every line that he delivered was punctuated by a roar of helpless laughter from the crowd. Cody spoke nonstop for over a minute. I never got to speak a word. I just stood there, mortified, trembling, no longer even able to fake a smile, horrified by the sight of all of those laughing faces, my entire community. Having to make a speech about charity and goodwill would have been humiliating, but having to stand there while he made a speech about wealth and excess made me feel stripped bare. The crowd saw straight through me, all of the greed and the narcissism and the ugliness. My morbidly bloated assets. I was what made the speech so helplessly funny, standing awkwardly next to him as he professed approval of hoarded wealth. I might as well have been a mannequin. I was there as an exhibit. I was there as a prop. When the principal rushed onto stage with a furious look to take the microphone, the crowd erupted into applause, whistling and cheering, a standing ovation. Kids were weeping with laughter. Cody didn't smile, didn't wave, didn't bow, didn't in any way indicate that the speech had been a joke, just glared at the audience as the microphone was taken.

I was already moving, dropping the notecards onto the stage, rushing down the steps to the grass, hurrying back across the empty football field, past all of the tables of heaped donations, trying to see through the watery blur of tears in my eyes, feeling nauseous, feeling hideous, leaving the crowd behind. I broke into a run at the edge of the parking lot, ran back through the streets and across the intersections with my dress whipping with gusts of wind, ran until my lungs were burning and my legs were aching and my mouth tasted like blood. My neighborhood seemed horribly peaceful compared to the feeling inside of me. I had lost my flats on the way home. I came walking into my house with dirty feet. Panting, sweating. My hair was wild from the run, with strands hanging down around my eyes. I could still hear the laughter. I was still holding back tears. I slipped past the doorway to the great room, where my parents were watching television with my sister, calling hello to me without turning to look. Walking calmly into the kitchen, I rooted through a drawer, found a matchbook, grabbed the matchbook, strode down the darkened hallway to my turret, climbed the spiral staircase, marched into my bedroom, and tore the clothes in my closet down from the hangers, tossing the clothes onto the rug at the center of my floor, a heaping mound of lush fabrics, seersucker and linen and gingham and silk and paisley and denim and lace and cashmere, a tangled mess of sleeves and legs and collars, and then grabbed bottles of essential oil, lavender, eucalyptus, orange, rose, then dumped the oil onto the clothes, and struck a match. I dropped the flame onto the pile. In the dim twilight streaming in through the windows, the fire was strangely beautiful, burning radiantly through the clothing, consuming the belongings at a breathtaking speed, converting the objects to heat and light, growing in intensity as cars with lit headlights occasionally drove past the house out on the street. I remember coughing as the smoke began to cloud the air. How the space suddenly brightened as the canopy on my bed burst into flames. By the time my parents came running into my bedroom, smelling the smoke, the flames had spread to my cedar chest, my stool, my vanity, the rafters on my ceiling.

"What happened?" my father cried, glancing around the room with a look of terror.

"I don't want to be rich anymore," I said, as if somehow that would help my parents understand.

★ ★ ★

I can imagine now how we must have looked to other families. On a cool spring weekend that year before, torrential rains had fallen across the state, whole feet of water in a day, and the river had surged over the banks, flooding neighborhoods across the city, stadiums, theaters, the honky-tonks on Broadway. Streets had been flooded. Alleys had been flooded. Houses had been flooded. Basements. Bathrooms. Kitchens. Bedrooms. Lawn toys and porch furniture had floated away with the murky water. Thousands had been left homeless. Before the floodwaters had even receded, other families had organized charities to feed and shelter the victims, to fund the replacement of essential belongings, to help to rebuild the destroyed homes. My parents hadn't donated to the relief efforts. My parents did donate to charities, but only for tax deductions, to maximize income after taxes, and not ever a penny more. Other families donated every last penny possible. There was nowhere in the country as spiritually healthy as the South, nowhere in the nation with such low rates of affluence as Tennessee. Volunteers delivered loads of canned goods to food pantries. Volunteers presented boxes of assorted clothing to new immigrants. Volunteers chipped in to finance the construction of trailer parks for the homeless. Architecturally breathtaking pedestrian bridges spanned the river, crowdsourced by volunteers. Bright daisies and hydrangeas bloomed in enormous flower beds in public parks, tended by volunteers with sun hats. Vibrant berries and squashes ripened in community gardens on every block, watered by volunteers with suede work gloves. Artists funded by volunteers stood on ladders alongside buildings and in plazas, installing colorful murals and gleaming metal sculptures. Engineers funded by volunteers walked about in hard hats, surveying the construction of glorious statues and magnificent fountains. Optometrists and dentists and physicians funded by volunteers held daily clinics, distributing eyeglasses and toothbrushes and medications throughout Nashville. Living among people devoted to the spirit of social cooperation, we must have seemed monstrously antisocial. We spent staggering sums of money on superfluous belongings, sums of money we could have given to charity, and as much as we spent on superfluous belongings, we had even more money sitting in the bank, accumulating interest like dust, pennies to the dollar. By voluntarily financing infrastructure projects, and housing initiatives, and healthcare programs, by financing the construction of art installations and grand monuments, other families were creating countless jobs, ensuring the health of the economy. We ensured only the health of our personal fortune.

I remember once sitting on a carousel at an amusement park as a child, surrounded by the neon lights of the fairground, gripping the mane of the pony for balance, overhearing a group of kids arguing behind me.

"Why don't we just force people like them to share?"

"That'd be, like, communism."

"So?"

"So communism's, like, crazy."

"You can't force people to be charitable."

"That's like the fundamental principle of volunteerism."

"Charity has to be voluntary."

I didn't have to be there in the car, days after the fire, when other teenagers drove past my house, gawking at the blackened ruins of the burned turret, the massive tarps covering the holes in the roof, flapping in the wind and the rain. I didn't have to eavesdrop on the gossip. I knew what the kids must have said. Burning the belongings was the same as throwing the belongings into a trash can, the same as buying the belongings in the first place. What a waste.

★ ★ ★

I had always been a spectacle at school, and must have been a legend after that. I'm sure that people from home still talk about me, telling the story of the fire. I'm sure that when people back home tell the story, the fire is portrayed as tragic. Sad. And yet for me, setting fire to the turret was a turning point, and was what finally freed me from the cycle of binging and purging. The turret had been gutted. My parents took my credit cards afterward, leaving me no way to binge, and my belongings had all been destroyed, leaving me no reason to purge. I felt fantastically light, like a tremendous burden had been lifted from me, and simultaneously fantastically empty. My sister eyed me at meals with a look of fear, as if expecting me to set fire to the house again at any moment. I was too ashamed to look my parents in the eye. My father barely spoke a word to me. My mother no longer reached to embrace me. I spent a week sleeping in the spare bedroom next to the laundry room, and then my parents came to me with a brochure for a boarding school. My parents claimed to be sending me away for my sake, to spare me the embarrassment of having to attend a school in the city, where everybody would know me as the freak who set her house on fire. I knew even then, though, the true reason that my parents were sending me away. I had crossed a line. I had put my family in danger. My family was afraid of me. My sister especially. My parents bought me a new set of clothing. I had no other possessions to pack. I remember standing in the rain on the patio of the boarding school, watching my family drive back toward the road during a thunderstorm. I knew even then my parents wouldn't pressure me to come home for holidays. I've seen my parents less than a dozen times since. My sister even less.

The boarding school was in the countryside, surrounded by hills and meadows, miles from the nearest store. I had to share a room with a chubby blond girl who snored. I was given no closet, just a dresser for clothes, with only enough space for a spare uniform, underwear, socks, pajamas, athletic apparel, a raincoat, and a casual outfit for weekends. A desk by the window, with a shelf for textbooks. A bed with a pillow, with a blanket for winter. I became accustomed to inhabiting nearly empty spaces. I was forced to learn to do without. On weekends we volunteered on local farms, building fences, repairing sheds, bagging dirt-crusted carrots and beets and potatoes to be donated to needy families. At night we watched movies together in the common room, or held dance parties in the dining hall, or traded comic books and fantasy novels from the library. I took walks alone through the countryside, tramping through the weeds and the mud. I cried myself to sleep almost every night that first year, silently. My roommate was gruff but kind to me. Eventually the sound of her snoring became familiar, even soothing. So much so that when sleeping with my husband for the first time in college, I was strangely comforted to find he snored too.

★ ★ ★

I live a different life now. A simple life, working at a farmers market, selling jars of raw honey. Middle age seems to suit me. My family owns perhaps more than we need, but our ratio is healthy, our house spare and tidy, a teal bungalow with a tire swing in the yard. I've learned to prefer this lifestyle. My children have never known any other. I buy pastries and greens to give to food pantries. I buy sweaters and peacoats to give to new immigrants. I help organize fundraisers to support renovations at the public library. I have friends who love me, who throw a birthday party for me once a winter. I try to find a healthy balance between volunteering and leisure. My husband is a lawyer for the city, a hulking cheerful man with thick dark hair who loves to rockclimb and waterski and volunteer at the animal shelter, bathing stray cats and dogs.

The house smells like dough and chocolate from the cookies my youngest daughter baked after supper. All of my children are asleep now. My husband is soaking in the bathtub. He's staring at me as he does, watching me gargle mouthwash at the sink.

I spit into the drain and say, "What?"

"You're beautiful," he says.

I know that when he says that, he means the inside of me as much as the outside. I am compassionate. I am generous. I am not wasteful. Like him, I find satisfaction in helping others. I am often happy.

★ ★ ★

But still, sometimes there are days when a dark terrible mood comes over me, a crushing sense of emptiness, a sense of utter misery, when the sound of my children choreographing a new play in the attic can't help me, when the sound of my husband singing while canning jam in the kitchen can't help me, when the sound of the bluebirds twittering on the birdfeeder in the backyard doesn't help me, when nothing seems to help, days that find me driving to the local shopping mall, days that find me driving back from the shopping mall, days that find me hiking out of desperation into the woods behind the house with a shopping bag full of boxes, in secret, alone.

I sit under the sycamore trees at the edge of the ravine deep in the woods, in the overlapping patches of shade and light, which ripple across the grass with the occasional gust of wind, dimming and then brightening whenever a cloud passes over the sun. I arrange the boxes next to me, and then peel off each of the wrappers, slowly, delicately, savoring the experience. The supple feel of the plastic. The synthetic scent of the plastic. The glossy shimmer. The plastic peels away with a beautiful frailty, as if begging to be removed. I set each crumple of plastic in the grass, and then gently slip a finger into the tab of each lid. I open each of the boxes. I reach into the packaging, taking out each of the products, carefully arranging the objects in the grass around me. A porcelain teapot. A tortoiseshell hairbrush. A pewter cocktail shaker. A brass pocket watch. A rose-colored bottle of perfume. Now the things are mine. I sit there with the objects until the excitement has faded. The luster fades. The newness fades. The objects are only objects. Tossing the junk into the bottom of the ravine, I go home.

The Sponsor

Less than a month before our wedding, our headline sponsor goes out of business, and just like that the money disappears. Jenna gets the call. Ty and me are sitting on the futon in tank tops and khaki shorts, gawking at photos of the new weight room at Gillette Stadium™, where he works as a trainer for the Patriots®; the sunrise is still tinting the sky, bluebirds are chirping happily in the trees, and then suddenly she bursts into the apartment with the news. Jenna, Jenna, dear sweet fragile Jenna, with her bright eyes and her snub nose and her chipped nail polish, standing hardly taller than a snow shovel, wearing yoga pants and a sports bra with her hair pulled into a ponytail and her mascara smeared from crying. The ad department left her a voicemail while she was in spin class. A recording spoken by a robot. The corporation is bankrupt. The sponsorship is canceled. Her voice cracks as she explains. "I tried calling back, but nobody's even there," Jenna says. In an instant, the budget for our wedding has been slashed in half. I try to sound optimistic. "Maybe we could just, like, scale back," I say. Jenna trembles. Verge of weeping. About to snap. "Brock, this is supposed to be the most important day of our *lives*," Jenna says, her voice squeaking. Ty wipes his mouth, sets a McMuffin™ in a wrapper down onto the table next to a cup of Folgers® on a coaster, and then says, "Realistically, you'll probably spend the rest of your lives trying to forget the wedding ever even happened. I mean, name a single wedding you've been to where the couple wasn't divorced within three years." Jenna is stunned. Her cheeks flush like she's just been slapped. She looks at me, then points at Ty. "This is your best man? *This? This?*" I'm like, "Ty, bro, get out." Ty leaves, but I wouldn't dare embark on a quest this desperate alone, so I secretly send him a message to wait for me, and then after consoling Jenna, vowing to her that I will save the wedding, swearing to her that I will find another sponsor, and kissing her goodbye, passionately, I meet him down on the street.

"I was just trying to keep the situation in perspective," Ty says, leaning against a parking meter with a squint.

"We're not like that."

"I know."

"It's the real thing."

"So true."

"Fuck, man, if we don't find a new sponsor, the wedding is going to be ruined," I say, starting to panic.

Ty takes me by the shoulders. I'm tall. He's taller. He looks me in the eyes. "Brock. I'm here for you. This is why you have a best man. Seriously. I'm going to help you save the day. Let's make some calls."

We sit on the hood of a station wagon sponsored by Walmart®, flip-flops flat on the pavement, dialing numbers shoulder to shoulder, just like we used to do when we lived next door to each other as kids, when we'd call around the neighborhood to recruit friends for a sleepover or a game of catch. The situation is grim. Jenna and me applied for and received all of the usual sponsors for decorations and regalia, but replacing any of those would have been simple compared to trying to replace the headline sponsor. With less than a month until the wedding, we don't have time to go through the proper application process. Ty and me are forced to call the corporations directly, angling to land an interview on the spot. We stick with companies headquartered in town, hoping the ad departments will take pity on a local couple. We switch to professional voices. We turn on the charm. Most of the receptionists hang up on me without even bothering to say no. Ty isn't having any luck either, cursing every time he gets rejected.

I've just about run out of ideas of companies to try when he hangs up with a whoop.

"I got us an interview at BJ's!"

"What the fuck is that?"

"You know, like Costco, or Sam's. Just worse."

I grimace.

"What?" Ty says.

"I just wish the name was different."

"Brock. You're not going to find another sponsor with this much cash. Honestly, bro, you're not going to find another sponsor period. I haven't even come close with the other calls. This is the play."

I imagine the name of the company on a banner at the ceremony, cringing, but then remember that a minute ago we didn't have an interview anywhere. The quest had seemed impossible. The wedding had seemed doomed. But we can do this. We still have a chance.

I offer him a fist-bump with a grin.

"I can't believe you got us an interview with less than a month to go," I say.

"Must be desperate, who knows, but the interview's in an hour, so let's hit the road," Ty says.

I dig through pockets, taking out keys with a jingle. Ty glances at his coupe, which is sponsored by Nike®, then looks at my pickup, which is sponsored by Denny's®. "We can't show up in that," Ty says. "No offense. I'll drive."

I grab the fluorescent binder with the wedding paperwork from the glovebox in my pickup, Ty stomps the clutch and punches the brake and hits the ignition in his coupe, and we drive through the city, Ray-Bans® on. We were supposed to work out at the gym today. We've got a tub of creatine riding in the backseat. I stare into the wing mirror, at my stubble and my neck and my shoulders and my arms and the road stretching behind the car in a blur of dark bricks and gray stones. Colorful kites are flying above the John Deere® Boston

Common. Tour guides in colonial costumes march along the Freedom Trail, presented by Twinings™. I love having ripped muscles, the sensation of tight abs straining against the shifting momentum as the car takes a turn, the feeling of pecs too firm to bounce as the car rolls over a speed bump, of tensing a rigid bicep, of flexing a hard tricep, of quads and calves that—

"We're here, bro," Ty says, shifting into park.

BJ's® has a black leather sofa in the reception area of the ad department.

"Let me do the talking," I whisper.

"Just don't make any blowjob jokes," Ty whispers.

"I'm not an idiot," I whisper.

"But seriously though," Ty whispers.

An assistant leads us into a boardroom to meet with a pair of ad execs named Paige and Katie, who both wear gray suits and browline glasses. We sit when we're invited. Oxfords clacking on the floor, the assistant takes the fluorescent binder from me, walks along the conference table, past all the empty chairs, to hand the wedding paperwork to Paige and Katie, and then leaves the boardroom. Sunlight shimmers on the glass walls.

"So you're interested in BJ's."

"Um, the company, yeah."

Paige and Katie flip through the paperwork in the binder.

"Tell us about the wedding."

I swell with pride on reflex. "Jenna, my girlfriend, or fiancee technically, she has a vision, she has an eye, she's been planning this since she was in kindergarten, and—"

"What's she do?"

"Ambulance technician."

"How about you?"

"Cement mason."

"Guest list?"

"Uh, four hundred and twenty-one."

"That's it?"

"We've also got some great-grandparents who're going to stream the wedding from their nursing homes."

"We don't care about senile guests."

"Oh."

"We're only interested in mobile consumers."

"Totally."

"These engagement photos are really lovely."

"Thanks."

"You make a very beautiful couple."

"Awesome."

"Let's talk about finances."

I feel a pump of excitement. "Well, between the photo booth, the fireworks, the dancers, and all of the complimentary taxis, to cover the reception alone we're going to need—"

"The finances of the guests."

"Er."

"Average income?"

"Uh, ninety-six thousand and fifty."

Paige and Katie lean in toward each other, murmur, then nod, and turn back to us with smiles.

"Sorry, fellas, just isn't going to work for us."

My heart sinks. Paige and Katie stand. I run my hands through my hair and over my mouth in distress and then suddenly am begging, "Please, we had a different sponsor, a legitimate national headline sponsor, we did everything like we were supposed to, we applied over a year in advance, we had to turn down other offers, and then our sponsor went out of business and didn't even tell us what was happening until this morning, and it would mean a lot to our friends and our families to hear that our wedding had been saved by a local company, you're the only ones that can help us," but Paige and Katie are already walking out of the boardroom, leaving the fluorescent binder with the wedding paperwork behind.

Jenna sent me a selfie of her binge-eating a pint of gelato, asking how much luck we're having. I send her back a sweaty-face smiley with a couple of thumbs-up emojis, saying that we're still looking. We're not. BJ's® was our last chance. There's nowhere else in town to try. I feel dizzy leaving the building. I stumble into a mailbox. I lean against a streetlight.

"Deep breaths," Ty says.

"This is a nightmare," I say.

Ty calls an emergency meeting at noon with the other grooms-men, Braden, Parker, and Alejandro. Braden and Parker are twins. Alejandro is an only child. When we were kids we built a fort out of used tires and scrap metal in Ty's backyard, where we'd go when we were dealing with bickering parents or dying grandparents or just wanted to hang out. Braden went to school at Energizer® Tufts. Parker went to school at Zippo® Emerson. Alejandro never went to anywhere and works in construction like me. As charcoal briquettes burn in the grill, we smoke a joint in neon lawn chairs in the dazzling sunshine on the stoop of Alejandro's house, which used to be sponsored by Budweiser®, fell into disrepair, plunged in valuation, and now is sponsored by Hellmann's Blue Ribbon Mayonnaise®.

"We tried literally every company in Boston," Ty says.

"I'm doomed," I say.

"You really are," Braden says.

"You totally failed," Parker says.

Ty reaches into the cooler and flings a handful of ice at Bra-den and Parker, who duck the cubes with a pair of grins. Across the street, kids in bright swimsuits run through sprinklers on the lawns of houses sponsored by Marlboro® and Drano® and Spam®. Rainbows fade in and out above the spraying water. Alejandro tears the plastic wrapper from a package of paper plates, delts bulging.

"It's not like the wedding is canceled," Braden says.

"There's still going to be a wedding," Parker says.

I explode, "You guys don't get it. It won't be the same. That spon-sor was like half of the budget. That sponsor was backing all of the highlights. The rest of the sponsors are just for props. Fuck, this cer-emony was her dream. You should've seen her face when she'd talk about it. The way she'd glow. I'm serious, this is going to break her heart. She doesn't deserve this, she's a good person, she's responsible, she's friendly, she never swears online, she never posts politics, she's nice to old people, she volunteers with cancer kids. And she isn't even like that to get sponsors. That's just who she is. She's perfect."

Braden and Parker get somber.

"The best a man can get," I murmur, trailing off.

A breeze drifts across the yard. The smell of freshly mowed grass. A couple of bottles clink together as melting ice cubes shift in the cooler, and then the street is quiet again aside from the occasional squeal from the kids across the street. Alejandro squats on the stoop, lays Johnsonville® brats onto the grill with a sizzle, pops the caps on some bottles of Heinz® and French's®, sets a bag of Lay's® chips by the plates, and then suddenly freezes with an expression of shock.

"Guys. Brock," Alejandro exclaims. "I just figured out how to save the wedding." He turns to me with an excited look. "You just have to talk to Simon."

My mind flashes onto a pale, skeletal, frightened face: Simon, the goth kid from the neighborhood, who used to wear eyeliner and lipstick, was known to hold seances in the graveyard across from the dollar store, got ass-beatings with a pathetic regularity, and never had even a single friend.

Ty squints. "Simon from the block?"

"No way," I say.

"Dude somehow landed a job at Mattel," Alejandro says.

"I won't."

"He runs the advertising department for Barbie," Alejandro says.

"I can't."

"He's living in Washington now. I ran into him last month. He was back visiting his mom. I got his number and everything," Alejandro says.

"He'd *never* help me," I say.

"Are you kidding? After you grew up in the same neighborhood? The same block? How could he deny a bond like that?"

"Because he *hates* me," I say.

"What, cause of the incident with the zucchini?"

"Man, that wasn't your fault."

"Yeah, you can't be blamed for that."

"Seriously, he's probably forgotten all about that by now."

Alejandro is already dialing the number. He's always been the runt of the group, jacked now but still the shortest. He loves any chance to act as spokesperson.

"Simon? Yo, what's up. Alejandro, from the block. Listen, we've got a situation. Do you remember Brock?"

Ty grabs me by the arms and looks me in the eyes with a grin.

"Bro, seriously, just imagine the annual budget for the ad department at *Barbie*."

Alejandro covers the mic on the phone.

"He wants us to drive down to talk about the deal in person," Alejandro whispers.

Ty does a fist-pump, high-fives Braden and Parker.

I grimace.

"This is going to be a hell of a Hail Mary," I say.

We hop into Alejandro's jeep, swing through a Speedway® for some Cokes™ and a Pepsi™ (Ty always has to be different), and then road-trip down the coast with hip-hop thumping over the stereo. Seagulls soar above the expressway. Models shimmer on the billboards. The sky is crystal clear. We hit the District at sunset, gliding through downtown with windblown hair. Tourists are snapping photos of the Goldman Sachs® White House. Flags billow majestically at the base of the Washington Monument, presented by Viagra™. On the sidewalk, beggars in ragged clothing sit slumped over hats full of change. A rabid-looking hobo with bloodshot eyes and a natty beard stands at a corner, tinted fluorescent red by a stoplight, holding a battered cardboard sign scrawled with a slogan: "Masters Brand Their Slaves."

The hobo bobs his head in rhythm with the music in the jeep.

"Turn that shit up!" the hobo shouts.

We laugh and cheer and then crank up the music, and for a moment an awesome, pure hope pumps through me, that the wedding is actually going to be saved. Jenna sent me a selfie of her pouting in a bathtub, asking if we've found a sponsor yet. I send her back a bouquet of heart emojis, promising we'll have a new sponsor locked by midnight.

Dusk is falling as the jeep coasts into Simon's neighborhood, a block of urban palaces whose stoops are flanked by soaring pillars. We all go quiet. The stereo is off. Stars glimmer above his driveway as his gate swings apart to let the jeep pass. Water burbles from a tiled fountain. The willow trees are becoming silhouettes. His convertible is sponsored by Rolex® and Chanel®. His mansion is sponsored by Facebook® and Google®.

"Shit, man, he didn't tell me he was living like *this*," Alejandro says, glancing from the convertible to the mansion with a look of awe.

Ty rings the doorbell as we cluster around each other nervously on the porch.

Simon's wife is a cadaverous brunette with a foreign accent, hauling apart the doors wearing nothing but a cucumber mask and a silk kimono. She must have known we were coming, because she never asks who we are, just greets us and leads us past a grand carpeted staircase into a wallpapered hallway lit only by the moonlight streaming through the latticed windowpanes. Music like a meditation soundtrack plays over hidden speakers. A bamboo flute. Some ringing gongs. On the walls hang monstrous landscape paintings, each caked so thick with oil that the surface has a visible texture. Between the windows stand figurative marble sculptures, each contorted into a posture so grotesque that the stones have palpable emotions. The rugs are as plush as sod. I feel out of place in a tank top and khaki shorts, flip-flops flapping on the floor.

She drops us at the doorway to a wood-paneled office where a Tiffany® lamp smolders next to an Apple® laptop glowing on a desk. Simon sits in a claw-footed chair, drinking wine from a crystal goblet, wearing a black tunic over black slacks. He cut the floppy ponytail that he always had when we were younger and now has wavy moussed hair parted at the side, but aside from that and some crow's-feet wrinkles, he looks exactly the same as he looked as a kid, pale and gaunt with light gray eyes and a freakishly weak chin. Above the desk colorful video clips from his life stream across a screen in a golden frame. He graduated from both Microsoft® Harvard and Amazon® Princeton. He's gambled at Bellagio presented by Mastercard®, skied at Vail presented by Swarovski®, and glamped in the Best Buy® Grand Canyon, the ConocoPhillips® Smokies, and the ExxonMobil® Everglades. His wedding was sponsored by Disney®, with hot-air balloons, horse-drawn carriages, and complimentary stained-glass slippers presented by The Magic Kingdom™. Seeing images from his wedding, him and his wife exchanging vows under blooming wisteria in a grove of blinking fireflies, him and his wife feeding each other dollops of frosting from a towering gold-leaf cake, immediately makes me think of Jenna. She's counting on me. This has to work.

"Simon, bro, it's great to see you," says Ty, who always loves everybody, especially anybody from the block, and sounds genuinely excited. "What a place. I'm lovin' it. So you sponsor weddings at Barbie?"

"Sure, we do weddings," Simon says.

He's staring at me with an expression of loathing.

He hasn't forgotten the incident with the zucchini.

This isn't going to work.

"Brock here is getting married next month, like we mentioned," Alejandro says.

"Best man," Ty waves, grinning proudly.

"And out of nowhere, the headline sponsor just fell through," Alejandro says.

"Braden, Parker, please don't touch that, it's very expensive," Simon snaps without glancing away from me. Looking guilty, Braden and Parker set an ancient-looking dagger back into a wooden stand on the bookcase.

Alejandro hesitates. "Anyway, we thought maybe you could help him out, you know, him being from the block and all."

Simon nods with a neutral expression.

Tentatively, I hold out the fluorescent binder. "I've got the head-shots, the guest list, the average income, all of that."

"That won't be necessary," Simon says.

"Oh." I lower the wedding paperwork, feeling confused.

Simon faintly smiles.

"Brock, do you remember that random pole in the sidewalk at the corner of the street?"

"Yeah?"

"I always wondered, why did each of you always slap the pole when you went by?"

I glance at the others.

"Um, just a tradition?" I say.

Simon folds his hands together in his lap.

"It makes me emotional seeing that all of you are still friends," Simon murmurs.

He turns to gaze at the moon out the window, the light of the lamp shining across his moussed hair, with a faraway quality to his voice suddenly.

"I went back to the block earlier this summer," Simon says. "Stayed with my mother for the weekend, showering in my old bathroom, sleeping in my childhood bed. It was strange being back. The way the neighborhood has changed. The cars. The houses. I didn't even recognize most the people living there. My mother said something during the trip that stayed with me, though. That the most important thing in life is integrity. You have to stay true to who you are. You always have to honor where you come from. That's what she said."

I frown.

"Wait, so you'll help me?" I say.

He blinks at the moon without turning from the window, his voice taking on a sudden eager intensity, the light of the lamp sparkling in his gray eyes.

"I always wanted to be friends with you," Simon says. "All of you. I used to watch you, hanging out together, playing basketball at the park. I knew that none of you were like me, but still, I used to fantasize about us becoming friends somehow. Everything that I did alone, I'd imagine us doing together. Reading tarot in the bathroom at school. Making poppets from twigs and shoelaces. Drawing sigils on sidewalks and trees. Ouija in the graveyard. You were always the ones I pictured. You've always been special to me in that way."

I squint.

"So, then you'll help me?" I say.

Simon glances at me.

"I'll help you," Simon says, "if, and only if, you do a ritual with me, taking a vow swearing your eternal devotion to the devil."

I'm speechless.

"Simon, that's pretty fucked up," Ty says, sounding genuinely scandalized.

Simon looks at him. "Wouldn't you agree something 'pretty fucked up' once happened to me?"

"He means the incident with the zucchini," Alejandro whispers.

"Brock, that *was* messed up," Braden says.

"You *have* to admit, bro," Parker says.

"I thought that wasn't my fault?" I hiss.

"Anyway, devil worship is a perfectly valid religion," Simon says, rising gracefully from the claw-footed chair.

"I'm not going to do any creepy rituals with you," I say.

"If you want a sponsor you're going to have to," Simon says.

I grimace.

Ty thinks, scowls, and then says, "Brock, it's *Barbie*."

Simon leads us through a carved wooden door, down rough concrete steps, and into a wine cellar lined with racks of corked bottles sealed with wax. The air down there has a chill, but then at the end of the wine cellar he takes us through a locked door with no knob or handle, only a keyhole, and we're hit by a warm breeze. We step into a hot dark chamber the size of a locker-room shower. Rippled black candles with charred wicks are arranged in a circle on the floor around a pentagram painted with white paint. On the far wall, a mildewed chest with rusted latches sits on a decrepit altar. Above the altar hangs a horned skull with gigantic eye sockets and nubby teeth. A skull from a goat. Otherwise the chamber is empty. No windows. No vents. No other doors. My neck and my arms are already slick with sweat from the heat. Simon lights the candles with a book of matches, looking delighted, and then motions for me to kneel in the pentagram. I don't want to kneel. I kneel. The floor feels rough under my knees. My nostrils flare at a musty smell. Ty and the others gather around the pentagram with nervous expressions. The scene reminds me of when we once took a shortcut as kids, strolling through the weedy ruins of an abandoned warehouse, where we suddenly stumbled onto a pair of teenagers in hoodies mugging somebody at gunpoint. That petrifying feeling of having wandered into someplace we shouldn't be.

I believe in three things in life: protein, weightlifting, and true love. I don't believe in gods and demons. I don't believe in hell and heaven. (Except for Jenna, my paradise here on Earth!) Still, my grandparents are all Catholic, and the pentagram freaks me out.

Simon stands beneath the goat skull at the altar.

"Repeat after me," Simon says.

"You know this doesn't mean anything, right?" I say.

"Brock, are you doing this or not?" Simon says.

"It's just words," I say.

Simon smiles.

The candles flicker as we do the ritual.

"I bow my head to the Prince of Darkness."

"I bow my head to the Prince of Darkness."

"I pledge my life to Lucifer."

"I pledge my life to Lucifer."

"I promise my soul to Satan."

"I promise my soul to Satan."

I don't feel any different afterward. My heart is beating faster than after any workout ever. I'm still me though. And it's done. It's over now. That's what I'm thinking, that the ritual is finished, when Simon turns to the altar to flip the latches on the ancient wooden chest. He lifts the lid. Mist pours out of the chest like fog from a freezer. Simon turns back toward the pentagram palming a dark red lump of flesh.

"What the hell is that?"

"The heart of a pig."

Simon reaches across the pentagram to offer me the heart.

"Eat it," Simon says.

"Fuck no," I spit.

"Brock, the ritual isn't complete until you do."

Ty and the others are watching from the shadows. Braden looks stunned. Parker looks nauseous. Alejandro's eyes have never been so wide. Ty nods, then whispers, "Just do it."

Beneath my tank top, a bead of sweat dribbles down my spine, slipping past my tailbone, soaking into the waistband of my khaki shorts. I think about Jenna's face. The little dimples in her cheeks when she smiles. I hesitate, then turn back toward Simon. My glutes are tensed from kneeling. My jaw is clenched together hard. My hands are trembling suddenly, which makes me feel ashamed. I'm afraid. I take the heart, cupping the raw lump of flesh between my palms. The flesh is frosted but isn't frozen. Wax trickles from the candles as the flames flicker. Simon looks ecstatic. I part my lips, then bend down and bite into the heart like an apple, twisting my head to tear off a mouthful with my teeth. The meat is cold and spongy. Flavorless. Gritty with crystals of ice. Blood dribbles from my mouth to my chin, dripping onto the floor. I'm the strongest man she's ever known. Jenna told me that once, the night we got engaged. That's why she loves me. Strong in spirit, strong in body. Eating a heart isn't any different than doing squats or curls. Each bite is another rep. I chew. I swallow. I fight the urge to gag.

Later that summer, in a tuxedo, standing at the altar in the cathedral at the ceremony presented by Neanderthal Princess Barbie™ as hired musicians make the strings on violins and violas and cellos sing, and trained swans nestle in pairs near the Gerber® archway of dried roses, and rented butterflies flutter in clusters between the Pampers® vases of fresh orchids, and live actors silently reenact the most significant scenes of our courtship in the sunlight streaming into the church through the stained glass, and our guests dab at tears with complimentary silk handkerchiefs in the pews, and Jenna walks toward me down the aisle wearing her Allstate® veil and her Verizon® earrings and her glittering Home Depot® dress, I think to ask myself, was it all worth it?

And it was. Of course it was. It really was.

One Big Happy Family

A sinkhole had appeared at dawn in the street across from the nursery, a sudden collapse of asphalt and plumbing that had swallowed a semi waiting at the stoplight, and the ensuing spectacle had distracted the staff all morning, clusters of caretakers gathering at windows on various floors of the nursery, pausing between tasks to gawk at the scene below: the water gushing from a broken pipe onto the cab of the semi, the driver being retrieved from the sinkhole by a crew of firefighters with a ladder, a highway engineer in a fluorescent safety vest placing a perimeter of neon traffic cones around the hole, oblivious traffic turning onto the street down the block and being forced to do a u-turn at the intersection, boxes of frozen crab cakes being hauled out of the trailer of the semi and rushed into the freezer of the convenience store at the corner to prevent the meat from spoiling.

Eleanor was standing at the window in her office when the new chief of security appeared in the doorway behind her desk, hat in hand, looking deeply ashamed.

"A child is gone," the chief of security said.

Eleanor stared at the reflection of the chief of security without turning from the window.

"How is that possible?" Eleanor said.

"We've already reviewed the footage from the cameras. The

abduction was premeditated. She had a keycard. She signed in with the guards for a visitor pass. She used the keycard to leave through the loading dock," the chief of security said.

Eleanor suppressed a feeling of panic.

"Which child was taken?"

"Marvin."

Eleanor knew the child. She had held the child personally. He was only a month old.

"I'll call the police. Nobody talks to the press. We'll prepare a statement," Eleanor said.

Eleanor had been the director of the nursery for nearly half a century. In that time she had overseen the care of thousands of children. She had stayed up through the night with children who had fevers. She had ridden along in the ambulances with children who had appendicitis. She had slept in hospital rooms with children who had fractured bones. She had protected the children with allergies. She had comforted the children with colic. She had never lost a child. She felt a rage growing within her. She turned to reach for her phone.

"Ma'am," the chief of security said.

Eleanor looked up.

"There's one last thing," the chief of security said. "The child was hers."

★ ★ ★

The kidnapper lived in a townhouse in Georgetown, an elegant home with shining granite countertops and polished hardwood floors. She wasn't there. Her computer was missing. So was her vehicle. Quinn arrived at the house after the others from the department, striding down the sidewalk with his derbies clacking on the pavement and the name of the kidnapper echoing through his head with every footstep. Daniela, Daniela, Daniela. Cherry blossoms were falling from the trees that grew along the curb. The petals that landed in puddles turned a darker shade of pink. Jared, his assistant, was waiting for him at the door with a to-go cup. Jared had a crush on him. Quinn didn't encourage this. Quinn was a professional.

"I got you a latte," Jared said, smiling.

Quinn took a sip from the cup and then grimaced and spat onto the stoop. "Is that soy?"

"It was a vegan place," Jared said, apologetically.

Quinn handed the cup back to him.

"She might have already left town," Jared said.

"We're going to find her before that happens," Quinn said.

"We've got the father in here," Jared said.

Jared led him into the townhouse, down a brightly lit hallway, past a bathroom with a modernist sink, past a bedroom with a modernist dresser, past a pair of police officers chatting among the gleaming chrome appliances in a kitchen, into a spacious living room where the father was sitting on a modernist leather sofa between a pair of gigantic ferns. Young and slender with a gelled crew cut and a mildly attractive face, the father wore suspenders and a silk tie over a light blue dress shirt with a white collar. He looked impatient. He'd been waiting. He probably hadn't wanted to be interviewed here. He was cooperating, though.

Quinn took out a ballpoint and a notepad.

"Can you state your name?"

"Charlie."

"Charlie what?"

"Roberts."

"Where were you born?"

"The Abraham Lincoln Nursery."

"That's where?"

"Illinois."

"Where were you raised?"

"Jacqueline Kennedy Onassis Academy."

"Where's that?"

"Milwaukee."

"You went to college?"

"Georgetown."

"Job?"

"Investing."

"Where do you live?"

"Downtown."

"Have you ever been to this house before?"

"Daniela came to mine."

"You're aware that your child was kidnapped earlier today?"

"Yes."

"When was the last time you saw your child?"

"Never."

"Not even once?"

"I pay my taxes."

"When was the last time you spoke to his mother?"

"When she told me she was pregnant."

"Where'd you meet her?"

"At a work party."

"Do you love her?"

Charlie laughed. "No."

"Does she love you?"

"We only hooked up a single time," Charlie said.

"You didn't answer the question."

"She doesn't love me."

"Ninety-nine percent of the time this happens, it's because the parents are in love," Quinn said.

"She never loved me."

Quinn said, "That's not an estimate of the frequency. That's an exact statistic from the database."

"We're talking about a one-night stand," Charlie said.

Quinn stared at the painting hanging over the piano, a massive impressionist landscape that appeared to depict the ruins of a classical temple on a sunny cliff above the sea. Greece. It was the only piece of art in the townhouse. The rest of the walls in the townhouse were bare.

"In all the years that you lived in the system, were you ever mistreated?" Quinn murmured, still gazing at the painting.

"I guess not," Charlie said.

The brushstrokes had faint shadows.

"I wasn't born in the system," Quinn said. "I grew up on a vegetable farm in rural Alaska. A wood stove, a water pump, completely off the grid. My parents were honest, decent people, and worked hard, but my parents were misguided. I had half a dozen brothers and sisters. Whenever a plane flew over the farm we would have to hide in the barn to avoid being seen. I can't even describe how lonely life was for us, compared to growing up in the system, and how meager of an education that we received there. My parents were anti-vaxxers. None of us had been vaccinated for anything. Hepatitis, meningitis, tetanus, rubella, polio, mumps, nothing. Not even my parents. My grandparents had been anti-vaxxers too." He frowned. "My grandparents lived in a rest home, an eldercare facility in the city, instead of at the farm, if you can believe the hypocrisy of that." He hesitated. "One summer my parents made a supply run to Juneau. Along with the rice and sugar, my parents brought back the measles. The outbreak swept through that farm like a fire. I watched the infection spread to each of my brothers and sisters, one by one, coughing and diarrhea and pneumonia and blindness, and then the infection spread to me. My parents were too sick to care for me. I spent a week in the hay on the floor of the barn, covered with rashes, drifting in and out of the fever, drinking water from a bucket meant for the cows. I survived. That fall the government raided the farm. I was the only child left alive."

Quinn felt a surge of anger.

"That's the other one percent. Radicals. Political extremists. People fundamentally opposed to universal childcare," Quinn said.

Quinn turned back from the painting.

"Do you know what's going to happen to that kid out there?" Quinn said.

"With all due respect, the kid isn't my responsibility," Charlie said.

"You're right," Quinn said. "He's not." Quinn stepped toward him. "He's mine." Quinn pointed at him. "I can promise you this. I'm not going to let what happened to me happen to him. I'm going to bring him home."

Quinn went into the kitchen. Jared was helping the officers search the cupboards for evidence.

"The father isn't involved," Quinn said.

Jared popped open the door of the microwave. A laptop was sitting on the turntable.

"I think she might have nuked her computer," Jared said, sounding amazed.

Her vehicle still hadn't been found. She drove a baby blue sedan with a rust spot the shape of a star eating into the numbers on the license plate.

"There's a bakery at the corner. Get me a whole-milk cappuccino. Triple shot. Extra foamy. And find her car," Quinn said.

★ ★ ★

The receptionist wasn't in the student center. Kyle rang the bell on the counter, but nobody came. How typical. Just classic. The one time that he had an actual emergency. He could hear voices further back. Kyle walked through the student center, past the cluttered desks where the receptionist and the counselor and the dean usually sat, which were all deserted. The voices were coming from the headmaster's office. Kyle peered in the doorway. The receptionist was in there, along with Ted, the counselor, and even Amy, the dean, all standing behind the desk, looking super concerned. Pops was there too. That was the nickname that all of the kids at the academy used for the headmaster. Pops. Pops was talking to a detective wearing a badge hanging from a chain. The detective had very interesting eyes. A sidekick in an actual cop uniform was searching through a filing cabinet. The sidekick looked like a newb. On the clunky television in the corner, a talk show was playing on mute.

Pops knew that he was standing there.

Kyle tried to interrupt.

"Pops," Kyle said, knocking on the doorframe.

Pops held up a hand, gesturing at him to wait.

"I just need a new deodorant," Kyle said.

"You know where to go to get that."

"I tried going to the janitor office but nobody was there," Kyle said.

"Then just go into the supply closet and pick out a new deodorant."

"It was locked for some reason," Kyle said.

"You're going to have to wait a second."

"But," Kyle said.

"Just hold on."

Kyle stood there and listened as the detective launched back into a question.

"She worked for a national bank, was working at the executive level, and you weren't at all suspicious when she said she wanted to leave all of that behind and take a job as an educator?"

"She was personable. She was intelligent. She said that she needed a change. She passed her background check with flying colors. And like we said, she never told us that she had recently had a baby, let alone a baby that had been placed at a nursery in the same district," Pops said.

"So how long did she actually work here?"

"Technically she was still training."

"And her keycard gave her access to all of the nurseries in the district too?"

"Once a week instructors visit the nurseries to teach the toddlers brief lessons."

"Is having keycard access to the nurseries really necessary for that?"

"We've never had an issue before."

"Why are you even still using keycards for door security?"

"Welcome to the wonderful world of government funding. We're still using a fax machine in the office, if you have any urgent faxes you need to send," Pops said.

"The kids all get new laptops every year, and we get used computers handed down from the park service," Ted said.

"Mine came with a sticker of a moose," Amy said.

Kyle knew who the detective was talking about. He had seen the new instructor taking a tour of the academy. He had known that there was something suspicious about her the moment that he had seen her. He had just been able to tell. Nobody ever listened to him though. What would he know. He was just an eleven-year-old meteorology enthusiast with a life-threatening nut allergy and above-average common sense. He felt bad for the baby who had been kidnapped. Even after the cops finally found the kid and brought the kid home, now the kid was going to be that kid forever. The kid who got kidnapped. He wondered if babies could feel embarrassed.

"Daniela hasn't been seen around here at all today?" the detective said.

Kyle glanced at the receptionist. The receptionist was staring at the television with an expression of shock. Before anybody could respond to the detective, she reached for the remote and hit the button for the volume. A sudden burst of noise leapt from the speakers. Breaking news. The host of the talk show was pointing at the corner of the screen, where a clip from a security cam was playing on slo-mo, showing a blurry figure in a sweatsuit carrying a baby into a loading dock. Next to the clip was a photo, a professional headshot of a woman in a blouse and a blazer with thick curly hair.

"This is an attack on the American family," the host proclaimed, looking outraged.

"Look, there she is," Kyle said.

★ ★ ★

Teagan worked for a fragrance corporation, developing avant-garde scents for younger consumers. She was at the showroom, introducing the employees to an assortment of new perfumes, when the news about the kidnapping hit the internet. Teagan wandered over to the waiting area in shock, tried calling Daniela, got sent to voicemail, left a rambling message. Teagan was still over there, skimming the bulletins, texting back and forth with Noelle, talking about how crazy the whole situation was, when a detective in a navy suit and horn-rimmed glasses came strolling into the showroom. He was gorgeous. His eyes were the most striking blue that she had ever seen. She was literally flustered by his beauty. She dropped a folder. He was accompanied by an assistant with a patchy beard, who looked super needy.

"You're friends with Daniela Ndukwe?" the detective said.

"Yeah, best friends," Teagan said.

The detective wanted to ask her some questions. Teagan squatted to gather her folder as the detective took out a pen and a pad. Sniffing sample strips, the employees snuck a glance at her, then turned back toward the perfumes.

"I know what everybody's saying on the news, but it can't have been her who took the kid. She wouldn't have done that. That's not who she is," Teagan said, smoothing her skirt.

"Have you heard from her yet today?"

"No."

"How long have you known her for?"

"Since college. Orientation weekend."

"How would you describe her?"

"She's happy. Beautiful. Amazing at her job. Insanely successful."

"Political?"

"Never."

"What's important to her?"

"Work. Friends. Sex. Croissants. She does yoga."

The detective licked the tip of a finger to flip a page in the pad. God he was cute. Teagan fantasized about cuddling with him on the deck of a sailboat, sharing intimate stories, laughing romantically together, exchanging emotionally supportive compliments, holding sparkling flutes of champagne.

"How long had she wanted a kid?"

"She didn't."

"Then why wasn't she on the pill?"

"She was. Daniela took those pills religiously. On the hour, every day, no matter what, without fail. We did a trip a year ago, Hawaii, staying at this resort on the ocean. Daniela takes the pill at nine in the morning. That's like the middle of the night there. We were all staying in a room together, piled onto a couple of king beds, and every night no matter how drunk we were we'd hear her alarm go off, and she'd roll over, take a pill, and then go back to sleep. That's how careful she was," Teagan said. "Last spring she picked up a case of ringworm at the gym. Athlete's foot. The doctor gave her a prescription for some antifungal meds to kill the ringworm. A couple months later she found out that she was pregnant. The doctor told her the antifungal meds must have interfered with the birth control. Hadn't mentioned that was a possible side effect. Girl was pissed."

"Why didn't she just have an abortion?"

"She wanted to, but she had a medical issue."

"What medical issue?"

"Hemophilia."

"Did you know that she recently changed jobs?"

Teagan frowned, getting an uneasy feeling. "To another bank?"

"When was the last time you saw her?"

"A couple days ago. We got brunch."

"Did she say anything unusual?" the detective said.

Teagan thought, remembering sitting there in the cafe across from Daniela, how the sunlight flashing off of cutlery and tumblers at other tables had glittered across her, and the pastel succulents in ceramic pots on the wooden shelves, purples and teals and greens. "She told me she loved me," Teagan realized. "I always make fun of her because of how stoic she is. She doesn't like to get sentimental. No matter how many times you tell her you love her, she'll never tell you she loves you back. But that day she told me she loved me as we were saying goodbye."

★ ★ ★

Noelle worked for a shoe brand, designing high-fashion sneakers for affluent consumers. She was in the lab, observing the gaits of testers jogging on treadmills, when the news about the kidnapping hit the internet. Noelle went over to the weight benches for privacy, tried calling

Daniela, got sent to voicemail, left a worried message. Noelle was still over there, reading the updates, texting back and forth with Teagan, who had gotten interviewed by some cop, when a detective in a navy suit and horn-rimmed glasses came strolling into the lab. His eyes were the most radiant blue that she had ever seen. He was flawless. She was literally dumbstruck by his beauty. She couldn't even speak. He was accompanied by an assistant with weak facial hair, who had a clingy vibe.

"You're friends with Daniela Ndukwe?" the detective said.

"Best friends, yeah," Noelle said, adjusting her wristwatch.

The detective wanted to ask her some questions. Noelle tried to gather her composure as the detective took out a pad and a pen. Still jogging, some of the testers glanced over at her, then turned back toward the treadmills.

"She didn't do it. She's not the type. If that's her in that video, then somebody else must have forced her to," Noelle said.

"Has she contacted you at all today?"

"Nothing."

"How long ago did you meet her?"

"In college. Freshman suitemates."

"How would you describe her?"

"She's beautiful. Brilliant. Crazy talented. Dedicated to her career."

"Political?"

"Nah."

"What's important to her?"

"Friends. Exercise. Dating. Work. She likes baking."

The detective licked the tip of the pen to get the ink flowing. Damn he was fine. Noelle imagined picking a fight with him about a flirtatious concierge, then having makeup sex in a hotel bathtub, clutching each other, murmuring passionate apologies, splashing water over the rim.

"How long had she wanted a kid?"

"She didn't."

"But she wasn't on the pill?"

"She was, but she was on other meds that interfered."

"Meds for what?"

"Ringworm."

"Why didn't she just have an abortion?"

"She couldn't. I mean, she could've, but there would have been risks. Daniela has a blood disorder. Hemophilia. A mild case actually. She's always been fine with cuts or scrapes. She didn't even find out that she had hemophilia until she had to have surgery to get a cyst removed. She almost bled out on the operating table. Anyway, the doctors still would have been willing to go through with the abortion, but when she weighed all the options, she decided just to carry the baby to term, rather than risk any complications," Noelle said. "We took this vacation a couple years ago. Honolulu, this ocean resort, very posh. One night we went to a party on the beach, and we got to talking with this girl who was anemic, who'd had bleeding complications after an abortion and almost died. I think that might have been why she was so paranoid about having an abortion. The story upset her. Daniela had only found out about the hemophilia that winter before."

"Are you aware that she recently changed jobs?"

Noelle hesitated, suddenly feeling concerned. "At the bank?"

"When was the last time you saw her?"

"A week ago. We met for dinner."

"Did she do anything unusual?" the detective said.

Noelle frowned, thinking about sitting in the bistro across from Daniela, how the flames of the candles at other tables had flickered behind her, and the pastel napkins standing in clamshell folds between the wineglasses and the cutlery, yellows and oranges and pinks. "She kept delaying having to leave," Noelle remembered. "I'd mention how late it was, and she'd change the subject, bring up some old story, start reminiscing about the past. She normally isn't like that, especially when she has to work in the morning. But that night, I don't know. It was like she didn't want to let me go."

★ ★ ★

A crescent moon hung in the sky beyond the windows of the penthouse. Teagan was still at work, Noelle was still working too, but everybody else was there at Ishan's, sitting on the sectional in the living room, wearing colorful headsets, in a virtual reality. Everybody except Daniela, obviously. The audio played over the surround sound. Chirping birds, crunching snow, a soundtrack of tinkling chimes. Max could hear the music from the kitchen. He couldn't do virtual reality. Virtual reality made him queasy. Which was fine. He'd rather be making drinks for everybody anyway. Yet again. Without so much as a please or thank-you. Daniela was the only one who had ever appreciated him, and now she might be going to prison, or gone forever. Max wondered where she was at that exact moment. He was dropping olives into the martinis when the doorbell rang.

A detective with intense eyes was standing at the door. A sidekick who looked vaguely feeble was standing there too. Max was crushed. He had thought it might be her.

Max brought the detective and the sidekick into the living room, where everybody on the sectional was making different expressions, gaping and sneering and pouting at the virtual reality.

"Um, there's some cops here?" Max said.

The detective wanted to talk about Daniela.

"Have a seat, she's all that we've been talking about all night anyway," Ishan said, ducking something in the virtual reality.

"Is she really a suspect?" Gabrielle said.

"Were you surprised to hear it?" the detective said.

"Yes, actually," Ishan said.

"What type of person is she?" the detective said.

"Like, the opposite of a criminal," Gabrielle said.

"She's a talker, super sociable," Bryce said.

"She's into networking, business cards," Liam said.

"She's ditzy," Ishan said.

"She is not," Gabrielle protested.

"Okay, not ditzy exactly, but she's shallow."

"You're such a jerk."

"I'm just saying that she's not the type of person you'd have a deep conversation with, about like metaphysical philosophy or whatever.

She's great. She's fun. She has impeccable taste in music. Incredible moves on the dance floor. I love her, you all know that," Ishan said.

"Could you take off the headsets?" the detective asked.

"Hold on, we're almost to a save point," Ishan said.

"Look at how pretty that unicorn is," Valerie exclaimed.

"Let's kill the unicorn with a spear," Raelynn whispered.

"I happen to have had a lot of meaningful conversations with her, personally," Gabrielle said.

"Daniela threw up on a priest once when she was drunk," Ishan said.

"Don't tell the cop that," Gabrielle hissed, swinging blindly at him, backhanding the couch instead.

"She's not the kidnapper," Valerie said.

"She's so innocent," Raelynn said.

"But then why hasn't she been answering her phone?" Gabrielle said.

"She's probably just too overwhelmed to pick up," Bryce said.

"She must be getting so many calls from reporters," Liam said.

"Do you really think she's going to be okay?" Gabrielle said.

"She's the type of person who always takes the last piece of pizza," Ishan said.

Max wished he hadn't mentioned pizza. Max was tired of being fat. He was on a strict diet. He wasn't allowed to have cheese. He wanted pizza so badly the desire felt almost erotic. Glancing over, he realized the sidekick had wandered off to search the rest of the penthouse.

"Did she ever talk about visiting her child?" the detective said.

"I actually had a couple of kids go through that same nursery," Ishan said, punching something in the virtual reality.

"You have children?" the detective said, sounding almost incredulous.

"I felt morally obligated to contribute these fine genetics to the national gene pool," Ishan said.

"He's only half joking," Gabrielle said.

"I love kids. Kids are awesome. I definitely wanted to have some.

Leonidas, the youngest one, just graduated to academy. He got to make a speech at the ceremony," Ishan said.

"Oh that's right, how was that?" Gabrielle said.

"I wasn't there. I had work. I think his mom might have made it," Ishan said.

★ ★ ★

Annie walked back from the clothesline carrying a plastic basket full of laundry, feeling a tenderness in the bruise on her thigh, from when she had bumped her leg. A detective in horn-rimmed glasses was standing at the door to the trailer with a badge hanging from his neck. His eyes were haunting. Behind him stood an assistant, who was smiling eagerly, like a traveling salesperson, and had this pesky aura that was irritating even from afar.

"You here to talk about Daniela?" Annie said bitterly, crossing the yard toward the door.

Annie let the detective into the trailer. The assistant came too. Annie set the basket down on the floor as the detective and the assistant scanned the trailer, probably judging all the clutter. She hardly had room for the cops to stand. The trailer didn't even have a closet. Her hallway was lined with cardboard boxes of clothing. Her cupboards were packed with stacked cans of food. She loved living in a narrow cozy space. The trailer was a chrome antique on a set of cinder blocks, with a rounded ceiling and a linoleum floor and crocheted seat cushions on all the chairs, and was crammed with all her treasures, the multicolored chakra crystals she kept over on the ledge by the sink, the mismatched knitting needles she kept in a carton by the television, the collectable stuffed animals she kept in a pile on the couch, the tarot decks and the moon charts she kept handy on the shelf over the bed. Sunlight shimmered on the dusty window overlooking the mobile homes next door. The center of the table was occupied by her latest bargain, an ancient cassette player with a working radio, which was surrounded by mounds of other finds, bisque dolls and painted doorknobs and nutcracker figurines and a baggie of vintage buttons from the flea market.

The assistant went to use the bathroom, probably wanting a chance to judge the decor in there too.

"Make sure you put the seat down afterward," Annie hollered.

"You're a housecleaner?" the detective said, noticing the uniform on the hanger hooked to the cupboard.

"A housecleaner, a cashier, a server. I've got more jobs than hands. The minimum wage in this country is shameful. You all should do something about that."

"I'm just a cop. I don't control the minimum wage," the detective said.

"Well, talk to somebody," Annie said.

The detective inspected a crate of yarn.

Annie said, "I flunked out of academy. I'm smart. I just don't test well. I get flustered. It all came down to a single history exam. I failed, big time. Got off track on the bubbles, filled in the answers for the wrong questions, didn't realize until the time was already up. That's the reason for having to work jobs like these. No degree. You happen to have a cigarette by any chance?"

"How long have you been separated from Deon?"

Annie reached into a drawer for a pack of menthols. "We split up before she was born."

"Daniela is your only child?"

"Yep."

"When was the last time you saw her?"

"Long time ago now."

"How long?"

"Would have been back around the time she graduated from college."

"Did you visit much when she was young?"

"Hardly at all."

"You weren't close with her?"

Annie shrugged. "I visited her more when she was in nursery." She lit a menthol. "She loved that place. She couldn't get enough. Making crafts, doing gymnastics, putting on puppet shows with her friends.

It's heaven for a kid that age. I loved watching her. But even back then, I just had all of these jobs. I mean, different jobs than now, but just as many. I sleep, wake up, drive to work, work all day, drive back home, collapse, and then just sit and recover. I would have liked to have visited her more. I just didn't have time. I didn't have the energy. At the end of the day, coming home, I would just be too exhausted."

Annie took a drag from the cigarette. She was so angry, so furious and disgruntled, a feeling that had been simmering in her the past few days. All of the times she'd had to watch that clip of her stealing the baby.

"As a parent you're supposed to do what's best for your child," Annie said, glaring at the rug. "That's what galls me, is just the unfairness. She knows better than this. She knows right from wrong. She's educated. She had all the benefits of growing up in the system. She knew exactly what she'd be depriving that child of when she did what she did."

★ ★ ★

Deon came out of the stairwell carrying a paper bag full of groceries, favoring his foot with the bunion, which always got aggravated when he wore his oxfords. A detective in horn-rimmed glasses was waiting at the door to the studio with a badge hanging from his neck. His eyes were soulful. Behind him stood an assistant, who was smiling intensely, like a virgin missionary, and for some reason just had this aura of utter incompetence.

"You come here looking for Daniela?" Deon said wearily, turning the key in the door.

Deon brought the detective into the studio. The assistant came too. Deon set the bag down by the fridge as the detective and the assistant scanned the studio, probably looking for signs that the baby had been there. Deon wouldn't have had anywhere to hide a baby. The studio didn't even have a closet. His clothes hung on a wheeled rack over by the shikibuton. His food was stored on a bookcase over by the electric stove. He loved living in a single open space. The studio was on the top story of a converted warehouse, with a cement floor and a vaulted ceiling and rough old brick walls, and had plenty of room for all of his toys, the astronomy telescope he'd been using to observe the stars, the tatami mat by the radiator where he'd been practicing meditation, the brewing kit he'd been tinkering with over by the boiler, the didgeridoo and the steelpan he'd been trying to learn how to play. Sunlight poured through the massive windows overlooking the river below. The center of the studio was occupied by his latest work, a gigantic figurative sculpture made of welded chains, which was surrounded by a sprawl of tools, band saws and tin snips and chipping hammers and a drafting table cluttered with sketches of past projects.

The assistant asked to use the bathroom, probably to make sure nobody was hiding in there.

"Jiggle the handle a little after you flush," Deon called.

"You're an artist?" the detective said, inspecting the fume hood on the ceiling.

"Always have been. I can still remember being brought a ball of clay for the first time back in nursery. That feeling of the clay in my hands. Being able to mash it up, squeeze it, flatten it, roll it. To make shapes. I've had a good long career. Pieces commissioned all over the country."

The detective crouched to examine a ukulele.

Deon said, "Being an artist is a time-consuming business. Demands all of your attention. Your every waking moment. I'm grateful for having gotten the opportunity though. That's the best you can hope for in this life, I think. To have a purpose. To get to contribute. Guess you'd understand."

"I'm just a cop. I don't have any artistic ability," the detective said.

"Oh, investigating must require some creativity too. You want a drink?" Deon said.

"How long have you been separated from Annie?"

Deon twisted the cap off of a bottle of kombucha. "We divorced while she was still pregnant."

"Daniela is your only child?"

"That's correct."

"When was the last time you saw her?"

"Many years ago."

"How many?"

"I suppose that would have been when she graduated from college."

"How often did you visit her back then?"

"Not much at all."

"You weren't close when she was young?"

Deon smiled. "You know how kids are. Parents are just a nuisance." He drank some kombucha. "I went to visit her once at the academy. She was still young then. I tried talking to her some, but she just looked bored. She'd hardly answer my questions, just say yes, no, uh-huh. She kept looking at the door. Finally she asked if she could go play. I stood at the windows and watched her running around out there with a huge group of kids, shooting squirt guns, laughing and yelling. She was happy there. She had great friends. She had so much fun. I didn't want to bother her. I didn't come around much after that. I was busy with the sculptures anyway."

Deon gazed at the sculpture. He was suddenly overcome with emotion, with helplessness and distress, as all of the sadness of the past few days hit him. All of the times he'd had to watch that clip of her taking the baby.

"I was proud of her," Deon said, on the verge of crying. "As a parent that's all you want for your child. She found a calling. She had a vocation. She was good at what she did. I don't know why she would have thrown all of that away for a baby. I just don't."

★ ★ ★

Mariela had just come down from the pole, striding back through the curtains, walking into the dressing room, where the lights above the mirrors had a soft white glow. Claire was waiting there. Claire looked strangely nervous.

"There's a cop asking for you at the bar," Claire said.

Mariela drank a cone of water from the machine.

"You want me to cover for you, say that you left, got sick or something?" Claire said.

Mariela dropped the crumpled cone into the trash can.

"I know why he's here," Mariela said.

"I'll lie if you want," Claire said.

"He's not here for me," Mariela said.

Mariela had seen him come into the club. She had been inverted, her legs wrapped tight around the pole with her hair hanging down toward the stage, that moment that the lights had caught his eyes in the door. A beautiful detective with a badge hanging from his neck by a chain. Leaving the dressing room, she strolled barefoot out into the club, past the clusters of patrons chatting in the shadowy booths around the stage, silhouettes holding fluorescent cocktails under the black lights. She had been working in the club less than a year. She liked the feeling of power that she got walking through the crowd. All eyes on her. The detective had a sidekick, she realized now, sitting there next to him. The sidekick looked like a total milquetoast. He was sipping a cream soda. He had probably never been laid. Mariela sat down next to the detective in the neon haze at the bar.

"You see that chick coming out to dance?" Mariela said.

The detective glanced at the stage.

"I'm back on again after her song is up. You've got until then. Ask what you want."

Claire climbed onto the pole as the song began to play, a fusion of bebop and techno with an almost noir feel.

"I'm looking for Daniela Ndukwe," the detective said.

"I haven't seen that chick in years," Mariela said.

"You were in nursery with her though."

"Yeah."

"You were at academy with her too."

"Yeah."

"You were friends with her there."

"Frenemies," Mariela said.

The detective watched her motion at the bartenders for a drink.

"Emphasis on the enemies," Mariela said.

Hunter came over.

"You can't drink while you're working," Hunter said.

"Now isn't a good time to say no to me," Mariela said.

Hunter poured her a glass of mescal.

"You heard about the kidnapping?" the detective said.

Mariela drank a swig of the mescal, then set the glass onto the bar, nodding.

"We already went by your apartment. We're going to have a patrol car stationed outside of your building in case she tries to come by. We could use your assistance here."

"She wouldn't come to me for help," Mariela said.

"Then who would she go to?" the detective said.

Claire twirled around the pole as the tint of the lights changed from purple to scarlet to orange.

"The chick is selfish," Mariela said. "She's a planner. She's a schemer. And she always puts herself first. I can't even tell you how many times that she used me to get ahead. We were the same class, born a week apart, grew up in neighboring cribs. Learned how to crawl together, learned how to talk together. Slept in the same bunk in nursery, once we were old enough to have beds. Lived in the same hallway in academy, once we were old enough to get rooms. We were inseparable. And we were charming. We were friends with everybody. We ran that social scene." She glanced over at the detective. "I don't know if you have friends like that from the system. Maybe you know what it's like. To be that close with somebody." She turned back toward the mirror behind the bar. "I was her first kiss. On the weekends we used to have sleepovers in the dorms. We would mess around sometimes after the other kids fell asleep."

"Daniela's bi?"

"I don't know if you need to put a label on it. We experimented sometimes. We were curious," Mariela said.

Claire slid down the pole with a look of desire as the beat of the song changed tempos.

"We were competitive too. With everybody, but especially with each other. We were like rivals. I've never had another relationship that intense. I don't know how to describe it. We were that way even when we fooled around, like we were both trying to outdo each other. Each trying to be the better kisser, to turn the other one on more. We were that way about grades, that way about extracurriculars, about sports and choir. And especially about other friends." The mescal shimmered in the glass. "We had a falling-out right before graduation. A pretty bad fight. Afterward we drifted apart." Mariela frowned. "We were headed in different directions anyway. I didn't even apply to college. I wasn't like her. She had always wanted to have some impressive job. I just wanted to be able to have adventures. To travel. I did, too. I went straight from graduation to an airplane. Picked up jobs here and there for cash. I've been all over the planet. Caribbean, Africa, Europe, Asia."

"How long have you been back?"

"I only came home to have a baby. I got knocked up a couple years ago. Thailand. Some college kid in a hostel."

"You decided against having an abortion?"

"Goddamn, you cops are nosey," Mariela exclaimed, reaching for the mescal, shooting the detective a look. "I'm a vegan. I don't even eat chicken eggs. I couldn't kill a human embryo. I'd feel guilty." She drank another swig. "Jada's her name. A cute kid. She's one now. Learning to walk." She held the glass. "I'm saving up to go back overseas. I don't know where next. I just want someplace new. Brazil, maybe." She downed the rest of the shot, swallowed, and then put down the glass again. "Life is about experiences. I think so, at least. I was never like her. Daniela, I mean. I didn't care about careers. Success didn't matter to me. I just wanted to experience as much as possible. Meet amazing people. See the world."

She glanced over at the detective again, then hesitated when she saw his expression, the way that his mouth had tightened. That desperate look in his eyes. This wasn't just a job for him, she realized. He actually cared. He was worried.

"She's been missing for almost a week. We've got roadblocks on every highway out of the District. Her car hasn't been seen once. The trail is going cold. We're running out of time. I need you to help me, Mariela. Please, I've seen what can happen to kids out there," the detective said.

Mariela scowled at the mirror as the lights turned blue.

"I'd do anything for her. I don't know why. After all of these years. After everything she did to me. I hate that it's true. I hate it. But it's true. The moment her face popped up on the news, I knew. I've traveled all over the globe, I've met all kinds of people, and to me she's still the most important person in the world," Mariela said.

Claire sank onto the stage in a split. The thumping beat of the song was fading. Mariela stood.

"But she's not going to come to me for help. And you might as well take down those roadblocks. Knowing her, she's already gone," Mariela said.

★ ★ ★

Robbie had never met the fugitive, but she had seen all of the newscasts and heard all of the podcasts and read all of the articles online, and she had been following the story all week with a sense of pleasurable suspense, munching on popcorn at night while browsing the internet for the latest reports, the way she had used to eat popcorn while watching television shows about outlaws as a child. She was withered and wrinkled with an arthritic neck and hands atrophied from carpal tunnel, a retired psychologist who had been born in the time before nurseries and academies, back before family had meant nation, back when family had meant relatives, when people had still tended to get married more often than not, and when the people who wanted children had still had time to raise children at home. She had grown up in a modest colonial with finger paintings magneted to the fridge, raised by a pair of shy accountants, who had not been perfect, who had occasionally criticized her opinions without invitation, who had sometimes made jokes at her expense, who had often failed to change the burned-out light bulb in her bedroom in a timely fashion, who had habitually forgotten to schedule her checkups at the dentist and the optometrist and the pediatrician, who had routinely brought home bags of takeout for supper despite her many requests for home-made meals, who had worn clothing that had clearly embarrassed her to public events, but who had tried, who had genuinely tried, and who had always treated her with kindness and patience and love. She knew the statistics, knew how many psychological issues could be traced back to the parents, knew how many children in those years had suffered from abuse and neglect and malnutrition, but still, she had loved living with her parents, and to her the idea of being raised in an institution had always seemed horrible. She had never given birth to any children personally, and to her friends she pretended to support the childcare system without reservation, but in her heart she believed that a child belonged with its parents. Daniela Ndukwe was a heroic figure to her, like a benevolent hacker or a principled bandit. Robbie had been secretly thrilled by her crime. Robbie had been rooting for her to escape. And yet, when she found the baby blue sedan abandoned in the empty field down the road where she liked to walk sometimes on the weekend to clear her mind, and she realized that both the rust spot the shape of a star and the numbers on the license plate matched the description of the vehicle that the fugitive had been driving, she hesitated only a moment before calling the police. After hanging up she was overcome by a sickening sense of regret. She couldn't explain why she had called the police instead of just walking away, pretending she had never seen it, pretending she had never been there. She had felt a sense of duty. She had never broken a law before. Or maybe that wasn't the reason, when she thought about it honestly. Maybe she had just had an overwhelming urge to be part of the drama.

A detective in a trench coat and horn-rimmed glasses soon arrived at the scene, escorted by an assistant and a pair of officers. The detective asked her some questions before ordering her to stand aside. Robbie watched with a sense of excitement, almost ashamed of how special she felt, getting to witness part of the investigation in person. The sedan had been abandoned deep in the field, in dewy grass that stood as high as the wheel wells. Snapping on a pair of disposable gloves, the detective searched the car, taking note of a thermos of cold coffee in the cupholder, a can of pepper spray in the glove compartment, a shopping bag full of rumpled clothing on the floor mat, a casino token lying on the dashboard, a squash racket sitting on the backseat, and an electric hair clipper in the trunk. The detective muttered. Then the detective stepped away from the car, glancing around the empty field, frowning now, looking perplexed.

"I can feel how close we're getting," the assistant said, nodding with conviction.

"Of all of the places, why leave the car here?" the detective murmured.

The detective turned with a look of horror at the sound of a train blowing a whistle in the woods beyond the field.

★ ★ ★

She rode the train through Appalachia, past misty shacks, past foggy huts, watching damp mining towns blur past from the chilly depths of an empty boxcar, periodically feeding the baby, that perfect beautiful child, who loved to be held, who loved to be bounced, who never fussed or cried, just smiled and babbled happily, grasping at her cheeks with his tiny fingers. She played peekaboo with him as the train clattered past a granite quarry. She played pattycake with him as the train flew over a rusted bridge. As the train crawled past the clanging signals at a crossing, the child spit up all over her hoodie, and her heart burst with happiness. When darkness fell she drifted off to sleep with the child wrapped against her chest in the cotton sling she had taken from the nursery, and later that night the child awoke her with a hungry squeal, and waking to find the child there in her arms was the most glorious experience of her life. Afraid of being recognized, she had buzzed her hair before abandoning the sedan, and the air was frigid on her scalp as she fed the child in the moonlight, but when the sun rose in the morning the air turned so warm and humid that she zipped off her hoodie, cradling the child in her lap as viny trees flew past the doors. Next to her in the boxcar she had a canvas rucksack full of trail mix and granola bars and bottles of water, stolen diapers and pacifiers and formula and a baby bottle with a rubber nipple, a flashlight, and a roll of toilet paper for emergencies. She also had a navigator, a handheld digital device that had been designed for hiking, which she had bought with cash to avoid being tracked. She used the navigator to follow the progress of the train, watching the blinking icon travel south. As the train screeched to a halt in a rail yard in Miami, she climbed down from the boxcar, wearing a running shirt and jogging shorts and a brand-new pair of hiking boots. She had the child wrapped to her stomach with the sling, carrying him where she had carried him when she was pregnant, with her hoodie zipped over the bulge, the bulge making her look pregnant again. Crouching in the shadows of a shipping container at the edge of the rail yard, she fed the child some formula, got him sucking on a pacifier, waited until he had fallen asleep, zipped her hoodie to her throat, and slipped on a pair of shades, and then she walked into the city, strolling down the sidewalk with an expression of calm, feeling tense and alert. She hailed a taxi at a hotel, praying that the child wouldn't babble or cry when he woke, but the child didn't wake once, sleeping through the entire ride, sucking peacefully on the pacifier. The taxi dropped her off at the dilapidated headquarters of a company that rented water-craft on the edge of a swamp, where she bought an airboat from a leathery man in snakeskin boots and a straw fedora. She paid in cash. The airboat was a single-seater with a gleaming propeller and a shining hull. The child was stirring. She dropped the rucksack onto the deck, anxious to get moving, eyeing the components that she knew from instructional videos online, the battery and the ignition and the steering rod. As the man was loading an extra jerrican of fuel into the airboat the child suddenly spit out the pacifier and made a noise beneath the hoodie, a curious shriek, and the man heard, swiveling, and he looked at her, and she looked at him, and in that moment she understood that he had just realized who she was, and that after all of her planning now her fate was going to be up to him, a stranger, and if she was found, it would be because he had decided to report her, and if she wasn't found, it would be because he had decided to help her. The expression on his face was blank and indecipherable. She zipped off the hoodie. The engine of the airboat came to life with a roar. She drove the airboat into the Everglades, where she had been told that there was a group of people in hiding, parents and children, living in secrecy.

Daniela felt a sense of relief once she was alone with the child again, gliding across the water under a sunny sky. She used the navigator to travel deep into the wetlands, steering the airboat along rivers and across ponds, past dragonflies flitting between lily pads, colorful orchids sprouting on oak trees, turtles clambering onto a log, otters floating in a creek, bobbing cattails, swaying rushes, a dark alligator with a round snout sunning on a rock, a beige crocodile with a pointed snout swimming in the sawgrass, bright pink flamingos soaring through the sky over a vast marsh. By twilight she and the child had reached the coordinates she had been given, a flooded grove of giant cypress trees with ghostly clumps of moss hanging from the branches. In every direction, that was all that she could see from the airboat, was water and sky and cypress trees. She had been instructed that the people who lived out there would meet her that night at those coordinates, so she waited, sitting there with her legs crossed, cradling the child in her lap. She had been told that she would know that an approaching boat was friendly if the people aboard held oil lanterns, but other than a crescent moon and the glittering stars above the canopy of the trees, all night the grove was dark, and no other boats appeared. She heard only chirping frogs, and the eerie shrieking of cranes nearby, and the frightening wails of distant loons. Water occasionally rippled against the hull of the airboat. Nobody came. At daybreak she fed the child and gave the child a change of diapers, taking some time to tickle him until he laughed, bouncing him on her knees, nuzzling him with her nose, trying to comfort the child, afraid he might somehow be able to sense her growing feeling of dread. That morning and the next she topped off the airboat with fuel from the jerrican, and then she drove the airboat out of the grove of cypress trees to explore the wetlands nearby, searching for some sign of the people who lived there. Both days she found nothing. Both nights she waited in the grove of cypress trees, at the exact coordinates she had been given, and no boats came, no oil lanterns appeared, and as the sun rose that next morning she realized finally that the people who lived out there must have never been told that she was coming, if there were truly any people living out there at all. She believed that there were, she needed to believe it, but now she understood the true situation. The commune wasn't going to find her. She would have to find the commune. The battery in the navigator had died. With a sense of desperation she drove the airboat out of the grove of cypress trees to begin searching again, and the airboat immediately ran out of fuel, the engine sputtered into silence, the propeller gradually spun out, and the airboat glided to a standstill at the center of a shallow marsh. The jerrican was empty. For a full day she sat motionless on the airboat, in despair, just helpless, fighting the urge to cry, using her back to shade the child from the beating sun, until her neck was sunburned and her ears were sunburned and her arms were sunburned and she was so thirsty that her tongue was sticking to her mouth and her lips were cracking, and then she knew that she had to keep searching, or else she would die and the child would die.

The water was black and warm and came to her knees, soaking her hiking boots. With the child wrapped tight against her chest, she waded to the shore of the nearest island as night fell across the scattered pine trees. Switching on the flashlight from the rucksack, she hiked across the island, keeping watch for some sign of human habitation, until finally the child began to fuss and she was too exhausted to keep walking, and then she sat against a stump, turning the flashlight off to conserve the battery. Her hiking boots were still wet. As her eyes adjusted to the darkness her heart leapt as she became aware of lights nearby, but then her heart fell again as she realized that the lights weren't of human origin. Neon green foxfire, a ruffled fungus glowing faintly on the trunk of a toppled tree just ahead of her. Pale yellow fireflies, a twinkling cluster drifting through the reeds along the banks of a stream far beyond her. Those were the only lights she saw that night. She dozed off. She barely slept. Whenever a twig snapped in the darkness she jolted awake again, shining the flashlight at the sound, bracing for an alligator or a crocodile, but wherever she pointed the flashlight there was nothing there. When dawn came she kept walking, ducking glittering spiderwebs, maneuvering cautiously through dense thickets, squeezing carefully through thorny briars, using fallen branches to plumb the depth of murky water, wading across shallow brooks to cross between islands, laying the child onto a stump or some grass for a change of diapers, then swaddling the child in the sling again. The next two nights she saw no lights at all. By then she was out of trail mix and granola bars and was down to a single bottle of water, and the battery in the flashlight was dead. She fed the child in the darkness. Without a flashlight the darkness terrified her. She talked to the child. She sang to the child. The child grasped at her chin. She felt delirious. At sunrise after changing another diaper for the child she staggered off of the dirt and kept going. While she walked she remembered her life. She had been bathed every day in nursery, and had bathed once a day at academy, and all of her life had lived indoors, in tidy rooms with dusted furniture and vacuumed floors, wearing freshly clean clothing perfumed with scented detergents and fabric softeners. She had never been dirty before, not truly dirty, not like that, with her arms streaked with dust and her fingers spattered with mud, the rims of her nails crusted with soil, her shirt reeking of sweat, burs clinging to her shorts, her thighs scratched, her shins scraped, her hiking boots caked with muck. She was afraid to eat any of the flowers or berries she saw. Mosquitoes hummed around her in a swarm, and she swatted at the air around the child to protect his flesh, and let the mosquitoes bite her instead. Her stomach gurgled painfully. Her lips tasted like blood. That afternoon as she came to the tip of a grassy island she saw what looked like a bright red tub of coffee grounds caught in the roots of the mangrove trees across a lagoon.

The sign that other humans had been there gave her a burst of hope, so intense that she actually grunted with relief, but the sight worried her, too. She was afraid that she might be hallucinating, because the coffee was the same brand that she drank back home. But no matter how long that she stared, the tub was still there, floating in the roots of the mangrove trees. Her arms felt weak. Her legs were quivering. The only way to get to the island with the mangrove trees would be to cross the lagoon. The water was bright and clear. She didn't see any animals nearby, not even insects. The lagoon was strangely quiet. She took the child out of the sling, holding the child against her chest, and then she walked out into the water. Her hiking boots filled as the water reached her ankles. She waded deeper into the lagoon, and the water rose to her thighs, then soaked her shorts, then rose to her belly, then soaked her shirt, then rose to her shoulders, until finally she was holding the child above her head with the water lapping against her throat. The silty bottom of the lagoon shifted beneath her feet with every tentative step that she took, terrified of losing balance, terrified of tipping over, of dropping the child into the water. She heard the child gurgle happily in her hands. She kept her eyes focused on the mangrove trees. Sunlight flashed across the ripples in the water. She was halfway across the lagoon when she felt something powerful knock against her under the water, a massive animal, and she jerked away from the movement with her heart beating wildly, twisting around in fear, but when she looked down into the water instead of the scaly body of a crocodile or an alligator she saw a pair of manatees, a gigantic adult speckled with algae and a beautiful calf with smooth skin, flippers gently paddling, tails lightly pulsing, lolling in the water around her, gazing at her with beady eyes, and in that moment, holding her infant above her head in the middle of a lagoon in the wilderness as a pair of manatees circled her, a parent and a child, she felt such a kinship with every animal on the planet that she was nearly overcome. Then the manatees drifted off into the lagoon, and she and the child were alone again.

The water around the mangrove trees was shallow enough that she could wrap the child in the sling again. The sun was setting. The tub was real. She peeled back the lid. The plastic still smelled like grounds, but all the coffee was gone. Dropping the tub back into the water, she squeezed through the mangrove trees onto the island in the lagoon, sloshing back onto land. She stood there. Water dripped from her fingertips. Water trickled down her legs. She didn't see any other signs of people. She swayed, feeling dizzy, and then she heard the child crying, and she looked down and saw the child smiling at her, and she realized that the child who was crying wasn't hers. She glanced up. She looked around. Palm trees. Purple sky. She followed the sound of the crying, shuffling through the palm trees, but then the crying went silent, and after that the island was quiet again. Feeling faint, she stumbled, leaning against a tree, head bent, breathing hard. A breeze blew softly. Dusk was falling, and through the trunks of the trees ahead she saw a light like golden torches. She staggered into a clearing where a pair of oil lanterns sat in the windows of a couple of rickety houseboats, anchored in a swampy cove next to a weathered shanty on wooden stilts. She could smell melting butter. She collapsed into the dirt.

She had never wanted a child. As an adult when she had seen children on outings standing in orderly lines at the entrances to museums and memorials, had passed the shining windows of nurseries where the staff were blowing bubbles with the children, had passed the fenced courtyards of academies where the staff were playing croquet with the children, she had never felt any form of desire. Getting pregnant had felt like a burden, like a misfortune, like growing a tumor, like having a tapeworm, being invaded by a foreign body that would leech the strength and the health and the nutrients from her body until finally getting removed. She had bought a customized wall calendar with landscape photos of her favorite beaches, counting down the days until her body would be hers again, when she could eat her favorite foods again, when she could wear her favorite outfits again, when she could have a normal workout routine again, when she could have a normal sex life again, when she could reach to shave her legs again, when she wouldn't have to literally waddle into the conference room for meetings, when she could sleep through the night without having to get up to pee. All of the parties she'd missed because of nausea and hot flashes. All of the parties she'd missed because of cramps and swollen feet. The heartburn and the brain fog. Her friends had planned a celebration for her afterward, sangria and dancing at her favorite bar, once the birth was finally over. But instead of feeling happy as her friends had chatted around her, she had sat there feeling bewilderingly lonely. How to explain that moment at the hospital, drenched in sweat, wearing a gown, still panting from the final push, the moment that she had first caught a glimpse of the child, a chubby newborn with a dark shock of hair and the dorkiest smile imaginable, when she had suddenly been struck by a savage and terrible sense of love. She had wanted to rip the child from the arms of the doctor, but then the doctor had turned, and the child had been gone.

She dreamed of that night again, she cried out from the nightmare, and when she awoke she drank cold pure water from a jar, gratefully, gulping, and then the jar was taken away from her and with water still dripping from her nose and her chin she reached for the child who had been brought to her where she lay on the cot in the creaking shanty, and she held the child in her arms, clutching him greedily, kissing his head, stroking his cheeks, whispering, "You're mine, baby, all mine."

Appearance

We sit in the parking lot and we wait.

We do not drive what you would expect. Some kind of van would be best, or a truck maybe—something dark-colored—but what my grandfather has is a white sedan.

Lights above the bar's back door cast yellow squares onto the cement. The back door is what separates the bar's kitchen from the bar's garbage. It is a metal door and from the outside has no handles.

We can take only one, sometimes two, per trip. My grandfather's trunk has its limits.

We do not listen to the radio.

Our problem is a problem of borders. Our house was built at the northern border of our property, and our property sits at the northern border of our town. Our town itself is at the northern border of our state—Rhode Island—which means that when we look north from the window above our microwave, all we see are borders, piled on top of each other, sharing the same space.

The cooks take turns throughout the night carrying loads of trash out to the garbage bin. Already a cook with dark dreads has taken his turn, and also Ryan Williams, who goes to my school, in the grade above me, and also is a cook. We are waiting for the Unwanted, who, like all of the Unwanted, we know will have skin so pale that the skin will be nearly transparent, and hair as white as his skin. The bar hired him several weeks ago. The bar's owner would not reason with my grandfather.

Understand that I know the proper terms for them. I know the terms used for them on podcasts and television. What I use are the terms my grandfather prefers—Unwanted, Squatters, Trespassers, Spares—the terms we hear at the supermarket, at the hardware store, on the porches of our neighbors. Unwanted can be both singular and plural. I've heard it used both ways.

The back door opens. A cook has shoved the door open with his butt, bent over dragging a pair of trash bags backward toward the garbage bin. Stepping between the squares of light on the cement, the cook props the door open with the brick the cooks keep there.

I'm wearing the white t-shirt of my high school's chess club, dark athletic shorts, and plastic sandals. It is December, but I am always warm. Even wearing only this, I am sweating. It is all the fat on me. I like to sit how my grandfather sits—with his hands on his stomach, the fingers of his hands interlocking—but my hands are so fat that I have trouble fitting my fingers together. When it happened, the Appearance, I was four years old. The Unwanted have been here with us for thirteen years, so now my age is seventeen.

Brett, get out of the car, my grandfather says, and then I know this cook's our man.

★ ★ ★

We have had the misfortune of taking three of them.

Two of them—the two Unwanted who stepped out after the cook on trash duty, one holding a lighter, the other carrying cigarettes— are in our trunk. It appears the bar had made some even newer hires. We duct-taped their wrists and ankles, then gagged them with their aprons.

The other cook is in our backseat.

He has spit out the apron we gagged him with.

Please, my name is Zachary, he says.

His hair is buzzed to the scalp—a style preferred by many Unwanted, as the color of their hair is one of the things that sets them apart. Beneath the skin of his face, pale blue veins are visible, the veins charting different territories on his forehead, his temples, his cheeks. This is the other thing that sets apart the Unwanted—those of us who were here before the Appearance, what's beneath our skin is hidden. The Unwanted often wear makeup, to make their skin more opaque, but Zachary, sprawled across our backseat, is not wearing makeup.

The other two had been.

Outside the stars appear in their various constellations.

My fingers are coated with the makeup from their throats.

My grandfather would be displeased if he knew I thought of this Unwanted as a Zachary. Names are something one is given when one is born, my grandfather has said. The Unwanted were never born, he says, so it is unnatural for them to take names. When my grandfather does speak to an Unwanted, he uses either You or Spare.

My grandfather wears old blue jeans, his work shirt from his job at the plant, and a dark cardigan unbuttoned over the work shirt. He prefers to wear his work shirt when we come for the Unwanted, as some kind of statement. He wears the cardigan, however, to cover the Edward stitched above the work shirt's breast pocket. He prefers the Unwanted not know his name.

Where are you taking me, Zachary says. I must finish my shift.

Brett, put the apron back in that Spare.

I can't reach it, I say.

The fields that we're passing now are some of the fields where the Unwanted first appeared thirteen years ago. My school, Zachary's bar, are both at our town's center. We are moving from our town's center toward the outskirts, toward our house.

I do not remember the Appearance. Some of the kids in my grade remember where they were, what they were doing, when they first heard. I don't remember the day at all.

What I do remember is a few years later, when I was seven, the day I heard my grandfather had been fired. Where I was, what I was doing, when I heard my grandfather had been fired, was herding stray cats into our shed. I liked to bring them there, keep them locked inside until they would start fighting. It wasn't my grandfather who told me he had been fired. A friend told me as he helped me herd the cats with sticks. Your grandpa isn't on vacation, my friend said. Your grandpa got fired, just like my dad.

My grandfather had been telling me he'd been taking sick days.

He'd been sitting in our kitchen, drinking juice and staring out the window, for a week.

Please, tonight I must take my daughter to her dance practice, Zachary says. My wife, she cannot drive.

Zachary's English is proficient—better than most Unwanted's.

I've seen videos online of the day of the Appearance. Ours was not the only state affected—most of the Heartland was, parts of the Southwest, some of the Northwest, most of New England. In Rhode Island, only eight or nine thousand Unwanted appeared. As everywhere else, they appeared out of nowhere, in fields, where before there had been nothing. None of them speaking English. None of them speaking anything. Some of them old, others only children, all of them naked. All of them walking in from the fields toward the lights of the nearest town.

Our state is not an island.

In the videos, the hospitals and the police stations are crowded with Unwanted.

Nobody knew what to do with them. The Unwanted could not tell us where they had come from, so we could not send them back.

Even now, now that many of them can speak English, the Unwanted will not say. If they remember anything from before the Appearance, they are not telling us.

Brett, my grandfather says, because Zachary is still talking.

Zachary's apron is on the floor of the sedan behind my grandfather's seat.

Zachary's wrists and ankles are still taped.

I am still sweating.

I lean over the gearshift and reach for Zachary's apron. Still I cannot reach it.

Use your shirt, my grandfather says.

I do not like to take off my shirt except for when I am alone. I cannot describe what it is like to be both fat and in high school.

The only thing worse is to be in high school and an Unwanted.

Zachary says, Please, if you want money, I have—

Zachary is gagged with my t-shirt.

My high school is eighth grade through twelfth grade. A few of the eighth-graders—born the year after the Appearance—appear to be at least half Unwanted, if not fully. Skin somewhat transparent, hair as white as their skin. But they were born here in Rhode Island, are citizens of the United States, and so the school's administrators cannot have them deported.

Rhode Island is still the only state where it is illegal to be an Unwanted. After my grandfather was fired, he fought alongside the other unemployed who brought the case to state courts. My friend, herding a straggling black cat into the shed, said my grandfather and his father had not been fired for being poor workers. They had been fired, he said, because their jobs had been taken.

Spares will work for anything, my friend said. Like a dollar an hour. Those *fuckers*.

My friend had often cursed in this way—emphasis always on the curse word, as if by its very nature it did not already have it.

Rhode Island was the only state to load the Unwanted onto buses and deport them to other states, but ours was not the only state affected. The job shortages are everywhere. In other states, factories are often fully staffed by Unwanted. The grocery stores. The gas stations. The kitchens of restaurants and bars. Even in our state, the law against them is not enough. They come anyway, taking the jobs that require no paperwork, no college or even high school diploma. The state does not have the money it would take to deport all of them.

A popular metal band is fronted by an Unwanted—the lyrics to her songs are often about her experience as an Unwanted, often critical of the ways they have been treated.

She does not understand.

We had not known they were coming.

I can only listen to her songs when my grandfather is out looking for work. And her band cannot come to Rhode Island, when her band is on tour.

First word they taught me was broom / didn't know where to put us, gave us vacant rooms / at Little Rock's airport hotels / had us sweeping and mopping to cover our bills.

In other states, the Unwanted were treated less charitably.

I have seen videos online I cannot even talk about.

Our sedan blows past our mailbox and our driveway and our house beyond it. The windows of our house are dark. Beyond it, our empty shed.

Zachary has spit out my t-shirt.

What did you do with Jamie and Paul? Zachary says. After you put me in the car—what did you do to them? Did you hurt them?

They're coming with us, my grandfather says. Brett, put the shirt back in.

Zachary has white stubble on his cheeks and his jaw. His eyes are a dark brown color. I have never before seen an Unwanted with brown eyes. Normally their irises are a pale blue, so pale that the irises may as well just be white.

I put the t-shirt back in.

We follow the road past more fields toward the border station. The border station is lit by lights that shoot cones of yellow into the sky. Before my grandfather pulls up to the border agent's booth, he has me roll Zachary onto the floor of the sedan. He tosses his cardigan over Zachary's head, then some unfolded maps over Zachary's body.

What we are doing is illegal. But in the same way that law enforcement in our state is willing to pretend that Unwanted are not living and working within the borders of Rhode Island, law enforcement is also willing to pretend that those same Unwanted are not sometimes disappearing. As long as we do not make it impossible for them to pretend, law enforcement will leave us be.

It is a matter of keeping them unseen, the Unwanted that we take.

This is why my grandfather prefers to take only one, sometimes two, per trip.

My grandfather's trunk has its limits.

It is easier when they are simply in the trunk.

We pull up to the border agent's booth. My grandfather puts the sedan in park, takes my license, indicates to the border agent that he cannot roll down his window, and then steps out of the sedan. Per my grandfather's instructions, I pretend to be singing along with a song over the radio to mask the sound of Zachary's gagged shouting. Our radio is not on. I am not a gifted singer. My grandfather shuts his door.

I am in here, in the sedan, with Zachary.

Zachary is on the floor under a pile of maps.

Door's closed, I say. Quit yelling.

Zachary quits.

What I want to know is, why even come here? I say to him. I talk through my teeth, without moving my lips, so that if my grandfather looks back over his shoulder he will not see me talking.

Zachary makes a sound.

You could go anywhere. New Hampshire, Vermont, Connecticut. There are lots of legal places.

Zachary makes another sound. My grandfather opens his door, sinks into his seat while shouting goodnight to the border agent, and shuts his door again. The border agent waves us through. My grandfather gives me back my license. We drive north.

Those *fuckers*, my friend said, helping me shut the doors of the shed. Why don't they go back to their own planet?

Like my friend, many believed the Unwanted were aliens who had migrated from some other planet—as if going on a vacation. Others, like our bus driver, believed the Unwanted were beings from another universe in our multiverse, beings who had somehow been taken from their universe and transported to our own. Others believed that hell was full up, and that the Unwanted were excess demons—others that what was full was heaven, and that the Unwanted were excess angels.

But even then, I knew the truth about the Unwanted.

That what they are is only people.

Are you listening to me? my grandfather says. Spare, are you listening?

Zachary makes a sound.

I spent five years in state court getting that law passed to keep you out, my grandfather says. And now they won't enforce it. So I'm going to enforce it. We're going to. Me and my grandson.

Zachary makes a sound, then no more sounds at all.

Our sedan passes the towns of those who live in Massachusetts.

My grandfather prefers to do it outside of Boston.

When my grandfather is driving he cannot sit how he likes—with his hands on his stomach, the fingers of his hands interlocking—but he makes a face that gives one the impression that he is still doing it.

My grandmother knows something of migrations, wherever she is—she left my grandfather when my mother was still only a child.

My grandfather's cheeks and jaw are spotted with white stubble.

I think this is what bothers him most about aging—that in some ways he is beginning to look like them.

I have always lived with my grandfather—my mother knows something of migrations.

And not even my mother knew the name of my father.

We park the sedan in the graveyard my grandfather prefers, on the outskirts of Boston, just beyond the city limits.

My grandfather puts his arms back into his cardigan, leaves the cardigan unbuttoned over his work shirt. We get out of the sedan, drag Zachary out of the backseat, then haul Jamie and Paul out of the trunk. Zachary spits out my t-shirt. I do not put it back on.

I take the aprons out of the mouths of Jamie and Paul.

They, like Zachary, have questions.

My grandfather takes out his knife.

Please, my name is Jamie, and—

My grandfather cuts the tape from Jamie's ankles.

You are not welcome in Rhode Island, my grandfather says.

My grandfather cuts the tape from Paul's ankles.

I know what my grandfather does not seem to. That anywhere we leave them will be somewhere they are not from. That they are not welcome here. That even where they are legal, they are still called the Unwanted.

Where are we? Paul says. Please, do not leave us here, my boyfriend is—

My grandfather cuts the tape from Zachary's ankles, saying, You can undo each other's hands after we're gone.

The makeup from Jamie and Paul's throats still coats my fingers. I cannot see it but I can feel it. The graveyard is not lit by any lights. I know that the veins in their throats are more visible than the veins in their faces, where their makeup has not been rubbed off. The moonlight outlines the shapes of the Unwanted, but not much more than that.

We walk back to the sedan.

To answer your question, Zachary shouts at me, because the money is in Rhode Island. And because Rhode Island is my home—just like you live there, I am from there too.

What question? my grandfather says to me.

I do not say a thing.

You are not from there, my grandfather shouts at Zachary. You came there from somewhere far away. Rhode Island belongs to me, and my family, the same as it always has. My grandfather lived there, and his grandfather before him. It does not belong to you.

We get back into the sedan.

I drape my t-shirt over the backseat, because it is still damp from Zachary's saliva.

Our sedan passes the towns of those who live in Massachusetts.

We drive back toward Rhode Island.

What I know about migrations is what I have been taught in school. My grandfather's grandfather did live in Rhode Island, and so did my grandfather's grandfather's grandfather. But our people have not always lived here. Before they came to the United States, they lived in what is now Germany. Before they came to Germany, they lived in what is now Turkey. Before that, somewhere else still.

Before our people lived in the state of Rhode Island, different people lived here—people with darker skin and darker hair—but even they had not lived here forever.

Why the *fuck* did they have to come to our planet? my friend said, peeking with me through the window at the stray cats inside the shed. My dad used to be happy.

But I had thought, *Why* wouldn't *they?*

The strays had not yet been fighting. Not until they got hungry, I told my friend.

He had not wanted to wait. He had begun pounding on the walls of the shed, trying to get the strays to fight.

It had been good to have a friend.

The bigger I had gotten, the fewer I had had.

Understand that I know why my grandfather and I need to deport the Unwanted, if law enforcement will not do it. In school I am in chess club. I understand that two pieces cannot share the same space—that they cannot occupy the same borders. When they do, one must kill the other.

I believe in what we are doing as much as my grandfather. We have a cause, and that has brought us together in a way that many families I know have never been brought. Few Unwanted live within our town limits anymore—we have taken that many of them away. In another year, or maybe two, my grandfather thinks, we will have driven away even the stragglers.

My grandfather's hands are trembling where he holds the steering wheel. It makes him upset to have to do what we have to do.

The border agent waves us through again.

Outside, the stars in their various constellations.

My heart skips a beat.

Goosebumps spread across my skin.

I say my grandfather's name.

What, my grandfather says, and then he sees them too—in the fields along the road, the shapes of people moving.

Then we see them, not along the road, but stepping into it.

★ ★ ★

No, my grandfather whispers.

He brakes the sedan, taking it from thirty to fifteen to five mph.

And then our car is stopped.

Our headlights cast cones of yellow onto the road. Beyond our headlights, people with transparent skin and white hair are coming from the fields. They are crossing the road in couples, in clusters of eight or nine. Some of them have veins so dark that the veins are almost purple. They are rubbing their arms, trying to warm themselves. Some of them have mud on their feet. Some of them have cuts on their feet. All of them are naked.

My grandfather says, I don't—

I do not say a thing.

Through our rear windshield, I see more of them crossing the road behind us, lit red by the lights of our brakes.

Is this what it looked like before? I say.

My grandfather does not speak. He only nods his head, and even then just once.

All of our work, he says. For nothing.

I do not remember the Appearance thirteen years ago, but I know this Appearance I will not forget.

This is where I was, I think. *This is what I was doing.*

A woman carrying a baby stops in the road. A man as fat as me stops there with her, and then another woman. They look toward the lights of our town beyond the fields, and then toward the lights that are closer to them—the lights of our sedan.

Trying to choose.

Then they are walking toward us.

My grandfather's hands are trembling as he locks the doors. The Unwanted are walking toward our sedan, reaching for our headlights, stepping into our headlights, as the baby cries and cries. My grandfather is shouting at them through the windshield to move, shouting because they are blocking our car. If we drive away, we will have to drive straight through them. They are standing at our headlights, and my grandfather is shouting move, and I am still sweating, but I am not afraid. I am not afraid, because our sedan has borders that cannot be crossed, doors that cannot be opened, doors locked from the inside. In here, inside of it, I feel almost as if we were in our own little world.

Lost Souls

Praise be to Yahweh, and to Allah, and to Buddha, and to Vishnu, and to Shiva, and to Brahma, and to Amaterasu, and to Jesus, and whoever else might hear our plea!

★ ★ ★

Naomi was working at the hospital the day that the empty bodies began being born. She was a nurse in the neonatal unit. The rookie. She had graduated only just the year before. Wildfires were raging in the mountains beyond the valley, and dark clouds of smoke had blown into the city, casting a spooky haze over the resorts and the casinos. Naomi had just clocked in for the day when the first infant was rushed into the neonatal unit. A pudgy pink-skinned newborn with bright blue eyes. The child hadn't been born prematurely. The child technically wasn't even ill. Its pulse was good, its respiration was normal, its temperature was fine. And yet something was clearly wrong. Its automated processes were working—its heart was beating, its lungs were breathing, its fingertips jerked in response to a prick, its pupils dilated in response to a flashlight—and yet the child didn't show any signs of consciousness. It wasn't moving its head. It wasn't moving its arms. It wasn't moving its legs. It wasn't crying. It wasn't squealing. It wasn't cooing. It wasn't moving its body or making any noises at all. Just gazing silently at the ceiling with an eerily blank stare. The physician on duty tried rubbing its back, tried spanking it, tried tickling it, and the baby still didn't respond. And then while the physician was standing there troubleshooting, the baby died. Just like that. It was just there and then it was gone, no pulse, no respiration, beyond resuscitation. Its eyes didn't glaze over. Its eyes didn't even close. Almost like sudden infant death syndrome, Naomi thought, except the baby hadn't been asleep. She was still looking at the dead newborn in confusion when another infant was rushed into the neonatal unit with that same blank stare. Then another. And another. The neonatal unit was chaos. A graveyard. Over half of the children born at the hospital that day exhibited the same symptoms. An utter lack of consciousness. Sudden death. Initially the staff assumed the phenomenon was restricted to that single hospital, but then word began to spread that empty bodies were being born all over Las Vegas. All over Nevada. All over the United States. All over Earth.

Naomi drove home in a state of shock.

"These aren't stillbirths that we're talking about. These are babies that were born alive. Physically all of the babies were perfectly fine. Just empty. Completely unresponsive. Like there was nothing inside," said a gruff voice on the radio.

"And all of the babies died within minutes?"

"I want to be clear that we're not talking about an extinction scenario. There's no reason to panic. Normal, healthy babies were born today, all over the world. Whatever this is, not all newborns seem to be affected."

"But what if the disease spreads?"

"We still don't know enough about the phenomenon to refer to it as a disease."

"Then what else could it be?"

"We don't know yet."

"Is it going to keep happening?"

"We just don't know."

Naomi had found out that she was pregnant the week before.

Ravens were circling in the sky above the entrance to her neighborhood. The street was empty. The sidewalks were deserted. An abandoned tricycle lay upended in a yard, the wheels still spinning. Tad was waiting for her in the driveway of the condo, wearing slippers and a bathrobe that was billowing in the wind.

"Everything's going to be okay," Tad said, wrapping her in a hug.

"I watched thirteen babies die today," Naomi said, and then he led her into the condo, where she got into the bathtub and wept.

Later she sat in a bath towel on the sofa with wet hair and a smoothie and watched the newscasters on every channel try not to have a nervous breakdown on live television.

"I could use a fucking drink," Naomi said.

"I'm sorry," Tad said.

"I just want to get drunk," Naomi said.

"Me too," Tad said.

"You're not pregnant," Naomi said, almost upset.

"I know."

"We still have that bottle of sake in the freezer."

"I know."

"At least one of us should be drunk for this."

"I'm not going to drink if you can't," Tad said, staring straight ahead at the screen, and he was so serious and earnest and simple that she felt the anger fade. She could never manage to get mad at him. She wished that she could have gotten mad at him sometimes. She would have liked to be mad at him. But it would have been like getting mad at a bandage. All he ever wanted to do was help. A baffled public health official in a checkered dress shirt was being interviewed on the television. Rama, the kitten, came wandering into the living room with a mischievous look, and then the whole family was there, Naomi and her husband and her cat and the baby growing in her womb, the baby that now was maybe going to be born only an empty body after all.

And though she would have preferred not to think about the possibility that there was an empty body growing in her womb, she was confronted with the possibility constantly, every moment that she was at work. Empty bodies continued to be born at the hospital that next day and the day after and the rest of the month, and each of the babies was rushed straight into the neonatal unit, and she had to stand there watching each of the babies die. Medications for catatonia had no effect. Electroshock therapy treatments had no effect. Out of desperation, in total secrecy, and despite that the symptoms that the affected babies exhibited weren't truly those of a trance state, the hospital brought in a professional hypnotist, who failed to induce any form of consciousness in the empty bodies. The halls of the maternity ward were filled with the wails of grieving parents. Meanwhile, back out on the streets, in forums on the internet, various parties were busy assigning blame for the epidemic. The environmentalists were convinced that the phenomenon was somehow related to widespread consumption of genetically modified foods, despite a lack of any supporting evidence whatsoever, while the puritans were convinced that the phenomenon was caused by widespread consumption of birth control pills, despite a lack of any supporting evidence whatsoever, and the prohibitionists were convinced that the phenomenon was thanks to widespread consumption of marijuana, despite a lack of any supporting evidence whatsoever, and the fact that humans had been getting blazed for millennia. Naomi wasn't an environmentalist. Naomi wasn't a puritan. Naomi wasn't a prohibitionist. Naomi was a scientist. She believed in logic. She believed in data. And for that reason the phenomenon horrified her. She had never before lived through an epidemic that modern medicine couldn't explain. Most researchers were pursuing studies that assumed that the phenomenon was caused by an infection, perhaps by a novel virus or a mutant bacterium, and yet even the scientists promoting these theories admitted that the theories were flawed, as the affected babies didn't display any of the classic symptoms of a viral or a bacterial infection, not to mention the fact that a virus or a bacterium would have had an origin, would have had to spread, while the phenomenon had appeared simultaneously across the globe. The utter lack of consciousness that the affected newborns exhibited seemed to suggest that the problem was neurological, or perhaps lay with the sensory organs, and yet autopsies showed no abnormalities in the brain tissue of the affected newborns, nor in the eyes nor the ears nor the nerves of the skin. The autopsies showed no abnormalities whatsoever. Science couldn't explain what was happening. The epidemic was claiming hundreds of thousands of lives a day, claimed millions of lives over the course of that first month, and still the best procedure that the medical community had developed for dealing with the phenomenon was just to catalog the deaths. To sit back and watch the babies die. Naomi had never dreaded going to work before, not ever, but the blank stares of the empty bodies terrified her. And yet the most frightening aspect of the phenomenon wasn't the empty bodies. The most frightening aspect of the phenomenon was its numerical precision. In Arizona, just across the border, only a state away, a famous gynecologist at a university medical center thought to turn to statistics. Examining the available data, the gynecologist discovered that the number of empty bodies being born per day was strangely consistent. The number didn't spike or drop the way that mortality rates would during a typical epidemic. The number did slightly fluctuate from day to day, but overall the number was constant. Almost as if the number was being regulated by a sentient force. That alone would have been eerie, but then the gynecologist thought to subtract the total number of empty bodies born each day from the total number of babies who were born daily, thereby obtaining the average number of babies born each day who were healthy and conscious. Then she compared that number, the adjusted global birth rate, with the global death rate. And the rates were equal. The number of humans being born each day now appeared to be approximately equivalent to the number of humans who were dying, stabilizing the global population at just over thirteen billion. Naomi felt a shiver of dread and awe, reading the paper that the gynecologist had published online. A Kabbalist, the gynecologist suggested that the phenomenon might somehow be related to the cycle of reincarnation. It was as if, the gynecologist said, the exploding global population had exceeded the total number of available human souls. The bodies seemed empty because the bodies were empty, just meaty shells, born without souls. Other scientists were quick to point out that correlation didn't imply causation, and that there wasn't necessarily a connection between the birth rate and the death rate. Yet in the absence of any viable alternative explanation, the theory was compellingly logical. It explained the symptoms. It explained the numbers. Within hours the theory had spread across the internet, being hailed as a breakthrough on the news, being discussed as a fact on the forums, becoming the prevalent explanation for the phenomenon worldwide. The Phoenix Hypothesis, the theory soon came to be called, named both for the city where the gynecologist practiced and for the mythological creature of cyclical reincarnation.

And yet to say that the theory was prevalent was not the same as to say that the theory was popular. The scientific community was upset by the implication that there was a spiritual realm, an invisible domain that couldn't possibly fit into the modern understanding of physical cosmology, unless human souls were composed of an as-yet-unobserved material, like dark energy or dark matter. The physics conferences that autumn were sober affairs. Beloved colleagues avoided even speaking to each other. Scuffles broke out between researchers who refused to give the theory serious consideration and researchers attempting to reconcile the theory with quantum fields. And the religious community wasn't any happier. The Christians and the Muslims, while pleased that the theory seemed to prove the existence of the individual immortal soul, seemed upset by the implication that human souls were reincarnated, which would fuck up centuries of theology. The Taoists and the Buddhists, while pleased that the theory seemed to prove the existence of reincarnation, seemed upset by the implication that every human had an individual immortal soul, which would fuck up centuries of theology. The Jains and the Hindus, of course, while delighted both that the theory seemed to prove the existence of the individual immortal soul and that the theory seemed to prove the existence of reincarnation, were distressed by the implication that the cycle of human reincarnation was separate from the souls of other animals, and, like the Sikhs, were profoundly disturbed by the notion that human souls could in any way be finite or quantifiable, which would fuck up centuries of theology. Everybody seemed to have been wrong in some way or another. The internet was haunted by angsty monks and clergy, gloomy specters appearing in interviews for newspapers and vlogs, bemoaning the bewildering state of the world. Even the Scientologists seemed troubled by the implications of the theory, although nobody except the Scientologists knew why the Scientologists would be upset, since nobody except the Scientologists had any clue what the Scientologists believed.

"I mean, if souls are real, and reincarnation is too, how do we *know* that souls don't move back and forth between humans and other animals?" said an acne-scarred janitor in the lobby of the hospital, helping to hang explanatory posters adorned with colorful infographics about the epidemic.

The data seemed conclusive. The phenomenon didn't appear to affect other species of animals. Cattle weren't giving birth to empty calves. Dogs weren't giving birth to empty puppies. Horses weren't giving birth to empty foals. The shortage only seemed to affect humans. And basic logic led to the same conclusion. Considering that humans had spent the past century exterminating countless species of animals from the planet, causing the greatest mass extinction event since the Quaternary, a shortage of souls in newborn babies was presumably only possible if human souls were separate from animal souls. Overall, although the human population had dramatically increased over the past century, the total number of living organisms on the planet had decreased considerably. If humans had been able to share souls with other animals, then there should have been a surplus rather than a shortage. Still, despite the overwhelming evidence to the contrary, an idea soon spread that killing animals might somehow liberate souls that could be used by human babies. Nowhere was this idea as infectious as in America. Within days of the theory being published, there were towns that had been whipped into a frenzy.

Towns out in the country, coal towns and farm towns, where the locals subscribed to mysterious folk religions whose curious belief systems combined elements of born-again evangelicalism, talk-show morality, gun worship, truck worship, bibliophobia, and pagan superstitions about college athletics. Towns where feeling ruled over logic. Towns where hearsay ruled over data. Towns where every nonhuman animal had been slaughtered, the bodies heaped into piles as high as haystacks. Corgis shot through the forehead, beagles shot through the forehead, terriers shot through the forehead, pugs shot through the forehead, cats slick with wet blood, horses bleeding in ebbing spurts, deer that had been rammed with cars, canaries that had been slain with hammers, parakeets that had been crushed with shovels, cockatoos that had been smashed with rocks, rabbits speared with pitchforks, beheaded chickens, mangled porcupines, groundhogs, raccoons, weasels, finches, cardinals, robins, woodpeckers, herons, and squirrels with snapped necks, a heaped mess of limbs and paws and hooves and tails and bloated tongues, being set ablaze at twilight in town squares as children in military fatigues marched about the burning bodies. The killings had no visible effect on the phenomenon. The killings kept happening anyway.

Babies fertilized in vitro were shown to be just as likely to be born empty.

Babies delivered by caesarean were shown to be just as likely to be born empty.

Meanwhile, the price to adopt a child had soared to over a million.

"Just because you've felt your baby moving doesn't mean that your baby is conscious. Most movements in the womb are involuntary. Or reflexes. There isn't necessarily any actual *control* involved," said a tech with auburn hair, pushing a patient in a gown down the hallway in a wheelchair.

With so few viable babies being born, the number of preemies in residence at the hospital had plunged. The neonatal unit looked like a motel on a dying highway. Full of empty beds.

By the end of that autumn, the hospital admin had decided to downsize the staff of the neonatal unit. Naomi was the rookie. She was first to go.

"We're grateful for the work that you did here," the human resources director said, offering her a handshake and a smile.

Naomi didn't bother applying for a new job. None of the hospitals were hiring for neonatal. She spent the week after losing her job sprawled across the sofa in underwear and a hoodie, crushingly depressed, binging on cream puffs and jelly donuts, watching the television with the curtains drawn. She was so tired of hearing about the phenomenon. Hearing about the phenomenon exhausted her. She kept flipping to shows about the phenomenon anyway.

There was an interview with somebody in a poncho.

"God was like, fine, you're going to legalize abortion? You don't want your babies anymore? You only want your babies sometimes? You're just going to start killing babies at random? Then so am I."

There was an interview with somebody with beaded cornrows.

"There's always been this assumption that God is good. Because that's what our scriptures tell us. But scriptures are just the word of God. We're taking God at its word. We're assuming that God never lies. If a man came to your door and told you he was good, and the only evidence he had for that was a book that he had written that said he was good, would you trust him?"

There was an interview with a weather-beaten rancher who had burned a hundred acres of prairie.

"Why burn all of the fields?"

"We're trying to kill all of the insects."

"You believe in reincarnation?"

"Been coming around to the idea."

"What about all of the evidence that humans souls are separate from other animals?"

The rancher grimaced, gesturing helplessly at the blackened stubs of grass.

"I'm willing to try anything at this point. My daughter's pregnant."

In the background a hawk flying over the ashes was shot out of the sky by a child with a rifle.

Tad stepped timidly into the living room, covering the mouthpiece on the cordless phone.

"Let's have dinner with your parents tonight," Tad whispered.

Naomi looked at him from the sofa. Rama had followed him into the living room, curling around his ankles, purring at his feet. Her parents lived in the hills above the city, in a modern villa with a shimmering infinity pool, with underwater lighting that cycled between shades of neon, violet and cyan and indigo and green. The house where she had been born. Tad liked her parents, but he had never spontaneously suggested having dinner with her parents before, not under any circumstances. He was just trying to help. To get her off of the sofa. To get her out of the condo. She decided to go along with it.

"You can say that we'll be there," Naomi said.

She took a long shower. She put on actual clothes. She still looked depressed as hell. Later that night she sat on a chair in the villa, sipping a virgin daiquiri across from her parents. Her parents were religious more out of habit than out of conviction, although the epidemic had inspired a renewed interest in religion for everybody, her parents included, and her mother had set out fresh flowers on the shrine. Her father wore a bright dastar with a charcoal suit. Her mother was wearing jelly sandals with a silk sari. Her parents were much older than she was, almost elderly now, and had no hobbies aside from making money and watching sports. Lately her father had been obsessed with professional paintball. A paintball match was playing across the television on mute.

"You look terrible," her father said.

"You really do," her mother said.

"I appreciate you saying that," Naomi said.

Warriors fist-bumped as paint-spattered enemies fell to the dirt.

"In a way, maybe losing your job was a good thing," Tad said tentatively, sitting next to her in a cream polo.

"Now you have the ability to travel if necessary," her father said.

"Now you have the freedom to explore every option," her mother said.

Naomi stared at her parents suspiciously, sensing a vague implication, a current of conspiracy in the air. Her parents were plotting something, she realized. Dinner tonight hadn't been spontaneous. Dinner tonight was an ambush. She glanced at her husband. Tad looked nervous. He was in on it. He had been scheming too.

"I hate it when you all make plans about me behind my back," Naomi said with a scowl.

"Please, baby, just hear us out," Tad said.

"There's a place out in the desert," her father said.

"A special place," her mother said.

"For pregnant women," her father said.

"Women looking for some type of assurance," her mother said.

"The facility is one of a kind. You can think of it as a precaution. We would live there until the baby was born, in order to ensure that it's born with a soul," Tad said.

Naomi scowled at him.

"I'm going to have the baby at home," Naomi said.

Tad glanced at her parents before turning back toward her with a hint of pleading in his voice.

"This is a once-in-a-lifetime opportunity," Tad said.

"We'd pay for it," her father said.

"It's really very expensive," her mother said.

"Absolutely not," Naomi said.

Her parents frowned with disappointment.

"Naomi. There's a body growing inside of you. You have a responsibility to do everything you can to give it a chance at having a soul," her father said.

"You're talking about the baby like it's not a person," Naomi said, getting upset.

"We have no way of knowing whether or not it has a soul yet, and without a soul, it's not," her mother said.

Naomi stared at the staircase to the basement behind her parents, at the scuff marks rubbed into the wallpaper by the rubber arms of the baby gate that had stood there for so many years. Naomi had been a sleepwalker as a child, awaking in the darkest hours of the night to wander the house with glazed eyes, brushing her hair in the darkness in the bathroom, holding her toys in the darkness in the playroom, sitting in her chair at the empty table as if expecting to be served a meal. Her parents had said that there was nothing to be ashamed of, that sleepwalking was simply a matter of the body waking too soon, before the soul. She remembered how embarrassed she had felt when her parents had installed a baby gate to protect her from falling down the steps while she was sleepwalking, and how furious she had been when her parents had said she didn't study enough to do premed, and how irritated she had been after dropping premed when her parents had suggested she might like nursing. How skeptical she had been when her parents had arranged the marriage with Tad, a goofy mathematician with a homely appearance. How certain she had been that there was no connection, even up to the very day of the wedding, convinced that the marriage would be lifeless and sad, but how afterward she had grown close to him, and how she had even come to love him. How sweetly and kindly he had cared for her every day since. How much she loved talking to him in bed before falling asleep, when his speech took on a temporary lisp from his retainer. Somehow her parents always knew what would be best for her. She looked at her mother and her father sitting there on the heirloom divan, at those tired and wrinkled faces, creased with worry and lost sleep.

"Coming to this country was not easy, but we did it, for the future of the family. And now, for the future of the family, this is something we must ask you to do."

Naomi felt the baby give a faint kick, and she hesitated, taking a breath, and then she turned back toward her husband.

"Could we bring Rama?" Naomi said.

A week later she was in the car, gliding along a desolate highway in the desert, gazing out at the sand and the shrubs and the massive ridges speckled with greenery on the horizon. Heat haze shimmered in the distance like flailing spirits. Rama was curled up on her lap, either napping or pretending to nap. Tad sat behind the wheel in a polka-dot dress shirt, occasionally glancing with a nervous expression at the clock on the dash, as her mother and her father chatted back and forth in the backseat, bantering about cryptocurrencies, both wearing shades. Following the instructions that the facility had given her parents, Tad turned off of the highway onto a dusty unmarked dirt road. For the next hour the car wound steadily through gullies and valleys and canyons without passing a single sign of life. Rocks ground under the tires. Clouds floated above the sunroof. The murmur of soul music playing over the radio gradually turned to static. After finally coasting through a forbidding gate, the car arrived at a gigantic concrete compound with a flock of buzzards perched on the roof.

Jane, the manager of the maternity center, was waiting at the towering doors.

"Welcome to the Oasis," Jane said.

Naomi was thirteen weeks pregnant.

★ ★ ★

In the immense hallway leading from the entrance of the compound into the inner chambers, a mass of faded prayer flags hung from the ceiling, fraying rectangles of colorful fabric, swaying with drafts of air. Jane was middle-aged, sporting a pair of heels with a blouse and a blazer and a hip haircut, and had the lively charm of a circus ringmaster, strolling ahead of the group to gesture enthusiastically at the highlights of the tour. Naomi and the others followed her through an arched doorway into a vast circular chamber, the altar room, where bright sunshine streamed down through the skylight on the vaulted ceiling, casting shadows behind pillars, making the space glow. Shimmery patches of sunlight trembled on the wall, reflecting off the glass in watches and spectacles. The chamber was furnished with over a hundred cots, radiating out from the stone altar at the center, each occupied by a withered body. Pregnant women sat on worn wooden stools throughout the chamber, murmuring together, giggling together, playing singing bowls over the peaceful sound of the life-support monitors, the quiet beeping of the electrocardiographs and electroencephalographs. The monitors stood on bedside tables, accompanied by bottles of pills and bottles of water. Incense in brass urns. Lilies in clay vases. Ancient statues spotted with moss and lichen were arranged like guardians along the perimeter of the chamber. Gods of childbirth. Gods of motherhood.

"A soul may be a spiritual entity, but that doesn't mean that it's magic, or can just do whatever it wants. This very epidemic proves that souls have limits, which means that just like an angel or a demon, a soul is still bound by the laws of physics. That's the key. A soul can't simply teleport into a new body. A soul has to travel through space and time. What we offer here is proximity. We're over a hundred miles from the nearest city. And on any given day we have over a hundred dying people in residence here. Many of those people are on life support, kept alive only by machines, and have given us permission to switch off the machines at any time, allowing us to guarantee that at least one person dies here every day. We also sacrifice a number of animals throughout the day. Typically a dove and a lamb at sunrise, a rooster at noon, a peacock at dusk, and a goat at midnight, although if you feel a special connection with another species of animal, we'd be happy to incorporate it into the daily cycle," Jane said.

Naomi glanced at the stone altar across the chamber, where a ceremonial dagger with a curved blade and an ebony handle rested on a stand.

"You'll give birth to your child right here at the Oasis, under the care of some of the finest obstetricians in the country, and between now and then every day you'll be surrounded by freshly departed souls in need of a new body to inhabit," Jane said.

Jane waved to a pudgy bearded cook in a spattered apron, who walked past the arched doorway carrying a tote bag brimming with leafy vegetables.

"That's Joaquin, the chef. The food here is exceptional. Bathrooms are communal. Towels are provided. The linens are washed daily. You'll be given a private bedchamber, although some residents occasionally prefer to sleep here among the dying, which can be arranged upon request," Jane said.

Naomi paused, watching a pregnant woman with beautiful golden hair, who sat on a stool near a cot, stroke the shriveled hands of a geriatric man with bloodshot eyes and a sallow complexion.

"Come to me," the woman whispered. "I've seen how you smile when you eat cookies. You like cookies. I'll give you all the cookies that you want. You'll have the perfect childhood. Disneyland. Malibu. Box seats at the Derby. Summer in the Hamptons. You'll have a trust fund. You'll have a sports car. We'll buy you anything you want. We're an important family. We have powerful connections. Exeter. Yale. We fought in the Revolution. We had ancestors on the Mayflower. Come to me when you die."

Naomi felt a sudden chill as the woman with the golden hair turned toward her, gazing at her with a jealous look.

"Naomi, time to say goodbye," Jane called with a smile, leading the group back toward the hallway with the prayer flags.

Tad said an overly cheerful farewell to her parents, Naomi gave each of her parents a tight hug, and then her parents left the compound, heading back to the city, and she followed him down a hallway lined with rough wooden doors.

The bedchamber was simple, furnished with a full-size cot draped with a beige wool blanket, a dresser, a mirror, a desk with a chair, and a bright salt lamp that cast a warm saffron glow across the room. No window. The door had a sliding lock. The bags had already been delivered. Rama was curled up in a satin cat bed on the floor, drowsing. Naomi sat down on the cot with a creak. Tad was organizing geometry books over on the desk.

Tad noticed her staring at him.

"What?" Tad said.

"You don't believe in any of this."

"I never said that."

"You're a card-carrying atheist."

Tad frowned, sitting down on the mattress, wrapping an arm around her.

"I haven't seen those empty bodies in person like you have. I've seen videos though. And it scares the hell out of me. I don't want that to happen to our baby. I'm willing to try anything. No matter how dubious its science is. No matter how much that it costs," Tad said.

Naomi was one of a dozen mothers living at the compound. Most of the fathers didn't have the ability to work from home, and only visited the compound on weekends, or once a month. Tad was the only father living there. He rarely left the bedchamber during the day, hard at work on a new proof in synthetic geometry, hunched over the desk with a mug of steaming coffee. Naomi spent the days wandering the compound alone. While the primary mission of the facility was to ensure the spiritual health of the babies by providing pregnant women with exclusive access to freshly departed souls, the facility was also designed to ensure the physical health of the babies. The daily agenda was wellness. The dining hall was stocked with wholesome nourishment, including freshly squeezed juices that the chef would make on command, pouring shimmers of pink and yellow and red and orange into crystal goblets, grapefruit or mango or watermelon or carrot. In the bathrooms, the rough stone counters were equipped with jars of prenatal vitamins and antacid tablets and gleaming amber vials brimming with fragrant bodywashes and shampoos and exfoliants and cleansers and moisturizers and creams. A maid cleaned the bedchambers and washed dirty laundry. A masseuse offered massages, gently kneading the oiled skin of women splayed across towels. A yoga instructor drove in each day to lead yoga classes in the yoga room, strolling between the rubber mats as women held rigid poses. A meditation teacher drove in each day to lead meditation classes in the meditation room, coaching women sitting on embroidered cushions through soothing breathing techniques. Women exercised on stationary bikes in the fitness center, drinking purified water from glass water bottles embedded with colorful hunks of quartz meant to dispel negative energy and impart positive energy and help calm the mind, while others reclined with diaries on the benches in the greenhouse, journaling together in the clean pure steamy air. Jane worked spiritedly throughout the day to ensure that each of the residents had whatever was needed, running to and from the supply room in the manager office to fetch body pillows and belly bands and eye masks and maternity bras and boxes of truffles. If not for being located in a desolate wilderness of sand and shrubs and scorching heat in the middle of the Great Basin, the maternity center would have been heaven. Naomi felt spoiled and lonely. Rama trailed after her sometimes, mewling at residents in passing. Other days the cat stayed back in the bedchamber with Tad, or snuck off to prowl through the compound alone. Regardless of whether the cat was with her, the other residents never spoke to her, just smiled tightly in passing. Emily, the pregnant woman with the beautiful golden hair, was the belle of the compound, always surrounded by happy chattering companions, the center of attention. Emily was tall and slim and elegant, dressing in haute couture garments made from lush magnificent fabrics, with an intense hungry gaze and a harsh angular face that was pretty the way that a storm could be pretty, and wore her hair in fantastically intricate buns and chignons and braids that were as geometrically complex as figures from a textbook. Strands of gold would twinkle in the light as she passed through a room. Packages of new clothing arrived at the compound for her almost daily. The other residents fawned over her. Like her, the rest of the residents seemed to come from prominent families. Socialites, and legatees, and scions, and heirs. Naomi was an outsider. She was the outcast. When she tried sitting with the other women in the dining hall, none of the women ever made conversation with her. When she arrived in the dining hall before the other women, the women sat at tables across the room from her. Emily seemed to whisper about her sometimes, glancing at her as other women broke out into cackles. Naomi became accustomed to eating breakfast and lunch alone.

Naomi had never been frightened by pain or suffering or death, but there was something eerie about the altar room. Most of the terminal patients were comatose. Withered atrophied bodies that were fed intravenously. The rest of the terminal patients were bedridden. Elderly bodies reduced to withered husks. Dying figures coughed and moaned and muttered and called out from cots as the medics on duty emptied out bedpans and changed drip bags and spooned mashed peas and chunky applesauce between trembling lips. The smell of incense and lilies was thick in the air. Although even the patients who were conscious were generally too addled by dementia or pharmaceuticals to carry on much of a conversation, residents were encouraged to socialize with the dying, and all of the women visited the altar room at least once during the day, sitting on worn stools beside the cots, holding the hands of comatose patients, wiping the brows of bedridden patients, praying at the feet of the ancient statues, quietly playing singing bowls with wooden mallets. Joaquin, the chef, came through the altar room periodically to deliver refreshments. Silver platters heaped with persimmons. Trays piled with plump pears. Chilled bottles of water, infused with lemon wedges or sliced strawberries. Emily was often in there, murmuring in the ears of comatose patients, reading fairy tales aloud to bedridden patients, prowling through the cots with a covetous look. Naomi avoided being in the altar room when she was there, and though death had never frightened her, violence of any kind profoundly disturbed her, and she avoided being in the altar room during sacrifices too, when the sharp curved blade of the ceremonial dagger would be drawn across the tender throat of a shrieking rooster or a struggling peacock, and dark blood would spatter across the rough pale stone of the altar, taking hours to evaporate into the air. Every afternoon a comatose patient was chosen to die, removed from life support by the medics, vanishing from the world to the sound of a flatline. Emily was always there, hovering nearby with a hopeful expression as life left the body, and whenever a bedridden patient suddenly died without warning, Emily would rush to the altar room to be as near to the freed soul as possible, followed by an entourage of women. Naomi liked to be in the altar room at quieter times. Liked to be helpful. To rub the arms of comatose patients to prevent bedsores, to scratch the legs of bed-ridden patients to soothe itches, and to sit listening to the peaceful beeping of the life-support monitors, which made her nostalgic for the hospital. Yet even then there was something creepy about the altar room. Pregnant women and terminal patients had both occupied the same building at the hospital, of course. But still, the juxtaposition of the pregnant women and the terminal patients in the altar room troubled her, and she felt followed sometimes by the empty stares of the decrepit statues along the wall.

There was something eerie about the birthing room too. The birthing room was across the compound, a vast circular chamber the exact same size and shape as the altar room, but instead of a hundred cots radiating out from a stone altar, the birthing room was completely empty aside from a single hospital bed, shining under a spotlight at the center of the chamber. Rather than having statues standing along the perimeter, rustic wooden shelves were arranged along the wall, lined with gigantic healing crystals, lumps of amethyst and topaz and citrine and quartz that glowed in the faint underlighting of the shelves, casting glimmers of color across the floor. Dust twinkled in the air. Nobody was ever in there. None of the residents were due for months. Naomi sometimes peeked in through the arched doorway, placing both her hands on her stomach, feeling her baby move under her fingers, imagining giving birth to the child in there someday. If she shouted, her voice would echo through the chamber, the sound reborn every couple of seconds with another bounce off the wall.

That was how she passed days at the Oasis. Getting periodic medical exams by the doctors, doing yoga with women who ignored her, practicing meditation with women who ignored her, eating mochi, drinking lassis, getting massages, and wandering the compound. A clanging bell announced when dinner was served. Tad ate dinner with her every night, babbling excitedly about whatever podcast he had listened to while he was working. After dinner she would hang out with him, playing board games from the entertainment room, or video-chatting with her parents, or streaming new romcoms together, or reading popular science magazines. Some nights he would have sex with her. Some nights he wouldn't have sex with her. Each night he dutifully inserted his retainer before climbing under the covers to go to bed, mumbling his final thoughts for the day as he drifted off to sleep, faintly lisping. The concrete walls were thick. Naomi never heard any noises from the other bedchambers. Tad slept peacefully, probably dreaming of lines and shapes, the shifting measurements of changing angles. Naomi slept fitfully. When she couldn't sleep, sometimes she took walks, padding barefoot through the compound in the darkest hours of the night, when the hallway was lit only by the dim emergency lighting above the doorways to the bathrooms. Jane lived at the compound too, but she was never awake that time of night. The only staff on duty that time of night was whatever guard was in the security office and whatever doctor was in the medical office, there in case of emergencies, getting paid to sit quietly. Naomi liked to climb the central stairwell to the tiled patio on the roof, where the other residents sunbathed during the day. To sit there under the moon. Just to look at the stars. She missed Vegas. She had never imagined that was possible, but she did, missed the neon and the noise and the heat and the traffic, and the celebrity imposters, and the ridiculous billboards, and the tourists stumbling drunkenly down the sidewalk in skintight clothing, and the gambling addicts waiting in line at the pawnshops, and the newlywed elopers parading out of kitschy chapels, and the cheapskates strolling out of buffets with purses full of stolen pastries, and the catcallers, and the gangsters, and the missionaries, and the doomsayers, even the putrid stench of the garbage baking in rusted trash bins in the alleys. Being able to drive around, and run errands, and grocery shop. Lounging around in her condo. Getting to visit her parents. Smelling sauteing garlic, taking a bath while her husband cooked brunch. Rama sat with her on the roof occasionally, watching intently as bats arced over the compound. Naomi never saw anybody else up there that time of night. Sometimes she would stay on the roof until dawn, when she would hear the station wagon that the chef drove arrive in the parking lot with a crunch of gravel, and then she would slip back down the stairs, heading toward the dining hall to get some breakfast.

Naomi was rummaging through the video collection in the entertainment room one day when she heard a group of residents stroll through the doorway, plopping onto couches, sinking into armchairs, chattering with Emily, who took a seat on a plush leather ottoman, grinning wickedly at the others, hair cascading from an elegant waterfall braid.

"Hold on, which guard?"

"The young one," Emily said.

"Chase, with the gauges?"

"We did it in the greenhouse once," Emily said.

"Wait, you've hooked up with him more than once?"

"I couldn't take it anymore. I was completely losing it. I've been super horny since the first trimester. Danny knows that. If he didn't want me to sleep with other people then he should have been here. Money isn't an issue. He chose to keep working. He decided not to come."

"I'd rather just use a vibrator."

"I haven't been horny at all."

Naomi fumbled a cassette, which hit the floor with a clatter. Emily glanced over at her, then turned back toward the others.

"I mean, it's whatever. He's the best of what's around. The other guards are too old. And the cook is just creepy. I'd be afraid of catching a case of eczema or something, hooking up with him. You just know his back is hairy. You don't even have to look. And the other options around here are just as unattractive," Emily said, looking over at her again with a faint smirk.

Naomi realized that she was talking about Tad.

Naomi stormed back down the hallway in a blind rage, not even paying attention to where she was going, furious both to have had her husband be considered an option for seduction and to have had her husband be deemed too unattractive to fuck. She trembled with barely contained anger. She went back to the bedchamber.

"I can't do this anymore," Naomi said.

Tad looked up from the desk.

"I want to go home," Naomi said.

Tad took in a breath, then let out a sigh. He set down a pencil. Rama mewed, peering out from the shadows under the cot.

"I don't want to be here any more than you do," Tad said.

"I really don't think that's possible," Naomi said.

"Trust me," Tad said.

"Nobody here will even talk to me," Naomi said.

"Baby. We're so close. Just hold on. We only have to make it a few more months," Tad said.

And she tried, but the situation only got worse. When she ran to get a drink of water during yoga class, Emily took her place, forcing her to move to a mat at the back of the room, where she couldn't even see the instructor through the contorted limbs of all of the women who shunned her. When she ran to take a pee during meditation class, Emily edged out her cushion, forcing her to move to a place at the back of the room, where she couldn't even concentrate on the teacher over the distracted whispers of all of the women who shunned her. Emily organized a sleepover in the entertainment room, ordering a dozen sleeping bags online, buying stovetop popcorn, getting pizza delivered, and then invited every resident except for her. Naomi tried approaching the other residents when the women were alone, trying to make friendly jokes, trying to make superficial banter, even just trying to exchange some fucking pleasantries about the weather, and the women rebuffed any attempt at conversation, as if acting on orders to exclude her. When she went to the medical office for a checkup at her scheduled time, Emily was there instead, insisting that she needed to be examined at that very moment in order to make a session with the masseuse, insisting that stress could be incredibly harmful to a child in the womb, insisting that the massage was absolutely crucial to the health of her baby, and she threw such a tantrum that the doctor finally caved and pushed back the appointment with Naomi.

Jane found her afterward, looking apologetic and embarrassed.

"I'm so sorry about that," Jane said.

"I'm paying to be here too," Naomi exploded.

"I know," Jane said.

"I shouldn't have to deal with this catty shit," Naomi exclaimed.

"I'm sorry. You've been so patient. Thank you for that. Truly. I know how hard it can be to deal with her. There's nobody here who visits my office as often as she does, every day, even during the night, always with some new problem or demand. There's no excuse for it. I just try to remember that she had a difficult upbringing. There are mental health issues. She's under a lot of pressure from her family," Jane said.

Naomi went into a bathroom, the only place she knew she could be alone at that time of day, and shut the door and slapped the lock and sat cross-legged on the floor under the sink, blasting trance music over her headphones, letting the noise shake her, letting the sound consume her, like she'd done as a teenager whenever she'd been so frustrated that she'd wanted to scream. She hated how important that minor interactions could seem in an isolated social setting. She had friends back in the city. Friends from college. Friends from childhood. On an intellectual level, she knew that she was likable. On an emotional level though, she felt like a loser. Back at home, in real life, she wouldn't have given a fuck what women like that thought about her, but having to live with the women, having to share space with the women, seeing those women and only those women every single day, she would have given her life for a smile. Being rejected by the other women there felt like being rejected by all of human society. It was absurd. It was crushing. That was all she wanted, was a friend.

That next evening a new couple arrived at the compound, a woman in a holographic jacket with thick bleached hair and a man with a muscular build wearing a black tracksuit, who both looked vaguely familiar. Naomi was sitting near the altar with Rama, petting the cat behind the ears. Eavesdropping as the couple took a tour of the facility, Naomi realized that the woman was a celebrity tennis player, a gold medalist, a world champion, and that the man was a supermodel. Naomi had seen his face on billboards downtown, in pouty advertisements for peacoats and underwear. He had grown up in Newark. She wasn't sure where she had read that, and was embarrassed that she had.

Annabelle, the tennis player, wasn't pregnant yet.

"We don't get to have sex while you pull the plug on somebody?" Annabelle said.

"That actually isn't necessary," Jane said.

"But what if a soul enters a new body at the moment of conception?" Annabelle said.

"It certainly might," Jane said.

Annabelle frowned, looking at the withered figures sprawled across the cots in the chamber. "So then shouldn't he be trying to come in me at the exact instant that one of these guys flatlines?"

Jane smiled awkwardly. "Fertilization doesn't occur the moment that the sperm enters the vagina. Conception happens anywhere from an hour to a week after sex. It's impossible to predict the exact moment that you'll become pregnant." She clasped her hands together. "For that matter, we don't know how to identify the exact moment that a body has died, either. Medically we used to consider a body dead after the heart had stopped, but that definition has become problematic, now that we have defibrillators that can start a heart back up again. Many physicians now define death as the moment that all electrical activity ceases in the brain, but even that definition is problematic, as various organ systems within the body can continue to function long after brain death occurs." She spread her hands wide. "And even if we could pinpoint the exact moment that a body had died, we don't know how these matters work spiritually. If a soul remains with the body for a time, or leaves the body instantaneously."

Spencer, the supermodel, looked totally lost.

"So, like, why did we even come here, if we're not supposed to fuck while some dude gets terminated?" Spencer said.

Jane handed the couple the key to a bedroom.

"You're paying a lot of money to be here, and that money ensures that this facility has a steady supply of dying bodies. You can start trying to conceive whenever you're ready. Tonight, if you want. And on the day that your child is conceived, and at every other stage of your child's development, we can guarantee you that there will be freshly departed souls nearby, looking for a healthy human body to inhabit," Jane said.

Naomi briefly fantasized about becoming friends with the new couple, doing group activities, doing double dates, which she knew was ridiculous. It seemed ridiculous. But the next day she was sitting alone in the dining hall when the tennis player approached her with a tray of food.

"You want to be alone?" Annabelle said.

Naomi stared.

"You can sit," Naomi said.

"Why aren't you eating with the others?" Annabelle said.

Naomi hesitated.

"There's a certain hierarchy here," Naomi said.

Annabelle rolled her eyes, setting the tray down on the table, sitting down in a chair with her hair tied back in a messy ponytail. With a shock, Naomi saw that she had a bowl of cereal. Naomi gazed at the cereal in amazement. Geometric marshmallows bobbed in the milk, colorful triangles and circles and squares. Naomi had been craving cereal for months, but the dining hall didn't have any, and she had been too embarrassed to ask for any or order any online.

"Where'd you get the cereal?" Naomi said.

"Smuggled a box in. Figured all of the food here would be natural or organic or probiotic or whatever. I would have starved to death. I need a balanced diet of artificial flavors to get through the day," Annabelle said, and then took a bite.

Naomi watched her with a sense of longing as she chewed and swallowed the cereal.

"I've never actually seen you play tennis," Naomi admitted.

"I'm a typical baseliner," Annabelle said.

"I don't have a clue what that means," Naomi said.

"I hit at crazy angles," Annabelle grinned.

Naomi's heart leapt at the sight of a smile. She glanced across the dining hall, where the rest of the residents were gazing at Emily, listening to her tell some story, and then she turned back around toward Annabelle, watching her gulp a sip of chocolate milk. Naomi felt ecstatic suddenly. She felt extraordinary. She felt fantastic. Joaquin was flipping omelettes behind the counter.

"I heard an interesting rumor last night," Annabelle said through a mouthful of marshmallows.

"What rumor?" Naomi said.

"That most of the people who die here used to be homeless," Annabelle said.

"I thought everybody who dies here is getting paid?"

"Well. Their families are. Which seems fair. I mean, imagine if you had some junkie uncle who'd been living on the streets the past fifty years, totally refusing to go to rehab, refusing to give up the drugs, occasionally hitting your family up for money or favors, and then suddenly he's in a coma at a hospital, hooked up to life support, with no chance of resuscitation, and some company comes along offering you a huge windfall of cash just to take him out into the desert to pull the plug."

Spencer, the supermodel, wandered into the dining hall with mussed hair and wrinkled pajamas, yawning glamorously.

"I hope it's true. I was a runaway as a kid. I lived in a shelter a while. I had a lot of friends there. It'd give me a weird sort of satisfaction, knowing that all of these rich people were going to end up giving birth to children with the souls of homeless people," Annabelle said.

Rama had snuck into the dining hall. Silverware rattled as the cat leapt onto the table. Naomi set the cat back down onto the floor. Rama slunk off toward the buffet with a sulky look, heading for Spencer, who was filling a plate with bacon.

Annabelle glanced back toward the hallway with an expression of admiration.

"Genius, in a way, figuring out how to monetize all of this," Annabelle said.

"Nobody's even given birth here yet," Naomi said.

Annabelle looked at her.

"That's what's been keeping me awake at night. I mean, we don't even know if this will work," Naomi said.

★ ★ ★

Rain was falling on the roof. Naomi sat over a board game in the dining hall, across from Annabelle. Tad was sitting across from Spencer.

"Do you think a soul gets to choose its new body after it dies?" Annabelle said.

"Totally," Spencer said, losing a turn, passing the dice.

"That actually wouldn't make any sense," Tad said.

"Don't get all mathy on us," Spencer said.

"It's not math. It's just logic. Nobody would choose to be born to an abusive meth addict living in a shack in a slum in a country ruled by a totalitarian regime. But some people are," Tad said.

Naomi rolled the dice, reaching for a soldier piece, trying to launch a war. She was twenty-nine weeks pregnant.

"Maybe souls have, like, different criteria," Spencer said.

★ ★ ★

Dust was blowing past the windows. Naomi stood over the foosball table in the entertainment room, next to Annabelle. Tad was standing next to Spencer.

"Can any of you remember past lives?" Annabelle said.

"Nope," Tad said, spinning a bar, missing the ball.

"I had a super intense dream about being a sailor once," Spencer said.

"I don't think dreaming about sailors counts as a past life," Tad said.

"I had all of these skills, though. Like tying knots. And catching fish. And then everybody on the boat accused me of stealing a bagpipe," Spencer said.

Naomi twisted a handle, making the goalie backflip, kicking the ball down the court. She was thirty-one weeks pregnant.

"I have trouble with the idea that we're something separate from these physical bodies," Tad said.

★ ★ ★

Naomi was slumped on a bench in the greenhouse with Annabelle, passing a bowl of dry cereal back and forth.

"It was hilarious. My parents have always been totally opposed to things like that. People who do yoga for exercise, or do meditation for mental benefits, like to increase productivity or whatever. My parents think it's a corruption of Indian religions. Seriously, whenever they drive past the studio by their house, this total silence falls over the car. You'd think they'd just driven past a Confederate monument. They've been that way my entire life. I got really into yoga and meditation back in college. I caught so much flak from my parents for that. But when they took the tour here, they were so into the idea of this place that when they saw all of the women doing yoga and meditation together, they were like, 'Yoga! Meditation! Naomi, this place is paradise!'" Naomi said.

Annabelle threw her head back and laughed.

"I want to meet your parents so bad," Annabelle said.

"You'll definitely get to. They're going to drive up the second my water breaks," Naomi said, chewing some marshmallows.

"I can't wait to hang with those two," Annabelle said.

Beads of water glistened on the colorful peaches and plums and nectarines hanging from the branches of the fruit trees across from the bench. Tad was working. Spencer was napping. The warm steamy air in the greenhouse felt refreshing.

"I wish you would have gotten to meet my mom," Annabelle said.

"Me too," Naomi said.

★ ★ ★

Annabelle found out that she was pregnant a week later, months after arriving at the maternity center. Naomi went on a walk with her afterward. Naomi had never seen her so radiantly happy. Annabelle kept laying her hand on her stomach, which was still as flat as an axis. Naomi was bulging through her sweatshirt, with pains in her back from all the extra weight. She felt gargantuan. Annabelle sat next to her by the stone altar in the altar room.

"I'm really going to miss you when you're gone," Annabelle said.

"I know," Naomi said.

"I'm still going to have so long to go," Annabelle said.

Emily was in there, dressed in a baggy linen tunic and leather huaraches with golden buckles, looking especially fervent today, playing a singing bowl near the cot of somebody who'd just died.

"We'll come back to visit you," Naomi said.

"You swear?" Annabelle said, glancing at her.

"I promise."

"Thank god."

Rama was staring at a blank spot on the ceiling.

"Make sure you bring that cutie, too," Annabelle said.

Rama kept staring at the blank spot on the ceiling.

"What are you looking at, Rama?" Annabelle laughed, reaching down to nuzzle the cat under the chin, but the cat ignored her, gazing intently at the ceiling, as if watching something that the humans couldn't see.

Across the altar room, a medic covered the dead body with a white sheet, preparing to wheel the corpse off to a waiting ambulance. Smoke rose from incense. Petals fell from lilies. Rama turned to watch something invisible glide down the wall, then backed away, crept forward again, batted at something invisible on the floor, and quick ran out into the hallway, as if chasing something.

"Cats are so dope," Annabelle said.

★ ★ ★

Naomi was stepping off of a treadmill in the fitness center later that night when she ran into Emily.

"Naomi, hi," Emily said.

Naomi hadn't had a single interaction with her in over a month. She froze, bracing for a confrontation. Emily was smiling at her, though. She looked genuinely happy to see her. Rather than workout clothes, she was still wearing the linen tunic and the leather huaraches, as if she had come into the gym specifically to talk to her. Her hands were cupped around the swell of her belly.

"You look so beautiful today," Emily said.

"Oh," Naomi said, taken aback.

"You're like literally glowing," Emily said.

"Thanks," Naomi said, confused.

Tad was watching from a stationary bike, as if waiting to see if she needed to be rescued.

"I just had my latest checkup. Everything looks perfect. Everything looks great. And the baby has been really active lately. Moving around a lot. I know everybody says that that doesn't mean anything, but still, it's reassuring, you know?" Emily said.

Naomi was so stunned by this pleasant chitchat that she was briefly speechless.

"You're due soon too, right?" Emily said.

"Um, yeah, in a week," Naomi said.

"We don't know the gender."

"Us either."

"We want to be surprised."

"Us too."

"You're so lucky that you've been able to have your husband here with you the whole time. That's so special. That's so nice. Danny's overseas for another month, doing work things in Switzerland, but after that he's going to come straight here. He'll be here the last month, for when the baby's born," Emily said.

Tad had turned back toward the handlebars of the stationary bike, breathing heavily as he pedaled.

Emily abruptly turned toward the door, as if about to leave the gym, but then turned back around with an anxious expression.

"I'm sorry for being a terrible person. I should have been nicer to you. I'm such a monster sometimes. I honestly don't know why. Really, I've been like this my whole life. I just lash out at people," Emily said.

Naomi was speechless again.

"We could have been friends. I wish that we had. You're a real person. I mean, like, somebody who really thinks about things. From the moment you arrived, I could just tell somehow. You're the realest person here," Emily said, tucking a strand of hair behind her ear.

Naomi felt a bright warm glow spread through her chest, a sense of utter bliss, a powerful sense of reconciliation, being spoken to and apologized to and accepted by her finally after being rejected by her for so long. Emily suddenly seemed so vulnerable and insecure. Instead of the meticulously perfect braids she usually wore, her hair was lopsided, Naomi realized, with stray strands of gold hanging loose from a tortoiseshell hair clip. Her cheekbones looked oddly gaunt. Her eyes had puffy bags. Naomi almost wanted to hug her. Naomi didn't need her as a friend anymore. Naomi had other friends now to support her. But still, for some reason, being treated with kindness by her, being able to connect with her, made her intensely happy. The feeling overwhelmed her.

"It's okay," Naomi said.

"And sorry about your cat," Emily blurted.

Naomi frowned.

"About my cat?" Naomi said.

"Oh, I thought somebody probably must have told you," Emily said, laughing nervously.

"Told me what?" Naomi said.

"I know everybody says that humans can't get souls from animals. I'm an overachiever though. I'm the type of person who'll do extra credit even when she already has a perfect grade. I'm like that with everything. Even if humans can't get souls from animals, I'd still prefer for the staff to sacrifice some animals during the day, just in case it might help. I actually think that it might. Anyway, I didn't even realize that the cat was yours at first. I thought it belonged to one of the staff. I've always felt a connection with cats. I don't know how to explain it. I just do. So, I don't know, I just got this idea into my head that the other animals weren't enough. That the cat needed to be sacrificed too. Jane said no, of course. I mean, it's your cat. This was back around the time that you first got here. I threw a huge fit. I was pretty embarrassed afterward. I was sure that you must have heard. Anyway, Jane got me some different cats instead. Every night for a week, that was the midnight sacrifice," Emily said.

Naomi stared at her in shock.

"I've just been freaking out a little. The stress makes me feel crazy. All of the pressure. We both have fertility issues, Danny and me. Especially me. I know we could just adopt, but my parents wanted us to have one that was ours, and that's what we wanted too. We spent over a million dollars on fertility treatments. We tried so many times. Over a dozen procedures, a dozen different embryos, and every single one failed. Every single one. Except the last one. This baby is a miracle. It's the most beautiful thing that's ever happened to me. I just want to do everything possible to make sure the baby is born healthy. I know it will be. I have faith it will. I just get nervous sometimes," Emily said.

"It's been a hard year for everybody. But everything is going to be okay," Naomi said.

"You really think so?" Emily said, looking at her.

Naomi nodded, and meant it.

"It's been super hard. But we're almost there," Emily said, squinting in happiness as she caressed her stomach with her hands.

★ ★ ★

The next day two of the residents at the compound went into labor, one at breakfast, one during lunch, and by evening both of the babies had been born, healthy and ensouled. After months spent living under a constant sense of fear and doubt and looming tragedy, a feeling of hope came over the residents at the maternity center, hearing the cries and babbles of conscious babies ringing through the hallways. Women kept spontaneously bursting into fits of relieved laughter. Naomi couldn't stop smiling. That night the staff hosted a celebration. Jane decorated the dining hall with golden balloons. Joaquin baked a pair of chocolate birthday cakes. At midnight a stork was slaughtered on the altar.

"And we know now that the methods at this facility really do work," Jane said during a triumphant speech.

Joaquin applauded along with the residents from behind the counter in the kitchen.

Naomi was expected to give birth next, but when her due date arrived, Emily went into labor instead of her.

Naomi was eating a slice of apple pie in the dining hall when a nurse appeared in the doorway with a frantic look.

"She's asking for you," the nurse said.

Naomi hurried down the hallway, following the nurse to the birthing room, where the rustic wooden shelves were still standing along the walls and the gigantic healing crystals were still glowing on the shelves and the rough concrete floor was glimmering with bursts of color from the crystals. The spotlight shone down onto the hospital bed. Emily still wasn't due for over a month. She was lying on the sheet in a satin gown. Jane was standing beside her clutching a manila file folder.

"Danny isn't here yet," Emily was saying, looking sweaty and frightened.

"Emily, he won't be here for weeks," Jane said.

"Call him. You need to call him. He can fly here today," Emily insisted.

"By the time he got to the airport, flew all the way across the ocean, and drove all of the way here, the trip would take more than a day," Jane said.

"We need to wait for him," Emily said.

"You cannot wait for him," Jane said firmly.

"But the baby isn't due yet," Emily said.

"The baby is coming now," Jane said.

Emily stared at her a moment with an expression that flickered between uncertainty and stubbornness and denial and fury. Then her mouth tightened, and her gaze softened, and she nodded finally, taking a deep breath. She wiped a sweaty strand of hair from her cheek.

"All that matters is the baby. I'm ready. Let's go," Emily said.

Emily hadn't asked for any of the other residents to be there. Only her. Naomi sat next to her throughout the delivery, rubbing her forehead, holding her hand. The labor was straightforward and effortless and lasted only an hour. The baby was born just after noon, a tiny rawboned child with fragile arms and delicate legs and wide round eyes that sparkled with beautiful flecks of blue. A child destined for power and wealth. The doctor clamped and cut the cord. Naomi stared at the child in disbelief. It wasn't moving. It wasn't crying. It just gazed at the ceiling in silence, breathing mechanically.

The body was empty.

"I'm so sorry," Naomi said.

Jane looked horrified. Emily looked fine. She reached for the child with an expression of reverence.

"He's perfect," Emily whispered.

Naomi and the others watched as she held the child, gazing into the blank eyes, tenderly cradling the empty body, murmuring lovingly. The child continued to breathe. Dust floated through the spotlight. Sweat was drying on skin. Emily began to look anxious.

The doctor moved to take the child back from her when the breathing stopped.

"He still doesn't have a soul," Emily said with a hint of confusion.

"It's too late," the doctor said.

The doctor hesitated before reaching for the child again.

"Just let me hold him," Emily pleaded.

"He's gone," the doctor said gently.

"Don't take him from me," Emily pleaded.

Naomi left. By then the news had already spread through the rest of the compound. Giving birth at the facility didn't guarantee a baby would have a soul. At dinner that night the residents were solemn, forking bites of salmon and broccoli in a gloomy silence, asking in murmurs for salt or butter to be passed. Spencer sat staring at a blueberry tart, in a daze. Annabelle sat hunched over a plate of meringues, looking just as somber. Spoons clinked against bowls. Emily was usually the center of attention in the dining hall, but tonight she wasn't there.

Tad wasn't concerned.

"Even if there's no guarantee, being here might still increase the baby's chances," Tad said, walking back to the bedchamber.

"I actually believed that we didn't have to worry anymore," Naomi said.

"The baby is going to be fine," Tad said.

Earlier that day he had discovered a new type of impossible object. A two-dimensional figure that couldn't possibly exist in three-dimensional space. A remarkable achievement. Back in the bedchamber, he tore a strip of masking tape from a roll, stuck a charcoal sketch of the impossible object to the wall above the desk, and then stood back to admire the drawing, gazing at the shape the exact same way that a parent might look at a newborn child. Tad had a blunt, ugly face, marred with blackheads, but when he was that proud, when he was that in love, there was something about him that was profoundly handsome. He was wearing the same polka-dot dress shirt that he had worn on the drive from the city.

"An impossible object only appears possible because of the limitations of the human mind," Tad said.

★ ★ ★

Naomi went on a walk later that night after he had fallen asleep. She wandered through the darkened passageways of the compound in a baggy cotton nightshirt, taking a moment to contemplate the withered bodies on the cots in the altar room, the blinking life-support machines, and then slipped into the stairwell, climbing the steps to the patio on the roof. She sat cross-legged up there for hours with her hands cupped around her belly, watching airplanes drift over the desert, watching satellites glide across the sky, looking at the stars, trying to decide what to do now that she knew the facility couldn't guarantee that a child would be born with a soul. Whether or not just to go home. Her baby was now one day overdue. Towels for sunbathing hung from the railing. A gossip magazine rustled in the breeze. Somebody had left the cap off of a bottle of tanning oil, putting the sweet scent of coconut in the air.

For a moment she closed her eyes, trying to sense the separate components of her soul and her body. Trying to imagine what it would feel like for her soul to separate from her body. Trying to imagine the course that her soul might have taken through human history. The lives it had lived in wealth, and the lives it had lived in poverty. The lives it had lived in war, and the lives it had lived in peace. The lives it had lived in health, and the lives it had lived in affliction. The lives it had lived in slavery, and the lives it had lived in freedom. She caught the sweet scent of the tanning oil again, which was her body that sensed that, though the awareness came from her soul. She wondered if she had a soulmate somewhere. And then she opened her eyes again, and heat lightning was flickering in the distance, and she remembered her baby, and that after all of the time that she had spent at the compound the child might still be born empty.

Naomi still hadn't decided whether or not just to go home when she went back into the compound. She emerged from the stairwell lost in thought, but then paused at the sound of a faint hum in the altar room. Electrocardiographs and electroencephalographs. The tone of a flatline. With the skylight dark, the only light in the altar room came from the glow of the candles flickering between the cots, and she could see the monitors from where she stood. Every last screen showed a flatline, as if all of the patients had died at once. Naomi frowned, thinking that the monitors must be malfunctioning, that maybe a power surge had fried the circuits, but then as she walked through the massive arched doorway of the altar room she realized that the monitors were functioning perfectly. All of the patients were dead. The bodies were mangled. The sheets were drenched. Blood was dripping from the cots onto the floor. The concrete suddenly felt cold under the soles of her feet. Frightened, she glanced toward the stone altar and saw that the ceremonial dagger was gone. Shadows flickered across the room with the flames of the candles. Naomi froze in place, watching the shadows carefully, afraid that whoever had stabbed the patients might be hiding somewhere in the room, behind or beneath the cots. The decrepit statues along the circumference of the room were silhouettes in the dim light, and she desperately tried to remember each of the poses that the statues held, paranoid that one of the silhouettes might be the killer posing as a statue. The flatlines kept humming. The statues were motionless. Naomi stood there in the doorway with her heart beating wildly until she finally believed that she was alone, that nobody was hiding in the room, and still she was afraid to move, but she forced her body to move, to go get help, and she padded off down the hallway with sweat trickling down the nape of her neck and a hot flash spreading across her skin. She felt sick. The walk to the security office seemed impossibly long, like minutes, entire minutes, and she felt a rush of relief when she saw light streaming from the doorway, the salt lamp that stood on the desk where the guards sat, but instead of sitting behind the desk the guard who was on duty was sprawled across the floor, stabbed so many times his uniform was shredded, with tinny music still playing over his earbuds, a chorus of trilling violins. Light was streaming from the doorway of the medical office too, the salt lamp that stood on the desk where the doctors sat, and instead of sitting behind the desk the doctor who was on duty was sprawled across the floor, stabbed through the thick fabric of her uniform, while a classic sitcom streamed across her tablet, accompanied by a laugh track. In the manager's office, Jane lay on the cement in a mound of silk, her neck slashed, her face rigid, her features contorted into a grotesque expression, surrounded by aspirin tablets that had spilled from a bottle onto the floor. Naomi felt a ripple of terror. There were no other staff at the compound that time of night. She and the other residents were alone. She had to warn the other residents. Tad. Annabelle. Spencer. There would be safety in numbers. She wasn't going to die. Her hands were trembling. She followed the hallway deeper into the compound, glancing behind her once, but nobody was behind her. Nobody was there. The bathrooms were dark. As she passed the bathrooms she caught the scent of the diffusers, jasmine and lemongrass, heard dripping water, and then she came to the residential section of the compound, where the rough wooden doors to the bedchambers stood at regular intervals in the hallway. At that time of night all of the doors were always shut, but all of the doors were open, as if each of the residents had been summoned from sleep by a soft knock or a familiar voice. Naomi stared down the hallway with a sense of horror. Madeline, a real estate heir with a brown bob cut and vintage spectacles, lay in a heap in the doorway of the first bedchamber, wearing madras pajamas soaked with blood. Limbs of other bodies extended from doorways farther down the hallway, hands and feet and shiny coils of hair. In the soft light of the salt lamps glowing in the bedchambers, the puddles of blood spreading from the doorways shimmered on the floor, forming an archipelago of black pools that extended off down the hallway, into the darkness. A ventilator came to life with a thump. Air creaked through a duct on the ceiling. Naomi padded cautiously down the hallway, stepping around the blood, with the nausea growing in her stomach with every body that she passed. The women had all been stabbed repeatedly in the throat and the belly. Spencer had fallen onto the floor with his hand stiffened around a bottle of absinthe, nude, bleeding from his chest and his throat. Annabelle had fallen to the floor in a bright kimono, bleeding from her neck and her belly, with her eyes wide with fear. Naomi was hyperventilating. As she walked toward the darkness at the end of the hallway she was crying now, silently, trying not to make any noise. Her bedchamber was the last one in the hallway. The salt lamp in her bedchamber was glowing too. Nobody was following her. Hesitantly, she stepped into the room. The satin cat bed was empty. Geometry books had been spilled across the floor. Metallic shapes glimmered on the covers. Silver grids of lines. The charcoal sketch of the impossible object was still taped above the desk. Tad was sprawled across the concrete in a horrible rag-doll posture, his mouth wide open, still wearing his retainer. Naomi spun away. Stars twinkled across her vision. She felt dizzy. The nausea rose in a stomach-churning surge of acid, and she squatted to vomit in the wastebasket by the desk. Afterward she sat panting on the floor by the wastebasket, catching her breath. She spat, trying to get the taste of acid out of her mouth. Nobody was in the doorway. She was shaking. She tried to think. She didn't have keys to any of the cars in the lot. She didn't have time to search all of the rooms for keys. She just had to run. She needed to run. Nobody was in the doorway. Still wearing her nightshirt, she knelt on the floor to put on her sneakers, but her hands were trembling so badly that she couldn't tie the laces. She swore. She fumbled. She knotted the laces. She wobbled as she stood. Nobody was in the doorway. Cupping her hands protectively around her stomach, she slipped back into the hallway, glancing in both directions, but the hallway was still empty. She was going to have to walk through the desert. She was going to need water before fleeing the compound. A canteen. Taking the quickest route to the kitchen, she cut through the greenhouse, through the shadowy jungle of flowers and vines and hissing misters, and then back out into the hallway, hurrying past the darkened doorways of the yoga room and the meditation room, the orderly stacks of mats and cushions. She could hear the distant humming of the machines in the kitchen now, the ice dispenser, the soda dispenser, the fridges and freezers, and her mouth was dry, and her palms were sweating, and the soles of her sneakers squeaked quietly on the floor, and then she came to the massive arched doorway of the birthing room, and her heart leapt as she saw a silhouette in the doorway, a living person, backlit by the glowing crystals on the shelves in the birthing room, the dazzling array of amethyst and topaz and citrine and quartz. Naomi froze, petrified. The figure stood with the eerie trancelike posture of a sleepwalker, gazing in at the stones, draped in an elegant gown. The figure shifted slightly. Then the figure turned. The dagger was clutched in a limp hand. She was cradling the empty body of a lifeless newborn.

Naomi took a step back.

"He still needs a soul," Emily said.

"Emily," Naomi said.

"All he needs is a soul," Emily said.

"Emily," Naomi begged.

"It's not too late," Emily said, and she was crying and smiling as she stepped from the shadows into the light.

★ ★ ★

Out in the desert, as the sun rose over the mountains, a dust devil spun in whirling circles, a twisting column of soil and pebbles. The desert was quiet. A jackrabbit with a dark tail sat chewing a thistle near a cactus, staring at the sun. A roadrunner sat on a cluster of eggs in a nest of twigs, looking at the sun. Flies hovered in a gorge. A flock of sparrows shot over the compound, soaring out across the desert, over the sand and shrubs, diving and fluttering through the brisk pure air above the land.

★ ★ ★

Lupe had fallen back asleep around dawn, and she was woken at noon by the baby moving, pushing and kicking in her stomach, and she got out of bed finally, slipping on her bathrobe. She washed her face. She brushed her teeth. She put on her glasses. Sparrows were chirping in the yard. Joaquin had left a dirty plate in the sink, and while she was scrubbing the plate she heard sirens, a caravan of ambulances tearing down the highway, and she imagined that there must have been some accident at the military base, where he had used to work before he had taken the job running the kitchen at the Oasis. Joaquin didn't like for her to do housework that late in the pregnancy, but she needed to do something to keep her mind off of the discomfort and the monotony, so she dusted the house, and she swept the house, and she plunged some hair from the drain in the bathtub, and by then she was exhausted, so she went into the living room to do some sudoku. When she got tired of the silence she got off of the couch and went over to the television to turn on the news for some background noise. She froze when she saw the image on the screen, realizing that she recognized the building. Joaquin had taken her there once, proudly touring her through the kitchen, showing off the industrial mixers and ranges. The maternity center. There had been a massacre at the maternity center early that morning. The worst mass killing in the country in over a month, and the murderer hadn't even had a gun. Over a hundred people had been stabbed to death, every last soul in the compound, before the murderer had phoned in an incoherent plea to an emergency hotline and then swallowed a bottle of meds. The only living creature that had survived the massacre was a cat. Footage of a firefighter holding the cat played across the screen, and then there was a clip from within the compound, a body lying on the floor of the dining hall, and the face had been blurred out, but she saw the hairnet, and she saw the apron, and she saw the colorful tie-dye t-shirt that he had been wearing when he had brought a glass of water into the bedroom for her before leaving for work early that morning, and then the screen cut to a shot of the compound surrounded by emergency vehicles with flashing sirens. Lupe had dropped the sudoku puzzles. She sank to the floor. She didn't weep or scream. She just stared at the television, in shock, as the same cycle of clips continued to play across the screen. A great wind blew through the yard, like a mass of spirits rushing across the desert toward the city, disturbing the chimes hanging over the stoop, agitating the laundry hanging from the clothesline, and a faint breeze escaped from the gust to slip into the house through the screen in the window, twisting gently around her body, sending chills across her skin. Advertising jingles rang out from the television, singsongy voices, peddling insurance and vacuums during commercial breaks. The phone in the kitchen rang and rang and rang and then eventually fell silent. Later, when the bright gold sunlight streaming through the windows had dimmed to the burning red of early evening, she curled up in a fetal position on the rug, staring at an empty power outlet in the corner as political pundits argued back and forth on a talk show.

"We should be grateful. We should be celebrating. It's solved the greatest problem of our time. I'm not talking about climate change. Climate change was just a symptom of the root problem. Pollution, famine, water shortages, those were all just symptoms too. The root problem has always been overpopulation. But we don't have to worry about the population growing anymore. Now the number is fixed."

"How can you expect people to be happy when children are dying?"

"If the religious community is right, and these babies are being born without souls, then technically there's nothing to mourn."

"But how can you ignore the lost potential of these empty bodies?"

Lupe was still lying on the rug later that night when the presidential debate came onto the television.

"We're in a time of crisis. Our scientists can't stop what's happening, and our prayers are going unanswered. God is sending us a message. It's up to us to act. God's chosen nation. A vote for me is a vote for your future. There's thirteen and a half billion people on this planet, and only half of a billion people in this country. America's children come first. We've got a military strong enough to carpet-bomb the rest of the world into oblivion. And that's exactly what we're going to do. We're going to release thirteen billion souls back into the ether all at once. A vote for me is a vote for your children. No more children are going to be born without souls in this land."

Lupe got up off of the floor finally and went into the bedroom, falling back asleep clutching his pajamas, which still smelled like his scent, as cicadas sang in the yard.

Her water broke early the next morning, and she drove through the desert alone, into Las Vegas, where she gave birth in a hospital with peaceful pastel colors painted across the walls of the maternity ward. Her child was born healthy and angry, shrieking and wailing at the sight of the world. Lupe raised the child back out in the desert. The child was angsty and listless and selfish, grumbling moodily about homework, complaining of boredom constantly, throwing blood-curdling tantrums in the parking lots of gas stations. He had the same hazel eyes as her, with that starburst pattern of brown and green, and the same bulbous earlobes as her father, and the same tilted snaggletooth as her mother, but more than anybody in the world the child looked like Joaquin. That exact same face, round and attractive. That exact same hair. That exact same smile. And yet in terms of temperament, the child bore absolutely no resemblance whatsoever to her, or her parents, or her husband. She tried to teach the child to work hard, to take pride in a job done with care and integrity, and instead the child did chores sloppily, shrugging indifferently when confronted with a poorly made bed or messily folded laundry. She tried to teach the child to be kind to animals, to find joy in petting and feeding other creatures, and instead the child threw rocks at chained dogs, laughing with satisfaction as the dogs yelped or whimpered in pain. She tried to teach the child about materialism and humility, to find contentment in the simple pleasures of life, to be grateful and appreciative for what life provided, and the child screamed and kicked on the floor of a supermarket, shrieking with fury, overcome with rage at being denied a new toy. Lupe had always believed in souls, even before the phenomenon with the empty bodies had started, and that was why. There was no explaining how different that a child could be from its parents otherwise. A child born to bookish parents, raised by bookish parents, who took no interest in learning whatsoever. A child born to outdoorsy parents, raised by outdoorsy parents, who loathed doing activities in the wilderness. A child born to frugal parents, raised by frugal parents, who wasted money on idiotically frivolous expenses. There was no explaining that by nature or nurture. Only by chance. The particular quality of a soul. Watching the child swinging on the playset in the yard, Lupe wondered about the soul that inhabited that body. She knew the theories that the staff at the compound had promoted. That a freshly departed soul would attach to the nearest available embryo or fetus. Lupe had been less than a dozen miles from the compound on the night of the massacre. The child might be inhabited by the soul of any of the people who had died. Even by the soul of the murderer. The person who had killed her husband. When she thought about it, when she honestly considered it, she was almost certain that that must be the soul that inhabited the child. Yet she loved him anyway. Lupe had always been taught that she should judge a person by what was inside, not outside. That she shouldn't judge a person based on physical appearances. That she should judge a person based on spiritual character. The child had a cruel, greedy, miserable soul. He pulled the wings from moths and butterflies for amusement. He spilled milk onto the floor deliberately. He hammered nails into the heirloom credenza. He called her horrible names. He screamed that he hated her. He stole earrings from her jewelry box, coveting the shiny nubs of silver and gold. He lied for fun. And yet she loved him, for no other reason than that the child had come out of her body, and vaguely resembled her, and resembled her parents, and resembled her husband. Because the child happened to look like other people she had loved. Lupe stood at the window in the kitchen, watching the child run around the yard. Maybe he would grow out of it. Maybe he wouldn't. The child might grow up to be an asshole, or a chauvinist, or a racist, or a killer. It didn't matter. It just didn't. She already knew that she would love him until the day she died.

The Tour

Professionally she worked under the name of The Master, but he knew her birth name from monitoring fan sites online. Born under the name of Zoe Abbott, The Master had been raised in Georgia, where she was rumored to have taken her first gig at a backwater brothel in the mountains, the type of enterprise with musty sheets flung over bare mattresses and empty light sockets in the halls, where she had soon developed a cult following, due partly to the hype surrounding her quirk of insisting that only paying customers be allowed to see her face. After working there exactly two years, she had disappeared, just straight-up vanished, without a trace. Two years later she had reappeared with scarred hands and a hooded cloak at a harbor on the coast, claiming to have mastered all of the arts of touch: massage, chiropractic, shiatsu, ashiatsu, and the manifold genres of sex. She had done her first indie gigs for journalists and bloggers, who had quickly spread the word that she was, as claimed, a master. Since then she'd been on one long never-ending tour of the country. She appeared only in continental cities, one town per week, one gig per town. There were no known photos of her face. When spotted in public, she always wore that same black hooded cloak, identified only by the scars on her hands and the presence of her bodyguards, a pair of bald giants who accompanied her everywhere. Her abilities were legendary.

Kaveh had crossed paths with her thirteen times on the road—Seattle, Portland, Dallas, Tulsa, Birmingham, Louisville, Manchester, Hartford, Philadelphia, Richmond, Fargo, Tucson, Cheyenne—and each time he had entered the lottery for a chance to buy the ticket, and each time he had gotten an automated email saying that he hadn't been selected.

"All those towns are *huge* compared to here," Rachel said.

"The odds are still one in a thousand," Kaveh said.

"But not *everybody* who lives here will enter," Rachel said.

Rachel was lying next to him on the bed as doves cooed in the field out the window. Her hair was dyed pale lavender. Her eyelids were dusted with glitter. Her skin had a deep tan. She was wearing the same perfume she always wore, a honeyed scent, almost like marzipan. She had been working at the brothel a year now, and claimed to be twenty, but looked younger than that, with a naive pretty face that seemed to glow in the light of the dawn. Drops of his come were drying around her mouth.

"But then you've got the people willing to travel here from different cities. Buffalo, Casper. Even from different states. Montana, Nebraska. You're going to have people entering the lottery from all over the place," Kaveh said.

"Damn, you're right," Rachel said, frowning.

The Master had just announced her schedule for that fall. In a month she was going to be coming through Wyoming. She was going to do a gig right there in Sundance.

"The odds are still fucked," Kaveh said.

Rachel gazed up at the canopy of the bed with a look of wonder. "I'd do anything for that ticket. To spend a night in a room with her. To get to study her techniques." She glanced over with a grin. "She's my hero, you know?" She turned back toward the ceiling. "I'm going to be famous someday too. Tour the country, do gigs at all the best venues. Just like her."

Kaveh felt a sudden grip of panic as the curtains around the window swelled with a breeze.

"Let's enter together, the same time," Rachel said.

And so he entered the lottery for the ticket at the exact same moment that she did, each hunched over a glowing phone, pressing the buttons to register simultaneously. After getting dressed again, he handed her a wrinkled hundred-dollar bill, she gave him a pat on the ass, and then he slipped out the door as she whispered goodbye. In the hall, a pair of prostitutes in silk robes were standing in opposite doorways, murmuring together, and glanced at him as he passed.

"Kaveh," Imani said, nodding.

"Kaveh," Penelope said, smiling.

Then he stepped out of the brothel, onto the rickety porch of the old ranch, where the sunrise was casting pink-orange light onto the massive hills on the horizon, and fluffy seeds were floating down softly from the giant cottonwoods in the distance, and the sagebrush and the cheatgrass in the meadow around the brothel were swaying gently with the wind, and as the ancient floorboards creaked under his boots that feeling of panic that was gripping his body burst into an all-out roar of fear and terror and imminent danger. He bit his cheeks to suppress the feeling and got into his truck and drove back into town, where some idiot was torching a heap of garbage that reeked of burning plastic in the alley behind the motel, and some moron in a crosswalk was holding up the traffic begging for hard-earned money with a bent cardboard sign, and some jackass in sunglasses was blasting rap over the stereo of a pickup at a volume so ludicrous that he could feel the beat of the bass in his chest, and the rage in his heart was so powerful that his hands trembled on the wheel. He went home. By noon he was showered and packed and back on the road, with a thermos of coffee in the cupholder next to the gearshift. He spent the next couple of weeks driving.

★ ★ ★

Kaveh worked as a trucker. He was named after his grandfather, an immigrant refugee who'd herded cattle. Instead of cows, he drove freight. He had a vintage rig with a sink and a fridge and a narrow bed at the back of the cab. He delivered all manner of merchandise. A shipment of cheese graters that could glow in the dark. A shipment of air fresheners infused with the scent of cigars. A shipment of alarm clocks shaped like puckering assholes. A shipment of plungers that dual-functioned as umbrellas. The inscrutable creations produced by the logic of a capitalist marketplace. Because he was a patriot, and because patriotism in his country meant an unquestioning faith in the greatness of capitalism, he treated these products with the reverence with which a humble monk would treat the mysteries of God. He had a reputation for performing miracles. No matter how bad the traffic was, no matter how bad the weather was, no matter if billowing clouds of smoke burst from the hood of the truck a hundred miles from the nearest town, he never delivered a shipment late. American flag decals were stuck to the windows of the cab. He was lean and solid and hardy, with dark buzzed hair and sharp facial features. He'd been driving almost a decade, ever since he'd come back stateside. He could live on the rig for months at a time.

At gas stations and rest areas, he sometimes crossed paths with traveling artists. Musicians with dreadlocks and topknots smoking blunts in a charter bus crammed with electric guitars and synthesizer keyboards and phosphorescent props, dancers in warmups and sweatsuits alighting limberly from the shining staircase of a grand coach with miniature cans of diet soda, comedians with bowl cuts and nose rings performing impromptu monologues about the rusted nail that blew a tire on a van, prostitutes in trench coats and designer aviators flipping through glossy fashion magazines in the plush leather lounge of a stretch limousine. On tour, crossing back and forth across the country just like him.

Technically he lived in Sundance, at the cabin he'd bought a couple years before. Aside from a foldout couch in the living room, a heap of dirty pots in the kitchen sink, a mangled tube of toothpaste on the bathroom sink, and a pair of boots by the door, the rooms were empty. The walls were bare. The counters were bare. He was never there. He spent money on nothing except necessities. Fuel, meals, alcohol, and sex.

Kaveh knew other truckers who used dating apps to get laid by random strangers, or even used the old-school method of hooking up with random strangers from bars, but to him sex with a stranger seemed unnecessarily risky, and was generally disappointing, too. He preferred to eat at establishments that were regulated by health inspectors, he preferred to drink at establishments that were regulated by health inspectors, and he preferred to have sex with somebody who had the paperwork to prove that they were free of venereal diseases, and who required the same paperwork from you. A professional, who wasn't going to fake an orgasm under you with pitifully unconvincing moans, or fumble drunkenly through some sloppy foreplay before using you for a quickie. Somebody with reviews. When he was home, he went to the brothel at the ranch every couple of days. While he was out on the road, he typically visited a new brothel after each delivery. He had an encyclopedic knowledge of the contemporary brothel scene. The Master had fascinated him for half a decade. He had exactly one hundred thousand dollars set aside in an account at the bank. The price of a ticket to see The Master.

He asked about her during those next couple of weeks on the road. In brewpubs, in taprooms, he met people who'd seen her. A geologist who'd spotted her and her bodyguards wandering the ghost town near Missoula; a ranger who'd spotted her and her bodyguards entering the pictograph cave near Billings; both times she had been wearing the hooded cloak, and neither the geologist nor the ranger had been able to catch a glimpse of her face. He met a tattooed bartender in Flagstaff who swore to have served a pair of old-fashioneds to her bodyguards, and at a cantina in Reno he met a rodeo star wearing a denim jacket over a rhinestone bra who claimed to have actually spent a night with her the year before.

"It was the most profound experience of my life," the rodeo star said, gazing into a glass of bourbon with a pensive look, but when

Kaveh asked what The Master looked like, she only smiled and then drifted away into the crowd.

A known vegetarian, The Master was rumored to be lactose intolerant. She was suspected to have an interest in voodoo. She was believed to have an aversion to incense. Her astrological signs were a mystery. Although the name of the school that she had attended was unknown, online there existed a scanned image of a blurred photocopy of a tattered report card for a student by the name of Zoe Abbott, which, if the same Zoe Abbott, revealed that in school she had struggled with dyslexia, had often fallen asleep in mathematics, and had excelled at art, history, psychology, and gym. She'd been an only child. She'd been a teenaged orphan. In the absence of any supporting evidence whatsoever, a rumor persisted that she'd been a weeaboo when she was young. Her bodyguards, who otherwise had never shown any signs of possessing a sense of humor, had once told a reporter that her favorite colors were infrared and ultraviolet. Video clips of her signing autographs, sometimes with markers, sometimes with pens, confirmed that she was ambidextrous. Nobody knew the story behind the scars on her hands. Whatever her motives were, she didn't seem to be in the game for money. She was a multimillionaire, the wealthiest prostitute in the world, and owned no property.

Sometimes while he was driving on a highway, he would glance over to find an automated semi in the lane next to him, coasting along the road with an empty cab. Prototypes, steered by algorithms and sensors, with no need for human drivers. He could tug the pull cord for the air horn, but the automated trucks never honked back.

He felt a connection with her in that way. A decade of legalization had produced a renaissance in her profession, and within a decade his profession would be replaced by computers. He was going to be out of a job.

In Omaha, leaving a convenience store he spotted a couple of teenagers spray-painting a war monument.

"What the fuck are you doing?" Kaveh shouted.

The teenagers bolted down the street.

"Huh?" Kaveh shouted, chasing after the teenagers with a rusted pipe from the gutter.

He spent a night with a prostitute named Beatriz in a wood-paneled brothel in El Paso. He spent a night with a prostitute named Nyala in a velvet-walled brothel in Sioux Falls. He spent a night at a brothel in Tombstone with a set of identical triplets, one with a bun, one with a bob, one with box braids, all double-jointed, who worked under the name Sibling Rivalry. He spent a night in Denver at a brothel called the Mile High Club, having a spontaneous orgy with an impromptu ensemble, Anastasia, Guadalupe, Bryndis, Brandon, Rhett, and Chastity, as a pink-green aurora shimmered above the Rockies. He delivered a shipment of suicide-bomber bobbleheads to a warehouse in Santa Monica, and then went to The Playhouse, a hip bordello on Venice Beach, where he spent the morning with an up-and-coming prostitute who worked under the name Goddess Of The Sun And The Sea, who could do tricks with her tongue like he'd never seen.

"Porn actors, cam stars, strippers, prostitutes, we're all performers," said the Goddess Of The Sun And The Sea, feeding grapes to him afterward as the dazzling light sparkling on the waves beyond the balcony twinkled across her face and her body and the sheet on the bed, which she'd soaked when she'd squirted. "Anybody working in this industry has my complete respect. But being a porn actor is the easiest, because you're being filmed, you can do retakes, you can make mistakes, and afterward the director can always just edit out any weird noises or expressions that you made. I was a porn actor a while. I did the cam star thing too. Being a cam star, that's not as easy, because then you're live, and it's even interactive, but still, you've got a camera between you and the audience, so you have a lot of control over the show." She had curly golden hair twisted into an updo, with a loose strand hanging down around the freckles on her nose. "Stripping, now, that's some hard work, because then not only are you performing live, but the audience is right there with you, in the room. Still, with stripping what you're doing is mostly choreographed, you're just doing a set routine, and you usually don't have to touch anybody. It's not that interactive." She kicked her feet back and forth in the air, playfully. "But this, this here. This is what's the hardest. Prostitution. There's no cameras, it's totally interactive, you're doing a live performance, and the audience is literally in the room with you, and isn't going to look away from you even once." She reached into the bowl on the nightstand, twisting a grape from the vine. "To perform under conditions like that, to achieve some level of artistry, that's the ultimate challenge."

She fed him another grape as palm trees swayed with a breeze beyond the balcony.

"Not all dancing is art. Not all movies are art. Sometimes a dance or a movie is just entertainment. I've been thinking about that a lot lately. Young Baby Elvis, this other hooker who's doing a run here, yesterday he said that the difference between art and entertainment is emotion. That art has an emotional component, beyond just your basic animal feelings like excitement or arousal. I mean, fuck, it's true. Even a squirrel can get excited. Even a possum can get aroused. But to touch another human emotionally, like only another human can be, that's fucking art," said the Goddess Of The Sun And The Sea.

A couple of seagulls squawked out on the balcony as she fed him another grape.

"I think that's why what we do is so valuable. Other performing arts, like ballet or theater, can basically be reproduced. But not what we do. Like a painting, or a sculpture, each fuck is absolutely unique. Irreproducible. A distinct work of art. What just happened in here was as much you as me," said the Goddess Of The Sun And The Sea.

She popped a grape into her mouth, rolling the grape around on her tongue for a while before chewing and swallowing with obvious pleasure.

"The Master is doing a gig in my town next week," Kaveh said.

She froze. A look of awe, almost even of fear, came over her face. The look gave him a chill. He had expected her to know the name, but he hadn't expected a reaction that intense. The very mention of the name seemed to have shaken her. She turned toward the balcony.

"Nobody else can do what she does," murmured the Goddess Of The Sun And The Sea.

That night he awoke suddenly on the bed in the cab with his heart pounding, his chest damp with sweat, his skin crawling with terror. He sat naked in the moonlight on the edge of the mattress with his face in his hands, breathing, and then once his pulse had calmed he washed his face with a splash of water from the sink. Midnight. He couldn't remember the nightmare.

He reached for the phone glowing on the counter. He'd gotten an automated email an hour earlier. He hadn't won the lottery for the ticket. He laughed, bitterly. He couldn't even win with a home-court advantage.

Rachel had called him. Kaveh called her back. She didn't say anything when the phones connected. He could hear owls hooting in the background.

"I got the email too," Kaveh said.

"I didn't get that email," Rachel said.

Her voice held a barely contained spark.

"You *won*?" Kaveh said.

He could hear the giddy smile in her voice as she rambled, "I tried calling you right away, I just needed to tell somebody, I've never won anything before in my life, and then, with odds like that, I win *this*?" She burst out laughing. "This is so crazy. I'm such an idiot. I can't even go. I can't afford it. I've got like a hundred dollars in the bank. I'm going to have to turn the ticket down." She exhaled. "I just keep sitting here, just staring at the email, in just like total disbelief. I only entered my name out of principle. I never thought my name would get drawn." She suddenly sounded wistful. "Still, though, there's something amazing about all of it. Like, even if we'll never meet each other, now she's at least read my name."

Kaveh jerked at the sound of glass smashing nearby. He peered out the windshield. Some fuckers in hoodies, probably unemployed, on unemployment, were throwing beer bottles against a garbage bin for fun. At fucking midnight, in the parking lot of a packed truck stop, while people with actual jobs were trying to sleep. Patriotism meant loving the traditions and the values of the country and hating most of the people who lived there. Not her though. He thought about the way she had looked in bed that night that she had talked about The Master, lying there in her bedroom with that shiny lavender hair and that smooth tan skin, her eyes glowing with ambition. He didn't know anybody else with a dream like that. He believed in her. She could be famous someday. She deserved to be famous. And this ticket, getting to spend a night with her hero, might make all the difference in her career.

"Are you still there?" Rachel said.

"I'll pay for you."

He heard a clatter as she dropped the phone, and then a moment later she was back again, breathless.

"Is this a joke?" Rachel said.

"I've got the cash."

Her voice was suddenly low and urgent. "Kaveh, if you do this for me, I swear, you'll never pay to see me again."

"I'll be back in town again tomorrow. I'll transfer the money to you then."

"Omigod." She squealed in excitement. "I can't believe this is happening." She laughed. "I'd give you the biggest kiss if you were here."

After hanging up he lay back down on the bed in the cab, picturing her sitting at the vanity in her bedroom as stars glittered above the meadow. Maybe someday when she was a celebrity she would hire him as a bodyguard. Maybe that was what he would do when the computers took over the roads.

★ ★ ★

The Master arrived in town at midnight, during a rainstorm, emerging from the dark backseat of a limousine with tinted windows, holding a shopping bag that appeared to be full of pomegranates. She was renting the historic hotel downtown for the week. Not just a room, but the entire building. Her bodyguards walked her to the door with a black umbrella and then jogged back to the limousine to carry her luggage, a pair of antique leather suitcases with gleaming brass latches, from the trunk into the lobby.

Kaveh was at the bar later that week as a crowd gathered in the multicolored light to gossip about sightings. Cash Taylor, who owned the hotel, had met her in the lobby that night that she had arrived to hand over a set of keys. As always, he said, she had been wearing the hooded cloak. The scars on her hands were pink and terrible and had frightened him badly. Although the cloak had hid her feet, he swore that he had heard the unmistakable sound of flip-flops flapping as she had crossed the lobby to the stairs.

"I can tell you this much, she never talks," said Bart, who had a business working as a tour guide for local attractions and had been hired to take her sightseeing the morning after she had arrived in town. Bald and beefy with a jawline of rugged stubble, Bart corroborated that she wore flip-flops, and moreover was able to add that based on the size of the footprints that she left in the dirt, her feet were large, same as her hands. Bart had spent a day with her, from sunrise to sunset, and hadn't heard her speak even once. He had taken her to the town museum, the truss bridge, the buffalo jump, and the windswept cluster of tents at the archaeological dig, where a blushing graduate student had begged her to autograph a dusty handkerchief. She had specifically requested to see Devils Tower, which of course he would have taken her to even if she hadn't asked, being the first national monument in the country. Standing there in the hooded cloak, The Master had gazed at the butte for nearly an hour, as if the site held some personal significance to her, and from there he had taken her even further into the mountains, to see the sights that only a native could have shown her, the local secrets that weren't on any map. Tiered waterfalls that cascaded down cliffs before scattering to mist in midair, smoking fumaroles that had stained the surrounding dirt the color of ash, and the secret thermal spring in the grove of ponderosas, where steam rose from the shimmering emerald water in the pool, which legend said was great for the complexion. Presumably she had removed the hooded cloak to bathe in the pool, but her bodyguards had kept watch while she soaked, telling him to wait further on down the trail.

After the tour was finished he had gone back to the pool alone, hoping that she might have forgotten something, maybe some hair bands, maybe some lip balm, some authentic celebrity belonging that he could auction off online. Instead she had left behind only an eerie silence.

"I've never heard those woods like that. The birds, the insects, everything out there had gone totally quiet. You could practically hear the heat rising from the water," Bart said.

Janice, who was gray-haired and stocky and worked as a librarian, had seen her on the side of the highway that next day. The Master had apparently gotten out of the limousine to examine a skunk that had been hit by a car. Janice had driven past her as she was standing over the carcass. Although her face had been hidden by the cloak, her shoulders had appeared to be shaking.

"What was she doing?" Kaveh said.

"Laughing? Crying?" Janice guessed.

"Shivering," Bart said, and the others around the bar agreed that the wind had been fierce that day, and that being from down south she just must not be used to the weather.

Sawyer had seen her carrying a tub of detergent into the hotel, Quint had seen her carrying a bouquet of tulips into the hotel, and Emilio, who worked as a prostitute out at the brothel at the old ranch, had not only seen her eat at the taqueria—she'd had chips and guac with the famous horchata—but afterward had managed to grab a napkin that she had used to wipe her mouth. Emilio had gotten the napkin framed just that morning, and had the napkin with him at the bar. Petite and effeminate, with elfin charms, Emilio was reputed to have the sweetest-tasting semen in the West. Kaveh had once seen him naked at the brothel, scampering down the hallway with a giggle, chasing a patron with a wooden paddle, and could attest firsthand that the prostitute had chiseled abs, sculpted buttocks, and a purplish cock of startling beauty and girth, which swung back and forth in the air with a profound gravity when he ran. Janice had recently announced to a crowd at the bar that he had once brought her to climax a dozen times in a single night, after which she'd had to sit on an airplane pillow at work for a week. Bart, who'd recently celebrated a silver anniversary with Janice, and whose sex drive was somewhat sluggish, often made emotional toasts in gratitude to Emilio, who he claimed had saved their marriage. Janice saw Emilio at the brothel about once a month. Bart and Emilio played checkers together sometimes on the weekends.

"Just think how much you could get for that online," Bart exclaimed.

Emilio clutched the frame with a rapturous smile.

"I'll carry this treasure with me for all my life," Emilio cried.

The napkin was smudged with a thick blotchy smear of bright scarlet, maybe from lipstick or salsa. Kaveh squinted, searching for some insight into the shape of the mouth that had made the mark. The mark was as inscrutable as an inkblot.

"I heard that cloak she wears is magic or enchanted or something," Maisie said.

"I heard she doesn't even take the cloak off while she's fucking," Tessa said.

"There's no way that's true," Kaveh said with a snort.

"That it's magic or that she doesn't even take it off during intercourse?" said Cash Taylor.

"I just still can't believe that one of us won," said Jezebel, plump and curvy with wild strawberry blond hair, who also worked as a prostitute at the brothel on the old ranch. Her specialties were anal, fisting, pegging, tribbing, and virgins of any gender. She'd taken his virginity in the meadow behind the brothel, the summer after he'd graduated, the week before he'd deployed, when he was still just a kid. Kaveh hadn't even dared to make an appointment. His father had thought he was riding trails. Kaveh had sat outside of the brothel on his muddy dirt bike, wavering, too scared to go inside, foot poised on the pedal, on the verge of kick-starting the engine to drive away again, and then a figure in a light blue petticoat had stepped out onto the porch, wrapped in a billowing linen shawl. When she'd seen that he was too nervous to go into the ranch, she'd offered to take him into the meadow behind the brothel, laying the shawl down under a fir tree as startled pronghorns had galloped off toward the hills. She was the oldest prostitute who worked there, long past fifty now, and liked to roleplay. He hadn't slept with her since coming back from overseas, and still, whenever she looked at him she looked at him like she owned him, with this coy smile.

"Rachel should play the stock market, that's how lucky she is," Owen said.

"Lucky to have such a generous sponsor," Harper said, glancing at him.

"Kaveh, do you have a crush?" Emilio cooed.

"It's not like that."

"Where is she tonight anyway?" Jezebel frowned.

"I think working."

Kaveh took a swig of lager, embarrassed that everybody knew he had financed the ticket for Rachel. When he thought about her going to the gig though, about her getting to meet her hero, about her getting to pursue her dream, the embarrassed feeling was trumped by a sense of pride. He had done that. He'd made that possible. To have been part of a moment that important was worth a hundred grand. The buzz from the beer made the lights in the bar seem to shimmer like nuggets of gold.

"I swear to god, The Master coming here is the most exciting thing that's ever happened to Crook County, and that includes the Sundance Kid," declared Cash Taylor.

A group of rednecks walking past the crowd toward the door of the bar called out some unsolicited opinions.

"That bitch should be run out of town."

"The same as the rest of you whores."

"Man, fuck you," Kaveh spat, slipping off of the stool to take a swing at the fuckers, but then he felt hands grabbing at him from behind.

"Hey there, kiddo," said Cash Taylor, holding him back as the fuckers filed out through the door, tipping the brims of camouflage ballcaps at the crowd in farewell.

Kaveh had a sighting that night after leaving the bar. Not of her, but her bodyguards. As he shuffled past the convenience store across from the hotel, he saw her bodyguards flipping through magazines at the rack by the doors. The sight stunned him. He'd seen hundreds of photos of her bodyguards before online, but her bodyguards were even more formidable in real life. One had light skin. He was rumored to be trained in jujitsu. One had dark skin. He was rumored to be a former boxer. Nobody knew what her bodyguards were named. There was a contingent of fans who desperately longed for her bodyguards to be lovers, maybe even to be secretly married to each other, but at the very least to be secretly dating, and having lots of sex, preferably in very steamy showers, while tenderly whispering sweet nothings into each other's ears. Fans who belonged to this contingent were referred to as "sbs," or "steamy bodyguard sex" fans. Whether her bodyguards were actually a couple wasn't known. What was known, what was verifiable, thanks to a somewhat blurry video filmed by a bystander, was that when a pair of obsessed lunatics had once rushed her with a couple of butcher knives, her bodyguards had leapt without hesitating between her and the attackers, ducking swipes of the blades, delivering swift blows to throats, dodging jabs of the blades, delivering quick kicks to chins, and afterward, panting over the broken bodies of the assailants, when her bodyguards had glanced over and had each realized that the other hadn't been harmed, her bodyguards had shared a poignant, arguably even romantic, look. Her bodyguards had also broken the wrists and fingers of countless fraternity brothers who had attempted to dehood her on dares. Videos that belonged to this genre were referred to as "bgo," or "bros getting owned" videos. For some reason sbs fans seemed to take particular pleasure in bgo videos.

The bell hanging from the doors jingled as he stuck his head into the convenience store.

"Describe her in one word," Kaveh slurred.

Her bodyguards stared at him, then responded to him simultaneously.

"Innocent."

"Immortal."

He took out his phone as he shuffled across the parking lot of the convenience store.

"Hello?" Rachel said.

"I just saw her mercenaries in the flesh," Kaveh said.

Rachel laughed. "You're so drunk."

"I believe in you."

"I appreciate that sweetheart."

"You're going to be better than she is."

"I think you might be biased."

"The greatest artist of all time."

When she spoke her voice held a barely contained joy. "You really think so?"

She had to go. Her gig for the night was coming back from the bathroom. She quick whispered goodbye.

As he was putting away his phone he saw the group of rednecks from the bar strolling down the sidewalk across the road.

"Fucking puritans," Kaveh shouted, and when the rednecks saw him the group rushed him, throwing a wild punch at him, wrestling him down onto the pavement, landing a kick to his ribs, knocking the wind from his lungs, and then he managed to scramble across the pavement to where his truck was parked, grabbing the tire iron stored under the cab, gripping the tire iron like a baseball bat, crouching next to the truck, threatening to knock the next person who touched him out of the ballpark, and then after the rednecks had taken the opportunity to call him a pussy, a dick, an asshole, and a socialist, the rednecks strolled back off down the sidewalk, flipping him off.

Panting, he dropped the tire iron onto the pavement, glanced at the convenience store, and then froze.

The Master was watching him.

Seeing her in person sent a tingle down the skin on the back of his neck. She was standing with her bodyguards by the doors to the convenience store. He hadn't even realized that she had been in the convenience store too. The brilliant fluorescent lights streaming through the doors behind her made her appear to have a dazzling aura. The hood of the cloak hid her completely, but from the direction she was facing, she was clearly staring straight at him. He was paralyzed by her gaze. He didn't move a muscle until she finally turned away.

He wiped some blood from his lip, and she crossed the road toward the hotel with her bodyguards both in tow, carrying a shopping bag full of toiletries.

Kaveh had been driving for almost a decade. By now he had seen the entire country. He had seen a solar eclipse darken the sky above downtown Des Moines. He had seen a rainbow shimmer in the sky above downtown Santa Fe. He had seen a sudden hailstorm in the parking lot of a diner in Baton Rouge, massive lumps of hail smashing windshields and denting roofs as the owners of the vehicles cried out in protest. The salt flats in Utah, both in summer, when the bright white salt cracked apart in patterns like honeycomb, glowing in the sunlight, and in winter, when the shallow layer of water covering the salt glistened like glass, reflecting the clouds. A sunrise burning over the rugged hills beyond the pink and green waters of Great Salt Lake. A sunset casting a gold and pink glow across the rolling slopes of the Great Sand Dunes. Moonlight shining across the striped pinnacles of the Badlands. New-moon stars glimmering over the towering mesas at Zion. The primitive colonial structures at Strawbery Banke. The ancient cliff dwellings at Mesa Verde. Elk grazing in a prairie in Colorado, pheasants with iridescent feathers bursting from a grassy thicket in Ohio, vibrant starfish clinging to crags in kelpy tide pools in Maine. Moose breathing steam in a snowfield in Wisconsin. Pelicans with bright crimson bills diving for fish in a rocky cove in Louisiana. Beavers with massive tails chewing bark from a beech tree in a forest in Virginia. He had seen a dust storm engulf the telephone poles and the streets and the traffic lights and the houses on the outskirts of Albuquerque. He had seen an ice storm crystallize the fire hydrants and the sidewalks and the power lines and the homes on the outskirts of Montpelier. Teenagers in tutus tossing batons during a parade in Cut And Shoot. Children in jackets waving sparklers as fireworks glittered above Truth Or Consequences. Surfers in dripping wetsuits carving the waves in Montauk. Crouching skateboarders zigzagging down the palmy boulevards in Hollywood. People dressed in alien costumes withdrawing money from a teller machine in Roswell. Celebrity impersonators waiting in line for a bathroom at a beach resort in the Keys. Burlesque performers in feathered hats taking a smoking break behind a casino on the Strip. Halloween in Oakland, Austin, Charlotte, Minneapolis, Topeka, Savannah, Jackson, Plymouth, and Hell. Conspiracy theorists standing with binoculars on the desert highway along Area 51. Internet influencers posing for photos at abandoned repair shops on Route 66. He had contemplated the glory of Old Faithful, inspected the candle-smoke signatures in the depths of Mammoth Cave, and regarded the majesty of Niagara Falls. Seen all of the inexplicable human spectacles, the mysterious sights that weren't in any guidebook, that were only possible to see once. A gangster in a bigfoot mask hopping into a getaway car after robbing a bodega in New Jersey. Somebody in a colorful aloha shirt throwing a pair of hightops with the laces knotted together onto a telephone wire in Mississippi. Somebody with a scuffed briefcase running off into an alley after lighting a garbage bin on fire behind a motel in Indiana. A family in mismatched pajamas fleeing from the doorway of a blazing duplex in Oklahoma. A rabble of distraught tenants huddling together as flames consumed an apartment complex in Delaware. Firefighters attempting to restrain a shopkeeper with a tousled combover who was fighting to enter a burning toy store in Washington. Kids watching from a window as a couple in bathrobes struggled to extinguish a cross burning in a lawn in Memphis. A couple with a stroller trying to use a cane umbrella to remove a noose hanging from a streetlight in Columbus. A sunburned man in tattered clothing perched on a milk crate on a sidewalk in Boise, shouting doomsday prophecies in a shrill voice. A blind woman with foggy eyes kneeling at the base of a drive-thru speaker in Providence, muttering an incoherent prayer to dead presidents. The shadow of a hand making obscene gestures in the light of the projector at a drive-in theater in Kentucky. A handful of pennies tossed from a roller coaster pelting down onto the crowd milling around a carnival in Missouri. Protestors in bandannas ducking behind parked cars as police in riot gear fired canisters of tear gas in Chicago. Pedestrians diving for the sidewalk as the windows of a strip mall shattered during a drive-by shooting in Orlando. A hit-and-run in San Diego, somebody in a roadster with neon sunglasses and windswept hair cruising off through a stoplight after sideswiping a cyclist. Rubberneckers gawking at the hole that a jackknifed semi had punched through the guardrail on a mountain pass in West Virginia. Somebody with an iced mocha keying the paint on an ambulance in the parking lot of a coffee shop in Oregon. Somebody in moccasins and a sundress screaming at a vending machine full of potato chips in Maryland, beating on the glass. Somebody in scrubs yelling at a clerk at a post office in Iowa, swearing to take revenge over a lost package. Somebody in coveralls shouting at a loan officer in a bank in Alabama, threatening to sue after being denied a mortgage. A holiday display toppling as a couple of shoppers grappled with each other in the aisle of an electronics store in Lincoln, fighting over a box of limited-edition headphones. Somebody throwing trash from the windows of a motor home on a turnpike in the Tetons, ignoring the horns of the veering traffic. Somebody drifting drunkenly between the lanes of a freeway in the Dakotas. Somebody speeding in the wrong direction down an expressway in the Carolinas. Somebody behind the wheel of a rusted minivan swerving to hit a rabbit on a highway in Window

Rock. Somebody firing a semiautomatic at a flock of ducks from a bridge over the Rio Grande.

The Master was a sightseer, the same as he was. She had been traveling nonstop almost half a decade. By now she had seen the entire country too.

Kaveh woke up at noon on the day of the gig, sprawled across the mattress of the foldout couch in his cabin. He felt anxious but no panic. He ate some cereal, did some pushups, did some crunches, did some squats, took a shower, got dressed in an indigo work shirt and some faded black jeans, and then went out to the truck. Rachel must have had the ticket by then, the actual physical ticket to the gig. Kaveh wanted to swing by the ranch to talk to her, just to see the ticket in person, and hear her geek out about getting to meet her hero, and make her swear to tell him all the details afterward, and maybe pitch her the idea about being her bodyguard someday, but just as he was getting into the truck his phone rang. Layne, his neighbor, needed help dragging an ancient water boiler out of her basement. Carrie, her new girlfriend, was over there to help with the water boiler too. So instead of driving to the ranch, Kaveh went next door and spent the next hour grunting and straining and wiping grease and dirt and flecks of rust from his hands onto his pants, helping maneuver the water boiler across the basement to the staircase. Like everybody else, Layne and her girlfriend wanted to gossip about The Master.

"Rachel won the ticket, right?" Layne said, sitting on the steps, taking a break.

"Rachel, like from the brothel?" Carrie said, leaning back against the banister, breathing hard.

Kaveh was resting against the water boiler, which was so massive that the bottom had gouged a jagged line into the cement floor. He still felt anxious but no panic.

"She's going to be famous someday too," Kaveh said.

"I slept with her once," Layne said.

"Rachel?" Kaveh said, turning to look at her.

"She really should be famous. Chick's got some legitimate talent with a clit. On a totally different level than the rest of the hoes at that place," Layne said.

Hearing that she believed in her too made him even more sure that the hundred grand had been well spent.

"Come on, let's get this upstairs," Carrie said, standing.

Kaveh helped try to hoist the water boiler up the staircase, but after another hour of struggling, the steps were scuffed, the banister was busted, and the water boiler was still in the basement. Layne finally announced that she was ready to quit. Carrie said that she was ready to quit too. Kaveh didn't want to let the water boiler win. As he was standing there staring at that massive cylinder of rusting metal, a car backfired out on the road, echoing through the house like distant gunfire, and the anxious feeling tingled across his skin, and now there was a current of panic. The sight of the water boiler suddenly made him angry. It infuriated him. It enraged him. It suddenly seemed to be threatening him. He wanted it out of that house. He wanted to try again.

"I'll just have to pay some people to come through and haul it out," Layne said, wiping sweat with a bandanna.

"We can do it," Kaveh insisted.

"Kaveh, there's no way," Carrie said.

"Just help me push," Kaveh snapped.

"It's too heavy, man," Carrie said.

And he kept arguing about the water boiler for so long that eventually the others actually got mad at him for refusing to let it go, and then he gave up on the water boiler too, and left. As he got back into the truck he sent a message to Rachel, asking her what time that she was going to head to the gig. He would have just driven straight to the ranch, but he was hungry again, and he didn't have any food in the cabin except for cereal, so he drove into town, where he swung by the bank to get some cash. The flagpole at the bank was bare. He tried not to get angry but he was already angry by the time he went into the lobby. He went over to the teller at the counter.

"What happened to the flag?" Kaveh said.

The teller smiled awkwardly. Gary, the custodian, was supposed to raise the flag in the morning, but he had called in sick at the last second, and none of the other custodians on staff had been able to cover his shift, and the other employees at the bank were all too busy to do his job. So the flag was folded up in a box in the broom closet, where the flag had been all day. Kaveh offered to go out and raise the flag himself, but the teller said that she actually couldn't let him raise the flag, because, like, legally the bank just couldn't allow that, because if he got injured somehow, like twisted an ankle or something, then he could sue the bank, and the bank didn't want that, obviously. Kaveh tried to convince the teller that he wasn't interested in suing the bank, that he was only trying to help, but the teller said that was exactly what somebody who was interested in suing the bank would say, and the bank was closing soon anyway, and then the flag would just have to be taken down again, and so there really wasn't any point. Kaveh was about to argue that yes, there was, but then a jackhammer started slugging pavement somewhere near the bank, making the knob on the door to the office behind the counter rattle, and the sound of the knob rattling made that feeling of panic rise, and he wanted out, so he gave up, just withdrew the cash and left. He went over to the grill to get a cheeseburger and sat next to a family with a kid who kept throwing plastic toys at passing servers, and whose parents did nothing to intervene. He went over to the creamery to get a milkshake and stood in line behind a customer with an eyebrow piercing who kept swearing at the cashier, and whose friends did nothing but snicker. Somebody had spilled a gallon of motor oil back out on the street, and then had just abandoned the mess, tub and all. The maddening pop music that had been blasting over the speakers at the grill and the creamery was stuck in his head. And that was why he hated being between jobs, hated being caught in a standstill back at home, not because there was anything horrible about that town in particular, but because that town was just as horrible as everywhere else.

By then the sun was sinking toward the horizon. Rachel still hadn't responded to the message he'd sent. He was walking back to the truck when he saw a couple of people in leather jackets jabbing a screwdriver into the tire of a convertible parked at the bakery across the street.

"Hey, what the fuck?" Kaveh shouted.

The people bolted, and he chased the fuckers, and the fuckers outran him, and hopped onto a motorcycle, and revved the engine, and both got away, speeding off toward the highway, and when he went back to the bakery to warn the driver that the tires on the convertible had been slashed, the convertible was already gone.

"Goddamnit," Kaveh murmured, staring at the empty parking space.

Rachel would have to leave for the gig soon. She didn't answer when he tried calling, which might have meant she was already on the way to the hotel, but he drove to the brothel anyway, still hoping that maybe he would get to see her before the gig. He kept expecting to pass her on the winding dirt road from the highway to the ranch, but he didn't pass anybody at all. Quail were darting between cottonwoods. The meadow was turning gold. Fuck, he was in an agitated state of mind. He bit his cheeks to suppress the feeling. All of the usual cars were parked at the brothel. Rachel's janky powder-blue hatchback was sitting in the shade of the hickory tree at the edge of the parking lot, with fallen catkins caught between the wipers and the hood. Dust exploded around his boots as he hopped out of the truck, heading toward the porch. He realized that he'd forgotten his phone in the truck when he heard his phone chime, but he was already moving, and he didn't go back. His phone was ringing in the truck as he stepped into the ranch.

"Is she still here?" Kaveh asked the bouncers, who were playing liar's dice in the lobby. Blake nodded yes, Wayne grunted yes, and then the bouncers went back to peeking at the dice under the cups. Delilah, the manager, was taking an appointment over the phone, jotting down info with a silver pen. Kaveh said, "Why hasn't she left?"

Delilah made a face at him, doing an eye-roll, as if he wouldn't even believe how ridiculous the answer to that question was, and then returned to logging info about the appointment.

Kaveh strode down the hallway. The hallway was dim, lit only by the sunlight streaming into the ranch through the windows back in the lobby. Every door in the hallway was shut. From behind each door came muffled noises. A giggle. A whimper. A moan. But when he reached the door at the end of the hallway, her bedroom was silent. He knocked, and waited, then knocked again, and then waited. Silence.

"Rachel," Kaveh said.

Finally he heard movement in there, the squeak of bedsprings, a creak of floorboards, as somebody came toward the door.

Rachel peered out of the bedroom into the hallway. He'd only ever seen her in silk robes, satin slips, hourglass corsets, lace babydolls, fishnet teddies, push-up bras, high-waisted panties, g-string thongs, leather pants so low on the hips that the dimples in her back peeked over the waistline, flimsy vintage dresses buttoned so low that her cleavage spilled over the loose hem of the neckline, jacquard bustiers strapped to ultra sheer stockings by garters so tight that the bands thrummed when plucked, bright lipsticks, colorful eyeshadows, diamond earrings, pearl necklaces, and bracelets and anklets made of lustrous gold, but tonight she wore a baggy soccer hoodie with the name of a nearby school district, wrinkled cotton shorts stained with a smudge of jam or chocolate, and a mismatched pair of socks. Her hair was a mess, her nail polish was chipped, and though he'd never seen bags under her eyes before, the skin under her eyes looked dark and puffy.

Kaveh stared. "Doesn't the gig start soon?"

"I'm not going," Rachel said.

Kaveh laughed. "What are you talking about?"

"I'm being serious," Rachel said.

Her voice sounded strangely monotone and depressed.

"What did you do with the money?" Kaveh said with a frown,

suddenly realizing that she must have spent the hundred grand on something else.

But she hadn't. Reaching into the pouch on her hoodie, she took out a ticket printed on metallic gold cardstock with glossy black lettering. She showed him.

The Master, Grand Hotel, June 1, 9 Oclock, Sundance, Wyoming.

Rachel reached across the threshold to tuck the ticket into the pocket on his shirt.

"What are you doing?" Kaveh said, staring down at the ticket in confusion.

"I already transferred the ticket to your name," Rachel said.

"No."

"You should have just gotten a confirmation," Rachel said.

"You need to get dressed."

"All you'll need is the usual paperwork," Rachel said.

"You're going to be late."

"I just called you to tell you," Rachel said.

"I can drive you there."

"Kaveh, I already decided, I'm not going."

"This is your dream," Kaveh exploded.

Rachel turned away from him with a look of misery.

"I'm not an artist," Rachel said sadly, and then shuffled into her bedroom, easing the door shut behind her.

"Rachel," Kaveh said through the door.

He felt the door shift in the jamb as she sank back against the wood.

"Rachel," Kaveh shouted, pounding on the door.

Troubled faces appeared in doorways just down the hall. Imani, Penelope.

"What did you two say to her?" Kaveh shouted.

Jezebel, Emilio, other faces appeared in doorways further down the hall.

"What the fuck did you all say?" Kaveh shouted.

He was pounding on the door to her bedroom again when the bouncers appeared. Blake grabbed him around the waist, Wayne grabbed him by the ankles, and he felt a heart-stopping lurch of gravity as the bouncers flipped him into the air and lugged him off down the hall.

"Rachel," Kaveh shouted, clawing desperately at the wallpaper, the faded runner, the wooden trim, the bearskin rug on the floor of the lobby, watching helplessly as her doorway at the end of the hall receded and vanished into the shadows.

The bouncers carried him out onto the porch and tossed him into the dirt. The steer skull hanging on the door clattered as the door slammed back shut. He coughed into the dust.

Meadowlarks flitted away from the roof. Crickets were chirping at the sunset. Looking at the linen curtains hanging in the windows of the ranch, the muted violet-orange light shimmering across the ripples in the handblown glass, he realized with a sense of despair that none of the other prostitutes at the brothel had said a word to her. Nobody had convinced her that she wasn't an artist. She'd believed that she wasn't an artist all along. She was the only person he knew with a dream, and she was too afraid of failing to try for it. She would die in that town.

★ ★ ★

He drove, pressing the pedal to the floor of the cab, catching air on the bumps in the road, slamming back to the ground with a thud, skidding around bends, scattering flocks of swallows, speeding back toward town in a whirl of dust and fury, with no time to swing by home, no time to bathe, no time to change, still wearing the indigo shirt and the faded jeans he'd been wearing when he'd tried to help move the water boiler, and when he'd gotten jerked around by the bank teller, and when he'd tried to chase down the tire slashers, and when he'd gotten thrown out of the brothel, streaked with grease and dirt and rust and dust, and he was still furious about the water boiler, and he was still furious about the bank teller, and he was still furious about the tire slashers, and he was furious at Rachel, but nothing, absolutely nothing, infuriated him like The Master. Her whole act, the hidden face, never talking, acting mysterious, it was all a scam, just hype and gimmicks, and the people who had spent a night with her were too scared to admit it, too afraid of the repercussions, too afraid of the humiliation, having dropped a hundred grand on a hustle. He was sure of that suddenly, and it filled him with rage, and he was glad that he had the ticket now, so that he could experience the letdown firsthand, and he could expose the truth to the world. When he got to the hotel he parked the truck in the middle of the empty parking lot, crookedly, because he could.

Her bodyguards were waiting at the desk in the lobby, both wearing tuxedos, both looking impatient.

"Boots off."

"Socks too."

Kaveh padded barefoot over to the desk. Her bodyguards scanned the black-light watermark on the paperwork from his physician, and then had him sign a liability waiver, which was standard, and a non-disclosure agreement, which was not. He was forbidden, among other stipulations, from taking photos of her, from recording videos of her, from ever making sketches or paintings or any other visual representations of her from memory, and from ever speaking publicly or privately about her, either out loud or in writing.

Her bodyguards stared at him.

"Kaveh, did you read this carefully?"

"Yes," Kaveh said.

"Then you understand what will happen if you break this contract."

"Yes," Kaveh said.

"You'll never be welcome at a brothel in this country again."

After he'd deposited his keys and his wallet and his phone into a lockbox, her bodyguards waved him with a metal detector, patted him down, looked him over, and then finally nodded with approval, gazing at him like a couple of farmers admiring a fleeced sheep.

"Don't talk while you're in there."

"And remember to mind your manners."

"Don't you need the ticket?" Kaveh asked, taking the ticket out of the pocket on his shirt.

He had never, ever, seen either of her bodyguards smile before, and when her bodyguards smiled at him, the smiles were horrible.

"That's your souvenir."

Kaveh climbed the grand staircase alone, tucking the ticket back into the pocket on his shirt. He'd lived in that town for his entire life, but he'd never once set foot in that hotel. A gigantic chandelier hung over the staircase. The wooden banister was riddled with a constellation of bullet holes, maybe from a shoot-out in the frontier era. Crystals tinkled softly as a draft passed through the chandelier. The hotel was eerily quiet. He felt nervous now that he was there. The doors upstairs were all thrown open, but every room was pitch-dark, except for the room at the end of the hallway, where lights were glowing in the master suite.

Aside from a tarnished mirror on the wall, a massive bed with a plain white sheet, and a pair of nightstands topped with flickering oil lamps, the master suite was empty. Beyond the windows a full moon was rising over the plains beyond the town. He walked over to the windows. He had only been standing there a moment when she entered the room.

Kaveh had forgotten how powerful of a sense of presence that she'd had in the parking lot of the convenience store. He had read once that just like stars and comets and planets had a gravitational field, every object in the universe exerted a gravitational force, even human bodies, but he had never felt the pressure in a room shift the way that the pressure in the air shifted around her. She was wearing the hooded cloak. From that close the rippled texture of the scars on her hands had a visible topography. He had seen scars like that before. Seared flesh. Burned skin. The mark of flames. Gracefully, so gracefully that she made no noise at all, she eased the door shut, and then she crossed over to the windows. She stood so close to him his pulse quickened, and as she reached toward him his heart leapt, but instead of touching him she tugged loose the braided ropes that had been tied around the curtains behind him, and the curtains swung across the windows. Then, before he could speak, could somehow greet her, she moved behind him. She reached around him, raising her hands toward the buttons on his shirt.

"I can do it," Kaveh said, but she hushed him.

Her fingers were nimble. She pushed buttons through holes with the care of a tea master straining clumps from a scoop of matcha, of a master mason scooping mortar from the crevice between bricks. She was careful to apply no pressure to him. She had touched only the fabric. She had not yet touched him. His shirt dropped to the floor in a heap of indigo, and then her hands moved down to his jeans, where her fingers deftly thumbed the button through the hole and then peeled apart the zipper, slowly, as if she was savoring every click of the parting teeth. His jeans dropped to the floor in a pile of denim, and then her hands moved down to the legs of his boxers, where her fingers pinched the fabric at the hems, gradually pulling his boxers down, past his hipbones, past the buzzed bristles of his pubic hair, over the fat round hump of his buttocks. His cock was hard, straining against the cotton, and as the waistband on his boxers slid down past the head of his cock, his cock bounced stiffly into the air. She let his boxers drop to his ankles, and then he stepped out of the mound of clothing, glancing over at his reflection in the mirror, trying to see his body like she would, for the first time. The buzz cut with the slanted line of bare flesh scarred into his scalp. His big eyes. His sharp jaw. His blunt chin. The shadow of stubble on his face. His wide shoulders. His curved biceps. His hairy forearms. The bulging veins on his hands. His hairy chest. His round navel. His knobby hipbones. The bulging veins on his cock. His smooth buttocks. His sturdy thighs. His hairy shins. The bulging veins on his feet. He looked like a feral animal. He heard the hooded cloak drop to the floor.

Kaveh turned. She was older than he had expected, seemed about the same age as him, and he was suddenly struck by the thought of her and him growing up in different parts of the country at the same time, newborns swaddled in plastic bassinets in different hospitals, toddlers staggering through sandboxes at different daycares, children chewing on pencils at laminate desks in different classrooms, teenagers smoking cigarettes secretly behind the loading docks of different malls, shaped by the same national triumphs and disasters. The complex routes that he and she had taken over the past thirty years to meet each other there at that present moment. She wore no jewelry, just a loose linen smock and flimsy leather flip-flops, and when she stepped out of the flip-flops he saw that the thongs on the sandals had left pale stripes on her feet, which for a moment he thought were tan lines until he remembered that her feet were never in the sunlight, and then he realized that her feet were dusty and that the stripes were the only places on her feet that were clean. She slumped her shoulders, letting the straps of the smock slip down onto her arms, and then with a shake of her hips the smock fell to the floor in a heap of linen, and she stood naked across from him. She had a narrow waist, average breasts, a slender neck, and a bizarre face. Only the uniqueness of her features made her seem beautiful. Her eyes, dark and beady, were too far apart; her nose looked smushed at the tip, and was too close to her mouth; her cheeks, high and bony, had a haggard look. Her hair was black and long and straight. Neither her fingernails nor her toenails were painted. Aside from eyeliner she wore no makeup. Her skin was almost frighteningly pale. The scars faded just past her wrists.

Online, some people claimed she was Romanian, other people claimed she was Egyptian, but to him she looked Iranian. The recognition startled him. He was almost sure.

Kaveh said, "Where do you come—"

"I will hurt you if you speak," Zoe said. She had a faint lisp.

Kaveh said, "You just look like—"

She jabbed a pair of her fingers into the tender dip of skin at the base of his throat, and he staggered back against the windows, fumbling at curtains, hacking for air.

"Fuck," Kaveh coughed, and she reached around his jaw to press her fingers deep into the hollow nooks of skin beneath his ears, sending a burst of pain through him so intense his knees wavered, but this time he bit down on his cheeks instead of shouting. She stared at him as if waiting to see if he would dare to speak again. His cock had gone limp between his legs.

"You don't want what you think you do," Zoe said.

She took him by the hand, not simply wrapping her palm around his palm but actually interlacing her fingers with his fingers, a gesture so intimate that he felt a rush of blood in his cheeks. Getting reprimanded had embarrassed him, had made him feel insecure, but being back in her favor exhilarated him. He was captivated. She led him over to the bed and laid him down on the sheet spread-eagle with his feet turned out and his arms stretched wide and his forehead resting on a pillow.

"Happiness was never meant to be pursued," Zoe murmured.

She blew out the oil lamps beside the bed.

"Adventure has always been superior to pleasure," Zoe murmured.

He felt the mattress dip as she got onto the bed, and then she straddled him in the darkness, lightly placing her hands on his shoulders with her fingers spread, with the poise of a pianist touching a keyboard before beginning to play. After being hurt by her he was wary of her, but being touched by her like that, gently, was electric, as if the very protons and electrons in the atoms of his skin were excited by her energy. He liked the soft touch of her fingertips on his shoulders, the sensation of her pubic hair on his back, the feel of her ass resting against his buttocks. She began to massage him, splaying her hands across his skull, tenderly running her fingertips over his scalp, then scratching his scalp with her fingernails, sending tingles of pleasure down his spine. She massaged his neck, kneaded the muscles in his back, stroked and kneaded his arms, gently caressed the ligaments in his wrists, rubbed his palms with her thumbs and the heels of her hands, even worked the pads of muscle on his fingers. Pressed between his abdomen and the bed, his cock was getting hard again. He was overcome by a sense of bliss. He felt the mattress shift as she swiveled on the bed, straddling him in the opposite direction. She massaged the pads of muscle on his toes, rubbed his soles with her thumbs and the heels of her hands, gently caressed the joints of his ankles, stroked and kneaded his calves, kneaded the muscles in his thighs, and then moved her hands to his buttocks. She found the tension where his buttocks met his back, the hard knots of muscle where all of the stress from driving had settled, the strain from sitting at a steering wheel from dawn until dusk every day, all the gridlocks and the pileups and the detours and the construction. She clenched her hands into fists, putting all of her weight into his flesh, pressing her lumpy knuckles deep into his skin, forcefully kneading the knots out of his buttocks. The release felt so pleasurable that his toes curled in reflex. She turned around again, and her hands glided across his back, moving across him in elegant strokes, just barely touching the skin. He couldn't remember ever having felt so calm. Serene. All of his muscles were relaxed. All of his tension was gone. His cock was throbbing.

"Think of someone you love who has died," Zoe whispered, and although he didn't want to think about his father just then, immediately that was who he thought of.

Her hands moved back to his shoulders, squeezing his flesh so tightly that pain spiked through his tendons, making him wince.

"Everyone you love is dead," Zoe whispered.

Her fingers clawed into his shoulders.

"Everyone you love is gone," Zoe whispered.

His tendons spasmed under her fingers.

"You couldn't save anyone," Zoe whispered.

He grunted in pain as her fingernails dug into his flesh.

"The planets are aligning," Zoe whispered.

Her hands lifted from his skin.

And then suddenly she seemed to vanish, any sense of another human presence in the room was gone, and he was alone in the darkness, lying naked on the bed as a sprinkle of raindrops pattered across his back and his legs—was that raindrops or fingertips, a spurting gleek of saliva?—and then another sprinkle of raindrops pattered across his neck and his back, suddenly, like after a rainstorm, when the fat beads of water that had gathered on the tips of the leaves of a cedar tree were shaken loose by a gust of wind, sprinkling the water across the figures resting below the branches, the soldiers in the laced boots and the camouflage fatigues. He grunted in surprise. The raindrops fell on him again, but before he could reach back to feel if his skin was truly wet, a spiderweb brushed against the skin on his neck and his face— was that spiderweb or fingertips, sticky wisps of licked hair?—and then another spiderweb brushed against the skin on his face and his ears, lightly, like the dewy webbing hanging between thick blades of grass, the massive spiraling orbs of almost invisible silk glittering in the bright light of the dawn beyond the distant gorge, brushing against the figures creeping quietly through the savanna, the soldiers in the camouflage fatigues and the chinstrap helmets. He was more curious than aroused now. His cock was getting soft. A spiderweb stuck to him again, and on reflex he reached to wipe the tangle of silk from his skin, but then suddenly he got flipped on the mattress, tossed by a pair of hands with the force of an explosive, and then he began to feel a pinching sensation, as if she was pinching his skin between her fingernails, except that he could feel the pinches all over his body, as if hundreds of hands were pinching him all at once, or as if instead of lying faceup on the hotel bed he was lying facedown on a gravel road, with the sharp jags on the rocks gradually pressing deeper into his flesh as the ringing of the explosion reverberated in his ears. He was afraid now. His cock had gone flaccid. The pain of the pinches became almost agonizing, he wanted to yell for her to stop, but there was no safeword. He flailed at the darkness, but he struck only air, and then he felt a horrible pressure on his temples, and he gripped the sheet, and he went still again, and then the pressure faded, and he was alone. He felt a growing sense of unease. He could see nothing, he could hear nothing, he could feel nothing, and then a warm breeze touched his face, like breath exhaled from hot lungs, or like the air blowing through the cracked window of a truck rumbling down a coastal highway as sunlight shimmered on the windshield, or like the blustery chinook that had melted the igloo that his father had helped him build in the backyard to mud overnight. Like the humid breeze rustling the uniforms of a group of soldiers getting assigned cots in a barracks, Andre tossing down headphones onto a pillow, Trevor making bets on a blackjack game a couple cots down, Rivkah taking challengers for a battle rap a couple cots over, Dennis neatly arranging a stack of farmer almanacs under the cot nearest the tent flaps, Kaveh sitting there too serious and shy to talk to anybody. The breeze played across his body, rustling the hair on his forearms and his chest and his shins, comforting him. A balloon bobbed across his chest, maybe the stretched skin of an inflated cheek, another balloon bobbed across his chest, and he actually cracked a smile in amusement, a wild cluster of balloons rushed past him, and then he was startled by a sensation like waxy leaves slapping against his body, slick strands of seaweed wrapping around his ankles, soapy wet bubbles popping gently on his face, a sandy beach towel landing in a tangled mound on his chest, the slippery polyester of a fluffy sleeping bag dragging lightly across his skin, twigs cracking under the soles of his feet, moss sinking under the soles of his feet, prickly burs poking his thighs and his shins, the metallic rings of a chain-link fence pressing into his flesh, and then a breeze blew again, cooler now, getting cold, and a wet spatter of sleet, or maybe slimy strands of drool, struck him in the face, and though he hadn't thought of the morning in years, he suddenly thought of the patrol to the village in the valley with Andre, how sleet had been falling that morning, and Kaveh had wiped the sleet from his face, and Andre had wiped the sleet from his face, standing under the weathered prayer flags snapping in the wind as an elderly widow had fed Kaveh and Andre challow, insisting on feeding the soldiers with her own hands, pinching clumps of the rice with her withered fingers, gazing up at the soldiers with a look of profound emotion, murmuring in a dialect so obscure even the translator couldn't understand, and how after being fed by the widow in the valley Kaveh and Andre had had this strange bond, had trusted each other, had become tight friends, and Andre had watched out for him around the base. He felt moist lumps clinging to his chest and his abdomen and his legs, like squishing tongues, or leeches, like the shiny dark leeches that he'd discovered clinging to his legs after wading through a murky pond behind a gold mine with Trevor, taking a shortcut to investigate the cloud of smoke rising beyond the ridgeline above the pond, and he remembered how Trevor had yelped when he had realized that leeches were clinging to him too, and how he and Trevor had stood bare-assed together in the wind on the ridgeline, burning the leeches off of each other with a fluorescent lighter and whooping in triumph every time that another leech dropped to the dirt, grinning at each other, and how later that week back at the base Trevor had come to Kaveh with a look of shame for advice about a corporal who kept harassing him, giving him creepy shoulder rubs, giving his butt gross pats, and how Kaveh and Trevor had stayed awake until dawn that night in the empty mess hall, hashing out the delicacies of his situation, and after that Trevor had always insisted on picking Kaveh as a partner for euchre despite how terrible that he was at playing cards. He felt soft fluff land on his chest and his throat and his head, like split ends, or feathers, like the downy white feathers that had erupted over his head as he'd scouted out an abandoned railroad station in the desert with Rivkah, startling a stork that had been nesting on the eaves of the station, and he remembered how he and Rivkah had stepped back from the eaves in terror, hearts pounding as the stork had flapped off down the train tracks, and how later that week back at the base Kaveh had accidentally walked in on Rivkah masturbating with a vibrator in a portable toilet, and how Rivkah had hunted him down afterward with a look of resolve, insisting no matter how much he protested that nothing could ever be okay again between him and her until she had seen him masturbate too, and so that night Kaveh had jerked off into a handful of crumpled tissues while Rivkah had watched from a stool with a bag of microwave popcorn, heckling him with sarcastic point-ers, applauding ironically when he climaxed, and how after that Rivkah had come to Kaveh whenever she was upset about drama back home, even with the secret about her sister. He felt a sensation like the clammy feet of a tree frog hopping across his chest, the bristly fuzz on a honeybee drifting across his body, the delicate wings of a butterfly flapping against his skin, and then a sensation like blown dandelion seeds scattering across his face, or maybe fluttering eyelashes, and he remembered the dandelion he'd found growing in the scorched soil of an oil field he'd been patrolling with Dennis, the only living plant visible in any direction, and how Dennis had taught a couple of oil workers how to blow the seeds to make a wish, and then Dennis had asked the oil workers a series of cringingly earnest questions about local traditions involving flowers, which had irritated Kaveh, that Dennis was always treating the army like a cultural exchange program, and how back at the base later that afternoon Kaveh had seen Dennis rereading letters from his parents with a homesick expression, and how later that evening as Dennis was taking a nap Kaveh had seen other soldiers huddling around the cot to tea-bag him, flies already unzipped, which hadn't been any surprise, considering how many times Kaveh had seen Dennis get towel-snapped and wet-willied, and how even later that night Kaveh had noticed Dennis eating alone in the mess hall, and how Kaveh had suddenly remembered life before the army, that feeling of loneliness, the feeling of rejection, never having even a single friend at school, always too serious and shy to fit in, and so even though Dennis was so nerdy that the geekiness sometimes gave Kaveh literal chills, Kaveh had ignored the soldiers calling out to him and had walked across the mess hall to eat dinner with Dennis, and after that Kaveh had made clear to the others that being friends with him meant being friends with Dennis too. A dragonfly alighted on his chest, he felt the wings gently folding against his skin, and he remembered the emerald dragonfly with the transparent wings that had alighted on his t-shirt while he was playing in the woods behind his house as a kid, and how he had held his breath and held his body as still as possible, gazing down at the dragonfly in awe, feeling profoundly special, as if the dragonfly had chosen him, and then he had heard the station wagon that his father drove puttering into the driveway, and the dragonfly had finally flitted away, vanishing into the evergreens, and he had quick run to the driveway, excited to tell his father what had happened. Craggy tree bark pressed against his cheek and his hands, brittle ears of wheat skimmed against his legs, mud squelched under the soles of his feet, the steps on a rickety fire escape, the rough wooden slats on a dock, the scaly fins of a new-born sea turtle flopped across his chest, the velvety heads of cattails bobbed against his chest with a breeze, suds dripped from a coarse sponge wiping dust from his face, pulpy timber rotted by termites crumbled to powder between his fingers, ferns brushed against his legs, toadstools squished under his feet, grasshoppers landed on his chest and then sprang away, he felt a furry cat nuzzle against his shins, he felt a dog pawing eagerly at his thighs, and then he gasped in shock as a crate of fish was emptied onto his chest, the heads and the tails of the fish beating frantically against his skin as the fish struggled to swim through the air, and then after the fish had floundered off of him a damp fishing net landed on his body, a canvas sail, a nylon parachute, he passed through a doorway hung with linen drapes, a doorway hung with glass beads, a doorway hung with papery stream-ers, a breathtaking storm of confetti, a burst of steam, a whirl of embers, the tumbling spatter of a waterfall beat down onto his head and his shoulders, a lasso cinched tight around his torso, and then he felt a sudden jolt of gravity, a bouncing bed. The hammock behind the barracks bouncing as the uniformed group of soldiers had gathered around him, leaning over his laptop to crowd the screen, cheerily crashing a video chat with his father, begging to hear some embarrass-ing stories about him. The truck bouncing over potholes on the pass through the mountains as the uniformed group of soldiers in the back had swayed, listening to him explain that he was there because he wanted to help the people who lived there, because he believed in freedom, because he believed in democracy, and because even though his father wasn't at all religious, even though he'd never been to mosque in his life, he'd always felt a special connection to that part of the world because of his roots, an almost telepathic understanding, as if he could understand the people there intuitively, and the other sol-diers in the truck had listened to him solemnly until somebody had brought up the fact that he was the one who'd thought a burkha was a type of animal, like a llama, and then the other soldiers had cracked up laughing at him. The cushions bouncing as the uniformed group of soldiers had dropped cases of beer onto the sofa in the lounge, making fun of him because none of the cases were for him, because he never contributed anything to the kitty, because he literally never spent money on anything, the ascetic, the angel, putting every paycheck straight into the bank, saving for the trip with his father. The other soldiers had huddled around him, making exaggerated faces of pity, dejection, gloom, pouting at him, oh, I have to save money for my vacation, oh, I have to save money for my dad. And then, because the others loved him even more than mocking him, the soldiers each shared a sip of beer with him, from every can whose tab got pulled back that night, and in that way had gotten him just as drunk as everybody. He felt hands suddenly, smooth, callused, clammy, cold, warm, strong, bony, fat, all over his body, lightly touching his ribs, grazing his abdomen, fingering his armpits, stroking the soles of his feet, tickling him, and he burst out laughing, feeling a genuine rush of ecstasy, but the hands kept tickling him, and he continued to laugh, hysterically, even as he begged for the tickling to stop, in discomfort and then distress and growing alarm, twisting, kicking, suffocating, desperate to breathe, out of breath, fighting to push the hands away, and then suddenly the hands vanished, and he panted for air in the darkness, frantically, uneasily, filled with dread now, with a sudden foreboding, and he felt a sensation like a gritty callus or a rusty blade dragging ominously across his throat, and then the quaking vibrations of the bells in a clock tower clanging nearby, and then a lurch of panic as a staircase collapsed under the soles of his feet, a trapdoor snapped, a skylight shattered, a hillside crumbled, a tightrope swayed, a ladder teetered, and he jerked in horror as a rat with greasy hair ran across his face, the leathery wings of a swarm of bats beat against his body, centipedes with wriggling bodies darted across his skin, scorpions with pointed legs scuttled across his flesh, spiny cactus needles pierced straight through his palms out the back of his hands, a swarm of flies bit his thighs and his arms and his chest, a swarm of wasps stung his arms and his thighs and his chest, a heavy snake with dry hard scales squirmed onto his abdomen and coiled up on his chest and then lunged and punctured his neck with a brutal set of fangs, massive vultures with hooked beaks tore strips of flesh from his body, bursts of static electricity shocked his skin, rusted barbed wire and razor wire shredded his shins, corroded nails drove through his earlobes, bent screws twisted into his kneecaps, scalding oil spattered across his body, hands slapped him across the face, hands shoved him in the chest, hands shook him by the shoulders, hands wrapped around his throat and squeezed his throat tight and started to strangle him and he writhed and thrashed and struggled to breathe in utter anguish and despair and desolation as hundreds of mouths bit down on him, sharp canines and snaggleteeth and broken incisors, snapping and gnawing at his skin as the laughter continued to echo hysterically in his ears, like the laughter he heard in nightmares, night after night. Andre cracking a joke about gay cowboys before stepping on an explosive, vanishing into a plume of sand and dust. Trevor laughing so hard at his own story that he cried, then getting shot in his neck the next morning, swatting at the wound with a look of confusion, as if he had felt a mosquito bite, and then stumbling sideways into Kaveh, burbling dark spatters of blood. Rivkah laughing so hard that she snorted juice out her nose, then getting her hands blown off the next afternoon, staring at the stumps in disbelief, as if seeing a magic trick she couldn't quite figure out, and then staggering helplessly toward Kaveh, hemorrhaging blood from both wrists. Dennis, who had been widely mocked around the base for having a corny sense of humor and had always embraced the ridicule good-naturedly, telling knock-knock jokes while clutching desperately at Kaveh, even managing to laugh, managing to genuinely smile, bleeding out next to a mound of sheep dung, waiting for an evac that came hours too late. Kaveh crouching alone on the dirt floor of a kitchen littered with rice and lentils and broken jars, pinned down, cut off, in terror, ducking potshots from the sniper on the rooftop across the market as the wispy curtains at the window had swelled with a breeze, and the floorboards of the staircase to the roof had creaked with the wind, and the wind had rattled the knob on the door to the street, and every time the curtains had swelled or the floorboards had creaked or the knob had rattled he had flinched or jerked and spun with the rifle, bracing for an enemy at the window or the stairs or the door, until finally a figure had appeared, but when it did it was only a child, a young girl in a brown dress standing barefoot out in the plaza, and when he had shouted at her to get down she hadn't understood, and he had hid in the house like a coward, paralyzed by fear, for whole minutes, just watching the child stand in the plaza as the gunshots had rung out across the market, until finally he had bolted from the house into the plaza, dodging an abandoned cart, hurdling a toppled moped, tackling the child to the ground and crouching over her to protect her, telling her that everything was going to be okay, and moments afterward the sniper had been killed, and the child had survived, only to get wasted by a drone strike a week later, along with her entire family. The corpse of a local contractor for the army, who'd loved to hula-hoop with the engineers, strung up by his wrists with nylon zip ties, hanging there swollen-tongued from a utility pole, with his throat slit by the rebels. The corpse of a local informant for the army, who'd just gotten married a month earlier, left by the rebels in a ditch with his back flayed to ribbons, raw meat, whipped with the blood-crusted electrical cord lying nearby. The elderly naan vendor with the vibrant green eyes, caught in a sudden crossfire, getting capped in the skull, spraying brain matter across the screaming grandchildren whose kite he'd been fixing just moments before. Those were the faces he saw in the nightmares, the vibrant green eyes of the naan vendor gazing at him with blood dripping from the tear ducts, Andre getting mailed to him in a cardboard box in bloody pieces like something meant to be put back together, Trevor dissolving with a horrifying scream in a vat of bubbling acid, Rivkah collapsing in the flames of a trash incinerator with terrifying shrieks, Dennis trapped under a frozen lake with the family of the girl in the brown dress, pounding desperately against the ice, Kaveh dying from a gunshot wound, Kaveh dying in a plane crash, Kaveh dying in a house fire, Kaveh being the one left alive. He had done a single tour, had spent half a dozen months overseas, and had been a mess of nerves by the time that the tour was done, too jittery to spread a pat of butter evenly across a slice of toast. He had dreamed of the relief that he would feel coming home. But by then the country seemed to have changed. The war seemed to have followed him. He could remember his father singing along with the national anthem at base- ball games when he was a child, how much his father had loved the country, how his father had loved the whole country, despite that his father had never traveled beyond the borders of Wyoming. How his father had sworn to him that someday he and his father would travel the country together, from sea to shining sea, even though he had always known that his father was too poor to afford a real vacation. Instead he and his father had taken modest day trips around Sundance. Like the morning that he and his father had gone snowshoeing on a trail in the mountains, stepping gingerly across the snowpack, wearing bright parkas and snowpants. Sunlight had glit- tered across the snow. Far ahead of him, his father had just arrived at a gigantic granite outcropping flecked with crystal veins of quartz. Kaveh had fallen behind, distracted by a bird hopping around on the snow, maybe a chickadee, maybe a goldfinch, when he heard a distant rumble, and he turned toward the mountain, saw the snow tumbling down the mountainside, saw the pine trees toppling, heard the pine trees snapping, and then turned toward the outcropping and saw his father reach back toward him with a look of horror, and when his father screamed he realized that his father was safe and that he was not safe and then the bird darted into the sky and the avalanche hit him, burying him alive. He woke in a dark chamber of ice, helpless, limbs frozen in place, panicking when he realized what had happened, hyperventilating, growing dizzy, feeling hopeless, imagining that he would never see his father again. Shouting for his father. Giving in to despair. He remembered squinting into the dazzling sunlight with a sense of overwhelming joy as bright red gloves had broken through the snow above his head, and his father appearing above him, and his father helping him out, and how afterward, lying exhausted on the snow together, he and his father had both laughed ecstatically.

"*Now* we have *been* somewhere together," his father had grinned, reaching over to pat his chest.

Kaveh had been haunted by nightmares the week after the avalanche, but each night after the nightmares had woken him his father had made him a packet of cocoa, sitting with him at the turquoise table in the kitchen, talking about baseball until he was ready to sleep again, and after that week the nightmares had ended. But by the time he had returned from war, his father had been dead, and there had been nobody to keep him company after the nightmares. He kept his hair in a buzz cut, exposing the slanted line of bare scalp where the shrapnel had cut him to the bone, and bought a truck with the money he had saved to travel the country with his father. Instead he traveled the country alone.

The dim pink light of daybreak was glowing out the windows beyond the bed. The curtains were parted. He could sense her nearby. He could hear her breathing. In the darkness he had come to think of her as a supernatural creature, a shapeshifter who could become rain, wind, sand, a swaying grove of bamboo, take any form she desired. But she had a body again. She was lying on the bed. In the faint light he could see her silhouette, the curve of her hip, the dip of her waist, the peak of her shoulder. She wasn't touching him.

"There is no hell, there is no heaven, in this universe there are only molecules and stars," Zoe whispered.

The bedposts were silhouettes.

"You have no purpose, you have no creator, the life of a human is as meaningless as the life of a moth," Zoe whispered.

The nightstands were silhouettes.

"Life is meaningless," Zoe sang softly. "Death is meaningless," Zoe sang softly. "Everything you've ever done, everything you've fought for, meaningless, meaningless."

The faint light gleamed on the glass shades of the oil lamps.

"Everything you've felt was real," Zoe said in a whisper.

He could finally make out her face again. He had missed her face in the darkness. Staring at her bizarre features, the disproportionate space between her eyes, the smushed tip of her nose, the haggard look of her cheeks, he felt a strange sense of reverence.

"*Here* you are," Zoe breathed with a sudden tone of recognition, of excitement, rising up off the mattress to gaze at him with a look of desire. Kaveh had lost any interest in sex, but because he was terrified and enchanted by her, being looked at by her in that way gave him a rush of adrenaline. Her face was flushed with sweat. Leaning over him, she kissed him gently on the mouth, lightly brushing his lips with her lips, and then she kissed him again, harder, pressing her lips to his lips with a sense of hunger, touching his face with her hand as she kissed him on the mouth again and again and again. She kissed his chin, she kissed his jaw, she kissed his throat, and then he felt her mouth sucking on his neck as her fingers roamed his skin, grazing his abdomen, circling his hipbones, fondling the buzzed bristles of his pubic hair, caressing his groin, squeezing his thighs, rubbing the grooves of skin between his thighs and his balls, fingering the sensitive patch of skin just under his balls, and then cupping his balls, gently stroking the skin of his scrotum. He was already hard again when she took ahold of his cock, not stroking him, just gripping him, tightly, sending intense ripples of pleasure through his body. Straddling his hips, she rubbed the head of his cock against her vulva, grunting quietly with satisfaction, and then she took his cock into her cunt, sinking onto his pelvis. She was so wet that he inhaled on reflex, gripped fistfuls of the sheet. She experimented until she found an angle that she liked, leaning forward to hold his waist in her hands, leaning closer to press her hands into his chest, and then finally sitting back with her hands on her thighs, rocking her hips on his body. She looked almost mystical in the strange light of daybreak streaming through the windows, but she felt profoundly real, the rough scratch of her pubic hair, the warm wet grip of her cunt, the solid weight of her thick ass. Her breasts swayed slightly with each rock of her hips. He was almost afraid to touch her, but after hesitating he cupped her ass in his hands, and she sank down onto him with her elbows on his chest, offering her neck to him as she moved on his hips, lifting and dropping her ass in the air, taking the tip of his cock to the rim of her cunt before plunging his cock deep into her cunt again, breathing quickly with each slap of pussy against pelvis. He sucked on her neck, her skin tasted pleasantly salty, and he kissed her collarbone, and he kissed her shoulder, and then he took her breast in his mouth, licking her tit until he felt her nipple harden under the tip of his tongue. She gripped his shoulders and pushed her body into the air to lock eyes with him, and a bead of sweat streaked from her temple down her cheek and dripped from her chin onto his breastbone, and he became aware that he could smell her, the potent vegetal odor of her armpits, the faint fungal odor of her feet. He could smell her breath, a bitter odor with hints of milk and coffee, and he realized that other lovers always smelled of mouthwash or mints, that he had never smelled the actual breath of a lover before, or the unwashed feet, or the undeodorized armpits, and gazing into her eyes as she rocked on his hips he was suddenly overcome by a powerful sense of intimacy. She had hidden nothing from him. This was who she truly was. She looked intensely vulnerable.

"Do you believe somebody can fall in love in a single night?" Zoe whispered.

He stared up at her as she moved on him.

"I love you," Zoe whispered.

He wondered if maybe that was something she said to every patron, but even if she did, the earnest desperate look on her face made him believe her, that she truly had come to love him over the course of the past night together, that she was the type of person who could be overwhelmed with love for a stranger, that the past night had been as much for her as for him, and in that moment he felt that he understood her, that he knew what it was to be lonely, that he knew what it was to be traumatized, and that he could understand the need to keep moving afterward, forever, to live on the road.

"I love you, I love you, I love you," Zoe said, each utterance somewhere between a cry and a gasp, spoken in rhythm with the movement of her body, and then he felt her thighs clamp hard around his hips as her cunt clenched down on his cock, and her eyes glazed over, and her mouth parted slightly, and her back suddenly arched, and she pounded him with a sudden urgency until the pleasure and the intimacy and the excitement overwhelmed him and he came, twisting his head back to groan into the pillow, and then she sank down onto him in exhaustion, panting for air, her bangs matted with sweat, her legs trembling from exertion, her heart beating in a frenzy against his chest, as between breaths in an exhausted voice she continued to murmur she loved him. He had come so hard that he had drooled onto the pillow. The orgasm had sent aftershocks of euphoria pulsing through his body. His cock was still throbbing. At first hearing her say that she loved him had made him pity her, but after everything he had lived through during the night, all of the sorrow and terror and grief and despair, he was overcome by a profound sense of comfort as she murmured the words. The intensity of the feeling amazed him. His eyes watered, his mouth tightened, and he began to weep, and she pressed her face to his cheek and held his head in her hands, whispering the words to him over and over and over, in a mantra.

The gold light of dawn was glowing above the hills. Dusty clusters of stars were still shimmering in the sky. His throat raw from all the crying, his lungs weary from the heaving sobs, the skin around his eyes crusted with salt from dried tears, he stumbled through the door of the hotel with his boots untied and his shirt unbuttoned, back out into the town. A flock of starlings rose in a mass into the air, twisting and swirling into different shapes above the rooftops. He felt like he had been gone for years. Somebody was dragging a whimpering dog across the intersection by a stretched leash, somebody in a sedan was holding down the horn outside of the bar, somebody in cowboy boots was firing a revolver into the air on the steps of the museum, somebody had vomited on the sidewalk and somebody had dumped a mattress in the middle of the street and a couple of people in ballcaps were grappling in the parking lot of the convenience store, but the country he had left was not the country he returned to. Looking around at the town, he felt only peace.

Why Visit America

THE ORIGINS OF THIS GREAT NATION

There wasn't anything special about us. We were just an average town. Porch swings, wading pools, split-rail fences, pumpjacks bobbing for oil on the horizon. Meetings at town hall were well attended, sure, but we weren't some hotbed of insurgents. We didn't subscribe to any one brand of politics. We couldn't even be plotted onto your basic left-right binary. Our town had everything: pro-lifers who supported gay marriage, pro-choicers who opposed gay marriage, climate-change deniers who owned solar panels, universal-healthcare campaigners who preferred private insurance, creationists with degrees in biology and geology, internet pirates whose views were unique to say the least, loyal conservatives, staunch liberals, moderates, radicals, and ornery retirees whose only real issue was guns. And yet that winter we found ourselves united by a common sentiment. We were fed up with our country. The executives were busy making donations that funded the campaigns of the politicians, the politicians were busy passing laws that protected the interests of the executives, and pretty much nothing else seemed to be getting done. We were anti-government, we were anti-corporate, but mostly we were normal people who couldn't afford to buy an election and had come to understand that our votes didn't mean shit. Hell, the executives were stepping down to take government appointments and the politicians were stepping down to take corporate positions so fast that we couldn't even keep track of who was which anymore, if there was any difference. There were libertarians among us who had been pushing for our town to secede for years now, but not until that winter, watching legal forms of graft being flaunted across the country like never before, did our town seriously begin to consider the proposition. The matter soon came to dominate our meetings. We knew that from a certain perspective seceding could be viewed as an act of treason, might mean arrest, might mean imprisonment, might even mean execution. And the debate at that final town hall meeting was appropriately heated. Most of us wavered back and forth, unsure which way we would vote until the very second that those slips of paper got passed around. Several of us were so nervous that we felt faint. Ultimately, however, the decision was unanimous. We would rather face handcuffs, jail, even a hanging, than spend another goddamned second living in that broke-down country. We'd voted to secede.

And so, on that day of January Thirteenth in the year of MMXVIII, we did. After the vote had been tallied, we sent notice of our secession to both local and global media outlets, along with the sheriff of Real County, the governor of Texas, and the president of the United States. As dusk fell across our streets, we filed out of the town hall, gathered around the poles in our yards, and took down Old Glory. We tucked the flags into our garbage cans, and then we sat in our houses, radios off, televisions off, computers off, sobered by what we had done. The initial thrill had faded. Now, exhausted, we felt only fear. Holding hands with our spouses and our children and our parents and our neighbors, we waited for the repercussions, for the arrival of the humvees and the helicopters and the tanks and the bombers, for our rebellion to be crushed by a show of force. But nothing happened. Nobody came. Nobody cared. At dawn, those of us who hadn't been able to sleep looked around and realized that our community was still standing. We were free.

Our town had been called Plainfield. Although we had liked the name well enough for a town, we were concerned the name wouldn't seem stately enough for a nation. And while we didn't regret seceding, we weren't ashamed of our origins either. In fact, we felt a great deal of nostalgia for our homeland. So, in memory of our former country, that was what we decided to name our new nation: America.

HOME OF THE TRAITOR

Though the vote to secede was unanimous, there had in fact been three abstentions: Alex Cruz, Tony Osin, and Sam Holliday, who had all been absent from that final town hall meeting. A group of us drove around that next morning to deliver the news about the secession. Alex, who lives in a motor home with flat tires behind the house where his grandparents raised him, is apolitical, an unemployed millennial, and absorbed the news with an expression of utter indifference before returning to a social media app. Tony, who works as a potter in the woodshed behind the house that his children bought for him, is apolitical, a proud alcoholic, and greeted the news with disinterest after being assured that the price of vodka wouldn't be affected. We knew better than to expect such a composed reaction from Sam Holliday, which was why we put off visiting him until last. A Vietnam vet who had dragged his wounded sergeant to safety through a muddy rainforest infested with vipers and cobras after being shot in his shoulder, who in his youth had attained the distinguished rank of Eagle Scout by constructing trail markers for canyons in a state park, and who later had worked for the federal government for decades as a bespectacled physician at Veterans Affairs, Sam loved the United States dearly, and had made clear at various town hall meetings in the past that he considered the proposal to secede a foolish enterprise. As we pulled into his driveway, he stepped out onto the porch in a denim shirt and a bolo tie with a shotgun in hand, a grizzled old widower with such rugged good looks that admittedly most of us were infatuated with him. The weather that morning was cool, only thirteen degrees centigrade, and some of us shivered, wishing we had brought jackets, but he looked perfectly comfortable with the temperature, standing strong and proud on the porch. Sam was a local hero, the most admired figure in our community, and we'd always imagined that if we ever actually seceded he'd be the one to lead the new nation, yet the more convinced we'd become that seceding was necessary, the more adamantly opposed he'd been to the very notion. A United States flag was waving on the pole in his yard.

Those of us there were led by Belle Clanton, a fiery libertarian who'd spearheaded the campaign to secede, whose voice that morning held a tremor of insecurity.

[Exchange as recorded in the journal of Ward Hernandez, barkeeper]

Sam spat in the dirt and then said, "What brings y'all out here?"

"Just wanted to let you know that we seceded," Belle said.

Sam gave us a squint.

"You can't," Sam said.

"We did," Belle said.

The tension in the air was remarkable.

"We notified the county, the state, and the federal government. Nobody made any attempt to stop us from seceding. Nobody even tried telling us that seceding isn't allowed," Belle said.

Sam sneered and said, "Because nobody is taking you seriously. You can't just secede by saying you've seceded. This land is still under the jurisdiction of the United States. You're still going to have to obey the traffic laws. You're still going to have to follow the health code. You're still going to have to pay taxes."

"I didn't even pay taxes to that country when we were citizens of it," Belle said.

"Ditto," Trent said.

"Same," Clint said.

"We're going to need you to take down that flag," Belle said.

Sam stared at us as if trying to gauge how many of us he could shoot before we would shoot him.

"Ward's had a Mexican flag flying at his place for years, and ain't nobody ever bothered him about it," Sam said.

We had to admit he had a point there. He watched spitefully as we drove back toward the road. The United States flag was still waving on the pole. Even after everything that's transpired in our nation since, visitors can still see that same flag flying in the yard when touring the home of Sam Holliday (see: MAP OF AMERICA, SITE OF HISTORICAL IMPORTANCE #7).

CULTURAL REFORMS

Visitors to our country often remark upon the unique culture here. Admittedly, when we realized we could do whatever we wanted, we were overcome by an astonishing sense of freedom. The possibilities were overwhelming. That town hall meeting the week after we seceded was just as crowded as the week before. Even Alex and Tony were there, looking curious about what would happen now that our town was a country. Sam Holliday, though, was once again notably absent, which made many of us anxious. Sam had never missed a town hall meeting before we'd seceded. He was an intelligent person. He was a respected person. And he was known to be headstrong. Belle Clanton kept glancing at the door from where she was presiding over the meeting, as if she was worried he might come storming into town hall at any second.

The first person who rose to speak at the meeting was Riley Whipper, who at the time was an all-star volleyball player over at the school, and was recognizable as being the only citizen of our country with a septum piercing and bright pink hair.

[Transcript as recorded by Pam Cone, secretary]

Riley Whipper: "I think we need to talk about whether we're going to continue to address each other by our genitals."

Crowd: (silence)

Riley Whipper: "Unless you all actually are as obsessed with your genitals as you seem to be."

Crowd: (murmuring)

Melanie Curbeam: "Riley, I think the rest of us need a little bit of clarification on what exactly you're talking about."

Riley Whipper: "You there, Bill Combs, do you consider your penis your defining characteristic as a person?"

Bill Combs: "Uh, I mean, I really—"

Riley Whipper: "And you, Terri Epps, do you consider your vagina your defining characteristic as a person?"

Terri Epps: "Now, I just, I mean—"

Riley Whipper: (points dramatically at crowd) "Or are we more than our genitals?"

Crowd: (looking at each other)

Riley Whipper: "Official documents to some people are addressed to a Mr. Official documents to other people are addressed to a Ms. I understand that these are meant as titles of respect. I do. I don't, however, understand why there has to be separate titles for us based on what genitals we have. Mr., Ms., that's what those titles are saying. 'Honored person with a penis.' 'Honored person with a vagina.' I mean, of all of the possible information about a person you could attach to a title, why is sex the information that we include?"

Adrian Moreau: "Um, arguably those titles are in reference to gender, rather than sex."

Presley Johnson: "Not all men have a penis, and not all women have vaginas."

Kendra Goldberg: "And while we're on the topic, those aren't the only genders anyway."

Riley Whipper: "Okay yeah and that's exactly the point. In the United States, there are two official genders, and you're forced to identify as and be identified as one or the other. And, I don't know, I just think that we should have a different system here. I think we should address each other by a neutral title, like Mx., so that people who aren't a conventional gender aren't mislabeled on a daily basis. So that people who are trans, who might be thinking about transitioning or might be starting to transition but might not be ready to tell other people about it, won't be put in a situation where you have to lie about what you are or reveal what you are before you're ready. I want to live in a decent country, in a country that treats every citizen equally. We could be that country."

Crowd: (whispering)

Riley Whipper: "I mean, seriously, are there any of you here who are so obsessed with your particular gender that you'd be opposed to being addressed by a neutral title?"

Mike Cooks: (raising hand) "I'm not here to naysay, I'm not against the idea, but I'd just like to go on the record and say that I actually do consider my genitals my defining characteristic as a person."

Bev Whittaker: (looking flushed) "Well. Well. That's just fine, Michael, thank you for sharing that."

The motion passed by a narrow margin. The next person to take the podium was Tim Kelly. Tim works as a furniture carpenter, has a reputation for fine craftsmanship, and that evening had dirty blond bangs sticking out from under the bent brim of a ballcap rippled with sweat stains.

[Transcript as recorded by Pam Cone, secretary]

Tim Kelly: "Do you know how many countries there are that don't use the metric system? I'll tell you. Myanmar, Liberia, and the United States. That's it. Those are the only countries that haven't gone metric yet. Literally every other country in the world is metric. I was reading about this just the other day. I don't know about the rest of you, but if you handed me a map of the world, I wouldn't be able to point to Myanmar, and certainly wouldn't know where to find Liberia, either. Am I even pronouncing the names of those places right?"

Angeline Ramirez: "Tim, are you saying you want us to switch to the metric system?"

Tim Kelly: "I think we got to ask ourselves, what type of country do we want to be? A modern, advanced, innovative country, at the fore-front of science and industry? Or a country like the United States?"

Morgan Banks: "If we were going to go metric, then we'd have to change all the signs."

Bob Tupper: (whistling) "Feet would become meters."

Pete Christie: (frowning) "Gallons would be liters."

Louise Banks: "We'd have to get a new scale for the bathroom, probably a new thermometer too."

Crowd: (mumbling)

Tim Kelly: (squinting) "What's that back there?"

Jesse Fankhauser: (tentatively speaking up) "Just sounds like a lot of work, is all."

Tim Kelly: "Oh come on, y'all know how to use a calculator. God knows most of your speedometers and measuring cups are already labeled with both systems of measurement anyway. You'd just have to start using the little numbers instead of the big ones."

Crowd: (muttering)

Tim Kelly: "I'm a carpenter, y'all. There's nobody whose daily life would be more affected by this than me."

Bev Whittaker: (slapping knee) "I say the hell with it, I'm ninety-one years old and I'm ready for some change, you know what I mean?"

The motion passed by a wide margin. The final person to take the podium was Antonio Vega. Antonio had formerly volunteered as the editor of the town newsletter, was now charged with the task of editing a national newsletter, and that evening had a shirt pocket lined with assorted pens.

[Transcript as recorded by Pam Cone, secretary]

Antonio Vega: "I've been running this bulletin a long time, and there's something that's always bothered me, and that's the issue of copyrighted words. Words that start out as brand names. Dumpster. Popsicle. Rollerblade. Laundromat. In the United States, words like that are trademarked by different companies, which means if you use it, then you're required to capitalize it, or you're liable to get sued."

Bob Tupper: (murmuring) "Popsicles are the most overrated food."

Pete Christie: (muttering) "Rollerblades were a truly strange fad."

Jenny Bergquist: "Antonio, you're saying that companies could actually sue people just for using lowercase letters instead of uppercase ones?"

Antonio Vega: (grimacing) "Language is supposed to belong to every citizen. Language is supposed to be a public good. Letting companies lock up certain words just infuriates me out of principle."

Rick Pinkney: "You know, there's always seemed something arrogant to me about capitalized words."

Caroline Russo: "I believe the technical term for that is proper nouns."

Julia Palmer: "As opposed to common nouns."

Rick Pinkney: "Well and now that's exactly the problem. That there is a class system. 'Proper nouns' and 'common nouns.' That's snobby is what that is. Invented by a bunch of coastal elites."

Deb Coots: "Kinda useful for words at the start of a sentence."

Adam Smith: "And the names of people."

Bev Whittaker: (wistfully) "I've always liked getting to be capitalized."

Antonio Vega: "I'm not talking about people. I'm talking about trademarks and copyrights. Heck, I don't know if our country even recognizes those things. But in the United States, that's what's been happening for years. I think we need to decide whether we're going to allow that to happen here."

The motion was passed unanimously. Dumpsters are now dumpsters. Popsicles are popsicles. Rollerblades are rollerblades. Laundromats are laundromats. Realtors are realtors, frisbees are frisbees, jacuzzis are jacuzzis, sharpies are sharpies, tupperware is tupperware, styrofoam is styrofoam, velcro is velcro, jello is jello, speedos are speedos, chapstick is chapstick, kleenex is kleenex, post-its are post-its, q-tips are q-tips, band-aids are band-aids, ping-pong is ping-pong, and vaseline, goddamnit, is vaseline. In the immortal words of Antonio Vega, now inscribed on a brass monument of a dumpster commissioned by Antonio Vega (see: MAP OF AMERICA, PLACE OF GENERAL INTEREST #17), "A word cannot be owned; a word is not property; on this day, in this country, let all words be free!"

For many of us, leaving the meeting that night was the first time we'd ever felt a true sense of nationalism. In a single session, we had reformed gendered titles, converted to the metric system, and overturned copyright law decisively. Meanwhile, across the border, the

United States government had been shut down for days, and was indefinitely. Capitol Hill couldn't even manage to pass a budget.

THE FIRST TOURIST

Visitors often seem surprised to hear it, but for us the transition from "town within the United States" to "nation bordering the United States" was relatively simple. The process was simplified by the fact that there were no foreign agencies operating within our borders. The United States Postal Service, which most visitors probably know is broke as hell, had long ago shuttered the only post office in town, forcing us to drive to the next town over to pick up our mail. The nearest police station was the next town over. The nearest fire department was the next town over. The nearest military recruitment office, secretary of state, and veterans home were towns away. Visitors to our country will sometimes see vehicles belonging to foreign agencies: police cruisers operated by Texas, fire engines from Real County, generally cutting through the country on the international highway that intersects Main Street. We don't mind these intrusions by foreign entities. Our country has a policy of open borders. Anybody is welcome to cross our borders at any time, regardless of citizenship, with no restrictions. Many Americans in fact still work in the United States.

Visitors sometimes express concern that the lack of checkpoints at our borders might pose a security risk. But we've found an open-border policy to have a variety of benefits for our country. After nearly a century of essentially no tourists whatsoever, we've experienced a relative boom. Notably, just over a month after our secession saw the arrival of our first tourist, a Dutch national named Johannes Dijkstra, who alighted from a semi that March and headed straight for the saloon on Main Street (see: MAP OF AMERICA, DINING AND SHOPPING #2). Just imagine, dear visitor, a foreign hipster with a handlebar mustache and a jaw of stubble stepping through the swinging doors of the saloon at high noon, wearing pastel shorts and a sweaty tank top with a pair of knockoff wayfarers hanging from the neck, carrying a banjo case plastered with chiquita stickers and a duffel bag coated in dust. Those of us at the bar couldn't help but stare.

"I am here to see America," Johannes announced, then added, "and to use an automated teller machine."

We were disappointed to discover that Johannes, who was midway through a meandering hitchhiking trip from New York to Los Angeles, actually was not referring to our nation but instead meant the United States. However, upon being informed that he was now in a different country altogether, Johannes was delighted. He was especially interested to learn that our nation was so young. Johannes wanted to take a tour, so Pete Christie and Bob Tupper, who are both retired and to tell the truth never really have much going on, offered to show him around the country. Johannes tossed his banjo and his duffel into the bed of the pickup, flashed peace signs at some of us walking by, and climbed into the cab, already chatting away. Pete and Bob spent the afternoon bringing him around: down to the town hall, to check out the signed Resolution To Secede hanging framed on the wall; over to meet Belle Clanton, who had recently been nominated for president, and who took a break from brushing the horses in her stable to talk with him a while; out to the coop behind the Garza place to see the heritage turkeys, pretty much extinct beyond our borders; out to the cellar at the Dylan place to hear the finer points of making cactus wine, our specialty; out to the skeleton of the abandoned stagecoach in the gulch, said to be haunted by a family of pioneers murdered by a couple of bandits for a pair of horses, where he claimed to feel some totally paranormal vibes; out to the plains, to the cluster of mounded burrows dug in the sandy soil by the ancient train tracks, where he got to feed peanuts to the prairie dogs, exclaiming with joy whenever a prairie dog nibbled a shell; down to the flooded quarry, where some teenagers who had cut school were busy swimming, and where after stripping nude he quickly mastered the art of the cannonball under the tutelage of Riley Whipper; to inspect the border signs that Walt Ho was building in his pole barn, with painted lettering on embossed wood, that would eventually proclaim Welcome To America; to examine the national flag that Bev Whittaker was stitching in her sewing room, a navy banner with a gold star, already fondly known as New Glory; down to the ice cream shop, shaped like an ice cream sundae, to treat him to an order of the famous "trough of ice cream" (see: MAP OF AMERICA, DINING AND SHOPPING #3). Johannes was amazed by everything. To be honest, there were some of us who had been feeling slightly insecure about our new nation, and his enthusiasm gave us a much needed boost of self-esteem.

Evening found him knocking back tequilas at the saloon, chanting drinking songs with a crowd of regulars, his arms around Pete and Bob.

"I love this country," Johannes shouted.

Johannes, whose tequilas had been on the house, finally staggered over to the teller machine back by the restroom to withdraw the cash that he had planned to get when he had originally arrived that afternoon. When he tried, however, he was refused. Those of us in the saloon tried to help him, gathering around and taking turns pushing the buttons, but no matter what we did, his card just got spit back out. The screen suggested he contact his bank.

After crashing on a sofa at the Whippers', Johannes returned to the saloon the next morning, eyes bloodshot with a hangover. Ward cracked an egg into a glass, threw in some worcestershire and tabasco, flicked in a pinch of salt and pepper, and slid the drink down the bar. Johannes drank the prairie oyster down with a gulp, set the glass back onto the bartop, and then stared into the glass with his elbows on the bartop and his hands in his hair, explaining the situation with an expression of despair. He had been on the phone with his bank since sunup. He hadn't realized how fast he had been blowing through money. His savings account was empty. His credit card was maxed. He had hit the limit for cash advances.

He had spent the last of his money, he realized, on a box of twinkies.

"I am very fucked," Johannes said.

Ward put down a dishrag.

"You want a job?" Ward said.

Johannes glanced up with a hopeful look.

"Here?"

"That's the idea."

"I do not need a visa?"

"Heck no, amigo, just grab an apron."

And thus our first tourist was also our first immigrant. Johannes eventually fell in love with Riley Whipper, left the saloon to be a full-time parent, and has since become a naturalized citizen of our country. Having authored a series of nationally acclaimed limericks, Johannes is currently the poet laureate of America.

HUMANITARIAN OPPORTUNITIES

Though we honestly don't mind when foreign agencies cross our borders, we have to say that we really did mind earlier this year when Corey Buber, an autistic entrepreneur with a chubby smile and a mild stutter who at the time was only nineteen years old, was abducted from our soil by federal agents of the United States. Crossing into our nation in the dead of night, and having made no request for extradition, these agents stormed into his house, raided his room in the basement, tasered him when he attempted to flee, and spirited him away to Texas. Currently being held in Houston, Corey is still awaiting trial, charged with operating an online piracy ring, possession of several million stolen songs, possession of several thousand stolen movies, and possession of psilocybin mushrooms, none of which are crimes in America. Visitors interested in contributing to the Fund To Free American Citizen Corey Buber From Illegal Detainment In The United States are encouraged to make deposits in the donation box at the town hall (see: MAP OF AMERICA, SITE OF HISTORICAL IMPORTANCE #1, PLACE OF GENERAL INTEREST #29). Corey's parents would also like to note that the agents left behind extensive property damage, including a turfed lawn and a busted door.

THE SUMMIT

Although our sovereignty is not yet recognized by the United Nations, nor by any of the member states of the United Nations, our nationhood is supported by multiple political parties in Catalonia, and we've received encouraging notes from diplomats belonging to the countries of Venezuela, Cuba, Afghanistan, Sudan, and the Democratic People's Republic of Korea. Emphatically, America does not officially identify as a "micronation," finding the "micro" to be somewhat disparaging, preferring to be called simply a "nation," but nevertheless, early on we did recognize the political realities of the situation, which was what led us to contact the various micronations of the world, in the hopes of forming an alliance, and was what led us to organize the first international summit of the United Micronations.

Just imagine, dear visitor, the grand scene of that momentous gathering, which has since been reproduced in countless paintings and recounted in multiple ballads. Belle Clanton, who earlier that spring had been elected president of the republic, hosted the summit at her hacienda, a bright white adobe with a rustic fountain burbling in the courtyard and flowering vines hanging over the walls. Ward Hernandez strode through the gathering in a tuxedo, serving caviar and gravlax and foie gras to a colorful assembly of besuited figures from across the globe, including representatives of the micronations of Sealand, Liberland, Akhzivland, Forvik, Elleore, Talossa, Seborga, Murrawarri, Filettino, Uzupis, Atlantium, New Utopia, Freetown Christiania, and Hutt River, who had all made epic journeys to reach this glorious enclave here in the Great Plains. As the oldest living person in America, Bev Whittaker offered a toast when the champagne was poured, saluting the revolutionary spirit of the summit. Johannes read a poem before the inaugural meal.

The summit was not without drama. Over the course of that week, Aubrey Ramirez was accused of stealing a diamond brooch by an emissary of Elleore, Daniel Curbeam got into a vicious argument about soccer with an envoy of Talossa, and Walt Ho, who is married, had a sultry affair with the ambassador of Seborga, which became a national scandal when a group of us stumbled upon him and the ambassador having a moonlight tryst in the vineyard behind the hacienda. Somebody with a lispy accent whose citizenship we never did manage to establish had a nearly fatal allergic reaction to a bee sting while giving a speech about trade pacts and collapsed to the floor mid-sentence before being revived with an epipen. Meanwhile, the prime minister of Uzupis, who apparently had a regrettably slow internet connection back home, skipped most of the summit to take advantage of the free wifi, spending the weekend in bed with a laptop, binging entire seasons of a foreign comedy show. To be perfectly honest, we had underestimated the variety of challenges involved in international diplomacy.

On the first morning there was also an incident with Sam Holliday, which only added to the tension for those of us from America.

[Exchange as recorded in the journal of Ward Hernandez, barkeeper]

We were sitting around the table out on the patio when we heard a horse neighing in the distance. Sam rode up to the hacienda a second later, squinting beneath the brim of a straw hat, reining the horse in the dirt just beyond the patio. He didn't dismount.

"Can we help you, Sam?" Belle called.

Sam gazed at us with a fierce look, staring long and hard at each of us sitting around the table, looking each of us square in the eye, as if verifying what he was seeing, that there truly was an international summit of micronations being held at the hacienda, that we truly had organized such a thing, and then he scowled and turned and spurred the horse, riding back off toward the vineyard without saying a word.

"Who was that?" said the ambassador of Seborga.

Belle stared as the horse galloped off through the vineyard toward the hills.

"He didn't want to secede," Belle said.

"Change is hard for some," said the ambassador of Murrawarri.

"Best just to shoot resisters," said the ambassador of Filettino.

"He is too sexy, he would be invulnerable, a bullet could never kill him," said the ambassador of Seborga, dabbing out a cigarette.

The primary goal of the summit was to form an official alliance, and yet finding terms that were acceptable to every micronation proved difficult, in part because the talks kept going off on tangents. Like us, the other micronations were preoccupied with achieving global recognition. The panel on whether to take an official position on fossil fuels, the panel on whether to take an official position on capital punishment, the panel on whether to take an official position on a two-state solution, all of the talks were inevitably hijacked by discussions about nationhood.

[Transcript as recorded by Pam Cone, secretary]

King Of Elleore: "We need more visibility."

Queen Of Talossa: "We need some type of political leverage."

Ambassador Of Seborga: "Maybe we micronations could ask for assistance from established nations that also happen to be micro. Monaco, Liechtenstein, Andorra. Singapore, Lesotho. Countries like these."

Bob Tupper: (shaking head) "None of those countries will even respond to us."

Pete Christie: (sounding hopeful) "Maybe if we tried again the countries would listen."

King Of Elleore: "We must somehow be seen as powerful."

Queen Of Talossa: "We must be respected."

Ambassador Of Forvik: "We should pursue the possibility of becoming tax havens."

Belle Clanton: "I don't think that would get us the type of attention we want."

Ambassador Of Forvik: "Then we should pursue the possibility of nuclear armament."

Belle Clanton: "I don't think that would get us the attention that we want either."

Prime Minister Of Uzupis: (wandering into dining room in pajamas) "Hasn't dinner been served yet?"

Regent Of Sealand: "The meeting's gone long, you can probably just watch another episode and then come back."

Ambassador Of Forvik: (slapping hand on table) "I think the only option is to create a joint space program. If we want visibility, want to be respected, then our citizens must walk on the moon. There is no other way."

Riley Whipper: "Honestly all you really need is a semi-intelligent social media strategy."

There were moments during the summit when we were sure that the talks would fail. Moments of defeat. Moments of despair. And yet through various miracles of diplomacy, on the final day of the summit, the gathered representatives met in the dining room to ratify a treaty, forming an official alliance. Known as the American Accord, the treaty is currently displayed in an airtight case in the very room where the document was signed, in the home of Belle Clanton (see: MAP OF AMERICA, SITE OF HISTORICAL IMPORTANCE #2). Visitors hoping to see foreign dignitaries should consult the official calendar for the United Micronations, as the alliance meets at the hacienda only once a year, on an irregular schedule.

THE LAST INDEPENDENCE DAY IN AMERICA

Even before that incident with him during the summit, many of us had been worried about Sam Holliday. Later that summer some of us drove out to his place, a group of us who had known him as children, who had gone to school with him, who had been friends with him forever, who had played wiffle ball with him in the schoolyard, who had played teeball with him, who had played football with him, who had learned to read and write with him, to add and subtract, to multiply and divide, had memorized the names of capital cities. A group of retired citizens, some wearing hearing aids, some wearing bifocal glasses, some walking with the help of canes. Standing there on his porch, we tried to convince him to come to the next meeting at town hall, but he just wouldn't budge.

"I will not participate in that foolishness," Sam said.

Grace Curbeam, who was cousins with him, and who knew him well, asked if he was acting out because he was still angry that his wife had died.

"This has nothing to do with that," Sam said angrily.

Eventually we gave up. As we drove away, a terrible sadness came over those of us in the car. Before we'd seceded, he'd been one of us, going fly-fishing with us, playing dominoes with us, playing mahjong with us, playing backgammon with us, drinking mojitos with us, sitting around a table in a kitchen or a restaurant eating sloppy joes or slices of lemon meringue pie, but now he avoided us like a bunch of communists. We missed him, and longed for some way to win him over. To be reconciled.

A week later another group of us drove out to his place, a group of adults who had volunteered to conduct a national census and were going around collecting information from people with official forms. Sam outright refused to participate.

"You have no authority to conduct a census on this soil," Sam said.

Becky Coots, who had worked under him as a nurse, and who still had a crush on him, asked him if maybe he could just fill out his data as a personal favor.

"I do not recognize the legitimacy of your government," Sam said.

Another group of us drove out to his place a week later, a group of teenagers who had recently written a national anthem and were going around performing the song for people a cappella. Sam refused even to listen.

"I have absolutely no interest in hearing your song," Sam said.

Cameron Ramirez, who had never met him before that moment, and who hadn't been properly warned about him, tried to explain that the lyrics would move him if he would only open his heart.

"You wrote an anthem for a country that factually doesn't exist," Sam said.

The next day was July Fourth, which is not a holiday in America, although all of us of course had celebrated the holiday back before we'd seceded. Throughout the day, we watched footage on television of the celebrations across the border. As always, the citizens of the United States looked depressed and weary, with bloodshot eyes shadowed by puffy bags, and all appeared to be drinking heavily, presumably as a form of self-medication, to cope with the stress of having to live under a dystopian plutocracy that viewed corporations as legal persons and treated citizens like mere merchandise. We could remember looking like that, and felt relieved to be free, and pity for those who weren't. The general mood in our country that day was one of quiet introspection. Or was, that is, until night finally fell across our town, when fireworks began exploding in our sky.

Somebody was celebrating July Fourth.

We knew even before we got there who was setting off the fireworks. For almost half a century he had personally funded the local fireworks show every July Fourth, and we found him where he had been every year before, at the bend in the creek just out of town, which offers the best vantage for shooting fireworks off over Main Street, but that year instead of being surrounded by a crowd of volunteers, Sam was shooting off the fireworks alone. He was wearing a bright white stetson and a bright red oxford tucked into a pair of blue jeans, United States colors, and had a revolver in a leather holster at the small of his back. He stepped away from the firework launchers as we turned the flashlights onto him. He looked tipsy, and was smiling, a frightening grin that had hints of rage and desperation.

A group of us were there, led by Belle Clanton, who we knew was still furious that he had turned away the census takers and the kids who'd written the new anthem. She had been looking for an excuse to confront him, and that was before he'd dared to set off fireworks. Those of us present were somewhat afraid of what she might do.

[Exchange as recorded in the journal of Ward Hernandez, barkeeper]

Belle trembled with a righteous anger.

"What do you think you're doing?" Belle said.

"Celebrating," Sam said.

"This is America. Those fireworks don't make you a patriot here. Those fireworks make you a traitor," Belle said.

Sam's smile faltered. He gazed at her a second before spitting into the dirt. Then he scowled.

"I'm getting tired of this game you're playing," Sam said.

"It's not a game. It never has been. If you love the United States, if you love it there that much, then go live in it," Belle said.

Her hand hovered over the gun holstered to her hip.

"You're welcome to leave any time," Belle said.

Sam stared at her. Water trickled through the darkness. Bullfrogs hooted in the creek. The tension in the air was terrifying. Those of us present watched him for any sudden movements, certain that guns were about to be drawn, but after a pause he simply turned away, trudging back toward the road in silence, vanishing into the darkness beyond the trees, leaving behind the rest of the fireworks, along with a flask and a lighter. Visitors can still see those crates of unused fireworks in the grass at the site of The Last Independence Day In America (see: MAP OF AMERICA, SITE OF HISTORICAL IMPORTANCE #6), although the fireworks have since been rendered unusable by exposure to the elements. And while that incident was resolved without bloodshed, most historians believe the episode was a turning point in the conflict, and was ultimately responsible for all of the drama that came later.

COLLECTIBLES

All forms of currency are accepted in America, including dollars, pesos, euros, yen, yuan, won, pounds, francs, rands, kroner, kronor, kronur, and rupees, but most businesses prefer that purchases be made with the national currency, the illustrious. While illustrious can be used to buy anything from a jeep to a slinky, the bills are also prized for the unique design, with each bill being printed on imitation gold leaf. Doomsayers who are convinced that the global financial system is on the verge of a total collapse pretty much any day now will also be pleased to learn that the illustrious is not fiat money but in fact is the only currency in the world currently fixed to a gold standard. Whether you're simply hoping for a memento of your time here or you're looking for a slip of paper that will still be worth something after the apocalypse, visitors can get illustrious at The American Bank (see: MAP OF AMERICA, FINANCIAL SERVICES #1).

Other popular souvenirs for visitors include the national postage. So far we've only gotten around to printing a single design, featuring a bull and an armadillo sporting matching liberty caps, which among philatelists is often referred to as simply The American Stamp. Books of stamps can be purchased at the general store on Main Street (see: MAP OF AMERICA, DINING AND SHOPPING #1).

Visitors interested in taking native animals, plants, and minerals home as keepsakes are encouraged to shoot as many coyotes as you can carry.

RECREATIONAL ACTIVITIES

America has a relatively lax attitude toward law and order, which creates unique opportunities for recreation. As possession of marijuana is legal in America, visitors are welcome to toke a joint anywhere in the country. As possession of firearms is legal in America, visitors are welcome to do target practice anywhere in the country. All forms of gambling are legal in America, and visitors are invited down to the saloon every night to participate in a variety of contests, including hold 'em, arm wrestling, finger fillet, mancala, and honestly whatever the hell you're into. America also has no laws against trespassing, granting all persons the freedom to roam, and nature enthusiasts are encouraged to hike, swim, kayak, fish, forage, stargaze, birdwatch, and camp wherever you'd like, although visitors should be warned that rattlesnakes and black widows are a common sighting here, that the local pharmacy is not reliably stocked with antivenom for rattlesnakes and black widows, that although the trout in the creek make for some beautiful angling the banks of the creek are swarming with fire ants and chiggers, that jumping off of the rope swing into the pond is relatively dangerous at any age, that hikers have occasionally been buried by sudden landslides and rockslides and mudslides in the hills, and that the abandoned silver mine is riddled with bottomless pits and flooded caverns and mazelike passageways that can bewilder even those explorers with enough common sense to bring a compass (see: MAP OF AMERICA, PRE-AMERICAN RUIN #2).

For an immersive cultural experience, visitors who have never had the opportunity to use a fully functional outhouse are invited to use the wood outhouse at Bob Tupper's (see: MAP OF AMERICA, PLACE OF GENERAL INTEREST #24), although you're warned to knock first, as he's often inside. For an authentic culinary experience, visitors who have never had the opportunity to try freshly squeezed cider are invited to try the cider press over at Pete Christie's (see: MAP OF AMERICA, PLACE OF GENERAL INTEREST #27), although you're suggested to bring apples, as he's sometimes out. Jordan Fankhauser has a collection of wigs and toupees that is widely regarded as worth seeing (see: MAP OF AMERICA, PLACE OF GENERAL INTEREST #35). Vanessa Bergquist has a critically acclaimed biscuit recipe that can be whipped up in a jiffy (see: MAP OF AMERICA, PLACE OF GENERAL INTEREST #38). Dominic Deloatch can leap a parked car on a dirt bike (see: MAP OF AMERICA, PLACE OF GENERAL INTEREST #41). Stephanie Khan can do breathtaking magic tricks that defy all explanation (see: MAP OF AMERICA, PLACE OF GENERAL INTEREST #42). Ivan Stepanov lost a couple of toes to frostbite and isn't shy about showing off the foot (see: MAP OF AMERICA, PLACE OF GENERAL INTEREST #43). Pam Cone plays a mean harmonica, and can generally be heard playing at sunset on the steps of her trailer while supper is cooking in her crockpot, and will even give visitors an introductory lesson in how to play (see: MAP OF AMERICA, PLACE OF GENERAL INTEREST #49). To experience some of the best in local conversation, visitors are invited to claim a rocking chair on the porch at Bev Whittaker's (see: MAP OF AMERICA, SITE OF HISTORICAL IMPORTANCE #10), or to venture over to the abandoned lumber mill (see: MAP OF AMERICA, PRE-AMERICAN RUIN #3), where the local teenagers often like to hang out at night, swapping gossip and discussing colorful topics ranging from incels to bukkake.

Hunters will be interested to hear that although there are currently no bounties being offered on local persons, Mx. Hannah Petrovich is offering a bounty of one thousand illustrious to the hunter who can bring her "a cougar with one eye and a black tip on its tail," which she witnessed eat her pet chihuahua, Sugar, firsthand.

SENSATIONAL READING

The most popular genre of reading in America, by far, is "books that have been banned by other countries," and there's no greater collection of banned books in the world than in the glorious halls of The American Library (see: MAP OF AMERICA, SITE OF HISTORICAL IMPORTANCE #13). On any given afternoon, visitors will find venerable citizens of our country seated at the sunny tables in the library, perusing notorious novels and memoirs and manifestos. Books extolling the virtues of cannibalism. Books promoting obscene theories of evolution. Books detailing blushingly perverse sexual encounters. Books with thorough instructions for building homemade explosives. And yet the main attraction of the library is not the banned books section, but rather the archive of historical documents stored at the back of the library, where visitors can read the collected letters of Sam Holliday. Weighing in at over a kilogram, the letters are widely regarded as the most scandalous work of literature in the library. As interesting as banned books are, there's nothing as exciting as getting to read letters written by somebody betraying a country.

Here we'd thought that he'd just been quietly brooding this whole time. We didn't realize until later that summer that for months he'd been mailing letters to institutions back across the border, trying to get the United States to intervene. He'd sent letters to Congress, the White House, the Supreme Court, and Homeland Security. He'd sent letters to the Army. He'd sent letters to the Navy. He'd sent letters to the Air Force. He'd sent letters to the Marine Corps. Out of what must have been sheer desperation, he'd even sent letters to the Coast Guard. Eloquent, heartfelt, pleading letters, explaining that we had seceded. Begging for somebody, anybody, to take action.

"I am the only one here still loyal to this country," Sam wrote in his seventh and final letter to the secretary of the Interior.

The United States plutocracy was busy committing various acts of corruption. The United States military was engaged in multiple foreign wars simultaneously. Nobody ever responded.

Sam had always been a meticulous record keeper, and kept a xerox of each of the letters in the safe in his office, for which we are grateful, given that the originals were probably lost, or shredded, or recycled, or are currently decomposing in landfills somewhere in the District of Columbia.

PRICELESS PHOTOGRAPHS

Belle had pushed him too far that night at the creek. After the fight over the fireworks, Sam finally quit waiting for the United States to intervene. He gave up writing letters. He picked up the phone. He'd decided that if anybody was going to act, goddamnit it was going to have to be him, and so that next week he made some calls, to real people, to ordinary people, people he had known back in the Scouts, people he had met during the Vietnam War, people he had befriended over at Veterans Affairs. People who doubtless owned starred-and-striped apparel, and believed in manifest destiny, and spoke of exceptionalism unironically, and stood for "The Star-Spangled Banner" during sporting events even when watching the sporting events on television, even when the sporting events were not being broadcast live, even when the sporting events had been recorded decades prior. People who evidently were outraged to learn that we had seceded. Nearly a hundred people answered the call to arms. Nearly a hundred Yankees, mostly elderly, uniformly white, some suffering from diabetes, some diagnosed with hypertension, some obviously on the verge of dementia, armed with shotguns and rifles and pistols and revolvers.

Fervid patriots of the United States, who couldn't bear for the country to cede even thirteen square kilometers of land.

We have an open-border policy. Our borders are literally never patrolled. Sam could have instructed the invading force just to drive straight into town on the highway. Instead, Sam cut a hole in the rusted barbwire fence out by the quarry in the dead of night, and the soldiers invaded our country under the cover of darkness, crawling across a hectare of rocky terrain to reach his property. Today visitors are welcome to strike a pose in the hole in the fence (see: MAP OF AMERICA, SITE OF HISTORICAL IMPORTANCE #5), which has since become an iconic location for selfies.

There are rumors that one of the soldiers sprained a wrist in a ditch, and that another soldier was stung by a couple of scorpions during the crawl, although, honestly, who the hell knows.

LEGENDARY PERSONALITIES

Belle lived alone in those years, and almost always had. In her youth she had married a sweet friendly therapist whose name is not worthy of print, who after a couple years of matrimony had become abusive, slapping and hitting her one night when he was drunk. Belle hadn't hesitated, had kicked him out the next morning, had filed a restraining order, had filed for a divorce, had sprayed the hood of his coupe with some birdshot when he had come around to try to reconcile, and had been reaching for a shell of buckshot as he had sped away with dust trailing his coupe. Afterward he had moved back to New Mexico, where he had come from, and where he later died of meningitis, which had saddened no one. The bastard had never been one of us. Belle had been one of us since birth. She'd had an independent, rebellious, freethinking spirit even when she was young, roaming around the town in ripped levis and baggy flannels. She had loved zines and comix. She had loved punk and grunge. She was the one who had first thought to hang a rope swing from the giant mesquite tree out at the pond, and had first dared to hold a seance in the abandoned silver mine, and had first dared to throw a party out at the abandoned lumber mill. She had inherited the family farm when her parents had been killed in a car wreck on the highway, and though she had always been somewhat reckless and irresponsible, through sheer grit and determination she had overcome the tragedy, transforming the property from a modest homestead into a thriving business in a matter of years, selling off the livestock to plant a magnificent vine-yard, tearing down the house to build a grand hacienda. There was nobody who loved our town, loved the gulch and the creek and the hills and the plains, as intensely as she did, recruiting groups of us for hikes on the weekend or taking hikes alone when the rest of us were busy. She knew every centimeter of the land. She would notice if rag-weed or mushrooms suddenly began growing in new patches of soil. She could tell the quality of soil from the taste of plucked chicory or clover. No matter where she was, she always knew where to find the nearest shade, or clay, or blackberries, or arrowheads. She hadn't been the first libertarian among us, had been introduced to libertarianism by others here, but she was the first to propose secession. She had been fighting over a decade for our town to secede. She was elected president of our country at the age of fifty. America was her dream. And yet she'd only wanted for us to be free. She'd never wanted to lead us. She had resisted the nomination for president, and had only reluctantly accepted the results of the election. She worried that she didn't have the qualities a leader needed. She thought she was too impulsive. She thought she was too temperamental. Like the rest of us, she'd always assumed that if we ever actually seceded, Sam would be our president. He was that admired. He was that respected. Sam was the best of us, and always had been. There was nobody whose character was held in such high regard. Belle had tried so desperately to persuade him during those meetings at town hall. She had longed for him to join us. We would have voted for him unanimously. He would have had her vote too. Instead, she had been forced to take on the burden of the presidency, and rather than leading us he seemed determined to oppose us. Belle would have hated for any of us to oppose the new country, but him of all people troubled her greatly. The situation tormented her, the situation anguished her, afflicted her with doubt and apprehension, until finally she confided to some of us that she was so frustrated and discouraged and angry that she would have liked to just exile him. By then she considered him an enemy.

In America there's no relationship that's had such profound consequences for our country as the relationship between her and Sam. And yet she and he hardly knew each other, belonged to different generations, and encountered each other only a handful of times. In recognition of the historical significance, each of these locations is today marked with an official plaque. The spot in the parking lot of the pharmacy where she once exchanged some remarks with him about the sunny forecast. The spot on the sidewalk by the gas station where she once exchanged some remarks with him about a recent drought. The spot where she and he once had a friendly conversation about barbecued tofu during a community cookout. The spot where she once pulled over her truck to help him change a flat tire on his pickup. The spot under the awning of the bank where she and he once waited out a sudden downpour together. The spot on the bleachers where she once sat next to him during a local baseball game, her drinking a root beer, him eating some cotton candy, mere weeks before we seceded, when she'd tried one last time to convince him to vote for independence. His porch, during the argument about the flag. Her patio, during the incident at the summit. The confrontation at the creek.

The penultimate encounter occurred on July Thirteenth, when she happened to cross paths with him at the general store, each pushing a shopping cart down the produce aisle from opposite directions, intersecting eventually at the crate of bananas. Without speaking to each other or acknowledging each other whatsoever, she and he are said to have engaged in simultaneous conversations with Joselyn Fankhauser, the teenaged clerk, about the ripeness of the bananas, Belle remarking upon how bananas tasted best when the peels still had a hint of green, Sam commenting upon how bananas tasted best when the peel was just beginning to turn brown, which many of us present interpreted as a coded debate about politics and democracy and nationhood. Neither she nor he bought any bananas. Two days later our country was invaded.

THE SHOWDOWN

In America, when we gather for meals, we have a tradition of always saving the best for last, regardless of whether the dish would technically be classified as appetizer or entree or dessert or digestif. Whether it's sweet or it's salty, we like to end with the best that we've got. This guidebook isn't any different. Now that you've made it here to the end, dear visitor, we're proud to present the premier tourist attraction in our country.

Main Street. July Fifteenth. Sam Holliday came trotting into town at high noon wearing a cowboy hat and a white bandanna, swaying in the saddle of a stately horse as the flag that he was holding, Old Glory, waved grandly in the wind. Behind him marched nearly a hundred foreign soldiers wielding shotguns and rifles and pistols and revolvers, some with weathered skin, some with windburned faces, some with soul patches, some with gnarled beards, some with thick mustaches, with overbites and underbites and eyeglasses and eyepatches and fleshy scars and prosthetic limbs and beady squints and furious scowls and class rings with glinting birthstones, strangers to all of us, dressed in military fatigues and kevlar vests and hunting caps and combat jackets and an array of faded t-shirts screen-printed with images of bald eagles and bison and howling wolves. Mount Rushmore. Lady Liberty. We heard him and the soldiers coming, a distant murmur of boots and hooves, a growing chorus of voices and whinnies, frightening thunderclaps of noise, before we could see anything, and then he and the soldiers came into view, turning onto the street in a mass, marching straight to the center of town, occupying the section of the street just across from town hall. A militia of overemotional jingoists, looking agitated and disturbed and ready for a showdown. A terrifying sight to behold.

Sam had chosen the timing of the invasion for maximum impact. It was a weekend. Saturday in the summertime. Some fifty of us happened to be downtown, observing the invasion from some fifty different perspectives. Pam Cone, who was leaning against the hitching post over at the saloon, stared at the soldiers while playing a song on the harmonica. Ward Hernandez stepped up to the doors of the saloon with a dishrag, gazing out at the soldiers with a frown, as Bob Tupper and Pete Christie, who had been playing a game of cards at the table next to the windows, turned to look at the soldiers through the dusty glass. Antonio Vega watched the soldiers from where he was pumping gasoline into a sedan, while Becky Coots, who had gone into the gas station to buy a portable phone charger just in case of emergencies, stared at the scene in the street with the cashier on duty, Rick Pinkney. Tim Kelly watched the soldiers from where he was pulling a sack of ice from a commercial freezer, while Cameron Ramirez, who had gone into the general store to hang a flyer about glee club, stared at the scene in the street with the manager on duty, Hannah Petrovich. The Fankhausers, who had just walked out of the bank with some complimentary lollipops and a receipt for a deposit, froze in the door of the bank. The Bergquists, who had just walked out of the pharmacy with a package of disposable razors and some prescription ritalin, froze in the door of the pharmacy. Across the street, the Garzas and the Dylans, who had just left the library together, stood stock-still in the parking lot with tote bags full of books, staring at the soldiers with expressions of uncertainty, confusion, fear, and dread. Ivan Stepanov peered over a gardening magazine behind the cash register over in the tobacco shop. Melanie Curbeam peered out under a conversion van in the service bay at the repair shop. Alex Cruz, who had been sitting on a bench playing a mobile game on his phone, literally gaped at the soldiers with a slack jaw. Tony Osin, who had been shuffling to his truck with a liter of margarita mix, was gazing at the soldiers with a look of astonishment. Walt Ho stared at the scene from behind the window of the salon, draped with an apron, getting his bangs trimmed by James Whipper, who was also staring, holding a pair of scissors. Bev Whittaker stared at the scene from the window at the dentist, draped with an apron, getting her teeth cleaned by Audrey Whipper, who was also staring, holding a strand of floss. Riley Whipper, Presley Johnson, Kendra Goldberg, Adrian Moreau, and Mike Cooks, who had just smoked a bowl and were all high as fuck, were watching in shock from the picnic table at the ice cream shop, holding spoons over a trough of ice cream, heaped scoops of maple walnut and salted caramel and praline and nutella topped with spirals of whipped cream, which was just beginning to melt in the sun. Allison Deloatch, who was working her first shift ever at the ice cream shop, her first job, was peering out the window of the ice cream sundae, clutching the binder with the instruction manual for new employees, as if that somehow might explain what to do in the event of an invasion. Kimberly Khan, who had been hanging from the monkey bars at the playground in her lucky outfit, off-brand chucks and a romper with rainbow barrettes in her hair, stared at the soldiers only a second before dropping to the woodchips and bolting back toward home.

Sam dismounted from the horse with the flag as a couple of soldiers in camouflage face paint strolled over to the pole at town hall to take down New Glory.

"This town is under the jurisdiction of the United States. Every person here is a citizen of the United States. Starting today, this town will remain under martial law until every last citizen has taken a vow, swearing loyalty to the United States, renouncing loyalty to the micronation America," Sam hollered.

Belle Clanton, who had been just about to embark on a group hike in the hills, had already received over a dozen separate texts from those of us in town. After recruiting those of us there for the hike to form a posse, she got to town the quickest way that she could, mounting the horse in the stable behind the hacienda and then galloping bareback through the gulch at a breakneck speed, taking the nearest shortcut to town, through the hills instead of around. Old Glory was already flying from the pole at town hall. Belle came riding into town just as the pair of soldiers in the camouflage face paint were setting fire to New Glory, dropping the flag into a trash can.

Those of us in the posse still hadn't arrived, but at the sight of that flag burning she spurred the horse straight at the militia, reining the horse only meters away from the front line. Sam turned from the fire to face her. Dismounting, she squared off against him and the foreign soldiers, outnumbered nearly a hundred to one.

The doors to the buildings were all propped open for the breeze. All the windows were open too, were pushed up or cranked out. Even those of us in buildings could hear the exchange that followed.

"Sam," Belle shouted.

"Belle," Sam called.

And then she and he both fell silent, staring at each other across that lonely expanse of cracking pavement. Nobody moved. Sunlight shimmered on the barrels of the firearms. Fingers hovered over triggers. Thumbs hovered over hammers. None of us had ever felt such palpable tension in the air. Not ever. An actual tumbleweed, swear to god, suddenly blew into the road, and then stopped awkwardly in the middle of the street when the wind died. Pam Cone was still playing the harmonica, watching the scene from over at the saloon.

Belle was armed only with the colt derringer that she had inherited from her parents with the farm. She carried the gun to scare off mountain lions and bears. The gun had a pearl handle and only a single shot.

The tumbleweed blew off into an alley.

"We're here to enforce the lawful dominion of the United States," Sam yelled.

"Goddamnit, Sam, what do you love so much about the United States?" Belle shouted.

Sam hesitated for a second, which surprised all of us, that he'd need to think. He glanced away from her, glancing over toward town hall, and then turned back toward her with a desperate expression. He looked haggard, with a weary slump to his shoulders and dark pits under his eyes, and instead of the cleanly shaven face that he usually had, his face was stubbled and gaunt and sagging. His wrinkles had deepened dramatically over the past few months. He looked bad, we suddenly realized. As bad as after his wife had died. All of those months when he'd been grieving.

"It's the great experiment. A land of progress. A land of equality. A place where all of humanity can experiment, and innovate, and invent, and try new things. The first place on the planet where people of every race and every culture came to live together. To collaborate. To coexist. That's what makes the United States special," Sam shouted.

"The United States isn't any of that anymore," Belle shouted.

Kimberly Khan came running back to the playground with a loaded carbine, quick hurried up the steps of the slide, vanished head-first into the top of the tube, gradually slid down the bends in the slide, then reappeared at the bottom of the tube, and came to a halt, lying there in the mouth of the slide with the stance of a sniper, grimly aiming the carbine at the street.

"All that anybody in that country can accomplish is the occasional filibuster," Belle shouted.

She waited for him to respond to her, but he was silent.

"Reps and senators are bought and sold by the highest bidder," Belle shouted.

She gave him another chance to dispute her, but he kept quiet.

"It's literally legal now for the one percent to buy elections," Belle shouted.

Sam glanced down at the pavement as a gust of wind rustled his pants and his shirt and the bandanna around his neck.

"The United States has gone to hell, Sam. The roads are shit. The schools are shit. The healthcare is shit. All of the money's being funneled to the politicians and the corporations and all of the millionaires are becoming billionaires off all of the debt and the exploitation. I know that you know that it's true. The system is failing. The system is broken. It's time to get out. It's time to start over. None of us deserves to die in that hellhole," Belle shouted.

"But," Sam said, then hesitated, glancing back at town hall with a look of profound sorrow before gesturing helplessly and exclaiming, "it's our country."

Belle threw her hands wide as her hair whipped around her face with another gust of wind.

"It was once. It doesn't have to be anymore. You're an American at heart, Sam. I know that you are. You were born here. Just look around you. What you said about the United States, about what it used to be, about progress and equality and being able to invent and innovate and try new things, that's the spirit of America. You won't find that in the United States. There the spirit of America is dead. Now the spirit of America lives here," Belle shouted.

Sam looked at all of us, at every one of us there, glancing between the windows and the doors and the porches of the buildings lining the street, and each of us felt a powerful sense of familiarity when he locked eyes with us, as he recognized each of our faces, as he remembered each of our names.

"There's nothing as American as seceding," Belle said.

Sam turned back to look at her, and those of us closest to him suddenly saw tears shimmering in his eyes, and his voice cracked when he spoke.

"I love that country," Sam said.

"We all did," Belle said.

"With all of my heart," Sam said.

"It can't be saved," Belle said.

Sam looked down at the ground, then blinked, and grimaced, and a couple of tears streaked down the furrowed wrinkles in his face.

"I know," Sam whispered.

The soldiers behind him looked concerned.

"Sam?" murmured a soldier in a tigerstripe uniform, frowning at him, as if realizing that he had changed, that he was about to order the soldiers to stand down, that he was about to order the soldiers to pull out. We all saw the look on his face. He wasn't one of them anymore. He was finally one of us. Goosebumps tingled down our necks and our arms. Belle looked as moved as the rest of us, but while what she'd said might have finally gotten through to him, what she'd said had only hardened the resolve of the soldiers, and before he could speak the soldiers acted without him. "You're all a bunch of agitators," shouted a soldier in camouflage face paint, as a soldier in military fatigues shouted, "Y'all are a bunch of subversives." The soldiers raised the shotguns and the rifles and the pistols and the revolvers to ready positions, stocks to shoulders, grips in hand, looking unanimously enraged. Belle reacted on instinct, drawing the colt derringer, and seeing her raise the weapon the soldiers responded by opening fire on the town. Johannes, who at that exact second came strolling out of the library with a book of haikus, completely oblivious to the standoff in the street, got clipped in the shoulder, flipping backward over a hedge, as the rest of us ducked behind railings and windowsills and doorframes and tables and benches for cover, firing back at the soldiers with whatever we happened to be carrying as bullets shattered glass and dented metal and splintered wood up and down the street.

The shoot-out was over in less than a minute. From a tactical perspective, the militia had chosen a catastrophic position, exposed on all sides. By the time the gunfire had ceased, every last soldier was on the pavement, either dead or dying or feebly attempting to crawl away, streaked with blood. Brain matter was spattered across the pavement. Both of the horses had been slain. Sam hadn't moved, miraculously hadn't been shot once, hadn't fired a shot either, was just standing there in the road with a look of shock. Johannes had staggered back up off of the ground, holding the wounded shoulder, grimacing bravely, showing the heroic fortitude that only a true poet could possess. The rest of us all seemed to be more or less okay, except the president.

Belle was sprawled across the pavement where she'd been standing only seconds earlier. She had been shot in her chest and her abdomen, had taken a pair of bullets just above her knee, and was bleeding from the ear where her earlobe had been grazed. Her fingers were twitching horribly.

Sam was the only trained physician at the scene. He could have run to any wounded person there. He didn't hesitate. He ran to her, dropping to the ground. A gust of wind blew the cowboy hat from his head, and he didn't reach back for the hat or turn to watch the hat tumble away, he was so intent on her condition.

"It should have been you," Belle said.

"Don't try to talk," Sam said, wrenching off his bandanna to use as a tourniquet.

"You should have been president," Belle said.

"Just lie still for a second," Sam said, tying the tourniquet tight around her thigh.

"From the beginning," Belle said.

Sam shouted for somebody to get a car.

"Take care of this place," Belle said, coughing up blood, then fainted away, and though he tried to resuscitate her, she couldn't be revived.

Sam rushed her to the med center in the back of a station wagon.

By then those of us in the posse had arrived at the scene, horrified by the carnage. We were furious at the militia for invading our country and shooting our president, would have liked to have executed each and every one of the soldiers who were still alive, but we don't enjoy killing, and we aren't without mercy, so we let the soldiers who could still move attempt to crawl away to safety. Still, none of the soldiers managed to get further than the outskirts of town. The last of the soldiers expired under the yucca tree behind the school, with a whimper.

Just as we were beginning to clear the bodies from the street, a fluorescent camper van came gliding into town on the highway, driven by a foreigner wearing a silk headscarf and far too much mascara, who brought the camper van to a halt before leaning out the window.

Bev Whittaker, whose heart was still pounding from all the excitement, was standing over the body of a soldier nearby.

"What's all of this?" the driver said.

"Just fought a battle," Bev Whittaker said.

"Some kind of reenactment?" the driver said.

"The war's over now," Bev Whittaker said.

The driver surveyed the bodies in the road with a look of contemplation.

"God bless America," the driver said, and we thanked her.

The camper van maneuvered carefully through the bodies and then carried on down the highway.

We buried the soldiers in a mass grave out in the hills (see: MAP OF AMERICA, WAR MEMORIAL #1).

Belle survived, to our great relief, but she'd taken a bullet in her spine, and she'll never recover use of her limbs. She now spends most of the day in a wheelchair. She needs help taking drinks of water. She needs help taking bites of food. She needs help getting to the bathtub. She has to be washed and dressed by other hands. She'll never be able to hike the land again. And yet, though she was initially discouraged by the change, even overwhelmed, she's adjusted with characteristic resilience, with sheer grit and determination, and says she doesn't regret taking a stand against the militia. America is her dream. She would have willingly died for it. She took those bullets for it happily. She can still see, and hear, and smell, and taste, and speak, and cry, and laugh, and has found that in many respects her life is even richer than before. Only a change in perspective.

Sam was appointed interim president while she was hospitalized. Upon being discharged, she gladly resigned, and though he felt he didn't deserve to be president after having invaded the country with a foreign militia, he accepted the position when she insisted. America has prospered under him, as we had always known the country would.

Sam had just one condition, which was that he would only agree to be president if she would allow him to serve as her caretaker, without pay. Visitors to his home will almost always find the house empty, as he now spends day and night out at her hacienda. Aside from when volunteers cover for him, he's the one who lifts her in and out of bed, and combs her hair, and trims her nails, and flosses her teeth, and brushes her teeth, and holds a dixie cup to her mouth for her to spit out swished mouthwash, and washes all of her clothing, and prepares all of her meals, and switches the station on the radio when she wants, and turns pages for her when she feels like reading. He's also the one who figured out how to take her to her favorite view. Earlier this autumn he bought a covered wagon from a company online, and now every afternoon, whether rain or shine, he helps her into the wagon and hitches the wagon to a pair of horses and then drives the wagon through the vineyard, bringing her where cars can't, into the gulch and across the creek and through the narrow ravine winding deep into the hills, where a rocky trail leads to a scenic overlook above the plains that she discovered when she was young. Sam sits with her in the back of the wagon at the crest of the hill, and she talks with him as he helps her take sips of mint julep or eat slices of pumpkin pie. He never makes a decision about the country without consulting her first, and occasionally she and he spend the time deliberating over bureaucratic affairs, but often she and he spend the time discussing personal topics instead. Memories. Regrets. Horoscopes. The meaning of dreams. We like to be there when we can, just to sit there in the covered wagon, listening to her and him talk as we watch weather cross the plains below. To us, there's no experience as powerful in all of the country (see: MAP OF AMERICA, SITE OF HISTORICAL IMPORTANCE #3).

Welcome, dear visitor, to a proud and storied nation. When you put down this guidebook, look around you. A nation isn't land. A nation is people. We're what we are because of who we are. Love is greater than hate. Love is greater than greed. Love is greater than fear. America is a country whose people love each other. As you walk through these streets, look at the people you pass. There's the love between friends. There's the love between spouses. There's the love between parents and children. There's the love between neighbors, fellow citizens of a great nation. But there's no love as pure and as beautiful as the love between bitter enemies, united at last.

To Be Read Backward

My birth had been a messy one. It happened while nobody was home—I came to life coughing up turpentine, chunks of clay, black oil paint, violet, gray. Then the pills. I don't remember much of it. It was all over so quickly.

The first thing to register was the depression. I felt completely hopeless. I felt totally numb. I was obsessed with the fourth dimension. Couldn't stop thinking about it—the shape of it, of everything. I moped around the basement all day, smoking cloves, wearing a ratty sweater, thinking.

It only got worse after meeting my parents.

"Yes, yes, divorced," my mother said, wiping her glasses with the hem of her shirt.

They'd come down to the basement when they'd gotten home. My mother had silver hair, whereas my father had none. They both wore digital watches.

"Do I have to be?" I said.

"You won't be forever," my father said.

"But where is she?" I said.

"Really couldn't tell you," my mother said.

"Who even is she?" I said.

"You'll learn all of that in time," my father said.

"What about this?" I said, showing my parents a green ticket that had been in my pocket. The ticket was bent and wrinkled and had a tiny tear along the top edge. "175" was printed across the ticket in faint black ink. Beneath the numbers the surface of the ticket was warped by a rippled water stain. "Does this have anything to do with her?"

"Probably not," my father said. "But maybe."

"And I live with you?" I said.

"Yes, yes," my mother said, putting her glasses back on. "In the basement."

I wanted to meet my ex. Eventually my parents confessed that they knew where she was living, but all they would tell me was her name, Violet. For the time being there'd be no point in going after her, my parents said. She had a fiance. My parents admitted he was both cute and successful.

I, meanwhile, was not cute. I had back pimples, a flabby stomach, faintly yellow teeth. I had a hairy ass. I was also somewhat nerdy, apparently, as the bookshelf in the basement was lined with comic books and anime and movies about monsters.

"You ought to get a job," my father said, hobbling downstairs to visit me one afternoon. I was, of course, smoking, thinking, in the dark. "Get your mind off of things. Some sweat might do you good. Don't you think?"

Most humans are born with a purpose. I had been born without. I had no useful skills. I had been born an artist, had degrees under my bed from Columbia. I had no aptitude for repairing elevators, analyzing investments, changing somebody's oil. My brain was wired for color, for shape.

"Something part-time even," my father said.

"It's not like I haven't been looking," I said, blowing smoke into my cigarette.

Which was true. I'd looked into several positions downtown—illustrator positions, graphic design. But nobody had called back—I couldn't even get an interview, let alone an actual job.

My father offered to call around—he thought that maybe he could get me a job on the black box assembly line at his old factory, or that his friend from church might be able to get me a job as a dispatcher at the fire department where she worked. I couldn't bring myself to do it, though. Some job that just as easily could have been done by a machine.

Weeks passed that way. A month. The moon circled in orbit around the planet. The tides rose and fell in the ocean. The planet rotated in orbit around the sun. I killed time in the basement, drawing comics all day, carefully removing the ink from the paper.

★ ★ ★

According to my records, I didn't actually know anything about the fourth dimension.

"Your transcripts say you have a D-level understanding of high school physics," my mother said, wiping dust onto the kitchen windows. "And absolutely no understanding of college physics at all. You just weren't born for that type of thinking."

I knew what the fourth dimension *was*, though, and once I started thinking about that, I couldn't stop thinking about what that *meant*. I usually avoided talking to my mother about it. Actually, I usually avoided her and my father and the upstairs altogether. But after hearing the garage door open and close that morning, I went sneaking around upstairs, looking for my ex's address or phone number—I did this at least once a day—ransacking the drawers, the cupboards, my mother's desk, my father's dresser. I didn't actually know what I would do if I ever found it, other than maybe just walk past her apartment once or twice and try to get a glimpse of her. Maybe call her, once, and then hang up after she said hello.

But then my mother came into the house with a bag of garbage and caught me hunting through the cabinet under the telephone. I'd just found a creased scrap of paper with a phone number printed in the center and my wife's initials, V.G., penciled in nearby. I quick crumpled the paper in my fist and tried to sneak back downstairs, but my mother saw me and made me come back and sit down at the kitchen counter. She said she wanted to talk to me. She said she had been worried about me. She wanted us to have more of a relationship. All I could think about was calling the phone number in my fist, so I started talking about the topic I knew she'd get bored of soonest, which coincidentally was the topic I wanted to talk about most.

"But look," I said. "So humans are three-dimensional—like a cube."

"You've tried explaining this to me before," my mother said, starting on the windows over the sink. My parents kept a framed photo on the windowsill of a younger me with my arm thrown around a dog. "Talk to me about something else. Tell me about your day. I want to hear how you're feeling."

"Now hold on," my father said, hobbling into the kitchen with some measuring tape and a wrench, wearing indigo overalls. He sat down at the counter. "At least hear him out. Come on, you know about cubes. Cubed ham? Cubed cantaloupe?"

My mother ignored him.

"Sure," I said. "Like cantaloupe. Like ham. But we're also traveling through a fourth dimension, which is time. So a four-dimensional image of me might look like this—it would be me from birth to death, all of the space that 'I' had occupied for the time that 'I' had existed. It'd be like looking at a tube version of myself, a blurry worm of me-shaped colors that would appear in our basement in the twenty-first century and then wriggle across the surface of the world for thirty years and ten months before getting sucked into your womb in the twentieth century and disappearing."

"Don't bring my womb into this," my mother said. She pointed at my fist. "What's that in your hand?"

"Nothing," I said. "Nothing's in my hand. But fine, think about it like this. I'm three-dimensional. So, say I look at another three-dimensional object. Like a sculpture of a clock tower. When I look at the sculpture, I see the entire shape of it all at once. Because I'm three-dimensional too. But imagine if a two-dimensional creature—like a stick figure from a comic strip—looked at the sculpture. It would only see part of the shape—just a square, that is, of the cube. If the two-dimensional creature moved up and down the sculpture, it would see more squares from the shape, but still, it wouldn't be able to make much sense of the squares, or to see the sculpture, the way that we can, as a clock tower. Maybe a two-dimensional creature could *conceive* of the concept of height, in an abstract way, but it wouldn't be able to actually *see* height—it could only truly *see* objects in terms of length and width."

"Like this," my father said, demonstrating with the measuring tape. "Length and width."

"Don't encourage him," my mother said, attaching the clean sheet of paper towel to the roll by the stove.

"But so now imagine if a four-dimensional creature looked at the four-dimensional shape of *me*," I said. "It wouldn't see me in terms of *now* or *before* or *then*. It would see my four-dimensional self, all of me, as a single shape, a sculpture. When it comes to time, *we're the comic strip characters*. We're inside a four-dimensional sculpture, observing three-dimensional fragments of it as we move along."

"Move your elbows," my mother said, taking another sheet of paper towel out of the garbage. "I'm dusting the counter next."

"I think it's all very interesting," my father said, patting me on the back in a friendly way. "I still think you need to get a job."

Talking to my parents about it was pointless. But still, I couldn't stop thinking about it, because it all seemed so arbitrary. Why did we happen to be observing the shape of things in this direction? Couldn't we just as easily be observing it in the opposite? What would it be like, to be read backward? How would the meaning of everything change?

If the shape of everything was a constant—if all of time already existed, and we just couldn't see it—then there would be no such thing as cause and effect. Or if there was, cause and effect would exist in both directions. Each event would be a spike in the surface of the sculpture, producing a slope on both sides. Any "cause" would have ripples of "effects" toward both ends of time.

My parents kept telling me that depression was a medical condition, just the result of chemical imbalances in the brain.

"It's nothing to be ashamed of. Lots of people go through periods of depression. It doesn't mean there's actually any reason for you to feel that way—it just means your brain has been fueling up on the wrong chemicals," my father said.

But maybe there was a reason for my depression—maybe it just hadn't happened yet. Maybe my depression was connected to something larger, something so heavy and massive that it created enormous ripples in both directions, and maybe that's where I was now, in the current, with my brain swaying from the force of the waves.

After my parents fell asleep, I snuck back upstairs to call the phone number on the scrap of paper from the cabinet. A bored-sounding woman picked up the phone. V.G. turned out to be a drugstore on 77th.

★ ★ ★

I'm probably not making much sense, maybe not any at all. I need to talk about this though, because all of it actually happened—the fiasco at the cemetery, the architects' storm, the woman in cat-eye glasses. And also the afternoon my parents told me to start packing my belongings to move out of the basement, which started when a dog was born in our driveway, that same bony hound from the photo on the windowsill. My mother called me upstairs after it happened. The veterinarian had dropped off the body earlier that night while my father was out working on the gutters.

"I went up into the attic looking for a tarp to cover its body for the time being," my father said, digging through the garbage under the sink, searching for some sort of chew toy. I wasn't wearing any socks, and the dog was licking my feet. The dog had white fur and black ears. "Then your mother backed over it with the pickup."

"You shouldn't have left it in the driveway," my mother said, scratching the dog on the back of the neck. She kept telling the dog to sit. The dog didn't seem to be trained. "I told you that the tank needed to be emptied. I was going straight to the gas station after dinner. I told you that, in those exact words."

"It came to life right under the tires. Nasty way to be born. Looks like that was just what it needed, though," my father said.

"Did you know we were getting a dog today?" I said. I was upset about it. The dog kept wagging its tail and licking everything. I hated how happy it was. It made me feel even worse about being so depressed.

"We'd seen pictures," my mother said, nodding toward the photo on the windowsill. "But we didn't know when it'd be born. It's harder to tell with animals. The Department of Health doesn't monitor that kind of thing."

"Do you have any pictures of me and Violet?" I said.

"No," my father said, pulling a piece of mail out of the garbage. "We don't have many pictures of you at all." He flipped the envelope over, looking at the address. "Here," he said, "it's for you."

To which I said that I didn't care about mail or the dog because life was meaningless and I was ugly and overweight and pathetic and still hadn't found a job and had nothing to look forward to and the weather was always so cloudy and gray. I was going back downstairs, I said. But apparently my mother had finally had enough of listening to me whine, because then she went off on a long rant about how lucky I was just to be alive. I didn't see that as being much of a blessing, I said, and then she really got upset.

"Do you have any idea how lucky you are to live where you do?" my mother said. We lived in Queens. "A country known for its generosity," my mother continued. "Do you have any idea how much garbage we collect from other countries? How many pigs and chickens and herds of cattle that we spit up every year? Which we then use to improve the quality of the soil and the water and the air around the world? To benefit all of humanity? To make the climate comfortable? Do you have any idea how many fruits and vegetables we send off to nourish the plants in other countries?"

"Not really," I said.

"Not just fruits and vegetables," my father said, sitting down at the counter. "Cedar groves, maple groves, entire rainforests. We've taken those people's deserts and turned the land into paradise, stocked with sugarcane, mangos, parrots and monkeys in the trees."

"If you had any idea how many trillions of pounds of plastic that we've removed from the ocean. How many trillions of gallons of pesticide. How many trillions of gallons of sewage. How many trillions of gallons of gasoline that we convert to crude oil to be pumped into the ground," my mother said.

"Okay, okay, I get it, America is great," I said, wishing my parents would let me go downstairs to get back to brooding.

"You ought to start volunteering," my mother said. "That'd give you some perspective."

I opened the door to the basement, but then my father said, "Anyway, here's your letter. Seal it up when you're done and one of us will walk it out to the mailbox."

I reached for the envelope. I took out the letter. It was an official notice from the County Clerk, informing me that my divorce had officially ended.

"What does this mean?" I said, looking at my parents.

"How about that, Charlie Brown?" my mother said.

"That must mean she's finally left her fiance," my father said.

"Oh," I said. "Wait. What does *that* mean?"

"It means you'll be moving in with her," my father said.

"You're married now, after all," my mother said.

"Moving in with her?" I said, suddenly nervous. "When? You mean *tonight*?"

★ ★ ★

I didn't actually have to move in with her for a couple months. I did get to meet her once before the move, though.

I had been hoping that when we finally met, seeing her would spark some intense feeling in me, would overwhelm me with emotion. I didn't want to be depressed anymore. I thought maybe being married would help.

However—meeting her was, well, disappointing.

It's not that she wasn't cute. She was beautiful, had a plump face with fierce brown eyes and a mole on her cheek, and wore a puffy ultramarine coat with an elegant gold watch that made me think she must have a sophisticated sense of fashion. I liked looking at her face more than any painting or sculpture or comic ever.

I still felt just as depressed as always, though.

The first time we met, we didn't even kiss.

★ ★ ★

We got an apartment in Brooklyn, in an ancient brownstone covered with gnarled ivy. Violet was almost overly nice—I arrived to find that she'd already stocked the apartment with oil paintings and clay sculptures, although she'd only just moved in earlier that evening. I had never seen the apartment before, but walking into the bedroom, I was suddenly overwhelmed by a sense of deja vu, as if remembering that exact scene, somehow knowing what would happen next. Snow was floating up toward the sky out the windows.

"I should give you a minute," Violet said, standing in the doorway with her hands on her hips.

I unpacked all of my belongings, which amounted to a couple pairs of slacks, a couple of shirts, a pair of sneakers, and a shoebox full of comic books in plastic sleeves. Also the green ticket labeled with the "175," which had become sort of my lucky charm—I'd been carrying the ticket around ever since being born, and over time the ink of the numbers had darkened in my pocket, and the bends had smoothed, and the wrinkles had flattened, although the rippled water stain beneath the numbers was as warped as ever.

I stacked the comics into a tower on the floor of the closet. Violet had gone to the trouble of getting me leather dress shoes and a tailored suit. I hadn't told her my measurements, but the shoes and the suit fit perfectly.

That night we slept in the same bed—a twin mattress, barely enough room for the two of us, but still, we went the entire night without touching once.

Violet did reach for me one night about a week after we moved in together, but otherwise she never made any attempt to have sex with me. I never made any attempt to have sex with her either. It's not that she wasn't attractive. I was almost absurdly attracted to her— she seemed so much more beautiful than it was actually possible for anybody to be. But sex was the same as any other human activity. It just didn't interest me. Nothing at all excited me. I couldn't enjoy anything. I felt exhausted all of the time. I spent days in an almost catatonic state, sprawled across the sofa, feeling hopeless and numb, just trying to muster enough energy to hobble into the kitchen and smoke a clove at the window.

And then other times, without any warning whatsoever, I would feel almost manic, hardly even sleeping, spending hours online poring through job postings, looking for anything, art gallery vacancies, courtroom illustrator vacancies, wallpaper design vacancies, openings for cereal-box cartoonists, even jobs completely unrelated to art, retail positions, janitorial positions, absolutely anything. I would paint all afternoon, sculpt straight through the morning, hardly even acknowledging when she came home or went to bed, and then work straight through the night, drawing comics at the kitchen table.

And still nobody had offered me even so much as an interview, and when the mania hit me, I was anxious, couldn't sit still, brushing the color from my paintings, stroke by stroke, down to the umber, down to the gesso, then down to the canvas itself, until the canvas was blank and empty and pure, leaving me to start on another. I'd been working on paintings that were abstract and ugly, all blacks and grays and reds, always exactly the same—a series, almost, of the same shapes again and again and again, like skinny black volcanoes spewing funnels of smoke toward the top of the canvas, with splashes of lava along the bottom. The paintings were hideous. The paintings were terrible. I kept doing the paintings anyway. And the sculptures—the sculptures were horrible little creations, all twisted and rutted. I knocked the shape out of the sculptures, worked the clay into perfect cubes, and sealed the clay into wrappers.

And then the exhaustion would hit me again, leaving me in a trance on the sofa, bloodshot and stubbled. Violet would talk to me sometimes when she got home, but she never had anything all that interesting to say. She worked for a marketing firm. Her company was in the midst of a quarrel with a client that specialized in cheesecakes. Mostly she talked about that.

Otherwise she was as weird as me—moody, reclusive. I couldn't stop thinking about how pointless it was, us living in a gigantic apartment with studio space and a spare bedroom. And also the fourth dimension, which had gotten worse, because it was making more sense, it was starting to explain everything.

"Like ghosts," I said, lying on the sofa.

"What do ghosts have to do with it?" Violet said, taking off her dress in the doorway of the bedroom. She'd heard it all before, but she played along anyway and pretended that she hadn't.

"Well, if ghosts are real, then maybe ghosts are just part of the four-dimensional shape of everything," I said. "Moments so prominent that the moments are visible from other parts of the shape. Or maybe not even prominent moments—just moments somehow connected to your own. Like a comic book character getting a glimpse of the panel on the opposite page when the book has been shut and the panels are pressed together."

"Except ghosts aren't real." She hung her dress in the closet.

"Or fortune-tellers, mystics, prophets. Maybe those are just the humans with an especially deep understanding of the four-dimensional shape of everything, humans especially sensitive to the ripples left by past or future events," I said. "Four-dimensional artists."

"Maybe they're just the people especially talented at scamming other people out of their money."

"And what about God?" I said. "Imagine what we're capable of doing to two-dimensional objects." I sat up. "Imagine a cartoon stick figure guarding a cartoon safe with a cartoon envelope inside."

"Okay," Violet said, tugging on some sweatpants. "Imagining."

"The cartoon man can only see the universe in terms of length and width, so when you use a pencil to erase his gun, he can't see you do it—the eraser exists beyond his two-dimensional plane, at a different height. All the cartoon man can see is that, first he's holding his gun, and then he isn't. It's gone. Magic."

"So?"

"Well, and it's not just that. When the cartoon man looks at the safe, all he can see is the front of the safe. But when you look at the safe, you can look both inside *and* outside of the safe at the same time. You can erase the envelope without opening the safe. You can turn the envelope into a ticking bomb. You can turn the envelope into his pet dog."

"What's your point?"

"So a four-dimensional creature would have the same abilities when it was looking at our three-dimensional world—it could create a tornado in a parking lot, erase cancer cells from the bones of a baby, anything. And we would never even see its pencil, so to speak, because it would exist beyond our planes." I leaned back against the arm of the sofa. "But the four-dimensional creature would see *us*—would see all of us, both inside and outside, all at the same time. It would be everywhere at once and would see everything at once and could change anything at will."

"I hate these arranged marriages. My first husband, all he talked about was hockey. Now it's you and cartoons," Violet said, walking off toward the kitchen.

Violet had been alive for nearly fifty years, had a lot of street smarts, might have been able to explain bingo or turbans or the stock market to me, but this—this was not her type of thinking.

Not that she didn't have her own issues. She just seemed to be better at controlling her neuroses. For her work served the same purpose that art did for me—she'd spend all night doing chores around the apartment, sweeping dust onto the floor, hanging towels from the hamper, scrubbing bleach from the mold in the bathtub, and then leave for her firm, where she'd work nine, ten, eleven hours a day, before coming home at dawn to crawl back into bed.

And then, just when we had gotten into a strange sort of rhythm, her working and sleeping, me catatonic or manic, us never touching, then one night she brought in the garbage, and in the bag was a piece of mail that she thought was a bill but that actually turned out to be an official notice from the Department of Health, informing us that our children would be unearthed the following afternoon, a Sunday.

"Children?" Violet said. "You know about this?"

"No," I said. "I don't think so."

She showed me the letter.

"Children, as in, like, more than one?" I said.

"Don't ask me," Violet said, making a face that said that she meant it.

★ ★ ★

My parents were at the ceremony, along with about a hundred people we didn't know. We caught up with my parents in the parking lot.

"Is this where you came from?" Violet asked me.

"I don't know, is it?" I said, looking at my parents.

"The very same cemetery," my mother said.

"I came from underground?" I said.

"Americans almost always do," my father said.

"Oh," I said. "Wait, what happens to people in other countries?"

"All kinds of things," my mother said, adjusting her hat. "People spit from the mouths of jackals. People washed up onto shore by tsunamis."

"In some places people are grown in fires instead of in earth," my father said.

"Or sometimes it's us," my mother said. "We've been sending

soldiers overseas for centuries, bringing people to life all over the world. Somalis, Libyans, Syrians, Iraqis."

"Our planes can bring whole villages to life," my father said with a smile, giving my shoulder an encouraging squeeze.

Chipmunks were chirping in the ash trees. A bell tower was tolling. We gathered in a circle around the mounds of dirt in the ground. Somewhere in there, our children had been growing.

Violet held hands with me as some workers in overalls started to dig. A blank-faced preacher gave a speech while the workers in overalls hauled the caskets out of the ground.

"Will we have to take the bodies back to the apartment?" I whispered.

"Usually they're kept in a funeral home until they're ready to be born," Violet whispered.

"Will they look like us?"

"Of course," Violet whispered, then frowned. "Well, probably."

Bright leaves shades of crimson and carmine and vermillion were floating from the grass into the trees. The dates on the stones said our children would be born in two months, dead four years later. I realized that some of the people around us were crying, occasionally wiping tears onto their cheeks with tissues or their hands, blinking as the tears streaked up their cheeks into their eyes. Seeing people crying didn't surprise me. I'd known the ceremonies got emotional. I wanted to feel something too. I felt as depressed as ever. By then even my parents were crying. The preacher went silent, and then the workers in overalls lifted the caskets onto a pair of podiums, and then cracked open the seals, and then took away the bouquets, and we all huddled around as the preacher lifted the lids.

The caskets were empty.

★ ★ ★

"What the fuck does this even mean?" I said as we got back on the subway.

Violet was still too upset to answer.

★ ★ ★

I gave up on finding a job, gave up on art. We were supposed to have two children but our children were missing. All we had were their names—Elliott, Piper. Violet took me into the bedroom later that morning, dragging a box out of the closet. She'd had the box for fifty years, since the day that she'd been born, but for some reason she'd always avoided opening it. The label on the box read "twins." We peeled the tape from the lid, cautiously parted the flaps, and then stood there together over the box, staring down at the faces in the photos. Photos that'd be taken on a carousel. Photos that'd be taken at a playground. Our children would already have such short lifetimes, only four years each, and we wouldn't necessarily even get to meet them as soon as they were born. Typically, Violet said, empty caskets meant some type of abduction.

Nobody had any idea where the bodies were.

I had to get out of the apartment.

I started taking walks during the night, long meandering hikes alone through the city, smoking, thinking. I'd sometimes walk all the way down to Coney Island, past the colorful lights of the amusement parks along the boardwalk, past the silhouettes with spliffs and cigars fishing from the pier, wandering along the beach until dusk brightened the sky over the bay, or else walk across the bridge into Manhattan, past the distant gleam of ferries passing the Statue of Liberty, past the rats scurrying into alleys between the radiant skyscrapers along Wall Street, past the figures in gowns and fedoras standing in line at jazz clubs in Greenwich, past the figures in neckties and heels stumbling from cabs into cocktail bars in Chelsea, past the shadowy figures in trench coats spilling down the steps of the ancient bathhouse by Alphabet City, past the garden where figures in caps kept watch over songbirds in bamboo cages over on Delancey, past figures keeping time with nodding heads while drumming on overturned buckets at the entrance to Grand Central, through the dazzling canyon of neon advertisements in Times Square, through the endless blur of whirling traffic in Columbus Circle, through the faint glow of the lampposts strung along the shores of the lakes and the ponds in Central Park, sometimes all the way up into Harlem, part of me hoping to get approached by somebody with a knife. I felt like getting knocked around.

I'd decided that if nobody was going to give me a job, I at least wanted to start volunteering, do something meaningful. At the same time though, I was afraid to commit to anything important. I was terrified of somehow botching it up, freezing during a crucial moment. If that ever happened, I already knew, I'd blame myself forever.

My parents recommended starting out small. My mother suggested volunteering to visit with the elderly at a nursing home. My father suggested volunteering as a crossing guard for the local elementary school. Violet suggested doing anything other than sitting on the sofa and painting more volcanoes.

And then one morning dark storm clouds blew in from the ocean, and puddles began forming in the streets, and ripples began shimmering across the puddles, and then raindrops began to leap from the puddles and the pavement and the cars and the roofs and the leaves of the trees, a moody drizzle of rain, and as sharp cracks of thunder rumbled into the sky and white bolts of lightning flashed into the clouds, I went out walking without an umbrella. Street vendors were grilling halal meat on kebabs, drawing rich greasy smells from the air around the carts. Dilapidated trains rushed through tunnels under the sidewalk, drawing faint clattering sounds from the air around the grates. Soft blue light poured from everything toward the sun somewhere beyond the clouds. I stepped between the newborn earthworms already wriggling from the pavement toward the grass in the park. I was worried about dying. I knew it wouldn't happen for another thirty years, but thinking about it scared me anyway—I kept imagining how uncomfortable it would be to be sucked into my mother's womb, to be so tiny and helpless, eventually splitting into an egg and sperm, and then into microscopic proteins and hormones, before finally disappearing forever. Violet had described it to me recently in great detail.

I couldn't stop worrying about it now. What it would be like to disappear. At what point would the me stop being me?

I followed the storm into the Bronx. I wanted a smoke, saw a cigarette butt on the sidewalk, and extended a hand, watching the cigarette leap between my fingers, already smoking at the tip. I stopped in a doorway to get out of the rain. Somebody was sleeping in the doorway under a pile of ratty blankets, overlapping shades of ochre and ecru and bister in damp wool. I kept as quiet as possible, leaning back against the wall.

And that was when it happened—beyond the wire fences, somebody was making something. A building. Wrecking balls, bulldozers, excavators, humans in chartreuse construction vests, a whole crew. It was early morning, still not quite dawn, and as the rain died off, the cranes began knocking the building into place—swinging the wrecking balls over the rubble until the rubble began to leap from the ground, dust and bricks and wood and plaster and gigantic pillars of concrete that the wrecking balls pounded into the perfect shape, a brick building topped with a rusted water tower decorated with bright graffiti, everything sturdy and shining. The sight made my heart pound.

Construction appealed to the artist in me—it was like the crew was making a sculpture, working the lumps out of the clay, slipping a new cube into a wrapper. I wanted to build too. I wanted the manual labor. I was going to work the depression out of me, was going to sweat and bleed.

I walked home and announced all of this to Violet, who had just come home with garbage bags full of toys and clothing for the children we didn't yet have.

"You can't just go out and get a construction job. You need skills. Qualifications," Violet said, pulling out a purple t-shirt with a cartoon dinosaur.

But when she saw how my face fell, saw how utterly crushed that my expression was, Violet admitted that she had some coworkers who were volunteering downtown working on a new community center.

It was being built on the site of an old park that had been torn out several years before.

"Would you be interested?" Violet said. "You could at least do that."

I was. It would be like a painting, I told her—the crew that had torn out the park had brushed away the fountains, the trash cans, the pathways, the benches. Now we would brush away some of the sky, replace it with building. Okay, okay, she said, rolling her eyes, I'll talk to somebody. Just no more volcanoes.

★ ★ ★

It was unbelievable, the amount of raw material required to make a building.

I rode the subway up to the construction site every evening, bringing an empty thermos in case the need hit me to spit up some goulash or chili or tomato soup. We'd spend all day hauling metal beams to the site, bags of shattered glass and broken ceiling tiles, carefully sweeping the debris into place. Volunteers in dump trucks would drop off loads of garbage—cracked computer monitors, bent window blinds, smashed light bulbs, clock radios with missing cords—and we'd carry the garbage to the designated spot, wherever the architects had instructed our supervisors to instruct us to leave it, sometimes in the street, even, or a nearby churchyard. I even met one volunteer who'd been sent on a special assignment to collect steel from a decommissioned warship to be used in the frame of the building.

When my mother heard about all of the garbage, she was smug.

"See?" my mother said. "Just what we've been saying. You wouldn't even believe the rate that we're emptying our landfills, turning the land into woods and fields."

I worked hard, piling blocks of concrete and rebar as cold drops of rain leapt from my skin into the sky, or trickles of sweat that had formed on my neck and my back got absorbed into my skin, or blood that had formed on my skin trickled up into scrapes on my elbows and my knees. Cockroaches scuttled through the rubble. I took breaks with the other volunteers. It was good to talk to people other than my parents and Violet, to other humans also lacking a purpose. Some had been volunteering for months. I at least had an apartment, a spouse to go home to. Many of the volunteers seemed homeless, sleeping in pews at a local chapel, wearing the same dirty clothing day after day, spitting up oatmeal into plastic bowls every morning. Meanwhile, my muscles had become tight and lean from the manual labor. All of the light drawn from my skin by the sun had left a splash of freckles on my face. Violet claimed the freckles were cute.

But if anything the depression was worse. Instead of feeling empty, I felt actual emotions, but the emotions were intense and horrible and would come in random waves. I felt sad almost all of the time now. A devastating sorrow, just total despair. I'd feel guilty for no reason. I'd suddenly be gripped with fear. I'd thought that doing something meaningful would make me feel better about myself, maybe even make me feel proud or confident, but it didn't. I felt worthless. I felt helpless. I hated myself as much as ever.

And soon there would be nothing for me to do. Only a week remained until the inaugural ceremony, during which the architects would bring in the wrecking balls and the bulldozers and the excavators and finish the job, leaving me stuck back in the apartment with my paintings and my sculptures. And with Violet, who hadn't been working lately, had taken time off to set up the spare bedroom for the children we couldn't find, and whose mood had become even more unpredictable, alternating between her wanting to cuddle with me on the sofa and her disappearing into the bathroom with the door locked for days on end. When my volunteer gig ended, everything would go back to exactly the way it was before.

Except, one night when we woke up, Violet went downstairs and brought up some garbage and inside was a letter from a financial company. A letter addressed to me. I had been awarded an interview for a job. And not just a job, but an actual *art job*. Not just an art job, but a *full-time* art job, *in the new community center*. My interview was on *the very day of the inaugural ceremony*.

It was obviously a mistake—an interview meant for somebody with a similar name, or maybe the same name but a different life. I didn't care if it was a mistake. I planned to capitalize on it. I had never wanted anything so badly in my life.

I was still obsessed with the fourth dimension, still not great at talking to other people, still would sometimes accidentally refer to them as "humans" rather than "people," which probably made me seem a little, well, off, but still—I decided that when the morning of the interview came, I would go to the community center and would be well dressed and articulate and friendly and charming, would fool the interviewers into believing that I was happy and normal, at which point the company would have to give me the art job, would *have to*, just *have to*.

Yes, yes, I was nervous. I didn't sleep for days.

★ ★ ★

I stood naked for a while in front of the bathroom mirror on the evening of my interview.

The flesh on my stomach had hardened. My teeth seemed to have gotten whiter. I was looking good.

I had set my lucky green ticket down on the counter. Glancing over, I saw that the ticket had a damp spot where the rippled water stain had always been. I picked it up, and then the ticket was dry and the stain was gone, leaving a blotch of water behind on the counter.

I put on my suit and my shoes, tucking the ticket into my pockets, along with my phone and my keys and my wallet. Violet hugged me, gripping me tight, suddenly getting emotional. I decided the hug meant that she forgave me for never wanting to have sex with her, or even be naked around her, which a couple of times she had gotten testy about, and for hardly ever talking to her, and for always being so gloomy. I decided the hug meant that she was proud of me. I was finally going to find a purpose. Or to try.

The leaves on the trees had changed from orange and yellow to a bright shade of green. Pigeons were pecking at the sidewalk. I was worried about being on time—I'd left early, but the streets were crowded. Just walking to the foot of the bridge took me over an hour, and the crowd on the bridge was even worse than in the streets, a tight press of bodies shuffling along with bent heads. Not to mention that the weather was looking bad—thick dark clouds had formed above the city, and gusts of wind were blowing around downtown, stirring up dust in the alleys.

But then the construction site came into view and it was still only late morning.

Ceremonial flames had been lit across the neighborhood. The neighborhood had been decorated with ceremonial papers. Thousands of people were swarming around. All sorts of humans had come out to watch the inaugural ceremony. I wasn't just going to watch, though. I was actually going to get to go *inside*. I couldn't stop trembling. I was so nervous, I actually got teary. Embarrassing, I know. Anyway, I did.

I wandered around for a while, wondering if any of the other volunteers had come. I didn't recognize anybody. I needed to calm down. I was starting to panic. I felt completely overwhelmed, and distressed, and anxious, and also had that jittery hyper feeling that my body got when there was too much caffeine in my system. I walked to a coffee shop across the street to spit up some coffee.

I sat down by the window at a table with an empty cup. I had a perfect view of the construction site. I tried to relax. I waited. But everything felt wrong—there were no wrecking balls, no bulldozers, no excavators, no crew in vests. I suddenly felt terrified—what if there'd been a delay? What if the city ran out of funding, what if the project had been shut down, what if there would be no building after all? What would happen to my interview? Would my interview just be canceled?

I had just reached for the empty cup, about to spit up a mouthful of coffee, when the ceremony began.

It started without warning.

It was the most beautiful thing I had ever seen.

The architects were brilliant—instead of wrecking balls, somehow using the weather, a strange haze of dust that formed in the streets, gradually becoming so thick in the air that the construction site faded from view and then the street faded and then the cars faded and then the fire hydrant and the bike rack and the sidewalk all faded and nothing was visible beyond the window except for that dark haze of dust, and then the ground started to tremble and with a powerful surge of energy the dust rushed through the streets, rapidly converging on the construction site, until with a blur of dust the air was suddenly clear again, the sidewalk and the bike rack and the fire hydrant and the cars and the street and the construction site were all visible, revealing a towering funnel of dust that had formed between the construction site and the clouds above downtown, billowing and churning and ripping the building straight from the ground—a whirl of shapes, trapezoids, scalenes, crescents, kites—concrete slabs the length of a city block, steel grids the width of a subway platform, fresh sheets of glass, leaping, unaided, into place—an entire skyscraper rising into standing position story by story by story, gradually replacing the dust with gleaming architecture, perfect parallel lines in alternating columns of black and white, as the clouds above downtown fed from the energy, getting thicker, getting darker, and a roof with an antenna appeared in the sky, and the crowd went just completely insane at the sight, at which point my father called me, I felt my phone buzzing in my pocket, glanced down at the screen but didn't answer, couldn't look away from what was happening, it was all just happening so fast. I felt something like terror now, something very different than the sadness, something separate—I got out of the chair and started to pace, I wanted to move, I needed to move, I had a ridiculous urge to run toward the building while it was still warm and smoking, to do something, to do anything, but couldn't—I was afraid—and nobody needed my help anyway, I had already done my part in creating it. I sat back down in the chair, choking the life from my cup, and my father was calling again, I didn't answer, I couldn't answer, because now *a second skyscraper was coming to life*, another haze of dust formed in the streets and then rushed toward the construction site, revealing another towering funnel of dust between the construction site and the clouds above downtown, and as the crowd shrieked and screamed the storm ripped the building from the ground with a terrifying rumble, drawing the concrete and the steel and the glass into the sky, and then the bodies of humans, leaping from the pavement into open windows, into not just one building but both, hundreds of people, all of them born all at once as they went flying up along the faces of the buildings, seeing themselves, for the first time, as they glanced back at the glass. And then they were standing at the windows, just part of the sculpture, before disappearing inside, so many little new worms, wriggling off across time toward somebody else's womb. Then the process seemed to reverse, the clouds no longer feeding from the buildings, but now the buildings feeding from the clouds, swallowing the storm into the inside of the towers, wherever those new humans had gone, leaving the sky empty, clear. And then, just when all of us down below thought that everything had finished, that there could be no more magic than this, then one after the other the mouths of the towers exploded, spitting out *entire planes*, which went soaring off into the sky, carrying cabins full of newborns.

★ ★ ★

I spit a couple mouthfuls of coffee into my cup, waiting for the crowd to scatter. The wind had blown out all the ceremonial flames. The ceremonial papers had floated off into the air. The construction had taken over an hour, but there were still a couple of minutes before the interview. I sat watching the street, which was already swarming with bicycles and buses and delivery vans and cabs. Businesspeople in suits went flocking toward the new buildings, some carrying brief-cases, some carrying purses, some empty-handed or carrying bagels wrapped in tinfoil. A pair of people in matching hats, maybe teachers, herded columns of children into the plaza, pointing at the bronze sphere.

I spit a last mouthful of coffee into my cup, which was steaming now, full to the brim. I felt calm. Peaceful. I crossed the street and went into the first building that had grown out of the rubble, taking the elevator to the ninety-third floor.

A woman wearing cat-eye glasses was waiting for me at the door to her office.

"Come in, come in," she said, before she had even given me her name.

She told me to sit in an armchair across from her desk.

"So you're the artist?" she said, rifling through a drawer. I went to respond, but then she said, "Yes, here we go then, here's the folder for you."

"What folder?" I said.

"Your first assignment," she said, handing me a beige folder full of paperwork. "A bit boring—it's a promotional brochure about our different financial products. We'll need you to take care of this layout for the cover. Just do the best that you can. You'll have assistants eventually. We're still working all of that out."

"Wait, so that's it? I already have the job?" I said.

"Yes, of course. We're a new division—we've only started just this morning. So we've been hiring on in droves. Mostly newborns, including myself. I had heard that you were one of the exceptions, though. I was told you've been around for quite some time." She took off her glasses, rubbing her eyes. "I'm sorry if we seem disorganized. It's been an overwhelming couple of hours for all of us. We're still figuring everything out." She put her glasses back on, glancing at her clock, then back at me. "Speaking of new hires, I'd better go see how the newborns are getting along. You've got a couple yourself, yes?"

"Sorry?"

"Newborns. You should have a claim ticket—did anybody give you a ticket?"

"No."

"You didn't get one? A little green thing?"

"Wait," I said. "175?" I pulled the green ticket out of my pocket.

"Yes, that's the one. They'll be in the building across the plaza."

I had started out the day unemployed. Now, I had both a job *and* assistants. I took the elevator down to the lobby, then smoked a clove, walking across the plaza. I was nervous about meeting my assistants. My assistants wouldn't be scary, I decided. They would be boring. They would be polite. They would have cubicles.

But when the receptionist in the building saw my ticket, the receptionist pointed me away from the offices, down toward a brightly painted room at the end of the hall.

A guard with a nametag was standing at the door.

"175?" I said, giving the ticket to the guard.

The guard glanced back through the doorway, calling, "175!"

The corkboard beyond the doorway was pinned with messy drawings—snowy mountains, a bird next to a spotted egg, a stick figure wearing a police uniform. I heard some zipping noises, and then an elderly employee led a pair of children out into the hall, a boy and a girl, nearly identical, both carrying backpacks covered with tiny cartoon characters.

"Born just this morning," the guard said.

"We found them after we'd brought the other kids in for a tour of the new daycare facility," the elderly employee said, ruffling the children's hair. "Apparently they'd been hiding in a bathroom."

"They're the last ones left. It's late. Time to bring them home," the guard said.

I stared at the children. Those same faces from the photos, but in three dimensions now, blinking and grinning. The boy had a runny nose. The girl wore a rainbow scrunchie. I had never had a feeling like that before. It was breathtaking. In that moment, I felt so glad to be alive.

"Come on," I said, offering them my hands. "Let's go."

And so we went out to the street, and by the time we had hailed a cab they were already telling me stories, about the dark place they had woken up, and how confused they had been, and how uncomfortable they had been, and how long they had waited for the building to wake up too, and how awesome and pretty it had been when all of the walls had suddenly floated together and all of the lights had turned on inside, and about how much they'd already learned about sneezing, and how they'd gotten to work on some drawings, for just a couple of minutes, before they'd heard me arrive at the daycare, before it had been time to leave.

And then they wanted to know about where I'd been born, and what it had been like for me, how long I'd had to wait in a dark place of my own.

"Yes, yes," I said, "I'll tell you all about it."

I didn't, though. Instead, I lied—I invented a story, one which both was true and wasn't. I did not tell them about my own birth. I did not tell them about their empty caskets, or about the time before I knew their mother, or about how long I had waited at the table in the coffee shop, completely unaware that they were somewhere inside of the buildings growing out of the ground. I did not tell them any of that, and will not tell them, not now, not ever. And nobody can blame me for that, I think. Not even myself.

Thanks

To Libby Burton, my fearless editor. Your patience and wisdom are awe-inspiring. You deserve a monument in Central Park. I am forever grateful to you, to Gillian Blake, to Kerry Cullen, and to the rest of the fam at Henry Holt.

To the dream team: Sarah Burnes, the smartest and kindest agent a writer has ever had; and Michelle Kroes and Darian Lanzetta, who are hands down the most talented agents in Hollywood. You all deserve trophies, fireworks, and fountains of champagne.

To my teachers: Tony Earley, Lorraine Lopez, Jill McCorkle, Nancy Reisman, Heather Sellers, Danzy Senna, and Steve Yarbrough. There should be a national holiday on each of your birthdays. I did my best with these. I hope you like my book.

To Vanderbilt University, the Fulbright Commission, the Whiting Foundation, the MacDowell Colony, the Ucross Foundation, the Ragdale Foundation, Vermont Studio Center, Virginia Center for the Creative Arts, Blue Mountain Center, Prairie Center of the Arts, and Djerassi Resident Artists Program. Your support was life-changing.

To the editors and readers at *American Short Fiction*, *Conjunctions*, *Lightspeed*, *Michigan Quarterly Review*, *Missouri Review*, *One Story*, *Salt Hill*, and *The Paris Review*, who first believed in these stories. Special recognition is due to Jill Meyers, Callie Collins, Bradford Morrow, Micaela Morrissette, Michael Sarinsky, John Joseph Adams, Wendy Wagner, Jonathan Freedman, Vicki Lawrence, Speer Morgan, Evelyn Somers, Hannah Tinti, Will Allison, Jono Naito, and Emily Nemens. This collection would not exist without you.

To Netflix, Amazon Studios, Fox Searchlight, Fox, FX, 26 Keys, 6th & Idaho, Christina Hodson, Morgan Howell, Makeready, The Picture Company, Writ Large, and James Ponsoldt. Your enthusiasm and passion for these stories means the world to me. I've got a bowl of popcorn ready. Let's see what you all can do.

To my family, far and wide: living among the lakes of Michigan; in the forests of Virginia; in the plains of Texas; in the deserts of Nevada; among the mountains of Montana; among the swamps of Florida; among the fields of Illinois; in the woods of Ohio; in the hills of Kentucky; on the coast of California; and among the islands of New York; with special thanks to my sisters, for inventing games and inventing jokes and making home movies with me, and to my parents, for driving us all over the country in the summers when we were young.

And to Jenessa Abrams, the greatest living American.

About The Author

MATTHEW BAKER is the author of *Hybrid Creatures*, a collection of stories written in hybrid languages, and the children's novel *If You Find This*. Born in the Great Lakes region of the United States, he currently lives in New York City.